A Taste of Sprinkles

Morgan Briese

ISBN-13: 978-0-9966350-2-8
MorganBrieseWrites.com

DEDICATION

To all my readers on AO3, I never would've finished this without your constant support. Words are not enough to express my gratitude for sticking with me and my story for the past two years.

TABLE OF CONTENTS

KINDA AN ASSHOLE

Growing up, I was never really a further education type of guy, and I'm still not. I always believed I would enter my father's company and learn on the job while working my way up the ladder. I never intended to continue my education after high school, especially not in a field of my father's choosing. Don't get me wrong. He probably wants the best for me, but what he wants is not what I want. To Mr. Christopher Holt, my future includes nothing but mindless desk work and number crunching while my brother learns the ins and outs of the company he will inherit. Apparently, the ability to make money is more important to him than his second and youngest son's happiness.

Maybe that's why I rebelled – no, that's definitely why. At the first hint of my brother becoming the golden boy, I retaliated. The results were good, dare I say great, at first. I studied my ass off, to the point where I could spout useless algebraic equations in my sleep. A report of measly B's changed to straight A's, and I thought a 4.0 GPA would miraculously get my parent's attention. My mom was proud, gushing even, but my dad couldn't have cared less. It didn't matter what test I aced or what basketball game I won. Somehow, my brother was always better.

That's when my rebellion took a negative turn. It started out as missing curfew and sneaking out at night. I normally just hung out at a local park or watched a movie at the theater, but my parents didn't know that. They assumed I was out smoking, drinking, and having sex, and my father had no qualms about punishing me accordingly. I figured why take the punishment if I wasn't committing the crime, so I did exactly what they accused me of. I partied like a fucking rock star, and if that wasn't enough, I got a few piercings at sixteen and inked the day I turned eighteen (although it was nothing horribly delinquent, it was enough to disappoint the parents). The moment I graduated high school, my father shipped me out to Sodalis

University.

I can't really complain though. He pays my tuition, my off-campus apartment rent, and pretty much all my living expenses. I even get a nice chunk of spending money every month, although all that is probably on account of my over-caring mom. If it was up to my father, I'd be out on my ass in a heartbeat.

But I don't plan to mooch off my parents my whole life. I'll let my father pay for the education he most surely wants to take advantage of, but that's as far as it will go. I have my future in mind, and if that means deceiving my parents for the time being, then so be it. They'll be proud of my decision someday. Or well, my mom will. Hopefully.

That's why I frequent a small diner that is halfway between Sodalis U and my apartment. I work here on the weekends and am almost always here after my classes end. That's where I am now, sitting at the counter with an accounting textbook lying open and attempting to finish the last two problems.

"Scowling at an innocent book isn't going to help." My eyes snap up to spot one of my co-workers, Eli, leaning on the opposite side of the counter. "Need some help?" he asks.

"Please," I say, sliding both the textbook and worksheets across the counter. "The sides don't add up, and I can't move on until I find my fucking mistake."

Eli is a smart guy, probably the smartest university student I know. If this little blond genius can't find my mistake, then no one can. Of course though, the smart ass finds it in a quick glance. "You mixed up your debits and credits," he explains as he points them out.

"Ugh!" I groan in agony, letting my head drop to the counter. "This crap gets me every time. I mean, really, there must be an easier way to do this shit."

"Hang in there, Liam. You'll get the hang of it," Eli attempts to comfort me with a pat on my back. "I'll help if you want."

"No, no, I got this. Get back to serving nonexistent customers or whatever it is we do around here."

"Oi!" I cringe at the voice. "I heard that, Holt. You better watch your bratty mouth if you want to work back here on Saturday. I've got no problem putting you on the floor with Goldman."

I don't bother looking up from my worksheet, knowing full well the cranky head chef is glaring at me through the food window. "Yes, sir. Sorry, Simon," I mutter, erasing my chicken scratch of numbers to put them in their right place.

"Tch. You better be."

I continue righting my mistakes until I hear the muffled footsteps of Simon walking away. When the coast is clear, I heave a sigh. I can't afford to get on Simon's bad side, not now at least. I spent the last year trying to get in the kitchen of this diner instead of being a waiter on the floor, and I finally annoyed Simon enough for him to show me the ropes. I may be more interested in baking than cooking, but I'll take what I can get. I just want to learn from the best, and according to Quinn (another member of the kitchen staff), Simon is classically trained and is easily qualified to work in a five-star restaurant. It's a wonder why he works here, but to each his own I guess. It's none of my business what he does with his life.

Eli walks off to attend to an incoming customer as I focus on my calculations again. My fingers type the numbers on the calculator as fast as they can, and I hopefully add them up with no mistakes. I rule and prove the page before finally moving on to the next task. Writing all the account names is tedious and a pain in the ass, but I eventually get the long list down and move on to filling in dollar amounts. I don't bother checking their accuracy and leave that for tomorrow.

By the time I finish what is hopefully a perfect assignment, the sky outside has darkened and the street lamps switched on. I look up to find Eli flipping the open sign on the door to closed before collecting salt and pepper shakers from the tables to refill.

"Hey, Holt!" Simon calls from the kitchen. "Get your ass in gear and help, or get the hell out."

"I'm not on the clock though."

Simon's face pops up in the window, gray eyes narrowed. "Then get out," he says, pointing at the door with dish gloves covering his hands and forearms.

"Alright, I'll help," I concede as I pile my books and papers into my bag and leave the bag on my seat. I join Eli in collecting the shakers and bringing them to the counter.

"Did you finish the problems?" Eli asks while unscrewing the tops of all the shakers.

I begin filling the salt shakers and pass them back to Eli to recap. We've got a nice little assembly line going. "Yeah, I just have to check them tomorrow."

"Oh, that's right. You don't have classes tomorrow, do you?" Eli asks.

"Never do," I say smugly. "I loaded all my classes on Tuesdays, Wednesdays, and Thursdays. It sucks having twelve-hour school days, but it's worth the four-day weekend."

"But you work here on Saturdays and Sundays. Doesn't that cut your weekend down to two days?"

"Yes, my friend, but I'm getting paid for my time here unlike college where they take my money."

"Fair enough," Eli says as he starts putting the shakers back on the table and begins to wipe down the table tops.

I brush the spilled salt and pepper onto the floor before retrieving the broom to sweep up. We finish cleaning in relative silence before Simon and the kitchen staff are done. Simon tells us to *get the hell out* so I grab my bag, sling it over my shoulder, and walk out the side door with Eli.

"Are you working this weekend?" I ask as we walk down the sidewalk.

Eli shakes his head. "Darin, Miki, and Fae work on Saturday. I think Cody and Alex are scheduled for Sunday."

I groan. The thought of a whole shift with monkey see and monkey do makes my head hurt. Cody and Alex are bad enough by themselves, but put the two together and you've got a guaranteed headache. It makes a shift with Darin seem tolerable, but at least on Saturday I'll be in the kitchen and hopefully in minimal contact with him. Don't get me wrong. Darin's fine in small doses. Hell, we even get along, but the longer we're together, the more we run our mouths. I guess our inflated prides clash too easily.

"You have any plans for your weekend?" Eli asks as we cross the pretty much deserted street.

"Just the same thing I do every weekend."

Eli chuckles. "So nothing?"

"Oh, and do you have some almighty fantasy trip around the world planned?" I tease, only slightly offended at the jab at my lazy days.

Eli smiles, and I swear his eyes freaking sparkle. "Not exactly, but I am going home to celebrate my grandpa's birthday. He's turning ninety on Saturday."

"That's great," I say, slapping a hand on his back. "How's he been doing since his fall?"

"He bounced back really fast, but he's not too happy about having to live with my parents. He complains about not having enough freedom - like he's caged in by walls - but I know he likes the company. He did make me promise to take him to the lake, but I haven't talked my parents into it yet."

We stop in front of Eli's apartment building. "Have fun," I say as I wave my goodbye and continue down the sidewalk.

"I'll tell your family you said hi."

My eyes roll, but I don't stop walking. "Don't bother. It's a waste of breath," I call over my shoulder.

My stroll only lasts another ten minutes or so before I enter my own apartment building. It's nothing fancy, far from it actually, but it isn't a dump either. It's affordable while also being comfortable and spacious. For an outer suburb of Sodalis, it's actually quite nice.

The decor is pretty crappy though. The stairs are carpeted in a dull, 70's floral pattern and the walls of the stairwell are a dark, sage green. It reminds me of my dad's parents' house, and I hated their house. The hallways aren't any better. They're covered in ghastly wallpaper that has a really distracting swirl pattern. Whoever designed the place should be fired. Even I have better taste than that.

I pad up one flight of those ugly stairs and stop in front of the second door on my left. After fishing the key out of my bag, I unlock the door and enter the apartment. It's quiet when I flick on the lights and toe off my shoes.

Which is odd. Skyler's normally back by now, either watching some stupid reality TV show or sucking his boyfriend's face on the couch. Most often both. And if he's sleeping, I'd hear him 'cause he snores like a fucking bear. But whatever. He's probably back at the dorms with Emil, although I don't know why Emil doesn't move in with us. I swear he's here more than I am. I know for a fact he sleeps over most nights 'cause they're not exactly quiet.

And yes, it sucks having our rooms right next to each other. The walls are quite thin.

I toss my bag on the dining room table atop what's probably a week's worth of mail before heading to the kitchen. It can't even really be called a kitchen. It may have all the necessary appliances, but it's too damn small, barely big enough for one person. Now imagine the hulking, broad-shouldered Skyler and me, although much lankier, fighting to make breakfast in the same dinky kitchen. He can't grab the milk out of the fridge without slamming the fridge's door into my hip while I attempt to scramble some eggs. It was comical at first. Not so much now.

I dig in said fridge for the remnants of spaghetti I made earlier in the week, but it's not there. Damn that Skyler! I know we agreed to anything in the fridge being fair game, but I end up cooking way more than he does. I don't even remember the last time he made something edible. It was probably boxed mac n' cheese. And he even manages to fuck that up.

I decide on a sandwich because I'm too damn lazy to make anything else right now. I gather up the few ingredients I need and put them on the counter. After finally locating the mustard, I straighten up and slam the fridge door with a little too much force.

When I look up, I'm met with beady gray eyes that make me jump back, a startled squeak sounding from my lips that I will most surely deny. I scoff at the furry monster as it sits expectantly on the counter, right next to the package of sliced ham. It meows at me while its tail swishes back and forth, which is never a good sign coming from this beast.

"I don't think so. Get down." My hand reaches to push the cat off the counter, but it swipes its claws at me. The cat nicks my finger before I get the chance to pull away from it. "God dammit, cat! I said get down!"

But does the stupid thing listen? Of course not. It has the guts to paw at my ham slices and meow at me again like it didn't just bare its claws at me. But I'm not getting closer to the long-haired demon. I made that mistake before and learned my lesson, but don't think for a moment I'm giving up my meat. 'Cause I'm not.

I reach above the fridge, never taking my eyes away from the gray-haired devil, and blindly feel for a bottle I know to be there. After almost knocking it to the floor, my fingers wrap around it and hold it up for the cat to see.

I shake the bottle, and the cat immediately perks at the sound of its rattling contents. I point at the bottle. "You want this? I bet you do, but you're not getting it." I shake it again and begin to back out of the kitchen. "Come on. I know you want it." The cat lithely jumps to the floor and stalks after me into the dining room. It hops on top of the table and sits on the edge, silently eyeing me.

"Okay, no, this is where we started. Get off the table. Skyler may let you, but I'm not– Ah!" I spin around at the sound of another meow, startled until I spot the fat, orange tabby patiently standing by my feet. "Dammit, Simba, don't do that," I say but scratch its head nonetheless. "At least you behave." I direct a glare at the gray cat perched on the table, but it doesn't faze the beast. It meows again, pawing at the bottle in my hand.

I step out of its reach and pop the cap off the bottle to dump a few treats on the hardwood floor. The gray demon hops to the floor and joins the tabby in munching down the delicacies.

For the record, they're not my cats. They're Skyler's. He brought them home the first semester of our sophomore year of college. He said they were in a box on the side of the street, and he couldn't walk past them like everyone else did. That's just Skyler though. He likes taking care of things whether they're animals or humans. He does the same for me, kinda like the big brother I wish I had (although we are the same age). Actually, that's why we room together. Our fathers are business friends, and my dad thought Skyler would be a good example for me to be around. Too bad for him 'cause Skyler's a supportive guy, not a forceful douchebag like some people I'm related to.

Anyway, back to the cats. The gray haired demon is Furby, and in my opinion, it's aptly named. It used to be a fluffy ball of cuteness, but somewhere along the line, it sold its soul to the possessed toy it's named after. I have the scratch marks to prove it. Plenty of them.

The orange tabby is Simba, and I really don't mind it. It's fat and lazy and doesn't do much. That's my kind of cat. Every now and then, it climbs in my lap and takes a nap, and I don't have to worry about being mauled when it wakes up. Again, my kind of cat.

I sneak back to the kitchen as quietly as I can and make my sandwich. Leaving it unattended on the counter, I haphazardly put the ingredients back in the fridge and snatch my meal before the demon cat can. I pass said cat perched on the dining table again while I pad into the living room and plop down on the couch.

Crossing my feet on the coffee table, I turn on the TV as I scarf down the sandwich in a few quick bites. I flip through the channels and settle on a rerun of *Cutthroat Kitchen*. I may know who wins in the end, but it's always nice watching the competitors screw each other over. Payback's a real bitch sometimes, and I don't envy the competitors. I wouldn't want to be forced to cook in a tiny kitchen or have my cooking utensils taken away from me. I mean out of all the cooking competitions to choose, why pick this one? There are far easier ones to win where you won't get fucked over by your competitors. Personally, I'd choose Cupcake Wars. I make kickass cupcakes. Just ask Skyler. He loves them.

Speaking of the bulldozer, I hear the door squeak open, and it's gotta be him. I press the cancel button on the remote and check the time. Nearly midnight. It's pretty late for Skyler, especially when he's got class first thing in the morning. "Whatcha been up to? And if it has anything to do with Emil, I don't wanna know."

There's a strangled cough and an awkward clearing of a throat. "Sorry, Emil, I didn't know–" When I pull my eyes away from the TV and glance up, it's my turn to cough on choked breath. "What the hell's going on?" I manage to sputter as I jump to my feet. "Did you guys kill him? Do we have to hide a body?"

"God, Liam, no. Shut up," Skyler grunts as he kicks the door shut behind him. In his arms, he carries (more like halfway drags) the limp body of a man who appears to be our age or at least close to it. He stumbles past the cats, his demon child almost tripping him, and tells me to watch out. I step out of his way in time for him to lay the unresponsive lump of limbs on the couch. When he's disposed of his baggage, he heaves a sigh.

"Anyone going to tell me what's going on, or do I have to assume I've just become an accessory to murder? I'm sure there's a shovel somewhere, and we can go bury his body real quick. It'll take a half hour tops."

Skyler's shaking his head, but both he and Emil crack a smile. "You're stupid sometimes, Liam," Skyler chuckles.

"Did you just call me smart?"

Skyler rolls his eyes. "No, I said you're stupid. If you were smart, you'd see him breathing."

My eyes flick to the unconscious body. Sure enough, his chest rises and falls with each steady breath. "Okay. He's alive. Then why is he here?"

Skyler glances at Emil, and the two share an unspoken, wary conversation. Emil is sweating, his brow glistening more than usual, and his stance is stiff and rigid, like he's terrified, ready to flee the scene at the slightest slip up. Skyler walks back to his boyfriend and clasps his hand on his shoulder. "We can tell him," he says.

If my eyebrows weren't already shooting up my forehead, they are now. The more these two speak - or well, the more Skyler speaks - the more I begin to think the cops will bust down the door and slap cuffs on the three of us. Yeah, the guy is alive, but he's unconscious, and the last time I checked, assault is illegal.

"But I don't think he wants others to know," Emil quietly says, his voice almost a whisper.

"For fuck's sake, I don't want to know the guy's life story," I snap and immediately regret it when Emil flinches. Skyler gives me the stink eye, that I'm-disappointed-in-you mom glare. "Ah shit, I'm sorry. I just want to know his name, and like, is he okay?"

"His name's Nico, and he's fine. He passed out and needs a place to crash," Skyler explains.

"Shouldn't you take him to the hospital or something? I'm no doctor, but I'm pretty sure passing out is a bad thing," I say.

"No," Skyler shakes his head. "It's nothing serious. He ran out of stamina. It happens all the time."

"Then why didn't you take him to his place?"

"He doesn't exactly have anywhere to go."

"Huh?"

Skyler sighs, exhaling through is nose. "The truth is, he's been staying with Emil in his dorm, but the hall's R.A. found out and is pretty pissed."

"So he's gonna live with us?"

"For the time being, yeah."

I'm gonna admit that I'm kinda an asshole. The thought of a stranger taking up my couch doesn't sit all that well with me. Not only will there be less space for me on *my* couch, but he's a damn stranger. I don't know the dude. Hell, he could be a mass serial killer on the loose who's only pretending to be unconscious in order to insert himself into our lives and kill us in our sleep. And did I mention my couch? I mean, it's pretty damn comfy, and I spend a lot of my off days with my butt planted on its cushions. I don't give that up for Skyler, and I sure as hell won't give it up for this Nico guy.

"And you have to keep an eye on him tomorrow. Don't let him do anything stupid," Skyler says as he and Emil head to his room.

"What? Why?" I didn't sign up for this shit.

"Because we have classes, and you don't. Don't be an ass, and make a new friend. You could use a few." The door to his room clicks shut before I think of a smart comeback.

I can't say he's wrong. I can count my acquaintances on both hands and the people I consider friends on one. If it's not at school or the diner, I never really see anyone other than Skyler or Emil (sometimes Eli too). That never bothered me, and it still doesn't. I'm used to being alone, so I don't mind it.

I glance at the man passed out on my couch. His cheek is squished against the armrest, and dark hair falls across his forehead. One arm is wedged between his side and the cushions while the fingers of the other brush the beige carpet. Even with his legs bent at the knees, his sneaker clad feet hang over the other armrest. Freckles dot his face, neck, and the exposed skin of his forearms, being most heavily concentrated on his cheeks and the bridge of his nose.

Friends, huh? I can't say we'll get along or even like each other. Honestly, it'll be a miracle if we tolerate the other's existence. Either way, I'm gonna call him Sprinkles 'cause his cheeks remind me of cupcakes. It's a shame his freckles aren't every color of the rainbow. Then he'd really look like a cupcake.

And god fucking dammit I did not just think that!

I walk back to the entry hall and rummage in the dingy closet. When I finally find what I'm searching for, I wedge them under my arm and shut the closet's door as quietly as possible, but the damn thing still squeaks on its hinges. I grimace at it as I flick the hall light off and return to the living room.

Dropping the pillow in the middle of the floor, my ass plops down on it, and I cross my legs beneath me. I wrap the old quilt my grandmother made around my shoulders, a few patches torn or ripped, and settle down for one last episode of *Cutthroat Kitchen.*

Half an hour later and I'm engulfed, leaning toward the television screen and muttering words of encouragement for the kickass chef with the mohawk, as if the man can actually hear my stupid ramblings. It's another twenty minutes of nail biting and the occasional uttering of profanities before my bubble of a world pops, and my head snaps to eye the couch.

Sprinkles has rolled onto his back, his head propped on the armrest as soft snores whistle through parted lips. I try to ignore the low breaths, I really do, but who the hell thought snores could be so... musical. Aren't they supposed to be obnoxiously loud and unbearable. Like Skyler's. He cuts down fucking forests with his chainsaw snore. I mean kudos to Emil for tolerating that shit almost every freaking night, but it's annoying. Sprinkles, on the other hand, can pass as a bird chirping in the morning.

So I eventually get back to finishing the show. (Spoiler alert - kickass mohawk chef wins.) After a quick fist pump in the air for celebration, I turn the TV off and push myself to my feet.

Now, I may be an asshole, but I'm an asshole with feelings, especially at one in the morning. Maybe it's his peaceful exhaustion of a mind no longer conscious, no longer muddled with every thinkable worry a human can come up with. Maybe it's the way the room's light falls upon his skin, each freckle bold and vibrant. But most likely, it's because my mom always did the same for me.

I drape the quilt over Nico and leave the pillow on the floor near his head. I hit the light switch and stumble through the darkness into my room, shutting the door behind me. I strip to my boxers before sitting on the edge of my bed and crawling beneath the covers. I curl up on my side and let the bliss of sleep pull me under.

So I may or may not have slept in till noon (may - definitely may). It's pretty damn late even for me. Ten is normally the latest I roll out of bed. It's no 6 A.M. every day, but at least I attempt to be useful to society. I'm not, but I try. That's got to count for something.

My mind's still groggy with sleep when I rummage through the small pile of discarded clothes in the corner of my room. I locate a pair of sweatpants buried beneath countless other garments and slip them on to rest just over my hips. Halfway dressed at the crack of noon and that's all society is getting out of me today. Shirt be damned. It's not like I have to be presentable today. I'm the only one in the apartment after all...

Fuck. I already forgot. Sprinkles. Damn Sprinkles is ruining my no-effort day. What's the point in having a day off if I actually have to put effort into something? He better appreciate the extra energy I exert having to put a shirt on.

I'm still struggling to get my limbs through the right holes (half asleep so give me a break) when I miscalculate the distance between me and my door. I walk right into the damn thing, and the following rant of vulgarities would give a nun a heart attack. I piss and moan about the stupid door in my way even as I fling it open with unnecessary force. It bangs against the wall (thank god it didn't break through!), and my lips curl into a satisfied smirk at the echoing pang. That'll teach the door.

The smirk morphs into a grimace when my head finally pops through the right hole and I'm met with the back of the couch. Stupid Sprinkles. It's all his fault. I'm courteous enough to put a damn shirt on and look where that got me - my head pounding and for once not from a hangover. Not worth it. Next time, he'll be lucky if I'm in my boxers.

I step to bypass the couch but pause upon seeing it empty. Where the hell did the sprinkled freeloader go? I check the kitchen but find it empty as well. Not in there or the pathetic excuse of a dining area. The bathroom door is open so that's a no. I hesitantly peek into Skyler's room, barely cracking the door open and only letting my eyes sweep across the space once (because nobody needs to see the various unmentionables strewn on the floor). I even check my room because, I don't know, maybe I missed him while fighting with my door.

But Sprinkles is nowhere to be found. And here I put a shirt on especially for him. What an ungrateful freeloader he turned out to be!

BECAUSE I'M A BURDEN

It's early - far too early for any sane human, but then again, I'm not exactly human. Plus, I actually like mornings - love them even - but not today. I like mornings that warmly welcome me to consciousness. The soft glow of the sun's rays peeks through the window to dance across closed eyelids until its delicate fingertips coax my eyes to crack open. I awake to a peaceful quietness after a good night's sleep on an unaccompanied bed in my friend's dorm room. It was once foreign - a place I felt I had no right to invade - but now it's the closest to home I've ever known.

But as the tight knots in my neck demand to be felt, my eyes snap open to another foreign place. The couch I'm splayed on wouldn't even fit in Emil's dorm, and I don't recall ever seeing such an obviously homemade quilt in either of our possessions. And there's no way I would ever miss it, what with its mismatched squares and patched repairs. It drapes my body in a warmth that has nothing to do with the room's temperature. In fact, it is the only comfort in this foreign place that keeps me from fleeing.

I shift my weight, dislodging my right arm from beneath my torso and roll to lie awkwardly on my opposite side. I bury my face in the soft cushions in hopes of fighting against the unwelcomed light that shines over the back of the couch. Going so far as to pull the quilt over my head, I suck in a deep breath through my nose. The stale, dusty scent of the blanket is overpowering, but a sweeter scent - one that reminds me of freshly baked bread - lingers in the fibers. It's comforting, probably more so than it should be.

My eyes flutter shut, and I'm fully prepared to be pulled back into the bliss of unconsciousness, but the universe is unfair sometimes. The once streaming light disappears with a soft click only to be replaced by the far brighter lights shining from the ceiling directly above me.

I groan, loud enough for whomever turned the lights on to hear my displeasure. A deep, guttural chuckle answers me and gives away its owner's identity. Deliberately heavy footfalls echo in the tiny space and grow nearer as they round the couch.

Please just go away. Five more minutes. That's all I ask. Please.

"Eep!" Searing pain has me bolting upright, tangling myself in the quilt as I grope at my own backside.

"Shit, dude, I'm sorry. I didn't see it," Skyler apologizes as he hastily lifts his foot.

As soon as his weight disappears, my fingers curl around the smooth silkiness of my tail. I cradle it to my chest and tenderly poke at the affected length. If it wasn't naturally black, I'm sure it would be bright red to match the already puffy swelling. The tip of my tail flinches when my fingers brush against a particularly tender spot.

I glance up at Skyler, and if I hadn't been used to seeing him in his rosy pink boxers, I would've averted my gaze. But I am used to it. He spends enough time lounging around Emil's dorm for me to be used to his utter lack of shame. Not that it bothers me to begin with. I mean I'm not one to complain when it comes to showcasing muscles. He is the freaking *Hulk* after all.

"It's fine. I didn't even realize it was out," I tell Skyler.

"Nico," he sighs, and oh no, I know that tone of voice. It's his lecturing mother hen voice that he only seems to use with me because I've never heard him use it with Emil. "You need to take care of yourself."

"I am."

"No, you're not," Skyler disagrees as he points to my tail still clenched in my hands. "That wouldn't be materialized if you were, and you wouldn't have passed out in the middle of a conversation last night. You can't wait until your fangs and wings materialize to take care of it."

"It'll be fine," I insist, but neither of us is fooled. I've dealt with this unwelcomed aspect of my existence long before I fled to the human world, and Skyler's seen it numerous times as well.

"Okay, Nico, listen. I personally don't mind seeing you with your demon features. You can waltz around with them materialized all you want, but I have a roommate who has no idea you're an incubus, and you're going to need energy to keep it that way. Unless, of course, you want him stepping on your tail too," Skyler says.

The thought makes my tail throb, and I hang onto it a bit tighter. Skyler's right. He and Emil are the only two that know my secret, and I'd like to keep it that way. But that also means I will have to keep my energy up, and there is only one way for me to do that - involving an act I'm not proud to take part in. "I... I don't want that."

"Then you need to take care of business."

I know that. I know it better than anyone. It's easy for him to tell me what I already know because he's not the one who has to feed off of sex for energy. He doesn't rely on taking advantage of others in order to function on a daily basis. And even if (for some unforeseeable reason) he would be in the same situation, he has Emil. It wouldn't be a problem for either of them. Knowing Skyler, he'd probably use it in his favor, but I'm not Skyler and I'll never be him. I can't accept that vile part of me. No - it isn't only one part. My entire existence revolves around sexual acts and violence.

And I hate it. I hate me.

The firm grasp of his hand startles me when it settles on my shoulder. When I look up, I'm met with unshakable golden eyes. Their stare pierces through me, seeing everything I can't find the courage to say. "You can't change what you are," he tells me with the utmost sincerity in his voice.

"I know."

"Do You?"

"Of course I-"

"But do you accept it?"

"What?" What's there to accept? I'm a demon. That's nothing new. And yes, it's something I can't change. Again - nothing new.

It's Skyler's turn to sigh as his hand falls from my shoulder to hang at his side. He tries to hide his exasperation, but it's there. I can see it in the slight furrow of his brows and the miniscule quirk of his lips. He glances at the clock on the wall, and his resiliency - his will to make me see the light - slowly fades. But not completely. "Think about it," he says before going back down the small hall from which he came.

What if I don't want to think about it? What if I've already thought about it so much that there's nothing unknown for me to discover? What's left to contemplate?

When I hear a door click shut and two sets of familiar voices, I scramble to untangle my limbs from the confines of the blanket. I hastily turn on my side to face the plush cushions of the couch and bury as much of my body beneath the quilt as possible. I barely make it, my blood pounding through my veins, when Skyler and Emil walk by the couch. Their steps falter, pausing for only a moment. My heart races even faster with the passing tick of a few seconds until their pairs of footsteps continue to pad across carpet.

The door is pulled open, and the brightness of artificial lights disappears with a single flick. The darkness comes with an unnerving silence, and I finally suck in a deep breath in an attempt to calm my heartbeat. But the air freezes in my lungs when one last noise disrupts the quiet apartment.

"Have a good day, Nico." And then the door clicks shut.

Emil. He may not be as straight forward as Skyler, but he's quite observant. While Skyler's support comes in the form of blunt words and actions, Emil's is much quieter. It's that one little voice in your head - the one among many much louder shouts and yells - that whispers you'll be okay and you'll get through the day. It's that one stranger, engulfed in the sea of many, who takes the time to smile at you. It's the single star shining brightly in an otherwise black sky of night. You're not sure how or why that tiny star even bothers when it's all by itself, but it does. And it continues to shine until the sun takes over the following morning.

I appreciate Emil's kindness, Skyler's too, but sometimes I feel like it's misplaced. I dropped into their lives accidentally. By complete chance, they found me unconscious on the side of the road (which happens more often than I'd like to admit) and took me in as a friend with no questions asked. Neither one of them batted an eyelash when my tail and wings materialized the first time. They accepted them as unique features of a new friend.

That was over four months ago. And since then, I have lived with Emil in his dorm, but I guess that's short-lived too. All I've ever done is cause them trouble, but they never hold any of my faults against me. It's the complete opposite of the world I come from, and the concept of giving but not taking is new to me. But I like it. I like the world that Skyler and Emil live in, and I'd do anything to stay in this world as long as I'm allowed to.

Even if that means feeding on the sustenance of my kind. Once a week - that's the least amount of times I must feed to properly function. It's a small sacrifice to make in order to be with my new friends.

But not right at this moment. I'm tired, and I honestly don't want to, so I'll put it off as long as I can - even if it's only another hour.

It's quarter after eleven when I finally roll off the couch. The apartment is as quiet as when Skyler and Emil left earlier, so I assume the elusive roommate is either gone or still asleep. That's probably a good thing because I don't think my tail is going away any time soon.

Which reminds me of my half-conscious resolve to fix that problem. I groan at the thought but know I can't put it off any longer. Reluctantly, I stand and disentangle my limbs from my blanket cocoon and neatly fold the quilt to drape it over the arm rest.

I wander in the direction of where I believe the apartment door to be. As carefully and quietly as I can, I twist the knob and pull the door open. My head peeks out, scanning the hallway to find it empty. I sidle into the hallway, pulling the door shut behind me. I check the room number (in case I can't reappear in the same place) before letting my eyelids fall shut.

It's hard to explain how the travel between the human world and demon world works. The simplest explanation is teleportation, but I'm not sure that's right either. There's no magic key or summoning ritual (unless a human summons you). When a demon wants to move freely between worlds, they just do. They can pick any spot they want, and they'll materialize there. High ranking demons with thousands of years of experience can travel anywhere they please. I can't; I have to have been to the destination myself at least once before I can materialize there.

Which is why I always go back to the same demon when I have to feed because in all honesty, his lair is the only one I remember how to get to. When I open my eyes, that's where I am - surrounded by the dark, jagged stone walls that are lit ominously by the flickering flame of candlelight. The atmosphere is surprisingly cold despite the constant heat of fire, and it has an involuntary shiver running down my spine. No matter how many times I return to this place, it never changes. It will never cause a warm and fuzzy feeling. There will only be the freezing sharpness of shame.

"Well, if it isn't my favorite little runaway. And here I thought I'd see you a few days ago. Is my freckled Nico holding out on me?"

That would be my partner. (I honestly can't tell you his name. After all these years, I never asked, and he never told me. But I prefer it like that. It makes it easier.) I've been going to him for as long as I can remember. From the time I matured as an incubus to now, he's given me a way out - a way to feed without taking advantage of anyone else. We're not exclusive or anything like that; we're simply mutually beneficial to each other - we each get what we want. He gets food and pleasure while I'm allowed to keep the guilt about my whole existence to a minimum. My psyche doesn't walk away unscathed, but a small crack is more manageable than a shattered pile of self-loathing despair.

I picked my poison - choosing a labyrinth of intricate cracks over ending up as a forgotten pile of dust, because isn't it better to fight to live even if it's a miserable existence for the hope that maybe one day things will change, than to lie down and give up to forever wonder what could have happened? I don't know the answer myself, but I'm trying to find it. And isn't trying the first step?

I sure hope it is because they say the first step is the hardest, which can only mean it gets easier from here. Hopefully.

He lounges in his nest (the demon equivalent of a bed. Most are made of whatever foliage that can be found but this guy steals luxuries from the human world so his is a giant pile of blankets and pillows surrounded by stone borders). Onyx wings, surprisingly smooth despite their jagged and flared tips, fold into his back as he shifts to lie on his side with his elbow cocked so his hand can support his head. A thick, lizard-like tail is the same dark shade, and it flicks like that of an impatient cat. Two black horns protrude from his forehead, curving up and back with each ridged ring of bone. The unsteady burn of candles is barely enough to cast shadows upon the ashen skin of his unclothed chest and can't even touch what I'm positive is his nude lower half beneath the cover of a thin blanket.

"Are you letting loose this time?" he asks, genuinely curious as he tilts his head in wonder.

I follow the line of sight from his piercing silver eyes until my own orbs land on my tail. I shuffle to hide it behind my back, mentally scrambling to conceal the appendage; but no matter how much I strain, the tail won't disappear.

"Calm down. It's fine," he attempts to console as he sits up straight. The blanket slips from his lap, and sure enough, he's naked. "I like it."

"But... I don't," I say, barely a murmur.

He stands and shamelessly closes the short distance between us. "I know," he says softly, "but there's no reason to hate what you are."

"I could list numerable."

"Of course, you could," he shakes his head, a warm yet pity-filled smile softening his features. "But I'm guessing you want to make this quick."

I nod my head.

"Top or bottom?"

"Bottom."

He laughs, quiet and humorless. "Always is, huh?" When I don't respond, he adds as he takes my hand in his and leads me to his nest, "I hope you find someone you can feed with without feeling like you're taking advantage of them, because no matter how many times I tell you that, you don't believe me."

He guides me to the stone edge and gently pushes me down. I scoot back to make room for him as he crawls on top. With a hand holding him up situated on each side of my shoulders, he peers down at me, his silvery orbs reflecting the burning flame. He leans in closer, his lips hovering only millimeters above mine, each exhaling breath warm upon my skin. His hand - complete with long, pointed nails the color of coal - caresses my cheek, his thumb smoothing over my skin, as soft lips press against mine.

He is gentle - every time without fail. I should be grateful. Any other demon would be quick and ruthless like I asked, but he's different. He's slow and thoughtful, diligent in every last detail even as he skillfully pops the button on my jeans. He tugs them down past my hips until I can kick my legs free. His hand slides down my chest to toy with the hem of my t-shirt before he grabs the fabric and pulls it over my head.

For a moment, he just stares, and I wonder what he sees when looking at me. I wonder why he's so careful as he palms me through my boxers; but when he meets my cloudy gaze, I find my answer buried beneath a far too gentle smile that fails to reach his eyes.

He's gentle because he pities me. I can feel it in his every breath, his every touch. As his hand slips beneath the fabric of my boxers to swirl the precum on my tip, as he uses his now slick finger to slide between my cheeks to prod at my entrance, as he pushes the first finger past the tight ring of muscle. It's there in all of them.

I'd be offended if I didn't feel the same way. It's not that I pity myself, but I see where he comes from. Of course he'd pity an outsider like me - a demon who detests the existence of his own kind, his own world.

But that thought fades when he opens me up even more, adding a second finger and then a third. I clench my teeth at the slight burn, but when his fingertips brush against the bundle of nerves, I bite my lip to stifle a moan.

He leans down, his breath hot against my ear, and says, "It's okay to let go."

But it's not - at least not in my mind. I don't do this because I want it but because I physically need it, and there's a substantial difference between the two. I want to deny just how much I really do need this, but my body won't let me. It betrays me, relying on the pleasure to rejuvenate itself, but no matter how many times my body gives in to the pleasure against my will, my mind will stand strong. It's the one thing I can rely on - the one thing that constantly reminds me of the values I believe in, those same values that led me to flee the demon world in order to protect them, the values that tell me my existence is a nuisance to the universe.

So, no, I can't just let go like he tells me to. I refuse to.

But my inner strength and determination can only hold up for so long as my demon partner nips at my collarbone. He lavishes my chest with more nips, kisses, and sucks, marking me to his heart's content as he works his fingers in and out, successfully hitting my sweet spot with each practiced brush of fingertips.

I can't take it. The first unstifled moan slips through my lips, and my eyes go wide with the realization.

"That's more like it," he hums in satisfaction as he pulls another moan from my lungs. "I knew you could make some enticing noises."

My fingers grasp at the soft sheets beneath me and dig into the fabric. I whimper at the attention, because it's too much. He's doing too much, dragging it out too long. "Hurry up," I pant between sharp intakes of breath.

He smirks, and it's the smirk that says he knew I'd crack, knew I'd give in. "Why, of course," he says as he withdraws his fingers ever so slowly, loving the way the action makes me squirm.

He pulls my boxers all the way off and spreads my legs wider, pushing them until they bend at my knees. Positioning himself, he pushes into me slowly, giving me more than enough time to adjust to the slight burn of the stretch. He seats his entire length inside me and stills. "Tell me when."

He really doesn't know the definition of fast. "Now," I beg, and I hate that my voice pitches and squeaks with only one word.

And if I hate that, I downright despise the way my breath hitches at the first flick of his hips. It sets off that familiar spark of pleasure that grows with each practiced thrust. It's that buildup which clouds my mind and allows my demonic instincts to take over, the ones I fight so hard to suppress, but it's no use.

My boundaries fall even further with each moan and whimper that slips from my lips. I can feel my control slipping away, sliding between the grasp of my fingers. My last bit of self-control goes up in flames, leaving indistinguishable piles of dust in its wake. The proof spreads out beneath me, protruding from my shoulder blades to splay out at my sides. The final particle of dust floats to gently land atop the smoldering pile as a set of pointed teeth, once hidden away, breaks the skin of my bottom lip.

When his fingers curl around me to jerk in time with his quickened thrusts, it's over. My buildup of pleasure peaks until it bursts with a final strangled moan breaking its way from my lungs to bounce off the stone walls of the dark cavern. Before the echo dies away, he's giving into his own release, much more willingly than I did.

After a quick clean up and an even hastier redressing, I calm my thumping heart to the best of my abilities, but it still beats recklessly in my chest. I huff out a deep breath before sealing away my demonic traits, and thankfully they all disappear, even the notorious tail that led to my rude awakening this morning.

"Don't be a stranger," he tells me with a sideways smirk.

"We are strangers. We know nothing about each other."

"We can change that."

"No, thank you," I say without turning back to look at him.

"And why's that?" he asks.

My eyelids fall shut, and I engulf my mind with images of Skyler's apartment. I answer him, but I can't say he heard me. "Because I'm a burden."

The cold air of the demon world is engulfed by a welcoming warmth, albeit a little stuffy and stale. A calming breath of air fills my lungs and blows out through my nose as my eyelids flutter open. I'm met with the grain of light wood, and relief washes through me at the familiarity of the door and the silver plate showcasing the correct number.

The relief is short-lived, though, as I remember I don't actually live here, so I have no means of getting back into the apartment. I didn't lock the door, but what if the roommate left and locked it behind himself? I don't have a key - what with the whole I don't live here thing - and I never thought to look for one. And even if the door is unlocked, I don't have the right to waltz right in because, again, not my apartment.

But what if the roommate is home? Will he even open the door? Does he even know that I slept on his couch last night? Oh gosh, he might not. I'll knock on the door, and he won't know who I am. That's to be expected. I mean, I don't know him either. But then what do I do? I can't wait until Emil and Skyler get back. Well, I could, but how long would I end up sitting out here in the hallway? Minutes? Hours? Days? Okay, days is a bit much, but you get my point.

Or what if he's mean - like asshole mean - and knows who I am but won't let me in? What if we don't get along? What if he enjoys those same insufferable TV shows that Skyler constantly watches? What if he–

A muffled shout of *fucking hell* sounding from the other side of the apartment door startles me, forcing me to face the fact that, yes, the roommate surely is here. There's some slight shuffling and clattering that follows, but it quickly goes back to the relative silence of the hallway.

My hand raises, poised to knock. As my knuckles rap hesitantly on the wood, I prepare myself for the worst, completely ready to have the door slammed in my face. Every minuscule noise from within the apartment stills for a brief moment, and then footsteps pad closer, stopping not even an arm's length away, with only an inch or two of wood between us. The knob twists, and the door is slowly opened.

He's irritated, his lips pulled tight in a firm scowl. Light copper orbs glare at me, and I'm ready to flinch away until they soften with the slightest hint of recognition. He brushes a hand through sandy brown hair until his fingers scratch at the darker hue of his undercut, leaving a fine trail of flour in his hair. And actually, he's covered in flour. It's probably a good thing he's wearing an apron, even if it says *Kiss the Cook* across his chest.

He steps to the side and stares expectantly at me (and, okay, this isn't the door to the face that I expected). "Get in here, Sprinkles," he says as he returns to what he had been doing - cooking by the looks of it.

I'm left standing in the doorway like a complete idiot. Sprinkles? Where did that come from? How come he called me–

So this is a new one. I've been called Freckles, Speckles, Polka Dot, and another handful of nicknames, but Sprinkles is a new one.

MARTYR OR MURDERER?

Nothing calms me more than tying the apron strings around my back and cracking open my favorite cookbook, flipping to a page bookmarked with a yellow post-it note. With how worn the page is, you'd expect me to have the recipe memorized - and I don't mean to brag - but I do. There's just a comfort in having the book take up precious space on the limited countertop because what if I forget? It's perfectly reasonable to forget how much butter to add. I never do, but it could happen. Today's just not that day, though.

I cut along the line that marks 1/4 cup and fold the butter into the already measured flour mixture. This is one of my favorite parts, because a fork or a spoon never thoroughly mixes in the butter and a whisk or electric beater is a pain in the ass, which leaves my all-time favorite last resort - my hands. They delve in without a moment's hesitation, and my fingers work the slowly altering mixture together until I'm satisfied.

With bowl in hand, I stride the single step required to reach the kitchen sink. I use my elbow to nudge the handle up until water begins to dribble into the basin. I eyeball the few tablespoons I need (because who actually takes the time to measure each one out) before shutting off the water. Foregoing the use of any type of utensil, I stir the mixture that's starting to resemble dough with my hands, because why the hell not?

When I'm satisfied with its consistency, I scrape as much off my fingers as I can and lightly flour a small portion of the counter top (half of it ends up on either the cookbook or me). Then comes another of my favorites - kneading the dough. It's not technically required for the pie crust recipe I use, but it's the easiest way to add more flour to the too-sticky dough. And who doesn't like beating the shit out of something that won't punch back.

I finish kneading in the flour, cut the dough in two separate portions, and roll out the dough in remotely circular shapes. I line two pie tins with the dough and pinch around the edges to form the fancy looking fold in the crust. I prick the dough a few times with a fork before putting both pie tins in the already heated oven.

Now comes another of my favorites (okay, I love it all - it's all my favorite), and that would be the pie filling. I almost never make the same filling twice, and that's mainly due to my lack of grocery shopping. Although pies and pizza have become a Friday night tradition in this apartment, neither Skyler nor I ever prepare for it. Skyler doesn't concern himself with it because he doesn't have to cook, so it's natural he wouldn't have a clue as to what ingredients I'd be missing. He just shows up and is grateful to be fed at all. I, on the other hand, have no such excuse. I'm simply too lazy to go to the corner store and can't be bothered to write down a list for Skyler to go shopping. Honestly, it's a miracle that we even have a stocked fridge and pantry. I should probably thank Emil for that.

And I know the perfect way to - chocolate. I'll make one of the pie fillings extra chocolaty for him and Skyler to share. That should be thanks enough. But is there even any chocolate in the apartment? I know there's a container of pure cocoa in the back of one of the cupboards, but that shit's not to be messed with. I did it once and ended up throwing away an entire double batch of cookies because apparently cocoa is not as sweet as I once thought. Who would have guessed something so bitter makes something as sweet as chocolate? Obviously not me.

I begin the rummaging of the cupboards and am relieved to find packages of pudding mix on the first shelf. To my surprise, there's a hell of a lot. Like who uses this much pudding? Vanilla, vanilla, tapioca (gross), vanilla, banana cream (gonna use that one), yet another vanilla, and finally chocolate. I'm slightly appalled by the amount of vanilla pudding in an apartment where it is never eaten. Maybe Emil is trying to tell me something? Oh well. His secret message is going to have to wait for next week's pie because I've already made up my mind for today's.

Emil and Skyler are gonna love their chocolate pudding pie with a hazelnut spread slathered crust topped with peanut butter whipped cream. At least they better because that's what they're getting. And I know there's plenty of hazelnut spread and peanut butter - probably a year's supply that only lasts two weeks because even Skyler can't fuck up a pb&j sandwich.

But first thing's first. I gotta actually make the pudding. I fetch the jug of milk from the fridge and add it to the already cluttered counter top before retrieving two clean mixing bowls. I carefully push the milk across the counter, trying to make more counter space magically appear, as I set the two bowls down. Just when I think I've succeeded, the dirty bowl I mixed the dough in clatters to the floor, and the damn thing has the audacity to land right on my toes.

I jump back too late, even though my pinky toe has already fallen victim to the metal rim, and let a muttering of *fucking hell* express my displeasure. I stoop down to grab the bowl and toss it into the sink, its clash ringing and echoing in the tiny space. To prevent a similar tragedy befalling my toes, I clear the counter of anything I no longer need, quickly shoving utensils and dishes into the sink as well.

I reach for the jug of milk, but before my fingers grasp the plastic handle, there's a quiet knock at the door. Who the fuck could that be and why are they interrupting my cooking time? Heaving a sigh, my hand drops to my side, and I begrudgingly stride to open the door for whomever decided to waste my precious cooking time.

I pull the door open as I rake a hand through my hair. When my eyes finally look up at the person standing barely an arm's length from me, I'm pleasantly surprised to be met with the light dusting of freckles upon tanned cheeks. This little bugger is the reason for my mishap with the door this morning, but I guess he can be forgiven, what with his scared, lost puppy sheen to his russet colored eyes. It's understandable though. He hasn't been introduced to me, and I don't exactly come off as friendly.

So I'll let the poor guy off the hook.

I step to the side enough to let the guy in, and I try to make my tone as welcoming as possible, "Get in here, Sprinkles."

Okay, maybe that sounded a little domineering. Too commanding maybe? And, oh my god, I called him Sprinkles. What if he thinks I'm making fun of him? He probably thinks I'm an asshole. I am, but that's not the point. New roommates with the potential to be friends do not need to know the extent of my asshole attitude before they even know my name. Oh god, I just fucked up the first thing I said to him.

Yep, I fucked up. I'm gonna go back to the kitchen and pretend I never opened my mouth. And you know what, I look like an even cockier asshole leaving him in the hallway, but it's too late. I'd look stupid going back now, and I'd rather be an asshole, so sorry dude, but this is how it's gonna be.

I return to my awaiting pudding mix and tear open the chocolate pudding package. I dump it in the bowl and pour in a measured amount of milk. I dig in a drawer for a whisk and nearly jump out of my skin when I turn and spot Nico standing awkwardly in the entryway of the kitchen.

"Sorry, sorry," he apologizes as he takes a step back. "I didn't mean to sneak up on you. Um," he scratches at the nape of his neck. His hand drops to clutch at his opposite forearm. "I'm sorry to intrude. I'm not sure if you know me, but-"

"You're Nico, Skyler's and Emil's friend," I say in hopes of saving him some of the feeling in his arm.

I go back to the pudding and whisk the milk and powder together. Nico still looks uneasy, and I can't for the life of me figure out why.

No, wait. I take that back. I'm not only an asshole but a dumbass as well. "I'm Liam by the way." There we go. Make it look like I meant to forget to introduce myself. "I'd shake your hand, but mine are kinda busy and covered in flour."

He finally releases his grip on his forearm, and his stance relaxes, the tension fading from his shoulders. "That's okay. Do you want any help?"

Help? As in he'll help with cooking? I haven't cooked with anyone since I was a bratty little kid making Christmas cookies with my mom, dad, and Bryce. Those were the fun times before shit hit the fan, and then cooking became my release - a distraction from everyone else's bullshit, the one thing I was good at that no one could take away from me. I'm still not ready to share that.

I shake my head. "Thanks but no thanks. You can go watch TV or something."

"Oh, uh, okay." Nico slowly backs out of the kitchen, nearly running into the dining table. He offers a small smile that fails to reach his eyes as he turns. His hand rubs at the nape of his neck while he disappears into the living room.

I guess I can scratch the whole friend idea from my mind. Whatever. I didn't have any yesterday so what made me think I'd gain one today? One new person in my life isn't going to change that number. But who cares?

I finish making both the chocolate and banana cream pudding and set both bowls aside just as the oven timer goes off. You'd think with all my cooking experience, I'd finally be smart enough to let the heat escape the oven before I reach with an oven mitt to retrieve the pie crusts, but no. Apparently I don't learn from my mistakes because my eyeballs water at the burn of the heat. The minute I've got both pie tins on the stove top, I'm rubbing at my poor eyes. Note to self: don't do that again.

After my eyes finally stop watering, I go to the fridge in search of whipped cream. I hit the jack pot in the bottom drawer and find not only an unopened container of whipped cream but orange creamsicle yogurt. Oranges and bananas go pretty well together, and even if they don't, the two fruits are going to get along today or so help me. I straighten from my search and slam the fridge door shut.

Then something rubs against my calf, and I jump at least a foot in the air, dropping my spoils from the fridge as a high pitched squeal echoes in the kitchen. I stumble back, tripping over my two left feet, and my back hits the opposite wall before I fall on my ass. I glare at the damn thing that has the audacity to meow at me, and my sneer of *fucker!* is a bit breathless.

I'm still backed into the wall with my chest heaving when the hasty trample of feet on carpet turns to socks sliding on linoleum. His feet slip out from under him, and his back collides with the floor. A pained groan gives way to a soft chuckle as I gape at the unnecessary casualty pancaked to the floor, his right hand only a hairsbreadth from my feet. I'm frozen in shock, my arms wrapped around my knees to clutch them to my chest. When he doesn't even flinch when the hairball jumps on his stomach and paws at his t-shirt, I begin to wonder if he's hurt.

"Hey, uh-" but that's all I get out before his hand raises to scratch behind Furby's ears.

He turns his head to peer at me, worry bright in those rustic eyes. "Are you okay?"

I can't stop the laugh that bubbles its way from my lungs even when it causes Nico's eyebrows to furrow in wonder. I mean, really, this guy is something else. He falls flat on his back, probably hits his toes against the lower cabinets and most likely knocks his skull against the floor, but he asks me if I'm okay! Is this guy a saint? Or maybe a martyr? He throws himself in the line of fire, sacrificing himself to the villainous cat overlord that is Furby in order to save me. Is that what this is?

Probably not. Being a klutz is more realistic.

"What's so funny?" Nico quietly asks.

Oh crap, I'm still laughing. It's not funny. It really isn't, but I'm still laughing like a drunk seal. Come on, Liam, get your shit together. This is not the time to hurt Sprinkles' feelings anymore than I already have, and oh no, not that look. Please, Sprinkles, don't give me that dejected look. I'm not laughing at you. More like the whole situation, so it's not you. We're both pretty damn hilarious right now.

"Sorry, sorry." Dammit, Liam, breathe. Stop your damn giggle fit. "I swear I'm not laughing at you. I'm laughing at us."

Nico finally moves, pushing himself up until he's got his legs crossed beneath him and an abnormally affectionate Furby in his lap. "Then you're still laughing at me."

"Wait, no, I–"

He cracks a smile - a real one that has the corners of his eyes crinkling.

I do believe I'm dealing with a sprinkled little smart ass. "Are you sassing me, Sprinkles?"

He recoils slightly, his smile fading, and dammit if that isn't a kick to the gut. Was my tone too harsh? Did I come off as mad? Cause I'm not. I'm starting to believe that a friendship possibility isn't so impossible, but maybe-

"Sorry."

"Huh?" What the hell is he apologizing for?

"I said I'm–"

I cut him off, "I know what you said, but why'd you say it?"

"Because I made you mad."

"No no no," I shake my head as I slowly push myself to my feet. I extend my hand to him, steering clear of the now purring ball of fur. "That's me being a sarcastic dick. Trust me, you'll know when I'm mad."

Nico eyes me for only a moment too long before he carefully wraps his fingers around my hand. I give him a little tug to assist him, but he still struggles to his feet, what with him cradling the cat to his chest. Surprisingly enough, Furby is calm while practically being squished and nearly dropped when Nico hastily withdraws his hand from mine, and I can't help but be slightly disappointed at the abrupt loss of contact.

Instead of his fingers brushing the back of my hand, they run along the abundance of Furby's gray fur. When the cat's tail swishes back and forth, I step away from the pair, because that's never a good sign coming from this cat. I may not be the martyr that Sprinkles has proven himself to be, but I'm a decent enough person to warn the guy about the imminent danger he's in. Not before I'm out of harm's way first, because I've got to look out for myself. No one else will. Okay, maybe Nico, but one case of failing to save me from a demon cat isn't much to go by. I guess it's enough to repay the favor, but that debt is going to have to wait. Because no amount of saving my sorry ass will be enough for me to put myself between him and a pissy ball of demon possessed fur with sharp teeth and even sharper claws.

But like I said, I warn him. "You might want to be careful with that one."

He cocks his head, peering at Furby like a loving parent gazes at their newborn child. "Why?" he asks, his voice full of wonder as he continues to stroke the cat.

I warned him. I really did, so whatever injuries he procures from this point on that are inflicted by Furby are in no way, shape, or form my fault. "'Cause he's a demon."

He stares at me, his expression blank, but he laughs only a short moment later. Sprinkles' laugh is quiet and yet musical - both short and sweet - as if I've missed some inside joke that he shares with himself. "So we're kindred spirits," he murmurs to the cat.

Even though I'm positive that comment wasn't meant for my ears, I reply to it anyway. "Does that make you a savage beast that attacks innocent victims?" For good measures, I add the most playful smirk I can manage and hope to god it doesn't end up looking like a pained scowl.

It must have been closer to the latter, though, because Nico's face drops, the soft smile and any remnants of the joyful laughter disappearing faster than me at a dinner with my family. He forces one of those awkward laughs that's reserved for jokes you don't find funny but laugh at anyway so as not to hurt the jokester's feelings.

"It depends who you ask." And Sprinkles leaves it at that, backtracking from the kitchen and taking the whole cause of this little exchange with him.

As I retrieve my dropped ingredients from the floor, I can't help but contemplate his answer. What the hell does it mean? Is he not as reserved and saintly as he appears to be? Are there dark desires hiding behind the splatter of freckles? Oh my god, what if I'm right about him? The innocent looking Sprinkles is secretly a serial killer who's acting like a good samaritan in order to gain our trust. A week from now, after Emil, Skyler, and I accept Nico's presence as pure and good-spirited, he'll turn on us in our sleep. And then no one will find us for days because it's not that odd for the three of us to miss school together.

It'll probably be Eli who finds our lifeless bodies strewed throughout the apartment, blood adding to numerous stains on the beige carpet. Hopefully Sprinkles isn't too sadistic to write some insane message on the wall in our blood. Poor Eli would be traumatized for life, not that he wouldn't after finding us mangled on the floor, but a menacing message in blood is pushing it too far, and Eli doesn't deserve that. Well, nobody deserves to find their friends murdered by a new roommate, but least of all Eli. He's too nice of a guy, and honestly, that whole ordeal would probably send him spiraling into his own psychopathic break down. And unlike your common killer, Eli's smart enough to get away with it. It's scary just thinking about what he'd be capable of if he lost it, so I better warn Nico not to even think about killing us (assuming he is a serial killer).

No, you know what, screw that! If Nico's evil enough to write a message in my blood (disrespectful little prick), then he deserves what's coming to him. It'll be a fight between the malicious freckled serial killer and the revengeful psychopathic best friend, and I've got my money on the best friend. I can sit on my ghost ass eating popcorn that'll go right through me while I enjoy the massacre. Cause that's what it's gonna be; there's no way those two will go at it without leaving a trail of casualties. Bodies will keep piling up until the only two people left are Eli and Nico. Then, as they face off for the final showdown, the world will explode into trillions of tiny pieces, leaving the two of them to duke it out in the endless vastness of space.

Yep, that's how the world - no, the universe - as we know it will come to an end.

By my calculations, I've got about a week (give or take a few thousand years) before Earth explodes, or in other words, this could very well be the last pizza and pie Friday I ever have the pleasure of partaking in. With that terrifying thought bouncing around in the confines of my mind, I put my all into finishing the last two pies I will ever make.

I don't mean to pat myself on the back, but I might as well since no one else will. They turn out far better than even I could have imagined. Kudos to me for being fucking fantastic! Both are masterpieces! Skyler and Emil's turns out just as I planned - a layer of hazelnut spread lining the crust with a chocolate pudding filling and topped with a peanut butter whipped cream. Mine, although more eccentric, ends up far better than I had hoped for.

Apparently, bananas and oranges are best buds because they taste amazing together. A fluffy, flaky crust with a banana cream pudding filling is good by itself, but add a mixture of orange cream yogurt and whip cream and you've got perfection. A light sprinkling of cinnamon and sugar turns perfection into over-achievement.

And I'm an overachiever. It saddens me to have to place my masterpieces in the fridge, because I'd love nothing more than to dig right in and give into the gluttonous rumble of my stomach. But I've got enough self control to keep my craving in check - not enough to stop me from swiping a finger through the peanut butter whipped cream for a final taste, but oh well. The baker has every right to taste test his goods. I've gotta make sure they're edible. Yeah, that's my excuse, and I'm sticking to it.

I brush my hands on my apron before reaching out to the love of my life, grasping a green sticky note and flipping to the marked page. Glancing at the time on the stove, I deem it alright to start making the pizza. It'll be done around the time Skyler and Emil get back so hopefully Skyler won't have to complain about it being too cold or having to wait too long for it to be done.

But I've got one problem - I'm out of mixing bowls. Now, some may ask, Liam, why don't you reuse the bowl you mixed the pie crust in, but to them I say I have too much pride as a chef. Five star chefs don't reuse dirty pots and pans so neither will I.

I push the dirty dishes in the sink to the side in order to put the stopper in the drain. I flick on the water and squirt dish soap all over the bowls and utensils. Might as well wash all the dishes while I'm at it so I turn to search the apartment for any spare spoon or cup, but I make it all of one step.

Simba - that fat little angel - sits patiently before me, staring at me with wide, innocent eyes. Behind the orange tabby, the gray demon strolls almost cockily (if cats can even be cocky) to pad lightly across the linoleum, but it's not the cats that have my treasure hunt for dirty dishes stalled.

It's Sprinkles, yet again, as he freezes on his hands and knees, his fingers reaching out to Furby; but the cat's bushy tail slips through his grasp. His arm hovers above the floor, and he lifts his head until his eyes meet mine.

"What are you doing?" I ask.

"Uh, I," he stammers, his hand falling to the floor. He straightens himself to his feet and makes a show of brushing the dirt from his knees. He points to Furby as if the simple gesture will answer why he was crawling around on the floor. "The cat– I was trying to keep it out of your way, but it kinda got away from me."

"Oh, well thanks, I guess." That's it? How am I supposed to remember he's a serial killer in disguise when he continues to act all goofy and dorky? Like what murderer crawls around on his hands and knees in pursuit of a cat? Sprinkles apparently - that's who.

Nico rubs at the nape of his neck and adverts his gaze. "Are you sure you don't want any help?" he quietly asks, his attention on the running water behind me.

I should probably turn that off before the bubbles have a chance to overflow and trail down the cabinets. I shut the faucet off and dip my fingers into the suds. "Do you really want to wash dishes that badly?" I joke.

"It's better than sitting around being useless," he shrugs. His tone is logical, like it's fueled by reason, but the hitch in his voice when he says *useless* suggests his argument is anything but logical. And there's that frown upon his lips that showcases poorly veiled disappointment in himself, the disappointment which nags at the back of your mind and says you're worthless unless you accomplish something great each and every day, like your life depends on never wasting a single second. But the disappointment comes from past mistakes - past time wasted - because you never know when your failures and inadequacies might catch up to your present; and the only thing you know for sure is that you don't have the stamina to outrun them much longer.

And I hate seeing that despondency steal away the light from another person's eyes, even if that person is my potential murderer. Hell, especially then. Because if he's gonna kill me, I at least want him to enjoy it. There will be no point in my death otherwise.

I flick the suds on my fingers at Nico to regain his attention, and the startled squeal I get in response is priceless. "Could you wash one of the mixing bowls for me first?"

"Yes!" This guy responds so fast and cheerfully that you'd think he's just won the lottery, but all he's won is the (dis)pleasure of hand washing dirty dishes. He's stepping around the cats and has his hands in the water before I can fully get out of his way, causing our shoulders to bump together.

I chuckle. "I can go find more dishes for you if you're that excited."

"Go ahead."

Okay, then, I'm going to do exactly that. I search high and low, between every cushion of the couch, going so far as to venture into Skyler's personal lair. I return with a rather pitiful assortment of spoons, forks, and a single cup.

Nico scoots over as I drop my acquisitions into the soapy water. I grab a towel from its respective drawer and dry the awaiting mixing bowl sitting patiently in the drying rack. I could probably wait around and dry the rest of the dishes, but Nico needs something to keep him busy for a while. When I'm finished with the now damp towel, I drape it over Nico's shoulder and pat it in place.

I ignore the way his muscles tense beneath my unexpected touch and take my mixing bowl to my own counter space. There's not much room for maneuvering between us, but hopefully it's enough so I don't startle Sprinkles with every reach of my arm.

I'm in the middle of measuring flour when Nico initiates conversation, even if it's slightly hesitant. "So... what are you making?"

"Pizza." I answer, and then a rather important question of my own pops into my head. Honestly, I should have thought of it sooner. "You're not allergic to anything, are you?"

He shakes his head and glances at me over his shoulder. "No, why?"

"Because I'd feel bad if something I made sent you to the hospital because I wasn't smart enough to ask about allergies."

"Makes sense," he agrees. "Can I ask what kind of pizza?"

"A taco pizza. It's got spaghetti sauce, *Doritos*, ground beef, lettuce, tomatoes, and a shitload of cheese."

"How much is a shitload?"

I think I like sassy Sprinkles. "About five huge ass fistfuls."

"And a huge ass fistful is..."

"It's like that stupid crane game, but the crane is your hand and the stuffed animals are shredded cheese. You just kinda go for it and snatch as much cheese as you can possibly hold while dropping half of it on the floor."

Nico stops scrubbing the plate in his hand and stares at me, dumbfounded. Maybe that wasn't the best analogy, but it's all I could think of. "So a lot?"

"A lot."

He smiles at that, the corners of his lips turning up and his eyes crinkling slightly.

We go about our own duties in relative silence that doesn't have to be filled. It's more companionable, the two of us satisfied with our few exchanges over the afternoon and completely fine with focusing on each of our respective tasks. It's no surprise that Nico finishes first, leaving the dishes to air dry in the rack.

I half expect him to go in search of Furby or Simba, but he doesn't. He hops up on the counter, planting his butt on the slim strip of counter top before it dips into the sink basin. His legs dangle like a five-year-old, the heels of his feet continually colliding with the cabinets. He hangs onto the towel, if only to have something in his hands, but he doesn't make a single peep, the only sound being his steady breaths.

I can feel his eyes on me, watching every move of my hands as I form the dough to the rectangular sheet pan. His gaze follows me to the fridge and right back to my little pizza station with a half-filled jar of spaghetti sauce. He watches the sauce pour over the dough more than I do and follows every flick of my wrist as I spread it evenly with a spoon. Nico only averts his eyes when I ask him to scoot over so I don't hit his shins when opening the oven door.

The minute I straighten, his gaze returns to me; and it's rather unnerving. Like I said earlier, I haven't cooked with anyone in years, and it's become a solitary activity. Having eyes watching my every move adds a whole new pressure I'm not used to, the pressure that makes simple tasks you've grown accustomed to seem almost impossible. It's evident in my struggle to cut open the ground beef package and glaringly obvious as I attempt to brown the meat, continuously spilling it over the pan's edge.

I deal with it and keep my mouth shut, though, because Sprinkles seems fragile, as if one wrong word from me will shatter our hopefully blooming friendship. Plus, he appears perfectly content in swinging his legs back and forth without a care in the world.

When the meat's done browning, I gather the rest of the ingredients. By the time I pile them on the counter, the dough is ready. I pull the pizza crust from the oven and rip open the bag of *Doritos*, stuffing a few cheddary chips into my mouth and offering Nico a handful. He cradles a precarious mound in his open palm and munches on them like a chipmunk.

The more I watch him, the more I'm having a hard time imagining his dark side. How could this overgrown five-year-old have a dark side? It's a good facade if he really is a serial killer, because in all honesty, who the hell would think this guy is capable of murder?

He is a thief, though, stealing another handful of *Doritos*.

I'll let it slide because I'm eating just as many. Only half the bag actually ends up on the crust. I spoon the meat over the chips and then toss the pan and spoon into the probably cold dish water.

Nico slides from the counter top and being the ever diligent dishwasher, returns to his task, his eyes finally focusing on something other than me. Almost magically, my dexterity returns to my fingers the moment his gaze no longer bores into my back. With my renewed motor skills, I dice up a tomato before the weight of peering eyes has the chance to chase away the precision I desperately need if I want to keep all ten of my fingers.

I sprinkle the diced tomatoes over the meat, followed quickly by shredded lettuce and cheese. "Nico," I say to gain his attention. He finishes rinsing the pan before turning to me. I carefully (very carefully) grasp the blade of the dirtied knife and offer the steel handle to him. "You can drain the water after this one."

He nods and gingerly takes hold of the knife. He makes no attempt to pull the knife away until my fingers release their grip and return to my side.

While he dutifully wipes down the knife with a washcloth, I retrieve plates from the cabinet, grabbing three by instinct and having to go back for a fourth. When I go for the forks, I count them one by one so as not to make the same mistake. I pile them beside the plates as Nico safely places the knife in the drying rack, blade down.

Right on cue, as if the pizza had called out to him, the apartment door swings open, and Skyler storms in, followed by a much quieter Emil. "Smells good, Liam. What kind is it today?" Skyler asks far too loudly as he drops his bags atop the dining table.

"Taco."

"I meant the pie," he says as he strolls into the kitchen as if there's plenty of spare room for his hulking form. He doesn't wait for an answer, though, instead choosing to pull open the fridge door and pin me into the corner of the counter top. He retrieves both pies and nudges the fridge shut. Giving both of the desserts a quick sniff, he chooses to keep the chocolate one (like he always does) and hands the other one to Nico.

He leaves a bewildered Nico to wonder what he's supposed to do with the pie and peeks out of the kitchen to the living room. "Emil, did we make it in time?"

Here we go.

"It just started," comes Emil's reply as the ever familiar tune of Skyler's favorite game show bounces off the walls of the little living space.

Skyler scoops up the plates and forks and all but dashes toward the couch. "Hurry up, Liam! Grab the pizza and get in here!"

I roll my eyes but do as I'm told, plus I grab a pizza cutter. "Come on, Sprinkles," I say as I lead the way from the kitchen.

Not even a minute has passed since Skyler bounded to the living room, and yet he already repositioned the side stands in front of the couch to hold our food and got comfortable on the couch beside Emil. His speed no longer surprises me because I know Skyler's shows are near religious. He wouldn't miss a single second of them even if the apartment is burning around him.

"Hurry up, hurry up!" Skyler prompts as the host introduces the families.

I set the pizza down on the little table before plopping onto the couch cushions. Normally I'd have plenty of space all to myself, what with Skyler and Emil practically on top of each other, but tonight there's one more ass to fit on the cushions. I scoot over until my shoulder bumps with Skyler's and pat at the space next to me. "Have a seat, Sprinkles, and enjoy the Friday night tradition of *Family Feud.*"

He sits down in the offered space, squished between me and the armrest. It's not the most comfortable arrangement - far from it actually - but it'll have to do, what with the lack of furniture.

I begin cutting the pizza into bite-sized squares as the host asks the first question. "Name something people put plugs in."

"Ears."

"Ass."

"Walls."

Emil, Skyler, and I (in that order) answer before either contestant even presses their buzzer. When the quicker of the two does answer with *ears*, the number one slot on the board flips and her family gains control, choosing to play.

"Ass, it's up there," Skyler insists.

Disappointingly enough, it's not and Skyler has no problem expressing his displeasure at the missed opportunity.

At the first commercial, Skyler hands out the plates and forks. We all stock up on pizza and begin stuffing our faces. We're so busy scarfing down food that we miss the only allowance time for casual conversation (as deemed by Skyler).

The next question says, "Name a kind of crack."

"Crack head."

"Butt crack."

"Cocaine."

In case you couldn't tell, Skyler's obsessed with asses. He even cheered, nearly dropping his plate on the floor, when *plumber's crack* is revealed to be number two.

The host reads the next one, "Name something that never works when you need it most."

"Cellphone."

"Dick."

"Car."

Even Nico chips in on this one. "People."

I'm going to ignore Skyler's answer (he likes to find a sexual answer for every single one) and instead focus on Sprinkles' answer. It's a good one that I never would've thought of (because I've already given up hope with people), but the way he says it suggests a deeper meaning - like earlier today when he made the comment about being useless. It makes me wonder even more what his story is, what he's been through up to this point. I mean, there has to be a reason why he's here, depending on Skyler's kindness instead of his family's. But it's not my place to ask.

Neither his nor Skyler's answer is in the top five.

By the time the second episode rolls around, not a single piece of pizza remains. We each lick our forks clean and pile our plates atop the empty pan, Skyler and I snatching up our respective pies.

I plunge my fork through the whipped cream and pudding, shoveling the first bite into my mouth. And damn, it's as good as I remember it being - no, it's even better. I offer the tin to Nico, and he stares at it questioningly. It's not until I push it into his hands that he digs his fork in and takes a bite.

With bated breath, I await any sort of reaction. It's not often that I cook for anyone other than Skyler, Emil, and occasionally Eli; and they always tell me the same thing. *It's delicious* or *it tastes great*, and I appreciate each and every compliment. Hell, I live off of them, but they're friends. That's what friends are supposed to say. I've heard the same things from people I trusted and loved only to find out they were lies. That nagging feeling of betrayal has stuck with me like a parasite, feeding off every compliment until it turns negative and morphs into insults that cut deep into my being.

But Nico's different. He owes me nothing, and we're little more than acquaintances, strangers until only a couple hours ago. I can't imagine him telling me it's disgusting, but I also don't believe he'd lie to me. He has no reason to protect my feelings, and even if he did, he's pretty much an open book. One way or another - whether it be through words or body language - he'd tell me the truth.

All thoughts, all worries vanish faster than they materialized when the dull despondency washes from his dark irises, the orbs brightening as his lips close around the mouthful of pie - the pie that I made. And in that moment, he doesn't have to say a single word because the dopey smile upon his face as he chews and swallows is more than enough for me.

MEANS A LOT TO ME

I can hear them - Skyler and Liam - arguing... about me. From the looks of it, Emil can too, although to give him credit, he's not sweating as much as he normally does in uncomfortable situations. He's not exactly doing a great job of masking the furrow of his brows or the frown that spreads across his face every time a new portion of the others' conversation drifts into the living room - which happens to be almost constantly - but then again, I'm fairing no better.

I try to focus on the sweet deliciousness of chocolate chips as a local news station drones on in the background about current weather patterns. The two cats - who I now know as Furby and Simba - sit on either side of me on the floor, my back resting against the couch. The tubby tabby is content being curled up against my thigh and receiving the occasional scratch behind its ears. Furby, though, really wants one of my cookies. It paws at my forearm as I take another bite, meowing its protest.

I wish the quiet roar could drown out the voices from the kitchen, but the walls are thin and the apartment is small, so the kitchen really isn't that far away. When the tension rises and their voices grow louder, Emil attempts to the best of his abilities to be even louder, commenting on a news story about some human celebrity I don't know. I want to listen to him - I really do - but my ears tune into the conversation I'm not meant to hear.

"I have work today," Liam insists for what is probably the fifth time.

"Take him with you. Let him hang out at the diner and introduce him to your friends," Skyler says, also not for the first time this morning.

"Why don't you take him with you and Emil?"

Skyler heaves a sigh loud enough that even Emil stops rambling for a moment. "Emil and I are meeting Naomi to go watch a play that sold out months ago. Remember - the one you said you didn't want to go to?"

"So what? Why can't he just stay here by himself? He's not some little brat that needs a fucking babysitter," Liam argues.

"I know he's not, but this whole arrangement is foreign to him. If you were in his shoes, would you want to be left alone in an unfamiliar apartment surrounded by unfamiliar things?"

Liam doesn't answer, or at least I don't hear him.

I'm not sure what the big deal is, because they shouldn't be arguing over me. I'm not worth their breaths, and I really don't want the two of them angry with each other. After last night's evening of laughs and carefree foolishness, this tense atmosphere feels wrong. If I wasn't here, none of this would be happening. Liam would've eaten all the chocolate chip cookies for breakfast instead of sharing them with me on the living room carpet, and Skyler and Emil would be getting ready to meet Naomi in a few hours. Liam would leave for work after calling out a goodbye instead of being pulled from his breakfast and herded into the kitchen by Skyler.

I'd be fine on my own. Staying here is no different from spending my days hidden away in Emil's dorm. I'd find something to do - playing with the cats, watching TV, or contemplating the uselessness of my existence. I'm used to it, and Skyler should know that. Why is he even bothering to convince Liam when me being alone is nothing out of the ordinary? And why doesn't Liam just leave? It'd be much easier than wasting his breath on an argument that isn't worth it.

If Skyler's doing this to make me feel better, he can stop. Because it's not. Hearing their thoughts on what to do with me only confirms what I already know - that I'm in the way, that I'm a burden. It's as Liam said - they're arguing about who will be my babysitter.

And by the crestfallen look on Liam's face as he slowly trudges to stand beside me, I'd say he's the babysitter.

"Um... Nico," he begins, "do you want to hang out at the diner today? It'll probably be boring, but, uh, my co-workers are pretty nice, and you might get free food out of it if you're lucky."

I'm ready to say no, to tell him I'll be fine on my own, but then I see Skyler with that broad grin of his and an excited twinkle to his eyes. That happiness isn't directed at me but at Emil. What right do I have to take that away from him? I can't say no, because their day with Naomi would be ruined. Skyler would spend it worrying even more about me instead of enjoying his afternoon, and that would take away Emil and Naomi's happiness too. None of them deserve to have their outing ruined.

But what about Liam? He doesn't seem overjoyed at the idea of me hanging out at his workplace - apprehensive even. And it's understandable. Who wouldn't be? We only met yesterday, and now we're practically being forced to spend time together. Not that I mind. On the contrary, I had more fun yesterday than I had in the few months being in the human world.

But who's to say Liam enjoyed it as much as I did?

"Sprinkles." I look up at Liam, and his uneasiness has all but disappeared, being replaced with a satisfied little smirk. He locks his gaze with mine before purposely peering to my right.

My eyes follow his to see Furby chewing on the half-eaten cookie in my hand. I jerk my hand back and stuff the last bite of cookie into my mouth, munching on it as I spitefully glare at the cat.

"Come on, Sprinkles," Liam laughs. "You better have your shoes on by the time I grab lunch, or I'm leaving you behind."

I swallow down the cookie and scramble to my feet. I hop over the still curled up Simba and race to the entryway with the laughter of Emil and Skyler echoing behind me. Plopping down in front of the door, I block the only exit while reaching for my sneakers. Liam is not leaving me behind.

"Oh my god," Liam smirks as he grabs a lunch box from the dining table. "Impressive speed, but I wouldn't actually leave without you." He toes on his shoes and then digs in the closet. "Here," he tosses a coat at me while I tie my laces.

The coat lands on my head, and I have to push it to the floor in order to tie my other shoe. Liam slips into a dark red hoodie with *Sodalis U.* written across its chest in white block letters as I push myself to my feet. Liam waits patiently for me to put the jacket on. It's a little snug as I zip it up, and there's that same scent - the sweet, baked goods smell - lingering in its fibers as on the quilt I use at night while sleeping on the couch.

"Bye, Liam. Bye, Nico," Emil calls from the couch with a little wave. "Enjoy your day."

"Yeah, yeah," Liam mutters as he reaches past me for the door knob. He waits for me to step back before pulling the door open and walking out into the hallway. Glancing over his shoulder at me, Liam pauses for only a moment and then heads for the stairs.

I move to follow after him, but Skyler has a goodbye of his own that has my footsteps faltering. "Let yourself have fun, Nico."

I fumble with the door knob and nearly trip over my own feet. A quiet *I'll try* slips from my lips as I pull the door shut. My eyes dart from left to right in search of Liam, and I can't help but feel all warm and fuzzy inside when I spot him standing a couple meters to my right, peering back at me.

Instead of leaving me behind, he waited.

I jog the few short strides to catch up to him and follow a step behind him when we descend the flight of stairs. One step in particular creaks almost silently - its quiet moan easily drowned out by a hushed conversation - but for some reason, it's comforting. It's that tiny little sound that somehow manages to be heard. Against all odds, it made its presence known, and while some may say it's an unwelcome nuisance - something that needs to be repaired - I disagree. It's homey; it's real. It's one flaw in a perfectly useable staircase, and a few flaws don't take away from its overall value and worth.

As soon as Liam pushes the door open and we step out onto the sidewalk, I'm more than grateful for the jacket clinging to my skin, even if it's only a light windbreaker. I still don't know much about seasons of the human world, but I've heard enough from Emil to know that it's unusually cold for late fall. The subtle breeze bites at my exposed cheeks, and I burrow my head as far as it will go into my jacket, retreating into the warmth like a turtle.

"Are you cold?" Liam asks, his words coming out as white wisps of breath in the morning air.

It's kind of impossible to not be cold. "You're not?"

He shrugs noncommittally even as his ears and nose are red, complaining that he is indeed cold whether his mind thinks so or not. There's no way he's not, what with only wearing a single hoodie that has less insulation than my coat. Or maybe I'm super sensitive to the temperature, and this is just typical for Liam's morning walks. He doesn't seem too bothered by the chilly breeze, so that's probably it.

We stroll down relatively empty sidewalks side by side, passing old brick buildings like they're commodities. They line both sides of the street, towering two or three stories into the cloud-ridden sky. That same architecture goes on for blocks until the sun-baked bricks abruptly end to be replaced by glass and steel - neither pristine nor polished but far more modern than the chipped and cracked bricks. It's a fine line between new and old, and with that line comes a change of atmosphere. What was slow and laid back shifts to quick and tense; and even the wind bites harder at my cheeks. The near-empty sidewalks grow crowded far too quickly with people bustling in and out of storefronts and businesses, to the point where I'm afraid of being separated from Liam.

The surroundings are unfamiliar to me, each street name a random jumble of syllables which fails to form any sort of map within my mind. If I lose sight of Liam, I'll be left in a maze of people, easily turned around and confused in a sea of strange faces. The first bump of an unfamiliar shoulder colliding into mine sends me into a flurry of apologies, but as I turn to face the person, they're already gone.

There's a tug on my jacket sleeve, and I attempt to pull away from it until I see the face behind the hand. "Stay close," Liam tells me as he releases the coat's fabric.

He may let go, but I grasp on. My fingers curl around the hem of his hoodie and hold on like my life depends on it. Copper orbs glance at the attachment, his cheeks coloring even more in the cold, but he doesn't protest. His pace slows slightly until I'm nearly walking on his heels, but I'm grateful for it - for him taking my feelings into consideration.

Liam silently leads me the rest of the way, and it's a pretty straight shot except for a single turn down a much quieter road. It seems to lead to a residential area, but before quaint houses have the chance to line the street, a small parking lot sits behind one of the buildings part of the busy main strip. The pavement is cracked and worn - the white paint of lines marking respective spots barely visible. The lot's reason for existence is to its right in the form of an elongated, rectangular building. A row of four windows - with a strip of red between each one - sits atop white paneling, is interrupted by a glass door, and then continues in perfect symmetry. Atop the raised, flat roof, a large white sign proudly displays *Scout's* in red block letters.

I follow Liam across the beaten pavement, finally releasing my grip on his hoodie when he opens a side door that says *Employees Only* across its face, and I'm thankful for the warmth that engulfs me. We enter into a small hallway, and Liam turns into another room, one that lacks any sort of door.

Hooks line the far wall, and a little circular table takes up most of the space in the tiny room. A refrigerator is plugged in against the left wall, and as my eyes scan the space, I realize we're not alone.

A petite young woman pauses in hanging her coat on one of the hooks, glancing momentarily over her shoulder. "Good morning, Liam," she says, her voice light and cheery, as she finishes with her coat. When she turns, she finally spots me, dazzling blue eyes landing on my form. "Oh, who's this?"

"Fae, Nico. Nico, Fae," Liam introduces, gesturing to us when he said our names. "Nico's gonna hang out here today."

"Nice to meet you, Nico," Fae says with a bright smile.

"Um... you too," I reply quietly, unable to meet those expressive eyes.

Liam slips out of his hoodie, pulling it over his head and messing up his meticulously preened hair, before gesturing for me to shed my outer layer as well. I'm a little reluctant because I'm loving the warmth right now, but with him being so considerate, I comply with the flick of his fingers and hand over the jacket.

As he hangs up the garments, Fae tells him, "Simon wants you in the kitchen pronto."

"He told you that?" Liam comments as he stores the lunchbox in the fridge.

"Not exactly," Fae laughs. "He heard me come in and thought it was you."

"And how'd that go?"

"He muttered something about *that damned brat* not showing up early like the rest of the kitchen staff."

My chest tightens painfully at her words. Liam's tardiness is due to my newly added presence in his life. If he and Skyler hadn't been arguing over who would babysit me for the day, he would've been here on time. He must blame me for that - I sure do - and it makes me advert my gaze as Liam turns from the fridge to face Fae and me.

Liam huffs in protest, and a quick glance catches a flippant scowl marring what can be gentle features. "Maybe he should get the stick out of his ass. It's not like we're open yet, and plus, I am here early."

"By whose standards?"

Fae is the only one who doesn't visibly flinch at the stern voice. I almost jump out of my skin, and I'm grateful I listened to Skyler's advice yesterday morning, because there's no doubt in my mind that my tail would be flicking nervously behind me. But at least I'm not the only one cowering in my sneakers. Liam physically cringes, recoiling back a step, and I swear I hear a quiet *fuck* fall from his lips.

But Liam's quickly let off the hook as sharp, gray eyes narrow at me. Despite the man's lack of height, his presence comes off as towering. It's as if he's seven feet tall instead of five feet and some odd inches. The piercing gaze of those narrowed eyes has my skin prickling, and I can't help but to grasp my own forearm to close in on myself as much as possible. Maybe if I can somehow become small enough, the little man in the crisp white chef coat will ignore me.

But, of course, I'm not that lucky.

"Who are you?" he demands.

"I...um...I'm-"

"He's my friend," Liam steps in - literally, as he moves to my side. "Is it okay if he hangs out here today?"

The man clicks his tongue but easily brushes me off. "As long as he doesn't make a mess," he says, and it has me breathing a sigh of relief. Those sharp eyes finally abandon me and lock on Liam. "If you're not in the kitchen in the next thirty seconds, you'll be on the floor for as long as you work here."

Liam blanches for a precious second before darting after the man. He pauses in the doorway, wasting more of his precious time limit, as his eyes peer at me. I wave him off, even though I really don't want him to go. He nods silently with a small smile to acknowledge my gesture before disappearing down the hallway.

And then I'm left with Fae, who takes it upon herself to cross the small space to stand at my side. Those brilliant blue eyes brim with a gentle kindness that is far too large to be confined to her small frame, and it's quite daunting to have such kindness directed at me. "Come on, Nico, I'll give you a tour of the infamous *Scout's*." She takes two small steps, then glances over a delicate shoulder to make sure I follow.

And I do, because it's better than being alone in the tiny break room to wait for even more awkward introductions all by my lonesome. That, and I'm pretty much a lost puppy who will follow anyone in hopes of finding an owner. I'm fully aware of that fact, but I'm not ready to abandon my collar to become an independent stray. I may never have that confidence.

Fae leads the way down the claustrophobic hall, a rather short distance until she has to pull open a door and usher me through. My senses are assaulted by a pristine brightness - one so different from the dull tans and browns of the employee area. The fluorescent lights shine off of nearly every surface, reflecting off the chrome of stools and the checkered black and white floor tiles. The plush red of booth seats lining the windows match the stools and the trim on the slightly off-white counter top. A thin strip of space - barely enough for two people to comfortably pass each other - lies behind the counter. Beyond that is more counter space that houses various appliances and machines - among them a soda dispenser tucked in the corner - and there's a window cut out of the wall that sees into a sliver of the kitchen.

"So this is the little diner known as *Scout's*," Fae tells me. "There's not much to see, but this is the dining area. The door right there leads into the kitchen, and the bathrooms are the last two doors on the left." She points out each one and then says, "That's about it, so feel free to have a seat." She pats one of the stools as if to entice me.

And it works. I slide atop the seat chosen for me and find the stool to be one of those swively ones. I can't contain the urge to spin in circles so I don't even try, grabbing hold of the cushion with my fingers and propelling myself in slow circles.

Fae rounds the counter, and by the time I make a full rotation on the stool, she's standing before me, an angelic smile pulling at the corners of her lips as she ties apron strings behind her back. Another rotation and she's stuffing a pad of paper and sharpened pencils in the apron's pocket. It's on the third rotation when she again initiates social interaction, and I'm glad, because I honestly have no idea what to say in this kind of situation.

"How long have you known Liam?" she asks as she goes about her morning duties.

About twenty-four hours. But how odd would that sound? What kind of twenty-four-hour relationship involves one party spending the entire day at the other party's workplace? Liam and I - that's who. But that truth sounds kind of stalkerish, even though Liam introduced me as his friend.

"Not very long actually." A little vague but still the truth.

"Then how did you two meet?"

Tread carefully, Nico. "Well, um, I needed a place to stay, and since I know Skyler, he offered to let me stay at his apartment so Liam and I are kinda roommates," I tell her, my words coming out a lot faster than I want them to.

47

"Oh, so you two are living together," she summarizes my jumble of words.

"Who's living with who?" an unfamiliar voice joins in the conversation as the door to the break room swings open.

My spinning on the stool comes to an abrupt halt, and I'm left staring at not only one new stranger but two, much like a deer in headlights. The one who spoke crosses behind the counter, his stride as casual as his question, and he leaves his companion to close the door behind him.

"So who's shacking up with who?" he asks again.

"Liam got himself another roommate," Fae says.

The newcomer laughs - no, downright cackles. "Who the hell would willingly live with Horseface?"

Horseface? That's Liam, right? I'm gonna assume it is and hope it doesn't make an ass of me.

Slowly, hesitantly, I raise my hand, like the shy kid in class that barely ever speaks but is marginally confident in their answer this time. "The *who the hell* would be me."

The brunette male didn't miss a beat as he flashed a cocky smirk my way. "So do you have to feed him hay or something? Maybe ration his corn and oats intake? Oh, I know! You ride him so he can get daily exercise!"

The air I had been so calmly breathing suddenly sticks to my lungs, and I have trouble coughing for more. The flush to my skin grows uncomfortably hot, so hot it feels like my cheeks are on fire. I gape at the man, fully intent on saying something, anything to deny his joke, but my ability to form coherent sentences disappears with my breathing functions.

"Shut the fuck up, Goldman!"

Liam's pissed off shout from the kitchen startles me into breathing again, but oh my gosh, he heard all that.

"What are you gonna do to make me?" the Goldman guy taunts, and it reminds me of childhood fights back in the demon world; but I really hope this one ends with less blood.

Liam bites back, "I'll shove my foot so far up your ass that– OW!"

"If I hear another word from either of you, you're both fired. Understood?" The little chef's voice echoes in the diner, leaving no room for anything but acceptance.

Both Liam and Goldman mutter a *Yes, Sir,* and it's followed by a muffle of laughter coming from what I assume to be more cooks in the back.

But Goldman isn't let off the hook so easily. His companion, a young woman with black hair that doesn't quite reach her shoulders, glares at him - that same I'm-disappointed-in-you mom glare that Skyler likes to use. "Apologize," she says, nodding toward me.

"I'm sorry, uh..."

"Nico," I supply for him.

"Darin. And this is my sister Miki." Miki gives me a small nod and a brief smile before walking off to do something else. "Again, I'm sorry."

"It's fine. I can take a joke," I brush it off to the best of my abilities.

"At least one half of the roommate duo can," Darin snickers.

Liam and I are already a duo, and it's only been one day. What are we going to be considered a few months from now?

"Darin," Miki calls from across the dining area, near the front entrance. "You should get to work."

Teal eyes that hide a hint of gray roll at her words. "Yes, Mother," Darin drones as he slips on an apron.

Miki flips the sign on the door to open and then joins the other two in doing whatever morning tasks they deem fit. There's a lot of menial cleaning of already spotless surfaces, and Fae even starts brewing coffee.

When customers begin trickling in a few at a time; Darin, Miki, and Fae take turns seeing to tables and taking orders. In all honesty, three waiters are too many for the number of people being served. One would be sufficient, two would even be understandable, but three leaves one of them standing around doing nothing, or in this case, conversing in small chitchat with me. At least they all take turns being the one with nothing to do, although I personally wish Fae would take a little more advantage of it. She's the easiest to talk to, although hearing Darin tell jokes that mainly poke fun at Liam is quite entertaining too - you know, when they don't involve sexual acts with me.

The morning passes by quickly without anything out of the ordinary happening. Business picks up marginally around noon, but it still can't be considered busy. The clock on the wall reads 2 p.m. when the lunch rush ends. It's then that Liam walks out from the kitchen only to disappear into the hall to the break room.

When he reappears with his lunch box in hand, he bypasses the entrance to the kitchen in favor of sliding atop the stool directly to my left. He drops whatever he brought for lunch on the counter in front of me; and the minute his hands are free, they drop to his side, his arms hanging limply as his head falls to the counter top, his cheek pressing against the cool surface. The exposed skin of his face, neck, and forearms has a flushed sheen, and eyelids veil his copper eyes.

"Are you okay?" I ask, reaching out to touch the feverish skin of his cheek.

"I'm too fucking hot," he whines as he shifts his head to rest his other cheek on the counter, and my hand retreats back to myself.

"Aw, Horseface can't handle the heat," Darin mocks. And, oh Liam, please don't retaliate and get yourself fired.

Liam sits up straight, spins on the stool to glare at Darin, and I hold my breath while waiting for the imminent outburst.

But, thankfully, it never comes.

"I'm just not used to it yet." And Liam leaves what could have been another yelling match at that.

He spins back to the counter and takes ownership of his lunch box. When he unzips it and pulls out its contents, I can't help but laugh. I expect some sort of leftovers or even sandwiches made that morning. Honestly, a few handfuls of chocolate chip cookies would have been less surprising.

"Keep laughing, and I'll eat yours too," he says, a slight pout to his lips.

"But don't you buy those for Skyler so he won't burn down the apartment trying to cook?" At least that's what Skyler always said when he'd bring them over to Emil's dorm - something about his roommate never forgetting the one time he melted a plastic bowl in the microwave while trying to make macaroni and cheese.

"Well, kinda–"

Darin cuts off Liam's reply, "Mr. Wannabe Cook always brings *Lunchables*. Makes me wonder if he even knows how to cook."

At Darin's words, there's a waver to Liam's eyes, one that showcases weakness - fragility. His jaw sets as if he's clenching his teeth, and his shoulders go rigid. But as fast as the vulnerability came, it's gone in the same blink of the eye. It's a moment so easily missed that it would have gone completely unseen had I not already been watching him.

"I don't have to prove myself to you," he mutters under his breath, and I'm not sure anyone else hears him say it.

But either way, Darin leaves him alone after that - actually, everyone leaves him alone. That's probably smart on their part because the scowl on his face rivals that of the cruelest of demons.

Even with a look that could kill plastered to his face, he gently nudges one of the pizza *Lunchables* until it sits in front of me. He silently tears his open and wastes no time in constructing miniature pepperoni pizzas. As he's squeezing equal amounts of sauce onto the little circles and spreads the sauce out with his fingers, his scowl softens; but the look of utter defeat that replaces it is far from an improvement.

I follow suit, building my own lunch; but as I do, I scour my brain for a way to cheer him up. Something about Darin's jibe cut deep into Liam's psyche, but there has to be something I can do or say that will cancel it out, or at the very least make him temporarily forget. There has to be something, anything.

And then I remember last night - when Liam offered me the pie he had spent the afternoon making. He had looked so nervous, so afraid of what my reaction would be. At the time, I brushed it off as normal, because who wouldn't be a little apprehensive about sharing something they put their soul into making with practically a stranger. But I didn't have to say a single word before Liam had sighed in relief and offered me back a grin brimming with pride.

So I know exactly what to say to cheer him up. "You're a great cook."

He pauses mid-bite through his second mini pizza. It's only a lapse of half a second, but I notice it, along with the renewed flush to his cheeks. He only replies with a slight nod of his head, but it's enough to watch his insecurity wither away.

We finish our late lunch in silence, and Liam's sipping on the straw of a juice pouch when a short woman with light auburn hair walks out of the kitchen. Her eyes roam the diner until she spots Liam at the counter, and she comes to stand across from us.

"Is this the friend you were talking about?" she asks.

Liam finishes off his juice pouch before answering, "Yeah, this is Nico."

The woman extends a hand to me, and my hand surrounds her much smaller one easily. "It's nice to meet you. I'm Stephanie," she introduces herself with a radiant flash of teeth. "I hope you're not too bored hanging around here all day."

"Not at all," I tell her, and it's the truth.

"That's good to hear. So, Liam, how are you liking working with Simon?"

With that one, simple question, Liam's eyes light up with unrestrained excitement, and he perks up instantly, leaning forward on the edge of his stool in his eagerness to tell. "It's amazing, like I thought Simon would be a total drill sergeant and wouldn't accept anything less than perfection, but he's not. He's actually really patient and is an amazing teacher. When I was messing up all those fancy cutting techniques, I thought he was gonna bite my head off, but he didn't. He walked me through step by step until I got the hang of it. I mean, who would've thought chopping onions for hours would be so fun?"

His words are fast, like that of a child telling their parents how they scored their very first point in a game at recess. And like that same child, Liam's elation surrounds him and all those around him, and the beaming smile upon his lips is contagious.

"If you think chopping onions is fun, wait until he trusts you to prepare dishes on your own," Stephanie tells him.

"Wait, he—" Liam stumbles for words, but he eventually manages a coherent sentence. "Do you think he'll let me work with him again?"

"Of course, he will. It may not seem like it, but Simon really enjoys passing on his trade. As long as you keep showing an eagerness to learn, he'll keep teaching you anything you want to know."

Speak of the devil, and he shall appear in the food window. "Steph, I told you to go get him, not have a leisurely conversation with him."

Liam's the one who replies even though the chef hadn't been talking to him, "Sorry, Sir, I'll be right there." He scoops up our combined trash and shoves it all in the lunch box to zip it up with lightning quick speed.

"Hurry it up then," the little chef, or Simon, says before going back to whatever he had been busy doing.

Stephanie laughs when Liam dashes to the break room and is back to stumble through the kitchen door in ten seconds flat. "I remember when that was me scrambling to please Simon's every whim," she smiles. "I better get back too. I hope you enjoy the rest of your day."

"You too." She walks away after that, leaving me with a little wave and a much larger smile.

The rest of the afternoon and the evening goes by much like the morning had. Around 5 o'clock, business picks up, even more than it did for lunch. By 7 p.m., the place is almost deserted again. It's an hour and a half later when Darin and Miki clock out for the night. Fae then begins cleaning up, stopping to serve the rare customer, and I help her any way I can - which is mostly wiping down the counter and booths.

Fae is just about to lock the front door when the tinkling of a bell announces someone's arrival. I turn in time to see her swept up in another woman's arms, and I avert my gaze when the two share a private kiss.

"Kari," Fae protests but makes no attempt to remove herself from the embrace.

"I've waited all day to see my dear Fae so I don't give a flying fuck who-" but Kari's sentence trails off as she spots me wiping down a nearby booth. "Oh my god, Freckle Buddy!" She abruptly drops Fae and races to sling an arm around my shoulder. She roughly bumps into me and squeezes me tight to her side.

"Kari, don't hurt Nico," Fae chastises her.

"I wouldn't dream of harming a single hair on my Freckle Buddy's head. Right, Freckle Buddy?"

"Uh, sure?" I hope that's the right answer.

"See, we're buddies!" Kari insists as she ruffles a hand through my hair.

"He doesn't even know you."

"Okay, okay," Kari says as she relinquishes her grip on my shoulder. "Hi, Nico. I'm Kari." With her introduction out of the way, her arm returns to my shoulders, and she grins broadly at me. "Is that better?"

"Um, yeah, I guess. Hi."

"See? We're already the best of buds," Kari claims as she claps me across the back.

"You should be more gentle with your Freckle Buddy."

Oh thank god!

"Liam, my boy! Long time no see!"

I huff a sigh of relief as Kari finally releases me for good and turns her sights to Liam. She races to him like she did to me, her arms wide open and prepared to wrap around Liam's midsection.

"I don't think so," Liam says as he steps out of her path. "And I saw you in class on Tuesday."

That's enough of a distraction for Kari to forget about her original mission of trapping Liam in her embrace. "Oh, that's right. I told you your banana looked like a penis. God, Liam, you really need to practice painting fruit."

"Yeah, and I told you that you have no idea what a dick looks like."

"That's right. Good times, good times. It's too bad you're such a poor loser."

"Yeah, yeah, you're right. Hey, Fae, do you need any help cleaning up? Otherwise Nico and I are gonna go."

"You two can go home. Kari will give me a hand, won't you?" Fae turns to her girlfriend and bats her eyelashes.

"Fine. Take my Freckle Buddy away from me. See if I care."

"Okay, goodbye, Kari," Liam calls as he motions for me to follow him to the break room.

"Bye, Liam! Bye, Freckle Buddy!" Kari shouts.

I reply much quieter with my indoor voice, "Bye." And I pull the door shut behind me.

Once again, Liam tosses the jacket at me, and I follow him out into the darkness of night. But this time, I don't feel like I'll get lost in the now nonexistent crowds. We can comfortably walk side by side without hindering anyone else, although I can no longer use him as a wind breaker in front of me.

"Hey, Nico," Liam says a little hesitantly when we're almost back to the apartment.

I wait, but he doesn't continue. So I prompt him, "Yeah?"

He's silent for another few steps until we're out from under the light of a street lamp. His gaze finds the ground, and he tilts his head away from me. "Thanks, for uh, what you said earlier. It, uh, means a lot to me to hear it."

I spend the next day hanging out at the apartment with Skyler, Emil, and Naomi (who stayed over last night and took my spot on the couch, so I camped out on the living room floor) while Liam is at work. We waste away the day watching game shows and (un)lucky me, there's an all-day marathon of *Family Feud*. I enjoy the show as much as any normal person, but Skyler's dick jokes get to be too much after one hour, let alone eight.

And I finally understand why Liam only trusts Skyler with *Lunchables*. When lunch time rolls around, Skyler declares he's going to successfully make macaroni and cheese. Then he sits down and gets absorbed into the TV... and forgets the noodles on the stove. They're not salvageable, so Naomi orders pizza, and we munch on that for the rest of the day.

"I've got to get back to the dorms," Naomi says around 8:30.

Emil agrees, so the three of them - although quite reluctant - leave me alone in the apartment. But it's not that big of a deal. I'm actually grateful for it because now I can change the channel without being permanently kicked out of the apartment.

The minute the door closes behind the trio, I snatch the remote and flip through the hundreds of channels. And then I finally find the one I'm looking for, and oh my gosh, *Too Cute* is on. I press the select button so fast that it would even rival Skyler's record.

I follow the life of fluffy balls of cuteness. A litter of fluff balls crawls around on their bellies - their eyes not yet open - and when they get too far, they cry for their mother. But it's not just their mother that answers them. Simba and Furby do too. Furby's head perks up, and it looks all over for the source of the crying, but it quickly gives up and returns to its nap. Simba, though, sits directly in front of the TV and intently watches the screen, more so than even me.

The baby balls of fluff grow into large balls of fluff in a matter of forty-five minutes. There's a lot of *aw*'s and *how cute*'s coming from me, but when the apartment door slams open with a bang, a shrill squeak falls from my lips

I scramble to my feet in time to see Liam storm past me, a small gift bag clutched tightly in his hand. His footsteps fall heavy against the carpet, and his hands are balled into fists at his sides. Eyebrows furrowed, he's wearing his typical scowl, but his bottom lip is between the bite of his teeth. Head down, he stares at the floor, but that can't conceal the wet sheen of copper eyes.

"Liam," I say quietly, taking a step to follow him.

But   he   stumbles   into   his   room   and   slams   the   door.

BONES AND BANANAS

Don't cry. Don't cry. Don't cry. Dammit, Liam! I'm stronger than this. I've been through this before. I've won this battle - this long, drawn out, tear-ridden, godforsaken shoot out - so why the fuck am I still fighting? Why does it still bother me so much? No, this isn't a bother; it's a wound that keeps reopening no matter how many times I sew it shut with a blunt needle or cauterize it closed with the lick of fire. How much do I have to bleed before the people I'm supposed to love - who are supposed to love me - stop twisting the damn knife in my back? Why can't they leave the wound to heal, or better yet, leave me the fuck alone?

Stop crying.

I told him not to bother. I told him not to waste his breath. No, Liam, this isn't Eli's fault. Don't kill the messenger. It's not his fault our families are old friends and next door neighbors. He brings something back from my family every time he goes home, because god knows I haven't gone back once since being shipped out to Sodalis. Of course, they haven't come to see me either. Apparently, all I'm worth is the occasional phone call or text from my mom.

Blink them back.

It's not my mom's fault I'm a piss poor excuse of a son. She should've stopped after her first child, but then again, there's no way she could have known she'd be stuck raising a worthless lump of flesh like me - someone who can't even forgive and forget, because what's there to forgive if what they said is true? They were right all along. I'm nothing compared to the almighty first born Holt child - the great Bryce Holt. And what family wouldn't want to celebrate their son completing yet another major he will probably never use. What's he up to now? Four? Maybe Five? How the fuck would I know? I'm never invited to those parties.

Breathe. Calm down. Don't lose my composure while still in the streets. Wait until I'm enclosed in the walls of my own room without any curious, prying eyes to see what will surely be another one of my monthly meltdowns. Come on, I can last another five minutes - four if I pick up the pace.

But my erratically racing heart refuses to still, not with the constant reminder squeezed between my fingertips. I shouldn't have looked in the bag, or I at least should've waited until I got home, but no, curiosity killed the fucking cat, and I'm that damned feline.

Why does a framed picture bring salty drops of betrayal and heartache to the corners of my eyes? Why does my chest tighten when I look through the thin layer of glass to see dazzling white smiles captured in a moment meant to be remembered, to be treasured? Why does the arm of my father draped across my brother's shoulders stir a pang of jealousy, and why does the kiss of my mother upon his cheek make me want to punch his skin beneath her lips?

But what's worse is the bitterness rising in my throat, because they are there too. The very people who are supposed to spoil their son's and daughter-in-law's children - the ones who knocked over the first domino in the intricate trail I had built my life upon, even before I rebelled against the golden boy - are grinning from ear to ear, celebrating one grandchild's life as if they hadn't had a hand in ruining the other's.

Stop. Please, stop. Stop digging up old memories that will only hinder every inch, every step of progress I've made since then. Please, mind, shut the hell up. I'm begging you.

But the picture encased in the extravagantly expensive frame isn't the only gift Eli brought back for me. The words of my mother, handwritten in her intricate scroll, reverberate in my head.

My Dearest Liam,

I hope you're doing well, both in your own endeavors as well as your academics. I apologize for being unable to call for the past few weeks, but I hope that can be forgiven. If you are free this coming Friday, I'd very much like for you to come home for a family lunch to celebrate your brother's achievements, but I also understand if you are busy. Please do not feel obligated to come if that is the case, but know that a place will be set on the table waiting for you. I look forward to catching up with you.

Sincerely,
Annette

The handwriting can only be hers, but the words are stiff and distant. They aren't the words of the mother I grew up loving, but that of the mother who took my father's side when I thought she was the only one I could trust. I still love her, I really do, but it's hard to read such formal language of my mother's public image. I don't want to talk with that version of my mother. I want the mom I talk to on the phone, the one who doesn't worry about public pretenses, the one who couldn't give two shits about what my father thinks about me, the one who offers gentle support from the sidelines.

But that mom's been fading over the past few months - ever since this last semester started and I once again failed to show my ugly mug at home in favor of working all summer. I guess my excuses became too much, and she decided I wasn't worth it too. I get it. I understand, because I'm beginning to feel the same way.

Open the door. Walk up the stairs, one foot in front of the other, come on, Liam. I'm so close. Turn the corner and find the right apartment. Five more steps. Four. Three. Two. One.

My hand grasps the doorknob and turns, throwing it open with far too much force, but who cares? I sure as hell don't. I kick it shut with my foot and set my eyes on my bedroom. I race for my personal space, not bothering to toe off my shoes or shed the jacket that has a distinctly sweet yet musky smell lingering on it. I only wish the scent could bring as much comfort as it had when I first put it on, before I tore open the tape holding the gift bag shut.

But I opened Pandora's Box, and now all that bad shit that had been locked up inside has free reign of my mind. The hatred, the doubt, the insecurity - they all burrow into my brain like parasites, eating what little confidence I built up over the years.

What's the goddamned point anymore? Who fucking cares what happens to me? No one does, so why should I care? I don't - or at least that's what I tell myself to make it easier to sleep at night.

"Liam."

Please, Sprinkles, don't let my name tumble from your lips like that. Go back to whatever you were doing and forget you ever saw me. Don't give me the hope that you actually care, because like a flea-bitten stray on the street, all it takes is a single bone for me to grow attached, and trust me, no one wants to have my sorry ass to deal with.

I dart to my room, stumbling across the threshold and slamming the door shut as I fall back against it. With the door clicking shut, the dam that held back the stinging tears cracks. It starts out small, merely a pinprick in the cement, but with each added thought of negativity - I'm worthless, I'll never amount to anything, I'm not good at the one thing I'm supposed to excel in, I'll never achieve the only dream I haven't given up on - the crack spreads. The cement walls crumble in a choking spray of dust, and I can't breathe.

My eyes burn, and my lungs ache for air, gasping for breath between the sobs I try so damn hard to stifle. But who am I kidding? My body racks with the weight I've put upon its shoulders. My hands shake, and I can hear the vibrations against the overly colorful paper of the bag.

This - all these useless emotions I thought I abandoned years ago - is all its fault. The goddamned picture. I didn't ask for it, and I sure as hell don't want it. What right does it have to dig up things of the past and leave a trail of dirt in my heart? Who gave it the right?

Crash!

The bag collides with the opposite wall, glass shattering upon impact. It falls in a heap on the floor, barely missing the foot of my bed, and it feels so damn good!

I stumble to my closet and rip the door open. There are more - dumped in a pile in the corner. One from every graduation I wasn't invited to, every Christmas I never attended, and every birthday I never celebrated - each one framed in hopes of them becoming keepsakes.

I grab one and let it fly, the fake smiles somersaulting into the same spot on the wall, but it's not enough. One after another meets the same fate of shattering into the wall until a corner of one of the frames breaks through the drywall. But that doesn't stop me, only makes me change tactics. I raise a picture from two Christmases ago above my head, clutching the frame with both hands, and smash it into the carpet with enough force to send a shard of glass across the room. I go through the entire pile until a mountain of glass shards lie at my feet.

It's gone - the high of the adrenaline - and all I want to do is pass out; and you know what, I don't really care if I wake up. I step through the glass splinters, their remains crunching beneath the soles of my feet, but I don't make it to my bed before my knees buckle, and I crumple to the floor. And that's where I stay, because I can't muster up the strength to drag myself onto my bed.

So I toe off my sneakers and fling them atop the glass shards, lazily discarding the jacket clinging to my frame at the same time. My body curls in on itself, knees pulling up to my chest and arms clutching them tight. I stare into the darkness beneath my bed, and for once, I'm not afraid of the demons that lurk there. Let them come. Let them take me. They can do no worse than what I already do to myself.

Because why am I blaming everyone else for my shortcomings - my failures - when it's all my fault? I choose not to go home. I choose to put minimal effort into everything I do because there's no point in expending 110% if nothing I ever do is good enough, if someone else is always substantially better than me. I choose to let other people's words cut me down again and again, because for some unfathomable reason, they echo in my head until the voice saying them is my voice. If only I would choose to not care - if only I were strong enough to, but I'm weak, someone who amounts to nothing, and until the day I choose to be more, I'll be stuck right here - a broken heap on my bedroom floor.

I try to let that darkness - those demons under my bed - lull me into unconsciousness, but even they ignore me. They leave me wishing I could fit under my bed with them because then they'd have to accept me into their world instead of abandoning me under the brightness of the lights I wish I never flipped on. The artificial brightness shines down upon the mess I will have to clean up tomorrow and only reminds me of the building guilt I'm trying to suppress.

So I shut my eyes and will myself to sleep, begging my inner voice to shut up and welcome the temporary death.

And it almost works.

A hesitant, light rap of knuckles knocks twice on my door. "Liam. Liam, are you okay?"

Save yourself, Sprinkles. Stop worrying about me. I'm not worth it.

The doorknob rattles, and the screeching squeak as the door's slowly nudged open rings inside my head. My entire body goes rigid, my muscles locking in place and freezing like a stone statue, and my eyes stay closed. I fight against the urge to gasp for breath and force air in and out of my nose as calmly and naturally as I can.

A sharp gasp sounds from Nico, and I guess anyone would be appalled at the destructive tornado that tore through my room. I expect him to back out to safety, but his footsteps pad closer. He stops by my back, so close I can feel the brush of his pant leg against my t-shirt. He steps over me, and my ears pick up the ruffling of fabrics.

And then a cool breeze of air washes over me. As Nico steps back, the familiar weight of my comforter settles over me, conforming to every inch of my body. His footsteps grow distant toward the hall, and the door creaks as it's pulled shut. Just before closing the door completely, the lights flick off, and the room is finally consumed by darkness.

I duck my head under the blanket and tangle myself in its clutches. My eyes moisten, but this time, there are no strangled sobs or choked-back cries. The tears simply fall, trailing down my cheek and into the carpet.

My poor Sprinkles, you have no idea what you've just done. By offering your hand, you have effectively gained a mangy stray to take care of. You should've ignored me - walk right by the starving mutt in the alley like everyone else, act like you never saw me digging through garbage for any scrap or bone I can chew on. But you didn't - you offered the stray a bone.

And I'm so sorry.

Crust breaks from my eyes as sunlight streams through a crack in the curtains. I blink against it, burying my face into the carpet. Unconsciousness didn't last nearly as long as it should have, and I doubt it will welcome me back now, not that I'd be able to fall asleep again even if it did. Collapsing on the floor is a terrible idea, and the aches ailing nearly every inch of my body remind me of that. I roll onto my belly, numerous bones in my spine creaking with the effort as if I'm an eighty-year-old man and not a twenty-year-old man-child. When I drowsily turn my head toward the door, I catch a glimpse of transparency lounging against the wall, the eggshell paint easily visible through the glass shard.

Nope. I refuse to deal with this shit so early in the morning, so before the guilt has its chance to settle into the pit of my stomach, I stagger to my feet, leaving the comforter in a lump on the floor. Dragging my feet across the carpet, I trudge like a living zombie to my door and pull it open, quickly shutting it behind me in a poor attempt to lock my problems within the room.

After a quick trip to the bathroom, I tiptoe into the living room, trying to be considerate of a potentially sleeping Sprinkles; but as I pass the couch, I find it empty. Suddenly, I'm awake, because he's gone again. What if he left after last night? What if he doesn't come back this time? What if-

The clattering of a pan breaks through my paranoia, and I breathe a sigh of relief I didn't know I was holding in. I pad to the kitchen, stopping beneath the entryway and leaning up against the wall to simply watch Sprinkles. He's standing in front of the stove, an empty pan on the front burner, but the lack of a little red light tells me the burner's off. The fridge door is pulled wide open, and it hinders my sight of Nico from his lower abdomen down. His eyes gaze into the fridge, a slight crinkle at the corners, as his lips purse in ponderment.

"You're gonna let all the cold air escape."

He startles, his broad shoulders flinching, and he slams the fridge door shut, spinning on his heels as he spots me watching him. A light flush darkens his cheeks but not enough to cover up the smattering of freckles. He reaches to rub the nape of his neck as he stammers, "I was, uh– Are you okay?"

I recoil slightly, and suddenly I'm wishing I was dealing with the freight load of guilt waiting for me in my bedroom. But it's too late for that, and how can I act like nothing happened in front of the saint of a man who practically tucked my sorry ass into bed (well, the floor) last night? "Yeah, I'm fine."

His eyebrow raises, and that's all it takes for him to call me out on my bullshit. "Do you want to talk about it?"

I don't trust myself to recall the events of last night - or more specifically what led to my sudden breakdown - without crying all over again, and I'm sick of spilling tears over the same damn thing. So I shake my head and release a little puff of air. "I'd rather not, but thanks anyway. I'm more interested in what you're doing." That's better - distract myself from reality with the daily antics of Sprinkles.

The blush that formerly lit up his cheeks is back tenfold. "Oh, well um, I was going to make you breakfast - you know, to try and cheer you up, but I'm not really sure what to make." Those dark honey eyes of his advert to the linoleum tiles, and he shifts his weight from foot to foot.

It's a good thing he's not looking at me because I can imagine the heat to my cheeks must match his. I can't even fathom why someone would want to cook for me, especially to cheer me up, because no one's ever cared enough to do anything like that in the past. But here's this guy - someone who randomly fell into my life only a few days ago - and all of a sudden I matter enough for him to wear his worry for me on his sleeve. It shouldn't scare me, but it does, because how long can it possibly last before - like everyone else - Sprinkles finds out I'm not worth the worry, not worth his kindness?

But until the day his great realization comes, I'll blindly accept whatever he has to offer because although I'm terrified of being abandoned, I'm also a selfish human being.

"Eggs and bacon would be nice."

Sprinkles breathes a little laugh, "Alright. I think I can handle that."

He thinks? "Have you ever made it before?"

"Not exactly..." he trails off.

"What do you guys eat over at Emil's?" I ask in awe, because who doesn't know how to cook some bacon and eggs?

"Pop-tarts and cereal mainly."

"What about before that - when you were a kid?"

Nico's silent for a minute, and just as I'm panicking because fuck, I shouldn't have pried, he quietly sighs. He looks up at me, his face wiped of any readable emotions and his eyes dangerously neutral - like he's distancing himself from what he says next. "I've kinda been on my own for years - actually for as long as I care to remember - and I'd take what I could get. So I wouldn't consider my diet to be normal in any definition of the word."

Yep, shouldn't have pried. You'd think me - of all people - would think twice about digging into someone's past, but no, I'm just an inconsiderate asshole. And I gotta fix it, because Sprinkles has been nothing but kind to me.

"Well, now that you're here, I'll feed you anytime you want."

He sputters as if trying to find words but doesn't manage anything more than gaping like a fish out of water. And damn does he flush red like an overripe tomato, the blush spreading down his neck and even to the tips of his ears. Dare I say it's endearing, cute even.

"I'll teach you how to make simple things too - starting with scrambled eggs and bacon, so scoot over a bit, please," I say, not giving him a chance to burst into flames from the heat radiating off his skin.

He steps back as I come to his side and swing open the fridge door. I retrieve the carton of eggs from the top shelf and an already opened package of bacon from one of the drawers, setting them on the tiny strip of counter space between the fridge and the stove. I grab a second frying pan from that little department beneath the oven door and set it on the bigger of the two back burners. "Okay, Sprinkles, I hope you're watching because I'm about to work some magic here."

Nico shuffles closer until he's standing practically beside me, peering over my left shoulder. He's so close I can feel each soft exhale of breath tickling my cheek, and in that moment, the realization of what I'm doing hits me hard in the gut. I'm about to cook with another human being, essentially sharing a private activity that's mine alone. It's not like at the diner. That's completely different because at *Scout's*, I'm working beside people who share my passion, but here - when I'm at home in my own apartment - it feels... kinda wrong, like I'm betraying a part of me I normally keep to myself.

But when I glance at Nico to see him peering back - genuinely interested in learning - and I'm close enough to distinguish each freckle upon his cheeks and each golden speck amidst russet irises, I think maybe - just maybe - sharing this part of me with Sprinkles won't be betraying myself, that all of this will be okay.

So I walk him through it step by step, explaining what I do and why I'm doing it just as Simon had done for me. I get four slices of bacon started on the back burner and crack four eggs into the front pan, whisking them together with my fork. I bump into Nico when I pull the fridge door open again, apologize for doing so, and then retrieve two slices of that amazing processed cheese. I tear the slices into even smaller pieces, tossing them in the still runny eggs and stirring them together.

"You're gonna take over, Sprinkles," I tell him, stepping back a bit so we can switch spots. "All you have to do is flip the bacon and stir the eggs every now and then so they don't burn."

"Gotcha," he says, determinedly picking up the fork I had been using, but I pluck it from his fingers. Before he can utter his protest, I slip a spatula into his hand.

"This'll probably work better."

He nods and goes about stirring the eggs while I grab plates and cups from the cupboard. I pour us each a glass of milk; and when I go to put the jug away, I have two cats meowing at my feet. Furby rubs up against my shin as if he's the sweetest angel on this earth, but that little bugger isn't getting a drop of my milk.

"Liam, I think they're done."

"'Kay, then turn the burners off," I tell him, and I bring both plates up to the stove, squeezing in between him and the counter. "Pile them high, Sprinkles."

After we both have a plate of eggs and two strips of bacon, we retire with our breakfast to the living room couch, the two cats right on our heels. We plop down side by side and dig into our food. It takes all of two seconds before Furby and Simba are crying at our feet and only about two more for Nico to tear off two bites of bacon and offer the pieces to the hairballs. They snatch up the meat and run off in opposite directions to chew on them.

"Now they're gonna come back begging for more," I say.

"Because they weren't going to anyway?"

"Point taken," I laugh.

And true enough, the cats are back for more, but by that time, Nico and I are already done with our breakfast and chugging down the last few swallows of milk. I take our dishes to the kitchen and abandon them in the sink. When I come back, Nico's got Furby purring in his lap, and I swear to god, he's gotta have some sort of supernatural powers to tame that beast.

"So what do you want to do today, Sprinkles?" I ask, perching on the arm of the couch with my feet planted on the cushions.

He shrugs, "I don't know. What do you normally do on your days off?"

I somehow doubt Nico would enjoy lazing around all day watching *Food Network*, and I really don't want to spend the entire day boring him to death. And then an idea comes to me. "Have you ever played *Mario Kart*?"

He shakes his head, peering at me with confusion clouding his dark eyes like he has no idea what I'm talking about.

"That's going to change then. Sit tight, and I'll get it set up real quick," I tell him as I hop from my perch and head straight to Skyler's room to retrieve the *Wii*. I step around his clutter and even have to toe a pair of underwear off the game console (cause there's no way I'm touching those with my hands). After unplugging all the connector cords and piling the controllers and a few games in my arms, I return to the living room to hook it up to that TV. I put the game disc in and plop down beside Nico again, dropping his controller in his lap. I give him a quick little run down of how to play and what all the buttons will do while I set up multiplayer.

"Pick a character," I tell him after I already claim Yoshi.

Nico scrolls through the unlocked options a few times before selecting Toad, and I can't help but think it's kinda fitting, 'cause you know, spots. We pick our vehicles and our teams, choosing to be on the same team until Sprinkles gets the hang of it, and I choose the Yoshi Falls track to start him off (okay, so I really like Yoshi, bite me).

So it turns out that he kinda sucks, like eternal 12th place sucks. He keeps taking the same waterway - you know, the only one that isn't meant as a shortcut - and falls to his death each time, but he doesn't seem to care about winning or losing. He chuckles each time he dies - which is a lot - and congratulates me for coming in second (damn that Princess Peach!), so I choose a course that is practically impossible to die on. We're racing through the mall, up escalators and around fountains, but he still manages to spin out on every dropped banana and races up the escalators that are going down.

"You're really good, Liam," Sprinkles says after I barely beat mini Mario to the finish line to come in second again.

"I'm only good at these tracks because they're my favorites. I suck at most of the other ones," I tell him.

"Na-uh," he says in disbelief.

"I'm even on par with your astounding skills."

He lightly - like super lightly, to the point of feather light - backhands my arm. "Ha, ha, so funny."

"No, dude, I'm serious. I'll prove it to you."

I choose Ghost Valley as our next course and tell Sprinkles to enjoy the show. I know I should be careful on this track - because I never fail to fall off the edge of the racetrack - but I have to show Sprinkles just how much I suck. So I race full speed ahead, taking the first turn far too fast, but I luckily collide with a wall and bounce back on course (that section of wall falls away, but I'll deal with that on the next two laps). Sprinkles must be learning from my mistakes, though, because he's going slow - like snail pace slow - but it seems to be working for him. I, on the other hand, barrel ahead of the pack, and it works... for all of ten seconds before I fall off the edge of the track and poor Yoshi flails his arms as he disappears into the dark abyss.

But hey, at least I'm still ahead of Sprinkles when I'm brought back to the track. Of course, that only lasts until the next curve, and I'm falling again. Now, I'm not saying I'm a poor loser, but I'm far from the laugh-every-time-I-die attitude of Sprinkles. It's more like muttering *fuck* that escalates to quite loud declarations of how much I hate this stupid fucking course and how much those ghosts on the track can suck my dick. And Nico's laughing at me - that deep, body shaking laugh that brings tears to the corners of his eyes - as he crosses the finish line in 11th place.

And guess who takes 12th place by default because he's an entire lap behind and fails to finish. This guy right here - a Mr. Liam Holt. Yep, I rock at video games.

Sprinkles is wiping at his eyes as he struggles to speak, "You really do suck."

I should be insulted - what with the whole sore loser thing - but I find myself laughing with him, and we become a pair of idiots gasping for breath and wiping tears of joy from our eyes.

We waste away the afternoon sucking it up at *Mario Kart*, munching on potato chips and chugging cans of soda; and when we get bored of that, we switch to *Super Mario Bros.* Sprinkles is marginally better, but I end up carrying him through most of the levels, or in cases where I can't, he goes into the bubble and waits for me to get past the obstacle. It's mainly me playing and him coming along for the ride, but he seems fascinated enough with watching the characters move across the screen.

"Do you play video games a lot?" Sprinkles asks during one of his sessions in a bubble.

I shrug, "Not nearly as much as I used to. I loved racing games and war games, but I sold off my consoles and games a few years ago. The *Wii* is actually Skyler's, and he agreed to let me play it whenever I wanted if I did the same with my *Sims*."

"*Sims?*"

I'm starting to think Nico's had a really closed-off childhood, because he doesn't seem to know things I consider to be pretty commonplace. But I'm not going to pry any more than I already have. "I'll show you what it is some other time."

"Okay," and he's satisfied with that as I let him out of his bubble so he can get the flag with me.

"What do you like to do with your days?" I ask.

"I enjoy reading, but Emil only had so many books to choose from. I've probably read all of his three or four times by now."

"Oh cool, so have you ever been to the Sodalis library?" I see him shake his head when I glance away from the TV screen. "You'd love it. I'll take you there sometime."

I'm not saying I'm good at art, but I have enough skill to paint fucking fruit - or something that is remotely shaped like a basket of apples, oranges, pears, and hey, there's a damn banana. But you know what would make this whole thing easier? Not having the original Freckle Buddy constantly hovering by my side. Like really Kari, do you not have your own piece to paint?

"How come the dick doesn't have spots?" she pesters.

"For fuck's sake, it's a banana. And why the hell would it have spots?"

She nudges me with her shoulder (thank god my brush isn't touching the canvas) and suggestively raises thin eyebrows at me. "Oh, I don't know," she slings an arm around my neck, tapping her hand against my chest. "Something about that freckled dick you're getting."

"What?" I fucking squeak far too loudly, and now I've got the eyes of every freaking student in the room on me.

"Don't play innocent with me, Liam my boy. You'd be a dumb fuck if you weren't tapping dat ass."

"Then call me a dumb fuck," I grumble as I trace my paintbrush up her forearm, leaving a yellow streak upon her dark skin.

But she doesn't budge from my side, barely even notices the paint trail - merely staring at me as if I've grown a second head. "Are you shitting me? He's good looking, and he's living with you. If I was straight and single, I'd be banging him so fast. So why the fuck aren't you?"

"Gee, I don't know. Maybe because I only met him recently and don't want to fuck up our blooming friendship," I drone sarcastically. A firm elbow jab to her hip finally does the trick of getting her to let me go. I gear up for her retaliation - a punch to the arm or a backhand to my head - but it never comes. Instead of looking pissed, she's smirking at me, slithering up to my side again but thankfully keeping her hands to herself.

"So what you're telling me is that you've thought about it but won't do it because you want him to like you. Cause that's what I'm getting out of this conversation."

"No, that's— You need to get your fucking ears cleaned." That's not what I said, and that's definitely not what I thought. Yeah, Sprinkles is handsome - what with his well-toned muscles and impressive build topped with a pretty face and the gentlest smile known to mankind - but we're friends, and I don't fuck my friends. I made that mistake back in high school a few times, and let's just say those people are no longer my friends, not even occasional acquaintances. Plus, Nico's the very image of innocence. I can't imagine him being anything other than a blushing virgin, and I'm not gonna take him to bed when he deserves more than a one-night stand or a convenient fuck buddy.

"Alright, alright," Kari finally concedes and steps back to her own canvas. "But I give it two months tops."

"Give what two months?"

"Till Cupid works his little cherub magic," she smirks, quite satisfied with herself.

I roll my eyes. "Yeah, yeah, whatever you say," I tell her. But when I return to my painting of fruit, I can't help but see dusted speckles upon the banana's peel.

The day drags by unbearably slowly, and I swear to god I've never sat through a more boring lecture on business ethics in my entire life. I mean, who doesn't know money laundering is wrong? How big of a douche bag does someone have to be to even consider misusing a business's funds? I didn't need to sit through four hours of a professor preaching how that can hurt a business. At least chemistry has the distractions better known as monkey see and monkey do, but even Cody and Alex couldn't make the class end any sooner (unless, of course, they make something accidentally explode, but today's just not that day).

I'm eternally grateful when my academic day finally comes to a close, and I can walk back to my apartment in the darkening night, watching the sun descend below the cityscape. It's a little colder than normal - to the point where I have to pull my hat over my ears (it's one of those with pompoms hanging from strings on the ear flaps and a little tuft of yarn on its top - thanks Skyler) and shove my hands in my pockets. By the time I'm within the apartment, my nose is bright red and numb, and I'm thankful for the heat that washes over me.

"How was your day, Liam?" Skyler calls from the couch as I close the door behind me and shed my outdoor wear.

"Boring. What do you want for supper?"

"Sorry, Liam, your housewife duties have been taken by Nico tonight. Grab a plate and join us before the show comes back on."

Sprinkles cooked? The guy who couldn't make bacon and eggs made supper. What did my little prodigy whip up?

I head straight for the kitchen but don't see anything waiting for me. There are no pots or pans sitting on the stove, and all the dishes I had left in the sink this morning are drying in the rack. Even the counters look like they've been wiped down. "Where is it?" I call.

"The microwave," Nico answers, followed by an obnoxious *shh*, so Skyler's show must have come back on.

I'm pleasantly surprised when I don't find pop-tarts sitting on the plate but a helping of spaghetti instead. I pluck a few noodles with my fingers and shove them in my mouth for a taste test, and my young grasshopper did a pretty good job. When I plop down in my spot between Sprinkles and Skyler (after being kicked in my ass to get out the way - thanks again Skyler), I nudge Nico and whisper a quiet *nice job*.

He nods, offering me a small smile in return, but the gentle gesture turns itself upside down at whatever crosses the TV screen. He turns his head to me, flinching from the ring of gunshots as he squeezes his eyes shut. Peeking through his lashes, those golden specks of his dart to the TV before realizing the scene isn't over and they're closed in a heartbeat again. The minute the scene ends and the bureau agents save the victim from what would have been his death, Sprinkles is fine - watching the happy ending as avidly as Skyler and Emil.

Which I can't help but grin at, finding this new information to be quite amusing. Mr. Darkside - the potential serial killer - can't stomach the violence of *Criminal Minds* but expects me to believe him to be capable of attacking innocent victims like Skyler's demonic fur ball. There's absolutely no way in hell my Sprinkles could harm a fly - that I'm positively sure about now.

But wait. My Sprinkles. No, no. He's not my Sprinkles - just Sprinkles, Nico. There is no my - only him. I chance a glance at him, and he's freaking glowing with glee - honey eyes bright and twinkling - while watching the reunion of the young victim with his parents, and all I can think of is a spotted banana.

Dammit, Kari!

WHY DO YOU CARE?

Coping mechanisms come in countless forms - some of which are healthy and others are detrimental. Humans and demons alike seem to gravitate toward one or the other, either finding productive or destructive methods of dealing with their realities - or in some cases, not dealing with it. The preferred choice would be one of production - creating art, running off the steam, or simply talking about the issue with a trusted friend - but too many times the method chosen is a destructive force - lashing out, emotionally shutting down, and denying it altogether. I can't deny that I often lean toward mechanisms of emotionally destructive, but I hate seeing others follow that same broken path, especially when that someone is a person of importance to me.

But Liam's walking down a beaten trail of his own, and he's lost - wandering in circles among the overgrown weeds. When we spend all of Monday playing video games, he stands still - trying as he may not to lose his way, but distractions can only work for so long, can only do so much. And they work until Wednesday. He wakes up that morning and doesn't say a single thing - not even his typical greeting - and leaves without eating breakfast. Skyler asks me if I know what's wrong with him; but I tell him I don't, because it's the truth. I only saw and heard the aftermath, but I have no idea what caused it. And even if I did, I don't have the right to speak of things Liam doesn't want others to know.

And speaking of the aftermath, the hazardous pile of shattered glass remains untouched on the carpet of his room. I know this because I check every day while Skyler and Liam are away at the university. It's probably an invasion of privacy - not to mention it's technically none of my business - but I can't help but wonder if those broken remains are the cause of Liam's sudden drop in his willingness to function happily and healthfully, or maybe they were simply victims of the anger he warned me about on our first meeting. But I didn't snoop out of curiosity or mere wonder - I'm grasping at straws to find the meaning behind my friend's destructive coping tendencies. I do not believe Liam to be a man of unwarranted rage, so why did he destroy the pictures and nothing else? If I'm wrong - and this is a case of spontaneous wrath - there were plenty of other objects within his reach that would have made far better victims and required less clean up (a rather large heap of discarded clothes in the corner wouldn't have left a hole in the wall).

It doesn't make sense to me, but then again, most emotions don't make sense to anyone other than the one feeling them.

I take a closer look at one of the pictures on Thursday; I know I shouldn't, but I do. A wooden frame is smooth against my fingertips, but the broken pane of glass is anything but. A jagged edge is sharp beneath my touch as my finger runs over it, the break distorting a man's face - cutting through a dark copper orb, across a prominent nose, and slicing the corner of upturned lips. It leaves the lines of his mouth to run across a younger man's broad shoulder and carves a striped tie in two, crosses through the abdomen before abruptly dropping straight down - drawing a perilous line between a black slack covered leg and a slimmer pair open to the room's air from mid-thigh down.

I see it in each of the three standing in front of an old brick fireplace, the flames crackling readily on the logs - that being characteristics I recognize, those I've come to know Liam as. Eyes of copper, which shine as bright as their metal counterpart, bore into me from the two males, frozen upon the paper on which they're printed; but there's a roughness around the edges - one that makes their smiles seem like daggered glares - that Liam didn't inherit. Instead, he received the soft corners of the woman with gentle, gleaming tawny eyes. He's got her hair too, at least on his darker undercut, but that's as far as the similarities go with her. Sharp cheekbones and an angular jaw match that of the two men, along with frames that are more on the slender side, but there's muscle beneath the pressed dress shirts. The younger of the males is a carbon copy of the older - but then again, Liam's pretty close too, but not quite enough to compete with his brother.

And every picture is the same - a mother, father, and a single son. There are a few in which an elderly couple is also present. Those seem to have taken the worst beating, if their cracked picture frames are anything to go by. The broken smiles obviously belong to Liam's family members - there's no denying the resemblance they all share - but then why is Liam not in a single photograph?

That has to be the reason for his sadness - no that's not quite right. I don't think he's sad or even truly angry. He's more... empty, like he's shutting down. And it's only gotten worse from Sunday night.

He comes home early Thursday - so early he beats Skyler by nearly two hours - and there's no way he attended all his classes. I may not know his class schedule, but Skyler briefed me on daily routines this past weekend, and Liam's last class doesn't get out until late evening. He shouldn't be back at 2:30 p.m.

"Hi, Liam," I greet him. He glances at me and gives me a minuscule nod before returning his gaze to the carpet. "Did you forget something?"

He shrugs noncommittally as he hangs his coat in the entry closet. Towing his school bag with him, he trudges to his room. The door clicks shut behind him, and he closes himself off for the rest of the day.

I want to go after him, to knock on his door - force my way in if that's what it comes to - and ask him what's wrong, but I honestly doubt he'd tell me. He brushed my concern off the last time I asked, so what would make this time any different? Constantly pestering him is only going to make him close in on himself even more, and that's the last thing I want. If all I can do is sit back and wait for the storm to pass, that's what I'll do. I'll wait until he's ready or even marginally willing to leave the confines of the prison he's made for himself within the walls of his room, because if he won't open up on his own, I don't have the right to force it out of him.

"What's wrong, Nico?"

I startle, jumping slightly and causing the TV remote to slip from my lap. My hands scramble to catch it, but the remote crashes into the carpet before I can grasp it.

"Dude, are you okay?" Skyler comes up beside Emil, hand on a cocked hip as he stares between the remote on the floor and me.

"Yeah," I spit out far too quickly as I retrieve the remote and carefully set it by my thigh (it's Skyler's baby - he'd kill me if I broke it). Settling into the couch, I clarify, "Yes, I'm fine."

"Then what's got you so jumpy?"

My eyes flicker to the hall. Should I tell them that Liam's home? I kind of have to because they'll find out eventually when Liam decides to come out of his room for food or a trip to the bathroom. My eyes return to Skyler. "Liam's back."

My hulking friend glances around the little living space as if he overlooked Liam's presence when he came in. He stares at me, disbelieving. "He wouldn't miss his pastry class," he states matter-of-factly, but there's an undertone of doubt as golden eyes drift away from me to linger on the entrance to the hallway. "That's his favorite course."

"But he's in his room," I tell him.

Skyler marches past Emil, calling out Liam's name as he disappears into the hall. "Liam, are you in there?" his bellow echoes out to where I sit.

I hold my breath waiting for some sort of reply, meeting Emil's gaze before both of us look at Skyler, barely able to make out his shadow in the hall. My ears strain to hear even the slightest of noises, but I fear I may miss his reply (if he gives ones, that is) with how loud my blood's pounding through my veins.

It feels like an eternity - and I nearly give up on hearing his voice - but an irritated *What?* finds its way through his lips to the door and down the hallway to my ears. The one word - even though it's laced with annoyance - pulls a sigh of relief from my lungs, because that's the first word I've heard him say all day. And I never realized how much I like his voice until he refused to use it, only communicating with head nods and a variation of grunts.

"Are your last two classes cancelled?" I hear Skyler ask, a hopefulness to his tone that that's the case and Liam is not skipping class.

But that hope shatters to dust with one word. "No."

"Why aren't you in class then?"

"Because I'm not. Just fuck off already," Liam bites back viciously.

I cringe at his tone, because while his angry irritation is obvious, there's a softer undertone that rings of desperation. It's kind of like when you're screaming at someone, but you're not sure why - a whole bunch of emotions swirl within your head and they become too much, to the point where you snap at an innocent spectator with the easiest emotion you can face. Too many times, that emotion is anger because it gives an easy way out, allowing the mind to focus on one feeling instead of a jumble of anxiety, self-hatred, fear, and disappointed frustration. But no matter how loud you shout or how hard your bite stings, you can't hide those deeper emotions and you know that. You hate the fact that you're taking the easy way out, but you don't see any other route.

Those emotions show themselves in his voice - in the exhausted profanity he throws Skyler's way.

"Come on, Liam, what's wrong?" Skyler says, surprisingly calm.

Liam's mumble of *nothing* is barely audible.

"It's obviously not nothing." There's a jiggling of a doorknob in a vain attempt to open a locked door. "Don't make me kick the door in," Skyler warns.

"Leave me the fuck alone!"

And there's the torrent of anger that has finally overflowed, rushing over the dams Liam had tried so hard to build. His words cut through the air like a sword through flesh and leaves just as big of a scar upon its victim.

Skyler trudges from the hall - a defeated warrior - and slides his arm through Emil's, pulling him to the couch and plopping down beside me. He snatches the remote and turns it to his go-to gameshow channel, but even the comedy of *Family Feud* can't lighten the tense atmosphere of the apartment.

And it feels so wrong - more foreign than nearly a week ago when I awoke on this couch to surroundings that have grown to be familiar and homey, but now are stripped bare to the bones.

The next morning, a hand nudges my shoulder until my eyes groggily blink open. The heels of my palms rub at the crust built up along them until the bleary figure bent over me takes more of a human shape, and the outlines of hulking shoulders and a square jaw become crisp and clear. The incandescent glow of artificial lights casts dark shadows upon one half of his face while catching in golden orbs to shine down on me. "You awake, or do I have to douse you with water?" he asks, his voice muffled due to the fact one of my ears is pressed against a rather flat pillow.

"'M up," I mumble, and it ends with a short yawn. I blink, trying to keep my eyes open to stare at Skyler in an attempt to prove I'm at least somewhat coherent, because I really don't want a bath so early in the morning (what time is it?) - and he'd do it too. I learned that the hard way.

"Can you do me a favor?"

"Now?" I drone like a five-year-old, expressing my displeasure in the most immature way I can muster.

"No, you asshat, just listen. Liam's been pissy and bitchy all week, and he won't tell me why he's moping around like the living dead, but he might tell you. Will you please find out what's wrong?"

The moment Liam's name slips from Skyler's lips and my sleep-hazy mind registers it, I'm all ears - suddenly more awake and willing to listen than the five-year-old me of seconds ago - but after hearing the whole request, I slump deeper into the couch cushions and pull the quilt over my head with the mindset of if I can't see him, he can't see me. It's beyond me why he'd trust me with such a task to begin with. After all, he's known Liam substantially longer than I have. If Liam won't even trust Skyler with the details of his personal life, what makes him think Liam will trust me? And I already tried talking to him, but Liam shut me out. What else am I supposed to do?

"Please, Nico."

There's desperation in his voice - similar to Liam's but with a slight difference. The root of Skyler's burden isn't caused from inner turmoil but from the external factor better known as Liam, so the pain isn't deeply scarred into the depths of his being. It's not a pain he's trying to hide under layers of scar tissue, but one he openly wears and shares. It's a cry of wanting to help but being unable to, not knowing what to do next after his proffered hand has been slapped away.

The portrait of Liam's family flashes in my mind, but the faces are different - the people are different. The crackling flames still lick at a pile of logs in the fireplace, but the people have changed and moved about to center around Liam. Skyler stands to his right with an arm slung around his shoulders, pulling Liam closer to his side even as Liam struggles to free himself - being more interested in arguing with Darin on his left. Emil's beside Skyler, attempting to muffle a chuckle at Liam's predicament but failing miserably; and Miki thoroughly scolds Darin, but her brother is more interested in being smug with his argument with Liam. Kari sits in front of them on the floor, cackling to her heart's content as she kicks Liam's shin only to be swatted on the head by Fae for doing so. There are two more off to the side, the little head chef and auburn-haired cook - Simon and Stephanie - the former looking utterly annoyed while Stephanie pokes his cheek in hopes of eliciting a smile.

This is Liam's true family. I'm sure there are far more people I have yet to meet - so many that they wouldn't all fit in the frame - but I don't believe Liam realizes just how big his circle of people who care for his well-being really is. He's so focused on blood ties that he can't even see the bonds formed through mutual trust and understanding, through shared laughs and cries, through friendships he chose to make - because unlike family, you can choose your friends, and those friends choose you too. It's a decision made by both parties to be there for each other in times of hardship and good fortune. It's far from the contract a person is forced into at birth, and from the looks of it, Liam was dealt a very strict, one-sided contract in the favor of the other party.

I peek out from under the quilt, only enough to squint at Skyler with one eye and nod my head. "I'll see what I can do," I say before ducking under the covers again.

"Thanks." And then there's pressure from his large hand ruffling the blanket where my head is. "I owe you one."

So I may have promised to do some investigating of Liam's behavior, but it's quite evident I most likely bit off more than I can chew. After Skyler left, I fell back asleep only to wake up to the sound of the shower running a few hours later. I think nothing of it and decide I should probably get up too; because if Liam's awake, it's got to be nearer to noon than to dawn. But when I say get up, I actually mean blindly reach for the remote on the side table and shimmy to untangle my legs from the quilt so I can sit up and cocoon myself in the blanket's warmth in a way which doesn't involve cutting off circulation to my feet.

I watch TV while the shower drones on in the background, but I can't focus on the show playing on the screen. What am I supposed to do when Liam comes out of the bathroom? How should I approach the touchy topic without pissing off Liam even more? Or maybe I won't even get the chance to. If he holes himself up in his room, I won't be able to talk to him without first getting him to open the door, and I somehow doubt he'd be very willing to let me in.

I'm so lost in strategizing thought that I don't hear the shower turn off, but I can't miss the loud thud and echoing shouts of profanity. The suddenness of the noise has me flinching in my seat and twisting to gape at the hallway, holding my breath for the storm that's sure to come.

When the dark clouds finally roll in, they're accompanied by the thunder of a door slamming into a wall and feet stomping on the floor. He comes to a deafening halt - bare chest heaving, hair damp and dripping - with one hand securing a towel around his waist and a pair of jeans balled up in his other. Sharp hips bones and the faint tone of abdominals (and is that part of a tattoo I see along his ribcage?) are a sight to behold, but the angry scowl and his snarling tone make the view hard to appreciate.

"Why are there fucking clothes in the bathroom closet?" he demands.

I hesitantly rise to my feet, because I don't like the looming, ominous feeling of an angry Liam shouting down at me. I wrap the blanket around myself and hold tight to its security as I quietly respond, "Skyler said I could–"

"I don't give a flying fuck what Skyler said! I own half this apartment, and I don't want my bathroom closet full of a fucking stranger's clothes!"

My fingers clench tighter into the soft fabric of the quilt, and oh let's pretend he didn't just spit those words at me, that he didn't revoke our friendship in a single breath. He's mad; he's hurting. He doesn't actually mean the words he's shouting, so I can overlook them. "I'm sorry, Liam, I–"

"I don't want half-hearted apologies or useless excuses!"

"Then what do you want?" Please, Liam, tell me what you want, what you need to make it better. I'll help any way I can, but you have to tell me how. I can't blindly search for an answer without making it worse, so please, tell me what's wrong.

He sucks in a small breath of air and his mouth falls open to respond, but he says nothing. He stares at me, copper orbs softening as the raging anger dissipates into nothing but pain - a hurting betrayal that threatens to overflow upon his cheeks. His chest heaves with each pant of breath he sucks in, and his body trembles with each gasp of air. His eyes lock with mine, and their watery sheen begs me for an escape.

But there's nothing I can give him. There is no easy way out of whatever maze he's stuck in. There are no shortcuts that will magically make each dead end a finish line. I'd be more than happy to go along for the ride, but I can't lead him out of a labyrinth he's made for himself. Liam has the map; he just has to figure out how to read it.

I take a single step around the couch toward him, but he flees like a spooked animal, dropping the pair of jeans in his wake; and his door slams shut before the denim hits the carpet.

I chase after him, because this conversation can't end here. It can't end with Liam destroying his possessions and sleeping in the first place he falls.

My knuckles pound on his door as I call his name. I reach for the doorknob, but my hand recoils as if it's been electrocuted. I can't be the one to open this door. I can't barge into space he considers safe and take the only secure place he has left away from him. I won't do that to him.

"Liam, please, talk to me."

My hand ceases its pounding, resting against the wood, and my fingers uncurl until they're splayed out with my palm flat on the grain. I wait, blood thumping through my veins and each calculated breath echoing in my ears.

"I don't want to talk."

His voice is quiet, subdued - barely a whisper - yet I hear it loud and clear, as if he's pressed against the other side of the door.

I'm getting nowhere. It's time to change tactics. "Then just listen." If he won't talk, I will. "I don't know what's going on or why you're hurting so much and I probably don't deserve to know, but I still care. Skyler and Emil care. Your friends from school and the diner care. That's probably not much consolation for what you're going through, but if you need a family, you've got one."

It's silent, save for my own words echoing within my head. Each ticking second that passes makes me question whether those were the right words or not. Have I overstepped a personal boundary by mentioning family or by assuming that's what Liam wants? And if I did, where is the line drawn between what I can and can't say? Does our friendship have to be a certain level before he'll trust me with details of his life? If this is something he doesn't feel comfortable confiding in Skyler, then he'd never open up to me about it.

"Please leave."

What? Oh no no no. I crossed that invisible line and made it worse. "Liam—"

"Just go! I don't want to talk! I don't want to listen! I want— Please leave me alone," his shouts turn to a mere breath of a request; and I won't deny him the only thing he's asked of me - of anyone - in days.

"Okay," I say, my hand falling from the door to hang limply at my side. "I'm going for a walk so please leave the door open for me."

I'm not going for a walk, but I can't tell him where I'm really going. Plus, it's probably better I go now before Liam finally decides to leave his room and sees a tail twitching from my backside. I'm about ninety-nine percent sure a scene like that will only make the situation worse, so I guess now's a good enough time as any to prevent that.

If he wants time and space to figure his own feelings out, I'll give him exactly that.

Labored breaths are warm against my ear, his words tickling the lobe. His fingers toy with the frayed ends of jet black wings which protrude from my shoulder blades, but I can't fathom why he enjoys running the pads of his fingers along the leather-like texture. He's wearing that self-satisfied smirk of his as his fingers trail up the edge of my wing, over my shoulder, and along my collarbone until they grasp my chin and nudge with gentle force to persuade me into looking at him.

"Are you ill? I feel like you are. What have you done with my shy, submissive little Nico who despises the very idea of showcasing the marvelous features which make him an incubus?"

I blow out a light sigh through my lips and run a hand through my ruffled hair, taming the strands to the best of my abilities. The flames of candlelight flicker within the silver of his irises, and for once, there is no pity, only amusement and genuine curiosity at my sudden change in behavior. And it's understandable. After all these years, I have never once entered his den without being dragged in by my instinctual needs, that is until today. Instead of looking like a beaten down victim, I walked in here with a purpose, albeit the same purpose as every other time, but I didn't deny it today.

There's no need to deny today because I have multiple reasons for my visit, and of those reasons, feeding is the least important. It's a byproduct of the other two - an activity that may as well be completed while I'm at it. It's substantially easier to accept when my mind is focused on far greater goals - as if it's a step one in a three-step process.

And with the first step completed, I can move on to the next (okay, maybe I should get dressed first. It's kind of awkward having a serious conversation in the nude).

"Woohoo! Nico!" he calls, waving his arm to get my attention. "As much as I appreciate the view of you bending over for your unnecessary scraps of cloth, I'd rather have you beside me." He pats the nest of blankets where I had been lying as an invitation to return.

I ignore his invite and take away his view of my freckled butt with those scraps of cloth he loathes so much, and he voices his displeasure with child-like *aw*'s and a pout directed at me when I finally face him fully clothed.

There's no round-about way to gradually bring up the topic I wish to discuss (and I've spent more than enough time away from Liam for him to collect his thoughts), so I outright ask him, "Are they still looking for me?"

The jutted lip of the demon's pout parts to heave a sigh. He rolls onto his back and stares at the stalactite formations hanging from the cave's ceiling. "Not as avidly as they had been."

"But they still are?"

"Yes, but–" he pushes himself into a sitting position - leaning back on his knuckles - and catches my gaze, "you don't have to worry. Avon doesn't have any real leads."

"Are you sure?"

"My freckled little incubus, as important as you are, you are not the only runaway demon. When it comes to priority, you are quite low on that list. Trust me, I'll be one of the first to know when you become the next target, so you can rest assured until then."

I have no choice but to believe him, even if he's one of those demons whose job is to track down and capture runaways like me. But I still trust him. He's had plenty of opportunities to take me into custody, but he's faithfully kept my secret. And for that, I am grateful.

Grateful for the friends I have made because of the freedom I have gained through him. And grateful I have the privilege to return to those friends.

"I'm going to hold you to that."

"Anything I know, you'll know," he promises.

I nod at that and leave him with a word of thanks.

So here I am once again, standing outside the apartment wondering whether or not I should enter, although my contemplation this time has nothing to do with being a stranger to Liam (because I'm trying really hard to forget the words he spat at me earlier).

I grab the knob and turn it, pushing the door in with the hope that Liam isn't watching TV on the couch and spooks at my entrance, but the situation I walk in on is far worse than any my mind could have conjured up.

Liam's seated at the round dining table in the chair closest to the left wall - the one we all hate sitting in because of how claustrophobic it feels being stuck between the table and the wall. His elbows dig into the tabletop to hold up his bowed head, and when I quietly close the door behind me, he doesn't move, doesn't hear or see me.

Because my minuscule noise is a pin drop in a bustling crowd compared to the verbal beating he's in the middle of taking.

"–disappointed in you. And how can you blame them? You stood up your own parents - the people who pay for you to be a success, but you're squandering their efforts. You're nothing more than a disgraceful failure, a smudge on the Holt name."

The man's not facing me, but the tailored suit jacket clinging to his slight frame gives me a good idea of who he might be. I recognize that shade of brown hair and even the confident, dominant stance which mirrors that of a man in a photograph.

"They were right about you. You're a worthless excuse of a hash slinger who couldn't cook his way out of a rundown kitchen, and the sooner you realize that, the better off your future will be."

Liam flinches at the insult and finally raises his head. Copper orbs water with both anger and betrayal - looking like he's ready to cry and punch someone at the same time. His lips part, fully prepared to defend himself, but the sheen of raging fire in his eyes dies the moment he spots me. The flames extinguish in that split second it takes him to register my presence, and a heartbeat later, the back of his chair collides with the wall. He's on his feet in a hurried frenzy and hangs his head low as he retreats to the safety of his room.

The man makes no move to follow him. He pushes the cuff of his sleeve up enough to check the time on an extravagant wristwatch and apparently decides he's done enough damage to his brother for one day. He turns to leave but pauses for a single step when he sees me. A dagger-like glare scrutinizes me from head to toe, and he makes no attempt to hide his appraisal. My worn jeans and borrowed band t-shirt must greatly disappoint him as he clicks his tongue and continues toward the door. I step out of his way and watch him leave - never once does his gaze follow after Liam's hasty departure.

I think I understand the situation now - or at least a part of it. The brutal smashing of family portraits makes sense. It's no wonder Liam took his anger out on objects which represent the cause of that anger. That doesn't make his actions right - because he did damage property other than his own - but it's understandable.

I can't imagine the hurt and betrayal he's feeling, because I never had a family to rely on. But if I compare that kind of relationship to the one I have with my demon partner, I know the damage he can deal to me if he was to ever break the trust we share would be life shattering. But multiply that damage by a lifetime of disloyalty and deception, of constantly being told family is the most important thing in your life only to have your family prove that wrong over and over again. There's only so many times broken shards of trust can be glued back together before the glue piles so high that it replaces the shard altogether. And the glob of hardened glue can never be the piece of trust it is meant to imitate. That trust will always be broken - lost - but worst of all, the people who broke it won't even notice.

I can't leave Liam alone this time, no matter how loud he may shout at me to do exactly that. His brother may have no problem walking away, but I won't let Liam believe no one cares - that everyone will eventually leave him when he needs them most - because they won't - I won't.

"Liam," I quietly call out to him as my knuckles lightly rap at his door.

His reply is muffled, choked back. "Go away."

I'm sorry, Liam, but that's not going to happen. Our friendship means too much to me for me to walk away when you're in pain.

My hand grasps the knob and twists, slowly pushing the door in, but I don't cross the threshold. His room is still a safety net for him, and I'll respect that boundary. I only want to talk, and as long as he can hear me, I'll stay in the hallway until he invites me in.

But seeing Liam curled in on himself atop his bed, facing the wall with his comforter pulled up to almost completely cover his head, is heartbreaking. It makes remaining in the hallway an impossibly difficult task when I want nothing more than to reach out a hand to soothe his worries, but my feet remain planted on the floor. Closing the distance when he wants to increase it will only end in more shattered shards of trust crushed against his carpet to lie beside the broken remnants of photographs.

"I can't leave you alone anymore, Liam," I tell him and pause for some sort of outburst, but it never comes. So I continue, "You're probably sick of people talking at you, so I want to talk to you, but if you don't want to hear it or don't want to listen, I'll shut up. All you have to do is say the word.

He says nothing.

"I don't fully understand what I just walked in on, but I heard things said that no one should have to hear. Please don't believe you're a disappointment because one person said so, and you're a great cook. If you weren't, do you really think Simon would take the time to teach you? He believes in you. Your friends believe in you."

I believe in you.

I can't say that's exactly what Liam wants to hear, or even if my opinion matters to him, but it's out there. I told him what needed to be said, and I'll tell him again if he tries to deny the talent he's put so much effort into honing and the worth that every living creature deserves to have. Because he has worth, no matter what his brother or his parents or anyone else has to say.

"Why do you care?" His question is quiet, near silently said, but it rings like an echoing cry in my ears.

Why do I care? I could blame it on human nature, but I'm not human. A demon - an incubus - wouldn't care, wouldn't even blink an eye unless the insults were thrown their way. And even then, the situation would end with one demon devouring the other. If you are lucky, you'll walk away with your life, but you'll still receive the beating of a lifetime. That's just how demon society works. It's survival of the fittest, every demon for themselves.

But the human world is different - or I thought it was before today. Skyler and Emil have shown me self-sacrifice that benefits someone other than themselves. They've shown me kindness and compassion towards both strangers and friends alike. Yet today, Liam's brother showcased the same selfishness which runs amok in my species. It's a characteristic I despise, a reason I abandoned that world.

I grew up watching violence between demons and humans on a daily basis. It was an everyday aspect of my life that made me cringe, but I only learned to loathe that cruelty because too many times I found it directed at me. That's when I began to notice the effects of such a lifestyle - of such a society. The most powerful demons aren't truly happy, and the weaker ones live in fear. It's a cycle of isolation that makes society anything but social. And the humans who call upon my species want one of three things - sex, compassion, or destruction - all of which demons contort until someone gets hurts.

When you've been on the receiving end of such cruelty, you value every word of kindness someone has to offer. You soak them up like your life depends on it, and you watch every word that spills from your mouth and every action that may affect another person. You're hypersensitive to the pain of others because you've been through it yourself.

"I know what it's like to hate myself, so I don't want you to go through the same pain."

My feet move on their own, backing further into the hall and away from what I just admitted. This isn't about me; it's about Liam. I don't want him feeling sorry for me when he's got plenty of his own problems to figure out. So I leave him in the safety of a blanket burrito, and that's sounding like a pretty good idea to me too.

I stumble over the pair of jeans still lying in the middle of the hallway but manage to plop down on the couch without falling flat on my face. Wrapping myself in the quilt, I burrow into the back of the couch and inhale deeply. The fresh bread scent still lingers in the blanket's fibers - not nearly as strong but still detectable - and it helps calm my scrambled thoughts.

Simba helps too when the tubby kitty decides to jump on me, falling quite a bit short and having to dig its claws into the quilt to heave its excess weight over my lower back and settle atop my hip. The tabby stretches out to lazily lounge atop me and meows loudly while pawing at my side.

I wriggle my arm free from beneath the quilt and wrap it around Simba. I pull the massive cat down between the back of the couch and my stomach, and Simba doesn't fight it. The cat curls up beside me and rubs its head against my hand until I scratch behind its ears. The rumble of the resulting purr vibrates against my abdomen, and it melts away the stress from my shoulders. The purring vibration is the very embodiment of peace.

And something so simple has me convinced everything will be okay

I COULD GET USED TO THIS

"I know what it's like to hate myself, so I don't want you to go through the same pain."

My shallow breaths catch in my throat at Nico's admission. I twist my torso to glance over my shoulder, but I only spot the back of a black t-shirt as he flees my doorway. Fucking hell. With a grumbled groan, I bury my head in the fluff of my pillow and pull the blanket up over my head.

I'm a fucking whiny little pissbaby. Here I am, wallowing in pity for myself over nothing new. It's not like I haven't heard everything Bryce told me before - from multiple people actually; I can think of four (including Bryce) off the top of my head. It honestly shouldn't bother me anymore. I don't care - I've stopping caring years ago - so why does it still hurt? Why are my eyes pricking with salty tears as my brother's words echo in my mind? I can't even call it betrayal anymore. It was betrayal the first time it left his mouth when I was fifteen. Now it's a promise - one he reminds me of every time I'm within hearing range.

But I was the dumbass who let him in. I should've known better than to think it was Nico knocking at the door.

Sprinkles. And fuck it - he's my Sprinkles. Everyone else be damned. He cares. He's a persistent little shit - pushing when I pull back, but he knows when I need to be left alone. For some unfathomable reason, Sprinkles hasn't abandoned my scrawny ass even though he has every right to give up on me - what with my temperamental attitude for the better half of the week.

No, it was far from temperamental - I was a fucking asshole. I spewed harsh words at everyone, both my roommates and classmates alike, but Nico took the blunt force of it. His bountiful kindness won't allow him to ignore anyone who's hurting, and such a respectable virtue put him in the middle of my rampant rage with a bright red target painted on his chest.

And boy did I hit hard. How big of an asshole do I have to be to lash out at a friend where I know it hurts?

I pretty much told Sprinkles I don't want him here - that he's nothing more than a random guy who sleeps on my couch - but that's as far from the truth as it can get. He started out as an acquaintance of Skyler - a friend of a friend - but it only took a single afternoon for him to be so much more. Something about him just feels right to be around, like all of his dorky quirkiness clicks with my grumpy prickliness. It's that first meeting where you're apprehensive about everything - how are you supposed to act, what is acceptable to say, can you swear without getting the reaction of a disappointed mom - but the moment the other introduces themselves, every mountain you dread to climb crumbles at your feet. Conversation flows naturally whether you let a *fuck* slip out or not, and the normally awkward lulls aren't so awkward. Talking and hanging out with them feels natural, like you've been doing so from birth instead of from two o'clock that afternoon.

That's what Nico is to me, and I'm a goddamned idiot to make him feel otherwise. I don't care how fucking angry or hurt I was, I had no right to let equally toxic words slip from my lips. I'm not my brother or father or grandparents - those are words they would utter. I don't want to be like them. I won't be like them.

I've run away enough. I've hurt Nico too much. I refuse to be the reason for his pain, for him to hate himself; because he's too good to have to endure such suffering. Sprinkles deserves a world in which the kindness he gives to others is bestowed upon him. He deserves to be surrounded by kittens and puppies while being served an endless supply of ice cream and *Oreo* cookies.

He deserves an apology.

Kicking free from my comforter, I roll out of my bed, dropping to the floor on my knees because I can't be bothered to get up like a normal human being. My rise to stand is slow, and I drag the soles of my feet against the carpet as I trudge a path around the shrapnel of glass. Rounding into the tiny hall I quietly pad the few strides to enter the living room, walking to stand an arm's length from the couch's armrest.

Midafternoon sun streams through a crack in the blinds that we never open and that have never failed to block out the day's light before. A single beam of brightness trails upon the carpet and climbs the couch to settle its thin strand of warmth over the bundle of body and blanket (and cat) that is Sprinkles. Chin tucked toward Simba's head, his freckled forehead burrows into the back of the couch, and gentle fingers stroke striped orange fur.

Gazing upon the saint that is Sprinkles, my heart aches to even imagine him hating himself. He's the epitome of all that is good in this world. He is kindness, patience, and gentleness which expects none of those in return;

but from my experience, people who always put the happiness of others before their own have a reason for doing so, most times because they know and have experienced the pain people willingly inflict upon each other and don't want to be the arbiter of similar suffering. Nico shouldn't ever have to feel that pain again.

"Hey, Sprinkles," I say softly, but not from hesitation. I don't have to apologize, but I want to.

Nico flinches, and damn does that hurt. I don't ever want to be the cause of that again. I don't want his fear - the same fear I feel upon the very mention of my family. I want his dopey grin to grace his lips as the corners of his eyes crinkle. I want the wet sheen of those honey orbs to be from joy, not sadness. Trails of bitter tears should never have the chance to stain the freckles upon his cheeks, and self-deprecating words should never pollute his mind.

He tips his head back just enough to catch my gaze, bangs falling to the sides. His eyes flicker away as he worries his bottom lip between the bite of his teeth, but he's listening. That's all I can ask for.

"I'm sorry," I say, and now it's my turn to glance away when widened eyes dart to my face. Don't look so surprised, Sprinkles. Even assholes can be remorseful. But I'm not done. Two words are not nearly enough to fix the damage I've done. "I was- no, I am a jerk, and I'm sorry. I didn't mean anything I said to you."

"It's okay," he murmurs.

"But it's not, and I shouldn't have said any of it."

"It's fine."

"Nico." I take a step closer, crouching down to meet his gaze. "It's not fine, and I don't want you thinking it is."

He stares at me, his eyes searching for...something. I'm not sure what, but whatever he finds, it causes his lips to upturn (or downturn since he's upside down) ever so slightly. "Thanks."

"What can I do to make it up to you?"

"Eh?" He sits up, pulling Simba into his lap. "This is enough."

Dammit, Sprinkles. It's okay to be selfish every now and then. Hell, I want you to be selfish right now. Give me a task - anything, I don't care how small and insignificant or enormous and daunting. Tell me what you want, and I'll do it without a single question or complaint.

But I should've seen his answer coming. He is Sprinkles after all. He would never think of inconveniencing someone with even his smallest desire, because how dare a living being want anything out of life. How dare someone want more than what life has already given them. You're said to be ungrateful if you do, because how can you want more without spitting on everything you already have?

Which is a line of total bullshit. There's nothing wrong with being selfish, with wanting more for yourself. Being dissatisfied with your life does not equal being ungrateful, and anyone who says otherwise has never been less than - less than a livable income, less than ideal health, less than society's standards of perfection.

I'm grateful for the apartment I share with Skyler and now Nico, but I still want my own house someday. I love my job at the diner (for the most part), but I want to be a baker. I hate having to rely on my father's finances and hope to be financially independent of him one day. But does that mean I'm not grateful for him paying my bills? Fuck no. I may despise the bastard, but he's still taking care of me, even if it's only by the force of my mother.

Does wanting these freedoms of home, career, and financial stability make me a bad guy? Absolutely not. Wanting a nicer car or fancier clothes doesn't make a person vain. It makes a person human. We all want better for ourselves, and there is nothing wrong with that. So be selfish and don't apologize for it. Don't let anyone tell you that putting yourself first makes you anything less than a glorious human being.

So, Nico, if you won't be selfish for yourself, then I'll have to be selfish on your behalf. I have no idea what you truly want, but from the reaction my toxic words brought out of you, I have an idea of how to fix it, of how to prove you're more than a random stranger and you belong in this apartment the same way Skyler, Emil, and I do. It won't be much, but I hope the significance behind it can overpower the shit I said.

I step away from Nico and head for the hall, pausing in its entryway. Stooping down, my fingers curl into denim and retrieve the pair of jeans that started this whole mess. I toss the pants at Sprinkles, one leg hitting the back of his head. He twists around, frown marring his face as he stares at his jeans. I say, "If you want, we can move your clothes from the bathroom to my closet."

He continues to quietly stare at his jeans, never once glancing at me. "Why?"

Because I'm going to be selfish for you, and I know you'd never ask otherwise. And honestly, I want to be selfish too. "Because this apartment is your home."

Nico looks up, the darkness of his eyes meeting mine. He's hesitant to believe me, and how can I blame him? But I don't waver, holding his gaze no matter how those searching eyes make me want to squirm. It feels like an eternity of staring each other down when it's only been a handful of seconds. After those few ticking moments, Sprinkles smiles, his eyes crinkling and his teeth shining.

"Come on," I prompt him.

"Now?"

I shrug. "Sure. Why not?"

Oh no, there goes that dopey grin of his. Why can't his smile remain permanently fixed upon his lips? Why must it fade to a nervous bite of his bottom lip, as if he's afraid to voice his objection?

"But it's, um, kind of dangerous in there."

Oh. Yep, that makes sense. Guess I should have thought about that before even making the suggestion, but no. I fucking forgot the remains of my tantrum scattered across the carpet. Of course Sprinkles wouldn't want to risk his own safety.

God-fucking-dammit, Liam! Because I can't get my shit together, I can't give Nico this one tiny sense of home. All I had to do was calm my anger like a normal human being instead of going on a destructive rampage. If I had to hit or punch something, I should've pummeled my pillow - leaving far less collateral damage.

I just want Nico to feel at home. Is his happiness too much to ask for?

"I'll help."

My thoughts snap back to Sprinkles. "Huh?"

"...with cleaning up. That is, if you want me to."

Shit. I wasn't expecting that. Do I even want his help? I'm not sure I want him seeing the evidence of my meltdown again, but then again, he's been the most comfort I can get. Maybe if he's there - picking up the pieces beside me - I won't feel so alone, so abandoned by the people in the pictures; because we all know how great I am when dealing with the past. With someone at my side, I'll be forced to keep my calm and at the very least have a distraction to hold me in the present, to keep me from reliving those buried memories.

And honestly, if it were up to me, I'd never pick up the pieces. But this isn't for me. It's for Nico. So let him give me the kick in the ass (or gentle nudge - it is Sprinkles after all) that I need to finally release my grasp on the jagged shards.

"I'll grab a garbage bag and the vacuum," I say before ducking into the entry closet and making a mess of it to find the two items.

When I walk back to my room, Nico's already on his knees, gingerly sorting through broken picture frames and the larger pieces of glass. He turns to me and holds up one of the least damaged photographs. "Do you want to save the photos?"

I shake my head, avoiding his gaze while kneeling beside him with the garbage bag. He's hesitant to throw away the picture - his hand hovering over the trash bag - so I do it for him, taking it from his hands and dropping it into the trash. Being able to let it go, to throw it away permanently, feels great. I watch it fall from my grasp and plummet into dark plastic confines, and it's almost justice. For once, it's not me trapped by the exaggerated smiles, but instead I trapped them. Maybe this is what I should've done in the first place, but at least now I know I can do this in the future.

Sprinkles doesn't throw away the pictures but hands each one to me, like he's giving me the power to decide, and I thank him for that. Because with each one I toss in the trash, a part of me celebrates its newfound freedom, its release from the chains which bind me to the past. It's not a quick fix, because those chains merely fall away, piling up at my feet. They're still here with the potential to tangle my limbs and weigh me down; but it's a start, and that's all I can ask for.

I'm not sure what inspired me to tell him - probably the simple fact that I know he'll listen - and when I start talking, the words flow easier than they ever have. "It happened when I was fourteen, just after starting high school. I lost a bet with my friends - Cody and Alex - and ended up having to let Alex pierce my ears. Seems pretty harmless, right? And it was only a stud in each lobe.

"Anyway, I came home around nine that night, which was nothing out of the ordinary for me, but I kinda forgot my father's parents were coming over for dinner. I knew I was screwed when I saw their car still in the driveway, so I tried sneaking in as quietly as possible. That didn't exactly work. My dad chewed me out for forgetting, and yeah, I deserved that. Then my grandmother spotted the earrings, and she flipped her shit. It started with *'How dare you defile the temple God gave you!'* and ended with *'You're a worthless human being who doesn't deserve to walk upon God's earth'*. I don't remember how it escalated so quickly, but it did.

"It really shouldn't've bothered me. She was bat shit crazy. For fuck's sake, she thought *Pokémon* cards were the devil's creation. But I share a birthday with her and grew up being told I was her favorite 50th birthday present. So much for that bullshit, right?"

Nico grabs my hand, and a piece of glass I don't realize I'm holding falls to the carpet. I glance down at the contact as he gently turns my hand palm side up. "Liam, you're bleeding."

Sure enough, Sprinkles is right. It's not a deep cut, but it's enough to draw blood.

"You should wash it and put on a *Band-Aid*."

"What about—"

Nico nudges my side. "I'll take care of this."

I consider it, deciding Sprinkles is right. "Thanks," I mumble and head to the bathroom.

It's a wonder I can even find a *Band-Aid* in the bathroom's vanity. I have to settle for a *Hello Kitty* theme because that's apparently all Skyler buys. I stick one on over the cut and another diagonally atop to form a plus sign just in case. As the thrum of the vacuum fills the apartment, I carefully pry open the door of the bathroom closet. It's stuffed to the brim with toilet paper, endless beauty products, towels, and the few changes of clothes Sprinkles owns. I dig out each scrap of cloth one by one, nearly knocking bottles of frilly shampoo on my toes (but I can't be mad, because that's my frilly shampoo).

I blindly find my way back to my room and drop the load of clothes atop my bed. I watch as Sprinkles drags the vacuum over the carpet, and he's done more than his fair share of work. Every last piece of glass has been picked up, and the trash bag is tied shut, resting against the wall. He stops, pressing the vacuum's off button, and it's suddenly too quiet. My words still hang heavily in the air, ringing in my ears, and I wonder if Nico hears the same echoes. But I don't ask him. I'd rather not know.

I move to my closet and slide the doors open. There's plenty of room upon the rack, what with the majority of my clothes piled on the floor. Even so, I shove my hanging t-shirts as far to the side as I can and collect the available wire hangers. I aimlessly toss each one over my shoulder.

Sprinkles squeaks in surprise as I let the last hanger fly. I turn in time to see a hanger barreling at my chest but too late to do anything about it. It thumps into me before falling to the floor, and all I can do it stare dumbly at Nico. His lips quirk into a smug smirk, and his shoulders roll in a shrug. "You started it."

And I laugh, even though it's not particularly funny. Sprinkles' smile grows wider, and he launches another hanger at me. I duck to the side, but it still skims my shoulder. "We're never gonna get done this way," I laugh, but I'm not opposed to starting a hanger war.

Nico pauses mid-throw and hums in contemplation, dropping the hanger to the bed. It seems he decided to work instead of play so I take a step to join him, but he throws a pair of jeans at me. The denim hits me in the face and drapes itself over my shoulder.

"What are you doing?"

"Helping," Nico says. "Put the pants on the hanger and hang it up."

I stare at him, because he's dead serious - as if I have no idea how putting clothes away works (and okay - there are enough on the floor to make that assumption reasonable). I don't have it in me to inform him otherwise and break his little bubble. "Yes, Sir," I say while making a show of fumbling to get the pants on the hanger.

We fall into specified roles - Nico tossing a hanger and piece of clothing for me to catch and hang up. His aim is crap though. He throws high and wide or far too low. It makes a spectacle of me lunging to catch every toss, but I'm 99% sure he's doing it on purpose because his last throw is spot on.

"How come you don't have piercings anymore?"

My arm freezes in its attempt to hang the last shirt, and I hope to god he doesn't notice. When I turn, Sprinkles is gathering his socks and boxer briefs into one pile, not even looking at me. But he's listening. And it's only fair I tell him after I dumped my baggage on him.

"I used to have a whole shitload on my ears and one in my lip, but I only got them to piss off my family. When I moved here I didn't see a reason to keep them anymore, so I just stopped wearing them. Most of the holes closed up nicely, but if you look close enough, you can see a faint scar right here." I touch the left side of my bottom lip to point it out.

"So you got them to be rebellious?"

I chuckle, "Yeah, I guess. Kinda stupid, right?"

Sprinkles shakes his head. "I don't think so. It's better than giving up and not doing anything."

I want to ask if that's what he did - because he suddenly looks pretty damn dejected - but it's not my place to pry. He had the decency to wait for me to open up so I can be respectful and return the favor.

"We all do what we need to in order to survive. Sometimes fighting works, but other times you just have to hide while the storm passes."

Nico considers my words and smiles. "Okay, Mr. Philosopher, where can I put my underwear?" And the little shit has the audacity to throw a pair of his boxer briefs at my head right after I try to cheer him up.

Yep, Sprinkles has great aim.

Being on the same shift with both Cody and Alex can be downright exhausting. We're friends, but I can only handle so many hours of their shenanigans in a row. A snack break would be nice. Or, you know, something to do considering this is my job. Another problem being on shift with them is the distribution of customers. With any other pairing, the waitstaff always takes turns covering tables, but it's different with Alex and Cody. Alex stakes claim to the counter while Cody covers the booths to the right of the entrance. You'd be surprised how many people turn right upon entering the diner. I get one customer for every five they serve, and yeah, I'm slightly bitter about it.

"Don't look so grumpy, my little Liam. Turn that frown upside down and maybe you'll get more customers," Alex singsongs from behind the counter, twirling in an extravagant circle.

"For the last time, I'm not frowning! It's just my face!"

Cackling laughter erupts in the small space, and not even Simon's shout to shut up can silence it. It's not until he calls my surname that Monkey See and Monkey Do fall silent. Both sets of eyes go comically wide as they turn to me, and their lips quiver in poor attempts to hide smirks.

A chorus of *oh*'s and *somebody's in trouble* follow me into the kitchen, and flashbacks of being in high school cross my mind. It's never good to get called to the office, especially if you're me. Outstanding students get invitations, but I get a summons. A feeling of impending doom settles in the pit of my stomach, and I can't help but wonder what I'm in trouble for.

I'm almost positive I didn't do anything wrong, but my mind is conditioned to believe otherwise. After years of only being called upon to get bitched at, it's become natural to expect some sort of scolding.

Simon doesn't pause with his fancy knife skills when he glances up at me. The blade chops through the carrot with swift precision even while his eyes are looking elsewhere. His skills amaze me, and I can't help but hope to someday be as talented as Simon is.

"I've got a proposition for you, Holt."

Wait, what? I'm not in trouble. The delinquent kid who always got called to the office finally gets an invitation. Is the world coming to an end?

"We're shorthanded back here so if you'll relieve Steph of dish duty, I'll teach you how to make twisted snail pastries. Yes or no?"

Holy shit. Is this the beginning of that trust Stephanie mentioned? Does this mean he'll ask me for my help more often when the kitchen is shorthanded? Yeah, it's only washing dishes, but even dish washing is an important element to any restaurant. Chefs can't cook and plate food without clean dishes to do so. Well, I guess they could, but that restaurant wouldn't be sanitary, much less in business.

"Yes or no, Holt?"

"Yes, Sir."

Some may think I'm insane to jump at the chance to be a dishwasher, but I'm too excited to care. I switch with Stephanie without a single complaint, and I find that kinda funny. I hate washing dishes at home and most times make Skyler do it. He'd think I'm ill to willingly accept the chore.

The duty itself is rather monotonous and boring, but it's far better than serving customers. It's kind of frightening to think I could get used to this, because it could be taken away in a heartbeat. Prior to Simon allowing me in his kitchen, the envied culinary career I want was only a dream; but now I can taste it. It's within my grasp, and I can finally visualize the future that will fulfill my dream. But it's scary to have your heart set on something, because you never know when the universe is going to send a big fuck you your way.

But the universe smiles down upon me today. A few hours of washing dishes fly by faster than any afternoon spent being a waiter. It actually startles me when Simon appears at my side. He calls out to Quinn to take over the kitchen while he leads me even further into the diner. I assumed the only thing in the back would be an office or two (which there is), but a short hall opens up to another work space - this one much smaller and tighter than the main kitchen. Two stacked ovens, a stove top, and cooling racks line the right wall while an industrial fridge with glass doors is up against the left. Dry ingredients are stored on shelves against the far wall. In the middle of the room are metal worktables with a large mixer sitting at the far end.

This is what my wet dreams are made off.

"I didn't know–"

Simon scoffs, clicking his tongue. "Did you think a classically trained chef and baker would buy pies and breads to sell instead of making them from scratch?"

"Wha– No. Of course not, I just– This is amazing."

A twitch of Simon's lips has him smirking smugly. "Don't just stand there gawking. Grab the box of pastry sheets off the middle shelf on the right side of the fridge."

"Yes, Sir," I say and do as told. When I set the box on the worktable, Simon sets down two straight spatulas, standing on the opposite side of the table.

"Grab the jar of jam as well," he instructs, pointing to its position in the fridge.

After I place the jam beside the box of pastry sheets, Simon says, "Snail twists are the simplest pastry I make here. I pre-make the pastry sheets and jam, so we just have to assemble them together." He reaches into the box, pulling out four rectangular pastry sheets and arranging them in two rows of two, their edges touching. Scooping jam onto each sheet, he explains, "Don't worry about making a mess. Slather the jam all over, and don't skimp on the corners."

I observe the flicks of Simon's wrist as his spatula spreads the strawberry jam before picking up my own to mimic his movements. Although he gave me permission to make a mess, I can't bring myself to carelessly dirty the tabletop, especially when Simon's side remains pristine. He finishes his two before I'm even done with one, watches me for a moment, then says he's going to retrieve a knife.

By the time he comes back with a rather large cutting blade - kind of like a giant dough scraper - I finish spreading out the jam (and I may have made a small mess of the tabletop in the process). Simon comes to my side, checking my handiwork and touching up a few places.

"Not bad," he says, and those two words have pride and confidence seeping through my bones. He could've told me a monkey could do better, and I'd still be overjoyed to be working under him, so his approval means the world to me.

"Lay another pastry sheet atop each, and I'll show you how to cut them."

I follow his instructions then step aside for him to take my place. Simon turns the stacks horizontally and centers the blade. A rock of the knife, and the blade easily cuts through the pastry sheets. "It's easiest to think in halves. Cut it in half, halve those sections, halve them again, and halve them one last time. Try to cut straight, but it's fine to eyeball it."

(I resist making a smartass comment about my sexuality, but only because he's my boss and I like this job.)

He finishes cutting one into identical strips before handing me the blade. Not gonna lie, I'm pretty shaky as I make the first cut, because what if it's not exactly half? But the paranoia slowly fades to confidence with each additional rock of the blade. Not every cut is completely straight, but Simon never steps in, so my cuts can't be that bad. He supervises until I get to the last sandwich of pastry sheets, and then retrieves baking sheets, preheats the oven, and collects the strips of pastry and jam into two piles. When I finish, he takes the blade from me and sets it far out of reach.

Simon picks up one of the strips and twists the ends before coiling the dough around itself to form its snail-like shape, holding it up the entire time to show me. I attempt to duplicate the actions, but it's far more difficult than Simon makes it seem. Twisting the strip is simple, but maintaining the twists while swirling the dough around itself proves to be an insurmountable challenge. I feel bad for the strip of dough in my hands because I'm torturing it and getting absolutely nowhere.

"It may help to do it against the table," Simon suggests.

Coiling the dough strip on the table is moderately easier. But hey, at least I finish one for every five Simon does. We line two baking sheets with them, and Simon puts them in the oven to bake for fifteen minutes. He washes the few utensils we used and tosses a washcloth at me to wipe down the tabletop. I scrub at the massacre of jam smeared on the metal, and it marvels me as to how Simon kept his side spotless the entire time. Probably something to do with not murdering his dough strips.

"What's that?" Sprinkles asks as he munches on a twisted snail reject (although Simon said they weren't terribly horrendous. I think he was trying to spare my feelings).

My cheeks heat up as my hand pauses in its scrawling across a recipe card. I glance at the homemade recipe book and regret my choice in decoration. At the time I made it (I was like 12), I thought green and white stripes with my name in block letters was cool. The miniature wooden spoon hot-glued down atop a twine bow had been my shining idea of artistic creativity. I loved my brilliant decoration skills back then, not so much now.

Especially now that my Sprinkles wants to know what it is.

I finish writing down the recipe and slip the notecard back into the photo slot. While clutching the book to my side, I walk over to the cluttered dining table and sit down beside Nico. I stare at the grain of the tabletop as I slide my precious book over to Sprinkles. "It's my future."

I chance a glance at him, because I can't resist knowing what kind of expression he's wearing. I half-expect the unabashed laughter which Skyler roared upon finding it stowed away in the cupboard, but watering eyes and gasping laughs are nowhere to be found. Instead, there's a fondness to the smile upon his lips and the softness of heartwarming eyes - orbs gazing at the sloppily made notebook as if it's a memento of his own. His thumb and forefinger gently thumb through the plastic photo sleeves, reading each notecard before flipping to the next page. When he comes to the last filled notecard, he turns to me.

"Do you want to be a baker?" he asks.

I nod, "And hopefully open up my own bakery someday."

If dark honey eyes weren't sparkling before, they are now - or maybe it's an illusion of the crappy lighting. Nope, scratch that. The lighting has nothing to do with the brightness of elation shining within his eyes. "That's awesome! You can definitely do it." He takes another bite of his pastry, chewing it like a chipmunk. "This tastes great."

"That's a reject," I point out.

"Well, this reject tastes fantastic." Sprinkles must be gaining some confidence because he sticks his tongue out at me.

"You'd be happy with anything sweet."

"Or grumpy."

What? "Why would a dessert be–" Sprinkles smirks and deliberately scoots his chair farther away from me. "Oh, you little shit! I am not grumpy!" Blindly reaching for whatever I can get my hands on, my fingers find another reject snail pastry and launch it at Nico's head.

Nico scrambles to catch it, falling out of his chair and hitting the floor with a thud in the process. To his credit, he does catch the pastry so kudos to him for being awesome. He lies flat on the hardwood, staring at the ceiling, and raises his hand with the pastry to his mouth, taking a bite. "Thanks for the reject. I love it."

Shaking my head, I stand and step over Sprinkles' sprawled legs. "Get up, weirdo. *Cupcake Wars* is on."

I glance over my shoulder to spot Sprinkles scurrying to his feet, rushing after me as he chews on another bite of dough and jam. "I kind of want cupcakes now. You should make cupcakes."

I plop down on the couch and turn the TV on. "Make them yourself."

"Liam!"

I laugh, thoroughly amused with whiny Sprinkles. He's not like this when Skyler and Emil are here, and my former moping stole these moments from me. I'd much rather hear the ring of my name as he begs for cupcakes than the shaking waver to his voice as he calls my name from outside my slammed door. I never want to put him or myself through that experience again, but I can be thankful that he's still my friend after it all.

I could get used to it - to this companionship with my Sprinkles.

The apartment's walls are too thin, and anyone who says otherwise has never tried to sleep on a night when Skyler and Emil come back from a date. And I was sleeping...till about five minutes ago when the *Incredible Hulk* and his giant beanstalk stumbled through the door at two in the morning. They're drunk - plastered - tripping over every shoe in the entryway and running into every surface standing between them and Skyler's bedroom. Emil's obnoxiously loud whispers to stay quiet are anything but and only result in a slurred response of Skyler who apparently believes he's as quiet as a mouse. That is if a mouse hiccups between each roar of laughter after running into the wall...again.

Breathing a sigh of relief as their bedroom door finally slams shut, I hope to find the bliss of sleep once more. I burrow further beneath my blanket, my eyelids falling shut. My beloved silence breaks when the first unstifled moan of many to come echoes in the apartment, and dear god just make it stop! I can't close my eyes tight enough or smother my head with too many pillows and blankets, because the noises won't stop. There is not enough cotton that can be shoved in my ears which would block out the lovers' throes of pleasure.

I have nothing against drunk sex when I'm one of the participants, but hearing two of my closest friends fucking with only a thin wall between us is like walking in on your parents doing it. It's scarring - like pour bleach in my fucking eyes and baptize me in holy water.

I should be used to it, be able to tune the lovers out, but holy fuck are they loud! Like seriously Skyler, must you narrate every fucking thing Emil does to you? I don't want to hear how great Emil is at sucking dick. Can't you, I don't know, try to be a few decibels quieter like a normal human being when he's got a roommate trying to sleep in the next room over?

And yeah, I've heard more of their sexual escapades than I care to admit, but this is pushing my patience. Emil normally keeps me in consideration by cranking up the stereo and bless his angelic soul for doing so, but his streak of embarrassment - which normally pushes him to do everything in his power to keep me from being scarred for life - flies out the window the minute alcohol enters his system.

And Skyler doesn't possess a single bone of modesty in his body. If it was up to him, he'd fuck Emil on my precious couch even with me sitting beside them. I swear to god, this is why none of the neighbors talk to us.

A quiet rapping on my door is a pleasant sound compared to the other noises clogging my ears. My door creaks open, and I can just barely make out Nico's head peaking in. "Liam? Are you awake?"

I sit up and cross my legs beneath me. "How can anyone sleep with those beasts going at it?"

"Can I come in?"

I pull back my blanket and pat the space beside me. "We can suffer together."

Sprinkles shuffles across the carpet, and I'm so fucking happy we cleaned up and he doesn't tear the soles of his feet open on glass. His hands feel for my bed, and when he finds it, he scoots in beside me.

I flip the blanket over us and scoot down until I'm lying flat again. I push my pillow over to share it with Sprinkles. "Get comfy. It's gonna be a while."

Nico groans. "Really?" My hum of affirmation convinces him, and he slumps back against the wall before wiggling his way further beneath the blanket. His half of the pillow dips down as he settles his head atop it.

And it's in this moment, when Skyler lets out a rather lewd moan that has Sprinkles and I giggling like virgin teenagers, that I realize how close we are. My bed's not small, but it's far from a queen or king. While sharing one pillow, the ends of his hair tickle my ear and his shoulder is smooshed into mine, but I'm not about to complain. The closeness feels normal, like we're best friends who have shared a bed since we were three. And Nico's pretty relaxed too, except for the occasional squirm when our housemates shout something explicit.

"Is this normal?" he asks in a hushed tone, staring at the ceiling.

"Sorta."

He groans again, shifting to drape an arm over his eyes.

"I guess you've never been subjected to this before, huh?"

"Not once."

"Lucky," I chuckle, and he is a lucky little shit. "I've been dealing with this for over two years."

Sprinkles yawns. "You're a brave man."

"Nah, I'm just too nice to bitch about it. Who am I to keep my friends from getting laid?" Even if I'm not getting any myself.

Nico covers his ears when the moans get even louder and squirms closer into my side, as if I can somehow shield him from the soundwaves. "When will it end?" he drawls.

"About thirty seconds."

Sprinkles peeks up at me. "How do you know?"

"When you overhear those two enough, you get used to the sound of their climaxes. Skyler's gonna blow first - give it ten seconds - and Emil will follow."

Nico leans back, staring at me through the darkness. "It's weird that you know that."

And then it's silent - no moans, cries, or mewls. The shouts of each other's names echo before dying down, and the peaceful quietness of the night finally returns. Yes, it's fucking weird that I know that, and it's not like I want to know it, but thankfully I'm right in this case.

Nico's breathy laugh as he flops back on my mattress startles me. "That's so weird," he laughs until the musical lilt morphs into a yawn. His breathing evens out, and those chirpy snores of his fill my room barely a minute later.

And who am I to wake him up and send him back to the couch at 2:30 a.m.? Cause I'm not gonna do it.

And fuck, I could get used to this.

"Ow! Fuck!"

I jolt awake from the unexpected hand hitting me in the face as Sprinkles rolls onto his stomach, stealing my pillow from beneath my head. And the little shit hogs the blanket too. No wonder my toes are so damn cold. And it's not like my ratty t-shirt is particularly warm.

Leaning on my elbow, I peer over Nico's shoulder to check the time on my alarm clock. It's six o'clock, and I probably won't be able to wrestle my pillow and blanket back to take advantage of the thirty minutes I have before my alarm goes off. Getting out of bed is a predicament as well - what with being stuck between Sprinkles and a wall - but I'm gonna give it a try. I could scoot to the foot of my bed and easily slide off, but where's the fun in the easy route? I'm a man who likes a challenge, so of course I'll carefully crawl over my softly snoring Sprinkles, calculating the placement of each hand and foot.

And then the little shit decides to roll...again - and knocks me off my own fucking bed. I land hard on my hip, a strangled cry falling from my lips. I lie on the floor, staring up at the ceiling and wondering why I'm not as pissed as I should be.

The bundle of freckles shifts on my bed, lifting his head to look at his surroundings. He blinks a few times before realization sets it. Bolting upright, the blanket falls from his shoulders. His eyes spot me on the floor, and he's even more confused. "What are you doing down there?"

"Contemplating my existence. Give me a hand up," I say, extending my arm and reaching for him.

Dark orbs narrow at my answer, staring at my waiting hand. I wiggle my fingers at him until he clasps the warmth of his hand around mine and squeezes gently. Half-heartedly tugging isn't nearly enough to haul my scrawny ass to my feet, but it's exactly what I'm hoping for. While he's still half-asleep - rubbing at his sleep crusted eyes - I overpower his sorry excuse of a helping hand and pull him off balance, until he tumbles to the floor beside me.

"We're even now," I say as he lies flat on his stomach, his cheek pressed into the carpet.

He stares at my face, not moving and not speaking for quite some time. Then he sits up, leaning his back against my bedframe. "That hurt."

I scoff, "Try waking up to a hand hitting your face."

His eyebrows furrow with confusion, and he questioningly points at himself. "Me? I did that?"

"Yes, Sprinkles. You need more practice sleeping with someone."

Honey orbs go wide, and his face flushes as red as an overripe tomato. And oh fuck, I can feel my cheeks heating up by the second. Why, oh why, do I not think before I speak? "That's– Uh– I didn't... well...you see... oh fuck it!" Smooth recovery, Liam. Way to speak like a fucking adult.

At least my inability to form a complete sentence brings a laughing smile to Sprinkles' lips. "I'll make breakfast to make it up to you," he says, pushing himself to his feet.

"So a bowl of *Fruity Pebbles*?"

He helps me up, this time careful not to be pulled back down, and shrugs his shoulders. "Maybe."

"It better be the best damn bowl of cereal I've ever eaten."

"I couldn't have hit you that hard."

Following him into the kitchen, I flip on lights as we go to illuminate the shadows of the early morning. Nico's in the middle of pouring cereal into two colored bowls when the cardboard box thuds against the counter top. "Uh, Sprin–" but the nickname dies in my throat when my eyes lock on the window above the sink that he's staring out. And then I see it, swirling among the branches of a lone tree and settling atop the roofs of tenants' parked cars.

Snow. The first snow of the season in late fall, and it's sticking to the ground, piling up as it continues to float down from the clouds. It's truly beautiful, sitting untouched on the cityscape, yet to be stepped and driven upon. In an hour, this beauty will be slush - a traveler's hazard upon the roads and sidewalks - but for now, I can understand the awe and wonder in Nico's gaze.

It takes multiple taps on his shoulder to draw his attention away and a tug of his night shirt to convince him to follow me into the living room. I open the blinds hiding the itty bitty balcony we never use and unlock the sliding door. After some forceful pulls, the glass door finally slides along its track, and the cold morning air seeps into the apartment.

I drop to my knees at the edge of the carpet, peering up at Sprinkles. "Do you wanna build a snowman?" I can't help but laugh at my own question because that stupid *Disney* song starts playing in my head. Damn *Disney* and its adorable family films.

Nico drops to his knees beside me with the excitement of a child on Christmas morning. His hands ball up the sticky snow like there's no tomorrow, cupping it in his palms to form the snowman's base while I work on its center. We make a good team, or maybe we finish quickly because the snowman is barely a foot and a half tall.

Sprinkles gasps and jumps to his feet. Lips parting, only a breath of air escapes before he shakes his head and gives up explaining himself. He motions for me to stay put, slowly backing away and then darting into the kitchen. The crinkling of cereal in its box rivals that of Nico's footfalls as he races back to me, dropping to his knees with a thud.

He thrusts the cardboard box at me to hold after grabbing a handful of *Fruity Pebbles*. With the precision of a practiced brain surgeon, Sprinkles presses the tiny flakes upon the snowman's face, giving him mismatched eyes and a rainbow for a smile. Nico's own beaming grin rivals the one he placed upon the overly happy snowman. With the remaining colored flakes in his palm, he sprinkles them atop the snowman's head and gives our little creation the most colorfully tasty hair I've ever seen.

"It's perfect," he beams.

I hum my agreement, but I'm not looking at the snowman anymore. There's far greater perfection kneeling beside me with that dopey grin of his and the morning sun shining down upon his speckled cheeks.

I could get used to this, and that fact alone scares the shit out of me.

MY SAFETY, MY COMFORT, MY BEST FRIEND

"Let's go to the library."

The door slams behind Liam; and he dumps his book bag on the dining table, staring expectantly at me while I play with Simba on the living room floor. His chest heaves as if he sprinted all the way home from the university (he is back a little earlier than normal), and snow dusts his hair and shoulders.

"The library closed at five," Emil says from his perch on the couch cuddled next to Skyler.

Liam's shoulders slump, and his fingers comb through his damp hair. He mumbles what's likely to be a string of profanities under his breath and turns back to the dining table in defeat. He leans against the back of a chair, his head tipped forward and brows drawn together in deep thought. A few long moments later, he perks up with a snap of his fingers. "What about that big ass bookstore next to the strip? How late is that open?"

"Until ten," Emil answers.

Liam pulls his cellphone from his pocket to check the time before shoving it back into his jeans. "We're taking the car, Skyler. I'll gas it up and bring you guys back something to eat."

"Keys are on my dresser," Skyler says absently as one of his many shows resumes from commercial.

"Grab a coat, Sprinkles. We're going on an adventure." Liam smiles, his eyes crinkling at the corners and his teeth peeking through his lips, before rushing to Skyler's room.

There's a skip to his step - a peppy excitement which rivals his typically gruff after-school attitude. And it's refreshing to see him hold his head high instead of staring at the ground, picking up his feet instead of trudging around like a lifeless corpse. Because Liam's not lifeless. He's full of spirit and ambition that those around him have attempted to squash; but each

99

time his flames are extinguished, a tiny smoldering ember remains. He protects the ember with every last ounce of strength he can muster and nurtures it until the flames ignite with reborn life - powerful enough to engulf the obstacles in his way.

And mesmerize those around him - or maybe that's just me - but either way, I'm willing to take the chance of being burned if it means I can remain at his side. Liam is worth that and so much more.

So I don't hesitate in springing to my feet, leaving Simba with one last scratch behind the ears. Retrieving my coat from the entry closet, I shrug into it and zip it all the way up, fishing a pair of gloves and a hat from its pockets. Or maybe I should say Liam's coat, gloves, and hat. After making our sprinkled snowman, Liam and I went out to the back parking lot to play in the fresh snow, and piece by piece, Liam gave up his snow wear every time a shiver racked my body. He made sure to say he was used to the cold and that it "never bothered me anyway." Since then, he's tossed his jacket at me every time we go out to fix our snowmen in the parking lot. I feel bad leaving him with nothing but a hoodie; but every time I try to convince him to wear his own jacket, he makes a joke about how he's hotheaded and doesn't want to overheat.

Liam comes up behind me, tugging down on the strings on the earflaps of the hat until the hat slides down to cover my eyes. He laughs as I fix it with a pout of my lips. "That suits you much better than me," he says, flicking the tuft of yarn atop my head.

I swat at his hand and duck out of his reach, only managing to stretch Liam's smile even wider. He steps around me and pulls the apartment door open, sweeping his arm in an overly dramatic gesture. "After you, Sprinkles."

I can't hide the small smile or light flush that surely dusts my cheeks, because what is this? Where has this dazzling excitement in Liam come from? He's taking me to a bookstore - probably one of the last places on earth he wants to be, if his complaints about reading his assignments are anything to go by - yet here he is, putting on a show about this great adventure he'll take me on. No one's ever done anything remotely close to this for me, so I burrow my head as far into the jacket as I can and comply with Liam's adventure plan.

I wait for him in the hallway as he pulls the door shut behind him, twirling a keychain with the car keys on his pointer finger. Liam leads the way down the creaky stairs, through the lobby, and out onto the sidewalk. The sky is pitch black - not a single star to be seen - and the few street lamps can only chase away so much of the darkness. It's daunting to be on the sidewalk during the eerie grayness of night, each whistle of the biting wind sending an involuntary shiver down my spine, so I stick close to Liam - so close I'm walking on his heels every other step. But he doesn't complain, simply leading the way around the building to its parking lot.

When we get to Skyler's old red beater (as he calls it), Liam bypasses the driver side door and races ahead of me to the passenger side. My steps falter, and I come to a standstill - only able to stare because, oh my gosh, I can't drive. I've only ever been in a vehicle - actually only this vehicle - five times tops, and most of those times were with me passed out in the back seat from a lack of feeding. It's probably considered weird by human standards that I can't drive, but there aren't exactly cars in the demon world as demons have no use for them because of the whole teleportation thing. How am I supposed to tell him that without making a fool of myself or putting a damper on our great adventure?

But Liam doesn't get in the car. He pulls the door open and stands back. "Your ride awaits, Sprinkles."

My breath of relief is choked off by a strangled laugh, because I've read enough of Emil's romance novels to know how cliché this is; and the mere thought of Liam extending this gesture to me has my cheeks flushing yet again. I pull the earflaps of my hat down even further in an attempt to hide my reddening cheeks and glance at Liam. When I hesitate to get in a moment too long, he shifts his weight and rubs at the nape of his neck, staring at the icy pavement. He quirks his lips in a shy smile, and copper orbs peer up at me.

It's endearing, even if it's quite embarrassing for the two of us to be freezing in the cold night with a flush to our skin, because even Liam can't wave it off as being caused by the bite of the wind. And I don't know what to say - don't know what to do - because how does one respond when you're the center of someone else's attention, when they go out of their way to cater to you? I've never had someone make me their priority - even if only for one outing - and I can't say I deserve it. But if it makes Liam happy, I'll gladly accept it.

So I scoot into the passenger seat with a quiet mumble of thanks as he pushes the door shut. I watch him through the windshield as he rounds the hood of the car, pressing the back of his hands to his cheeks while a wisp of white air is blown away with the wind. He hesitates outside the driver door - his shoulders slowing rising and falling with a single breath - and then he's sitting beside me, barely an arm's length away. With a few turns of his wrist, he convinces the car to wheeze to life.

And then we're bombarded with bubbly notes of music and a twinkling lilt of a feminine voice, so loud in the silence that we both jump in our seats. Liam utters an exasperated *for fuck's sake* as his hand darts to the volume knob. He turns it down so low that I can't make out a single lyric, and he might as well have turned it off.

Leaning back in his seat, Liam lets the car idle, turning his gaze to me. Even in the darkness of the car, I can't miss the quirk of his lips and the flustered sheen to copper eyes. "Will you believe me if I say Skyler listens to that crap?" he asks as he scratches at his neck.

A single puff of laughter blows from my lips, because Liam sounds genuinely concerned that I may think he listens to the same peppy music Skyler does, as if his taste in music will make me think any less of him. Of course, I know it's Skyler's music. I've heard him belting it in Emil's dorm too many times to count, and I've seen enough of Liam's t-shirts to know his taste is drastically different from Skyler's. But it's not often I get to see a flustered Liam, and by flustered I mean an endearing flustered, not a broken or sad flustered; and I want to see more of it.

"You like it too, don't you?"

Liam's eyes go wide, flailing his hands to slap away the very idea. "No, absolutely not! It's– Have you even heard it? It's crap - that's what it is!"

I laugh, because his sputtering explanation is far too serious for the topic. As my laughs grow louder, Liam catches on to my intentions, huffing out a chuckle of his own and flicking the tuft of yarn atop my head. "You're a little shit sometimes," he says, but there's a teasing edge to his tone - the same tone I often mistook for anger, but never again. We've spent enough time together that I can finally distinguish between his sarcasm and when he's being serious.

But it still takes getting used to. I understand he uses little shit as a term of endearment (along with every other insult known to man), but there's still a bitter aftertaste which rings in my mind. It's not Liam's fault, and I'll never blame him for it. He can't possibly know there's a voice in my head that tells me he's not joking - that he doesn't even consider me a friend and is only humoring Skyler and Emil. I know the voice is wrong, but when you grow up with negative remarks constantly directed at you, you become extra sensitive to them. It takes a long time to retrain your inner voice, and I'm still working on that.

And Liam's satisfied little smirk as he backs out of the parking space helps remind me that the voice can't possibly be right.

He maneuvers the car with ease, even with slush littering the streets. At the first red traffic light, he fiddles with the radio until he finds something more suitable for an adventure montage. The ride lasts for three songs, and I'm thankful when Liam puts the car in park. It's probably a good thing I was unconscious for all my other car rides because the motion outside the window makes my head spin. Any longer and I wouldn't be able to stomach it.

I unbuckle my seatbelt and reach for the door handle. "Wait, wait! Freeze!" Liam flails, leaning toward me to take hold of my wrist. The involuntary shiver which runs up my arm is a great improvement from my flinching every time Liam touches me. Again, my reaction isn't his fault. A gentle touch is just another thing I have to get used to.

When my hand slips from his grasp and drops to my lap, Liam gets out of the car and races to the passenger door. He pulls it open and waits patiently for me to step out before slamming it behind me. "What do you think?" he asks, pointing to the huge two-story storefront with stacks upon stacks of books in its windows.

It's the closest to heaven anyone has ever brought me, and I'm not only talking about the books. The books are great - fantastic even - but they're merely icing on the cake. I would have been more than happy spending the night watching TV and listening to Liam's sarcastic commentary, but this - a night which revolves around what I want - gives me a whole new meaning to the word happiness. When Liam had off-handedly mentioned he'd take me to the library someday, I never expected him to be serious. It's not that I doubted him as much as I doubt my importance to others. But Liam's doing his best to silence that doubt, and I can't help but be confused by it, because what did I do to deserve his rare act of benevolence.

"Why are you doing all this?"

Liam's smile doesn't waver at my question, simply softens at its corners. His copper orbs stare into mine, and there's not a single ounce of hesitation to his words as he says, "Because I want to."

That doesn't answer my question in the slightest, but before I can rephrase a new one, Liam grabs the sleeve of my jacket and gives it a gentle tug. "Come on," he prompts me to follow him, and there's still excitement to each step he takes as he constantly tosses broad grins over his shoulder.

The doors automatically slide open for Liam to lead me through, and it's not only the warmth of the building that has me rooted to the spot. It's huge, so much bigger than I imaged it to be. Shelves upon shelves of far too many books to count lay before me like a vast sea. Grand displays featuring popular picks and books recommended by the staff draw the attention of anyone coming in the door. There's a counter with four or five cash registers, but only one has a cashier checking customers out, which has one or two people always standing in line. Further back on the left, a carpeted staircase grand enough to be out of a fairy tale leads up to a second floor loft with even more books.

Every last inch of this place is beautiful - it's a bountiful expanse of knowledge hidden within the ink printed on paper. It's thousands of worlds coexisting under the same roof - the only boundaries separating them being front and back covers. These stories allow readers to experience aspects of the world that they otherwise would never get the chance to, and I'm no exception to that. Without books, I'd be even more ignorant about the human world than I am now.

But even with its beauty, this dream place is daunting. Huge and unknown - a strange place with a lot of people I don't know. I want to be excited - I am excited - but there's an underlying fear that makes me want to go home and disappear - one that says I don't belong here and everyone around me knows that.

"Nico," Liam calls my name softly, pulling on my sleeve with the same softness. His lips quirk in a fond smile as he says, "Let me show you my kind of book." He winks at me with a playful mischievousness that has my fear dissipating into fluttering butterflies in my belly.

He never releases his hold on my jacket, even when it draws the attention of a few other patrons. The questioning looks don't deter Liam from dragging me along behind him through the aisles of bookcases, not stopping until the carpeting turns to childlike blocks of colored patches. In this new area, the colors are brighter, the bookcases are shorter, and the soft melody of background music turns into a cheery tune of the alphabet.

Liam leads me to a reading section - a very tiny reading section, and by tiny, I mean miniature. There's a white coffee table with picture books sitting atop it, and it looks like it was built for a toddler. And did I mention the four beanbag chairs? They're tiny too, but still - beanbag chairs! Emil has one in his dorm, and I love it. Who doesn't love beanbag chairs?

Stopping in front of a blue beanbag chair, Liam releases his grip on my sleeve. "Have a seat, Sprinkles. It's story time."

I do as told and watch Liam drag the green beanbag next to me. He plops down like he's the five-year-old it was made for and wiggles to get comfy. Leaning forward, he snatches the first book he can grab off the miniature table before settling back into his beanbag.

Liam glances at the book he's blindly chosen, and copper orbs light up with a glistening recognition. "This was my fucking childhood!" he gushes, propping it on his knees to show me.

The title reads *The Very Hungry Caterpillar*, and an abstract-like drawing of the insect with little feet and bug eyes decorates the front cover. Liam makes sure I see the picture before flipping to the first page to begin his dramatic reading of a children's storybook. It's cute, and I don't just mean the story. Liam reads about a caterpillar munching its way through strawberries and oranges like it's the most interesting tale known to man. When he gets to the part where the caterpillar eats cake, candy, and ice cream; the excitement in his voice goes up an octave.

For once, the curious and sometimes degrading eyes of strangers mean nothing to me. Their stares don't bore into my back and weigh down upon my shoulders. I barely even notice the passing woman who makes sure to voice a nasty comment to her companion, because right now - in this moment - it's only Liam and me, no one else. It's only Liam's high-pitched reading voice and the broad grin he flashes my way with every turn of a page. It's the way he points out every little detail to make sure I don't miss an ounce of the story and how he sticks his pinky finger through the caterpillar's trail of holes and wiggles it to draw a laugh out of me. But most of all, it's how Liam makes me feel safe and secure in the strangeness of a world I know very little about.

Liam turns his brilliant flash of teeth to me once more and taps the picture of a very plump caterpillar. "That'll be you if you keep having cookies for breakfast."

I feign offense, placing my hand on my chest and giving him the best offended glare I can manage; but Liam only laughs and turns the page.

"...and he was a beautiful butterfly," Liam says with a single breath, never looking away from my eyes. He closes the book and sets it back on the tabletop before relaxing into the beanbag chair, but no matter how nonchalant he acts, the flush reddening his cheeks tells a whole other story.

"So what kind of books are you into?" he asks, his words rushing out with less composure than he'd like.

I shrug, "I like all books."

"Alrighty then," Liam says as he pushes himself to his feet, then offers me a hand up. "Let's go on a shopping spree."

A shopping spree equals money which I don't have, and I couldn't dream of burdening Liam with the bill. "But–"

"No buts, and don't feel bad about me paying, 'cause I'm not. It's gonna be courtesy of my father's finances."

"But–"

"Nope. Lead the way, Sprinkles," Liam gestures to the sea of stocked bookcases.

And I'm overwhelmingly lost again. Where do I go? Where do I begin? I don't know where anything is or how books are sorted, and I don't want to get in other customers' ways. Oh gosh, what do I do? I don't know, I don't-

"I'll lead. Stop me if you see something you like," Liam says, walking toward the nearest row of bookcases.

Before he gets more than a step away from me, I reach out to him, grabbing hold of the hem of his hoodie and falling in line behind him. He glances over his shoulder at my hand, but just like last time in the street, he doesn't say anything - only smiles and returns his attention to the books.

It seems the books are sorted by genre and then by topic. We start by the historical fiction and slowly wind our way through the fiction sections and eventually the nonfiction. I feel bad for tugging on Liam's hoodie to stop him when a book draws my attention, because I really don't want him spending money on me - even if it's not technically his money. But every time I show a liking to a book, Liam plucks it off the shelf and adds it to the growing stack in his arms. I eventually stop tugging on his hoodie, but he still notices every book I'm interested in and has no qualms in carrying them around.

After we glance through every bookcase, I follow Liam to the registers.

"I don't need any," I try convincing him, but he insists.

He flashes a credit card at the cashier. "Think of this as my rebellion. I'm giving my father a big fuck you where I know it hurts, and you're getting something you love. Sounds like a win-win to me."

Except his father loses, but I honestly can't find it within myself to feel sympathy for Liam's father. So my complaints fall silent, and I thank Liam for the books, snatching both plastic bags of goodies to carry before Liam can, but Liam doesn't give up without a playful fight. He's grabbing at the bags all the way to the car, and I'm trying my best to hold them just out of his reach, my slight height advantage coming in handy. Liam admits defeat with a huff, kicking at the slush, and then opens the car door for me.

I settle the bags of books in my lap and sit back as Liam finds a gas station to fill up the car. The ride is a little more comfortable if I close my eyes and don't look out the window, and Liam humming the tune of a song helps considerably to distract my mind.

"What do you want to eat, Sprinkles?"

I crack my eye open and glance at Liam, spotting a large golden M outside his window. I forget the name of the place, but Emil would always bring back burgers and fries for supper. "Anything's fine," I say, because I'm not picky (I also don't know the menu options).

My eye falls shut again, and a few minutes later, I'm listening to Liam order what sounds like far too much food, but it's not Liam's voice that hits me like a punch to the gut. The static voice of the person taking the drive-thru order has the hair on the back of my neck standing tall and my fingers trembling. I recognize that voice, and in the human world, there are very few voices which register in my mind and even less that are female.

But I know this voice. Runaway demons fear ever hearing this voice, and I'm a runaway demon. But what is she doing here, working at a fast food place? Why is she here - of all the places in the human world, why Sodalis? This can't be a mere coincident, because what are the chances a member of the deserter apprehension unit of the demon military would be in the same city as one of their targets?

I can't be found out. I can't be captured and taken back to the demon world. It's not a punishment I'm afraid of - because I will be punished - and it's no longer my values I'm afraid of betraying. I can lose my values countless times, and I'll always find them again; but I'll never find friends like Skyler and Emil. I'll never find someone like Liam again - someone who makes me feel secure and safe, someone who shows me I belong and makes me feel important. There's only one Liam, and I don't want to lose him.

Her words as she instructs Liam to pay at the next window send a chill down my spine. And oh gosh, please don't appear now. A tail and wings are the last things I need in this situation, but I can feel my control of them slipping away with my rationality. The closer Liam drives to the window, the more I doubt the trust I have(had) in my demon partner. He said I was safe, but how can I believe that with one of his co-workers dangerously close to me?

Oh no, there's the tail. And it won't go away! I can't let Liam see it. I can't let her see it. Oh, dear god, it can't end like this. I won't let it end like this.

While Liam's not paying attention, I shove my tail toward the car door, stuffing the end of it in the darkness between the door and my seat. I shift in the seat, doing my best to keep the base of my tail hidden, and rest my cheek against the coldness of the window. If she can't see my face, then she'll never know I'm here.

I listen to Liam pay and then be told to wait at the second window for his food, but even watching the distance between my assailant and me grow outside the window isn't enough to calm my mind. She's here, so close to taking away everything - everyone - I've come to love and cherish. I don't want to go back and lose the friendships I've formed. I don't want to say goodbye, and I don't think I can bring myself to. I don't want to be alone again - never again.

"Are you okay?"

I bristle at Liam's voice, every bone and muscle locking in place. He can't know about any of this - about me being a demon and the potential danger he's in simply by being next to me. I don't want to lie to him, but I can't tell him the whole truth. And actually, it's probably best I don't speak at all, because I can feel the sharp point of my fangs against my gums. So I shake my head back and forth to answer him.

"Are you feeling sick?"

I nod, thankful Liam supplied an excuse for me, and it's not far from the truth. My head is spinning with all the scenarios that have less than one percent chance of actually happening - the majority of them being bad endings - and it's making my head pound. Even worse is trying to maintain the concealment of my wings. I can hide my tail and fangs, but if my wings materialize, it's all over.

A coolness against my cheek startles me. It breaks through every bad scenario - crushing them into fine dust - and pulls me back to the here and now. The gentle press against my skin reminds me that I am safe and always have been with Liam by my side.

"You're a little warm," he says. "You should lie down when we get home."

And then his hand is gone, no longer pressing against my cheek. His attention goes back to his window to receive all the food he ordered, and instead of passing the bags to me, he sets them in the back seat. He turns his music down until it's a mere whisper of its former blare before pulling out into the street to drive home. He's silent the entire ride, but I can feel the weight of his flickering gaze constantly on me.

It's both reassuring and daunting to have so much of his attention. He cares, and that means more to me than any run-in with a captor; but it also means he's hyper-aware of everything I do. One wrong shift of my weight or flash of my teeth and Liam will know I'm not human. I'm not ready to face that obstacle, especially not in the dark confines of Skyler's car.

When Liam pulls into the apartment parking lot, he tells me to stay put. The moment he's out of the car with the bags of fast food and books, I scramble to hide my tail. I coil it into as small of a ball as possible, ignoring the ache of pain while doing so, and shove it under the waistband of my jeans. I hope to all that is holy that the tail of the jacket will cover the bulge in my butt, because if it doesn't, I'm in for a very awkward conversation.

Liam opens my door, and I slide out of the car, careful to keep my backside out of his view. He slams the door shut, and with his free hand reaches for my forehead. He presses his palm to my forehead for a short moment before dropping it to his side. "You're going to bed, and I'm not taking no for an answer."

I nod because I don't dare open my mouth to argue, not because he said so but because my fangs will show if I do (and I kind of slur my words when I try to speak with them). I follow after Liam, constantly checking over my shoulder for any people who may see my tail, but the sidewalk and apartment lobby are deserted.

When he pushes the door open and steps back for me to enter first, I have to swallow down the lump of protest in my throat. I pull the back of my jacket as far down as it will go and hope it's enough to hide my tail as I walk in front of Liam.

"We're back with spoils of war," Liam calls as he follows behind me, turning his back to me to close the door.

Skyler appears from the living room like a vulture to a carcass, zeroing in on the food in Liam's arms. He flashes me a broad grin, opening his mouth to voice a greeting, but whatever he plans to say dies in his throat when I purposefully flash my fangs at him. I point to my backside and mouth a silent *Help me!*

Skyler crosses the room with record speed, placing himself between Liam and me. As Liam turns toward us, Skyler slings an arm around his shoulders and steers him toward the kitchen. "What took you so long? I'm starving."

Liam struggles to shrug off the arm as I slink toward the living room, my eyes never leaving him and Skyler. I freeze when Liam whips his head around and catches my retreat. "You better be heading to my bed."

Skyler eyes me with an arched eyebrow, and all I want is to disappear from his questioning gaze - lock myself away and hide my burning cheeks. Liam doesn't even realize the unintended sexual innuendo he just said and probably believes the flush to my skin is from being ill. I can feel my face heating up even more under both their gazes, and the rise in temperature only adds to the discomfort of my aching tail.

I can't speak, so I nod my head in acknowledgement and continue toward the living room. Emil greets me from the couch with a genteel smile that morphs to concern when I don't say anything. I flash my fangs again, and he breathes a quiet *oh*, letting me continue to Liam's room without a question asked.

After closing the door behind me, I strip of my jacket and reach into the back of my pants. Gingerly, my fingers curl around my coiled tail and release it from the confines of my jeans. A sigh of relief blows through my lips as it uncoils and hangs freely behind me, the tuft of coarse black hair at its end brushing against the carpet. I kick off my shoes before flopping down atop Liam's bed, pulling the blanket up to my waist to conceal my tail.

My chest rises with a deep inhale. I hold the air in my lungs for a short moment, and then exhale through my nose, releasing with it today's worries, because I really don't want to remember the second half of tonight's adventure. The bookstore - that was amazing, an adventure I'd go on with Liam every day if I could. And it doesn't always have to be a bookstore. I'd be happy anywhere if Liam's there with me. It could be the most crowded area in the city, and I'd feel safe with him at my side. But today, running into someone from my past scared me, and I don't want to remember the fear. I want to remember the shy eyes peering at me as Liam held the car door open for me, the sputtering panic when he thought his taste in music was compromised, the carefree laughter as he cracked up over his own antics in the children's book section, and even the gentleness of which he pressed the back of his fingers to my cheek. Especially that gentleness in his touch.

At the sound of footsteps, I scramble to pull the comforter up to my chin and roll onto my side with my tail facing away from the door. My eyes squeeze shut, and my heart beats rapidly against my ribcage. Forcing air into my lungs at a natural pace is near impossible, but I try my best and hope the pounding in my head isn't as loud as it sounds.

The hinges creak as the door is pushed open and then clicks shut again. "You can stop pretending now."

Busted. I blow out a sigh and peek up at Skyler. I sit up and scoot toward the headboard, wrapping my arms around my knees as Skyler takes a seat at the foot of the bed. He directs his best all-knowing mom gaze my way, but I can't look him in the eyes.

I can already imagine what lecture is to come - the same one I received my first morning in this apartment, the one I've heard a thousand times. It's always the same - take care of yourself, do what you must - and yet here we are again back at square one. I feel like I'm running in circles, like I'm no different from the scared and dejected incubus who fled the demon world. The whole point of leaving that world was to change and become someone who I could be proud of, but I haven't changed at all. I've let myself down - disappointed myself - and if I'm disappointed, Skyler probably is too. He's been helping me try to grow, but all I've done is wither. How could someone not be disappointed when they put time and effort into nurturing a plant only for it to dry up and die? Because that's what Skyler's done for me, and I've let him down.

"Liam said he'll sleep on the couch tonight," Skyler informs me; and okay, that isn't the lecture I expected. There's not a drop of condemnation in his voice. It's conversational, like he's talking to Nico the friend and not Nico the pitiful incubus. It gives me the strength to pick up my head and meet his golden eyes - eyes that soften as he asks, "What's wrong?"

I fish my tail out from beneath the blanket, holding it in my palm as if I'm presenting evidence to a judge, and give him a quick flash of my fangs. "They won't go away."

"You know, maybe it's time to let Liam in on your secret."

My eyes bulge at the very idea, and my arms flail to shoo it away. "Wha– No, I can't risk that. He can't find out because... because..."

Because I don't want to lose him.

Skyler nods toward my tail. "Then what are you going to do about that?"

What indeed. I can't exactly go to my demon partner, not after having such a close call today. He said I wasn't high priority, and I trusted him. I depended on him to warn me, and he didn't. No sign, no message, no nothing. It's like he left me high and dry - threw me aside to fend for myself. I trusted him - thought maybe he was different from the typical demon. I guess I was wrong.

Not that I want to go to him anyway, and it's different than all the other times I didn't want to pay him a visit. I can't really put my finger on it, but now I get this aching in my chest - as if I'm suffocating with every breath of air - and it sinks into my stomach where it twists and turns until the very idea of feeding leaves me wanting to vomit. I've never been fond of feeding, but it's also never made me feel physically ill just by thinking about it. It'd be one thing if it's because I don't want to toss aside my morals and values, but I've already done that countless times before, so that can't be why. This feels more like guilt after a betrayal - not a betrayal of self but of someone else. But I don't get it. Who else would I be betraying?

"Do you love Liam?"

Skyler's words take a moment to truly sink in because I must have

110

misheard him. He couldn't have asked me what I think he did; but that's what I heard, and he patiently waits for some form of acknowledgement, staring at me with knowing eyes.

Is that why I suddenly feel like I'm betraying someone by feeding with my demon partner? Or more specifically - betraying Liam... because I... love him. Is that what this is? Is that why his smile warms my heart and his voice soothes my soul, his presence calms my trembling fear and his touch brings me ease of mind when everyone else's has me shying away? Is that why his happiness puts a smile upon my lips and his sadness pains me as if it was my own?

I don't know. Love is a foreign concept few demons have ever heard about, yet alone felt. I know what it is; I've read about it in so many stories, and I see it in how Skyler and Emil react to one another - to each other's silent gazes, gentle touches, and whispered words. I've been subjected to their more intimate relations, and theirs is so different from any I've ever known. To them, the act holds far more meaning than a mere demon could ever imagine - neither of them is taking advantage of the other, and maybe that's what I want. Maybe that's why I feel so ill when I think about feeding with someone I have no connection with - no bond with. Maybe that's why guilt eats away at me with just the thought of the betrayal of Liam - the one person I am bonded to.

But the only thing I know for sure is that Liam is the most important person to me, and I want to stay by his side in any way possible. I don't want to lose Liam - or worse, push him away - so I'm fine with what we have now, with this friendship where I can share in his joy and sorrow; and I'll cherish it as long as I can.

Without warning, Skyler pulls me into a crushing embrace, squishing my arms and tail against his chest. He squeezes gently and simply holds me, rubbing soothing circles between my shoulder blades. He doesn't say anything - doesn't seek a concrete answer to his question - but instead chases away every last ounce of tension in my body, enough for my shoulders to slump and my arms to go limp between us.

Skyler releases me with a pat on my back. "Are you feeling better?"

I nod.

"Good," he says, and then he pushes himself to his feet. The gentleness of his lips quirks into a mischievousness which matches a dangerous gleam to his eyes. He nods to the tail draped across my lap. "Do what you gotta do," he tells me with a wiggle of his brows and an obscene hand gesture before leaving the room.

I feel my face light up like a neon sign in the middle of the night. The mere thought of... jerking off in Liam's room - on his bed, surrounded by everything that screams Liam - has my fingers tingling and my tail twitching. It's a bad idea, and I know that; but my heart thumps faster and my temperature rises nonetheless. I shouldn't - I really shouldn't.

And yet, my hand reaches for my belt, undoing the buckle and releasing the button on my jeans. For every reason I can think of to not slip my hand beneath my waistband, not one of them makes me stop. As my fingers wrap around my length, a mantra of *to protect my secret, to remain beside Liam* races through my mind in a poor attempt to put myself at ease, but it only manages to conjure up images of Liam. My hand stops in its slow strokes, and I try to banish thoughts of Liam from my mind. I don't want to use him, even if it's only an image of him in my head.

But it's a futile effort. The battle is lost before it even begins, because everything in this room - the room itself - is connected to Liam. The heap of clothes tossed in the corner, the lone poster of his favorite band on the wall, textbooks left open on the floor, and even the hole he put in the wall - everything has Liam's name ringing in my ears. No matter how I try to clear him from my mind, he always returns.

I'll probably - no, most definitely - regret using him in the morning, but it's too late to go back now. In my head, it's not my fingers curled around my length; it's Liam's. It's far too easy to imagine Liam's weight dipping the mattress beside me, his hands exploring the naked flush of my skin, and his breath hot against my ear. My name could roll off his tongue in a heated moan, and I could taste those lips. I'd peer up from hooded, watery eyes to meet the glazed gaze of coppery orbs staring back. His touch - gentle and yet firm - trails a path of fire upon my skin, leaving me squirming and writhing beneath him.

I choke back a moan, trapping my bottom lip between my teeth and biting down. My strokes quicken with each image of Liam that flashes before my eyes, and my breath whistles through clenched teeth.

The walls are thin - I know this all too well - and I can't let my voice be heard. It's bad enough I lied to Liam, not to mention masturbating on his bed, but if he walked in on this, I'd never be able to face him again (that's assuming I'll be able to face him tomorrow).

But it's hard, so hard to hold back each breathless pant and stifled moan. Clenching my teeth doesn't cut it, and I can't risk drawing blood by biting any harder on my lip. I bundle up the corner of the blanket with my free hand and press the fabric over my mouth to muffle my voice. But then I'm overwhelmed by Liam's scent lingering it its fibers - a distinct sweetness mixed with natural musk.

That does it for me, sending me over the edge in a ripple of pleasure that leaves me scrambling for the box of tissues on the nightstand. I clean up quickly, thankful I didn't make a mess on Liam's blanket or sheets. I plop back on the bed to regain my breath, and as my breathing gradually returns to normal, my tail and fangs grow transparent until they're completely sealed away.

As I come down from my high, reality sinks in - the reality of what I've done and who I thought of while doing it. I don't want to face the light of day - not even the artificial glow of the room's lightbulbs - so I slip from the bed and flip off the lights. I stumble back to Liam's bed, crawl under the covers, and curl into a ball.

Who am I kidding? I do know what I feel for Liam. I know why I don't want to go back to my demon partner, and it has nothing to do with my fear of being captured. It's because of Liam, because I don't want to betray these feelings I have for him. So I won't go back to the demon world to feed - never again, even if I have to resort to the snacking of self-pleasure compared to the meal of sex. It's about the equivalent of starvation to a human, but I can still survive off it. It'll be rough, but I can do it. For Liam - and more importantly for myself - I can endure it, grow from it, and hopefully change into the man I want to be.

I drag myself out of bed the next morning, feeling the exhaustion that comes with improper feeding. Each step is sluggish as I walk to the kitchen in search of a bowl of cereal. Rubbing at my eyes, I blindly cross the threshold of the kitchen, knowing exactly where the fridge should be; but what I bump into isn't a household kitchen appliance. I step back, blink to clear my vision, and find myself face to face with Liam.

"Are you feeling better?"

No. "A little," I say.

Liam's eyes don't leave me. His gaze scrutinizes me from head to toe, his head tilted slightly. His fingers twitch, reaching out before falling back to his side. "What do you want for breakfast?" he asks softly.

"Fruity Pebbles."

"I'll get you some. Go rest on the couch, and we'll have a movie day." Liam grasps my shoulder and steers me back toward the living room.

I don't fight against his kindness and do as suggested. My feet drag against the carpet until my legs bump into the couch. The quilt and pillow I normally use are laid out and ruffled from Liam's night on the couch. I crawl under the blanket, folding my legs beneath myself and hugging the pillow to my chest. One night is all it took to make the pillow smell like Liam, and if that can't chase away a bit of my sluggishness, I don't know what will.

Liam joins me in the living room not long after, handing over a bowl of cereal before picking out a few movies. He pops the DVD in the player, snatches the remote, and then takes a seat beside me. I can't help but notice how close he is to me as he shimmies under the quilt and presses his shoulder against mine. It's far from the space that's normally between us, but I like it. I like feeling the warmth that radiates from him, and I like that he doesn't pull away from me.

The movie Liam picked out is some sort of animated musical that he's most likely watched far too many times. He knows the words to each song by heart and softly sings along to each one, even though I can tell by the light in his coppery orbs that he'd like to belt out each word at the top of his lungs. He refrains from doing so, and I'm grateful for that because I don't have it in me to tell him he's tone-deaf.

Liam nudges me in the side, a broad grin stretching his lips as another musical number starts up. He clicks his tongue in time with a character's knocking on a door, and then comes his enthusiastic singing. "Do you wanna build a snowman?"

He's so pleased with himself, grinning from ear to ear, and his smile is infectious. I remember that smug little laugh of his as he knelt at the carpet's edge, showing me the blanket of snow covering the balcony. He peered up at me with wonder and awe which matched my own and asked me the same question he now sings.

I sink further into the cushions of the couch and subsequently lean more against Liam. He side-eyes my movements, but his gentle smile never leaves his lips. I push my luck further and loll my head until it rests against his shoulder.

"Do you still feel sick?" he asks, his hand pressing against my forehead.

"Mhmm," I hum.

It's so easy to curl into Liam and listen to the vibrations in his chest as his soft singing turns to murmured whispers. The exhaustion of my body and mind is forgotten beneath the warmth of the blanket, and there's no doubt in my mind that Liam is my person - my safety, my comfort, my best friend. He's who I want to be beside, and I'll do whatever it takes to stay in this world - his world. I want to be a part of that world, even if it's only a small part.

RULE BREAKER

"Please!"

The dramatically drawn out whine grates at the remnants of my already dwindling patience. After ending my shift with a rude as fuck middle-aged woman (a Bible verse is not a fucking tip!), I'm in no mood to listen to the pleas of Monkey See and Monkey Do.

"No."

"Come on! Everyone else has met him. Why can't we?" Alex whines, slinging an arm around my shoulder and smashing me into her side.

Cody follows suit, yanking me like a ragdoll, and I find myself sandwiched between them, both numbskulls clinging to my sides. "We'll be on our best behavior," Cody says, but the poorly veiled snicker that follows isn't very convincing.

"No," I say with as much force as I can muster, which actually isn't all that much. I struggle to shrug them off - wanting nothing more than to trudge home, eat a decent meal, and go to bed. It's been one of those days where one little thing ruins everything (that fucking customer! Seriously! A Bible verse isn't going to pay for shit!); and now the day's been ruined for anything else I planned to do. Which wasn't much - consisting of a bowl of popcorn and a continuation of the *Disney* movie marathon with Sprinkles. But now I don't even want to do that.

"But Liam!" they whine in unison.

"No."

Absolutely not. Any other day - maybe. But definitely not today, and it has nothing to do with my dejected mood. If it did, I wouldn't hesitate to invite them over to get drunk with me; but it's not about me. It's about Nico. He's been under the weather lately, and I wouldn't dare subject him to the whirlwind that is Alex and Cody without preparation first.

"We'll help you study for finals."

That's a blatant lie. Alex's really grasping at straws to even suggest studying when we both know that's been a longtime pretext for partying.

She helped fool my parents back in high school, but I'm not as blind to her feigned innocence as my parents are.

"You haven't studied a day in your life. Now get off me and let me go home." Okay, maybe that's a little harsh, but it works. They release me from the human sandwich long enough to slip into my jacket (oh god, it smells like Nico).

When I turn back to them, the disappointed pouts I expect to see are nowhere to be found. The shitheads are grinning from ear to ear, whispering to each other - far too giddy for a pair who's been told no after a whole day of incessant begging. "What are you guys scheming?"

"Oh, nothing," Alex waves me off, and Cody bursts into laughter. Try as he may, Cody can't stifle his cackling, and Alex soon joins in. It takes all of five seconds for them to be in tears over whatever they're scheming, but I can't bring myself to care enough to find out.

I mumble a goodnight and leave the two of them in a state of hysterics; because I don't have enough patience left for their shenanigans today. I brush past the pair to exit the break room and leave through the employee door. It slams behind me as the whipping wind forces it shut, giving me half a second to jump out of the way or be clipped in the shoulder. Had I expected the freezing bite of the wind, I would've dug out a scarf from the closet before leaving the apartment today; but it wasn't this wild when I left this morning.

I'm halfway across the snow-covered parking lot, my sneakers crunching with each step, when the bang of the door resounds with the whistle of the wind. Knowing it to be Cody and Alex, I ignore it, choosing instead to burrow my face deeper into my jacket - far enough to cover the tip of my nose. I probably look like a turtle peeking its head out of its shell, but I'd rather be warm than look cool. Plus, it's both late enough and cold enough for most sane people to be indoors, so my badass image will stay intact (a dude can dream, okay!).

Or it would be deserted if not for the obnoxious cackles following behind me. If I didn't know otherwise, I'd assume the pair is drunk - what with their bursts of rambunctious laughter, their shushing of each other that's far too loud to be whispers, and their faltering stride on the sidewalk. I pause my steps, coming to a standstill and glancing over my shoulder. The two of them stop a little too late and collide into each other when they scramble to hide behind a lamppost, because, yes, that'll conceal their presence. Although I have to say, seeing them fall on their asses does improve my mood, and a quiet chuckle may escape my lips as a white wisp of air.

I watch as they oh-so-sneakily crawl one after the other - Cody after Alex - to hide behind the lamppost as if I haven't already spotted them. They peek their heads out on opposite sides of the pole, and two sets of large, doe-like eyes silently beg for my consent.

I suck in a deep breath - fully prepared to regret my new decision - and huff out a defeated sigh. "You guys can come over. You'll just follow me home anyway."

"Yay!" the two of them squeal in unison as they launch themselves at me, slipping and sliding on the icy sidewalk in the process. I brace myself for the collision and am lucky to remain upright when they wrap their arms around either side of me, yanking me into two separate hugs at the same time.

"Let's go, let's go, let's go," Alex parrots as she grabs hold of my forearm and pulls me along the sidewalk. When I don't increase my speed to her satisfactory jog, she enlists Cody to assist in pushing me from behind. To both of their disappointment, their actions do little more than ignite a streak of stubbornness in me that has my heels planting to the snowy concrete.

"There are rules."

That catches both of their attention long enough for them to straighten up and gawk at me like I have three heads. "Rules are made to be broken," Cody states smugly, earning himself a high five from Alex.

And a flick to his forehead from me. "I'm serious. Nico's been under the weather lately so you two will behave. You two so much as breathe wrong, and I'll kick your asses out. Understood?"

Now maybe that seems really extreme and rather rude considering Cody and Alex are friends - hell, we act like siblings - but I have to look out for my Sprinkles. He's finally warming up to me, and I won't risk fucking it up. He's become far too important of a person to me, and it's my turn to protect him in his time of weakness.

"Aye, aye, Captain!" Alex salutes me, but I continue to stare her down. I will not have them making Nico uncomfortable, and I'm not moving from this spot until they understand that.

"Dude, chill," Cody releases me and begins strolling backwards down the sidewalk. "We'll behave in front of your boyfriend."

"He's not my–"

"Yeah, yeah," Cody drones. "You're not smashing dicks, but you're cuddling on the couch watching movies."

I find myself stomping after Cody to set him straight, Alex still attached to my arm. "First of all, you don't smash dicks because that would fucking hurt, and I love my dick too much to kill it. Secondly, have you ever heard of platonic cuddling?"

"I have, but it ain't platonic if you wanna tap dat ass."

"Cody," I warn.

Holding his hands out in front of himself defensively - as if to protect himself from me - he says, "I know, I know. Rule #1, don't mention Liam's undying love for his speckled roommate."

"Damn right that's rule #1."

Alex nudges me in the ribs with her elbow. When I give her my full attention, I'm met with a smug, yet soft and endearing quirk of her lips. "You didn't deny it."

"Deny what?" No seriously, did I miss something?

She wiggles her eyebrows and purposefully bumps her shoulder into mine. "Your undying love for your speckled roommate."

Aw fuck dammit. I spent the entire day brushing off every comment about my feelings, not because I'm ashamed of them (cause I'm not), but because Alex and Cody will shout it from the rooftops. Not that that's a problem either, but I'd rather have Nico hearing it directly from me than from a goddamn side comment at the diner. And I'm not ready to tell him. I like how things are now; and I'm gonna savor every second of it while I work up the courage to confess to him and potentially fuck everything up. So yes, I don't want Alex and Cody - or anyone else for that matter - to find out and potentially ruin what I already have with Nico. The only one with the right to fuck it up is me, and I don't plan to any time soon.

"Relax," Alex says with a pat to my back. "You've got our support. Right, Cody?"

"Roger that. We'll be the best wingman and wingwoman in the history of this planet."

Oh dear lord. That's what I'm afraid of. "Can we just pretend this entire conversation didn't happen?"

Alex shakes her head. "No can do, Liam. Our little man has finally grown up, and I'm not about to miss out on his first love."

Little man? Wait no, first love? Sprinkles isn't my– Is he? I think back to every relationship I've ever had; and I hate to admit it, but Alex may be right. There were crushes and infatuations (a blonde volleyball chick and a dude on my varsity basketball team come to mind), but I can't say I loved any of them. I was a douchy little prick my high school years who only thought with his dick. Dates consisted of a movie spent making out in the theater and banging in the backseat of my father's *Mercedes*. Can't say it was comfortable, but I enjoyed it at the time. I don't remember a single relationship I had that involved my heart more than my dick.

Until now. I mean, yeah, I'd love to fuck - no, make love - to Nico, but who wouldn't? My Sprinkles is beautiful - drop dead gorgeous. But I want so much more than that; and if I had to choose between having his affection or having his dick, I'll choose his affection without a moment's hesitation. I could live my entire life without sex if it meant him being in my life for the rest of my days. I wouldn't have a single regret having him as my best friend who I get to live with and be all domestic with, and if that isn't love, I don't know what is.

"Fine, but what is rule #1?"

The two of them drone in an almost mechanical voice, "Don't mention Liam's undying love for his speckled roommate."

"Correct. Rule #2 - Don't make Nico uncomfortable. He's been sick, so if you buttheads stress him out, you'll pay for it tenfold. Got it?"

"Yes," came their bored reply.

"Rule #3–"

"How many rules are there?" Cody whines.

I raise my voice to emphasize, "Rule #3 - Talk shit, get hit."

"But wittle baby Liam stories are–"

"No."

"But–"

"No!" I interrupt Alex again, to which she quiets down with a pout.

"You can't stop me," she murmurs under her breath, but I don't miss it or the devilish smirk she directs at me.

"The hell I can't."

Cody reaches the apartment building first and holds the lobby door open for Alex and me. "You wouldn't harm a single hair on my head."

"I would if you had any."

"Hey, I've got some!"

"You've got stubble," I say with a cocky little grin, because maybe this is exactly what I need - my two numbskull friends being idiots. Maybe I don't want to go home and collapse on my bed while I curse the universe. I don't have to shut myself away and wallow in today's misery. I don't have to let that fucking customer be what I remember about today when I lay my head upon my pillow and give in to the bliss of sleep.

Cody seductively rubs his hand over his shaved head. "But is it pretty stubble?"

I shake my head as I unlock the apartment door, and an amused grin finds its way to my lips. "The prettiest."

"Aw, thanks," he says as he strolls into my apartment with Alex dragging me along behind her.

They walk in like they own the place, shedding their coats and hats to toss them on the dining table in a heap. They kick off their shoes, not caring where they land, and make a beeline for my fridge. "What's for supper?" Alex asks even as she rummages through the contents of the fridge while Cody finds an opened bag of potato chips in the cupboard.

"Get out of my kitchen, and I'll think of whipping something up," I say, tossing my jacket atop the heap on the table.

"Liam?"

My name draws my attention, but the voice behind it is what has my lips stretching into a fond smile. I turn to see Nico dragging his feet across the carpet, coming to a standstill just before the carpet turns into cold hardwood. He's got a blanket wrapped around him like a cape, one hand clutching the quilt while the other rubs at drowsy eyes. His hair sticks up in every direction, and I can only guess it's because he was sleeping.

He yawns, wiping away a stray tear that forms at the corner of his eye. "Who's here?"

I hear an excited gasp from the kitchen and immediately send a warning glare Alex's way. Her eyes light up like she's found the Holy Grail, and she sends me a very obvious thumbs up.

I step between the numbskulls and my Sprinkles to hopefully minimize any damage that's about to happen, because there will be damage. "Nico, this is Cody and Alex - my childhood friends slash co-workers."

Honey orbs turn to the entry of the kitchen, widening when he spots my dear friends staring right back, both having a hand in the bag of chips. "Um... hi," he says, but it comes out as more of a squeak.

"Hi," Alex parrots back to him with the broadest grin imaginable while Cody offers a wave of his hand, choosing to stuff a handful of chips into his mouth.

Before Alex gets the chance to say anything else (because she's nearly bouncing with excitement and I can see the mischievous spark in her eyes), I ask, "Where's Skyler?"

Nico looks relieved to have the spotlight off him, the startled puppy look relaxing back to simple drowsiness. "He said something about Emil being embarrassed after their last date night so they were going to spend the night in the dorms."

Normally, I'd be jumping for joy knowing I won't be overhearing sex in the middle of the night, but I could've used Skyler as a buffer between Nico and the monkey duo. Skyler's gotten along well with them ever since I introduced them freshmen year of college, so he could keep them in check if their shenanigans get out of hand. And I get the feeling Nico's going to need a little help, because he slowly scoots closer to me until he's right at my side.

"What do you want for dinner?" I ask, looking at Nico.

"Pizza!"

"Cheeseburgers!"

Neither answer came from Sprinkles, but I wait patiently for him to murmur, "Anything's fine."

Should've expected that, but there's no way I'm catering to Cody's and Alex's whims (that and I'm too lazy to put in that much effort tonight). As I'm thinking of an easy solution, Cody shovels another handful of chips into his mouth. And then a brilliant idea resurfaces from the depths of my memories.

"How 'bout some walking tacos?"

"Yes!" Cody yells around his mouthful of chips. He gulps them down

A TASTE OF SPRINKLES

before speaking more clearly, "It'll be just like in high school - celebrating a win by pigging out on leftover concessions. You remember, Lex? Those were the best stomachaches of my life!"

"And we always went to that old ice cream shop for root beer floats! It was the closest to beer we could get back then!" Alex laughs, joining in the nostalgic reminiscing.

I may bitch about my past a lot, but there are memories I'm rather fond of - most of them involving shenanigans with these two. I can still hear the buzzer sounding after I sink the winning basket and the collision of Cody jumping on my back in all the excitement. I piggybacked him all the way to his beat-up truck, stumbling every time Alex tried to hitch a ride from me too. Tires squealing, we raced out of the parking lot (which the principal later scolded us for) and sped across town to this quaint little ice cream parlor that had the absolute best waffle cones. We gorged on every flavor of ice cream until the kind old lady who owned the place had to close for the night, seeing us off with a complementary cone.

I remember wishing my dad's mother was as nice as the always smiling ice cream lady.

A light tap to my shoulder pulls me from my memories. "What's a walking taco?" Nico asks quietly.

"Only the tastiest gift to mankind!" Alex exclaims.

My eyes roll at the not-so-helpful answer. "It's something our high school sold at sporting events. You take a mini bag of *Doritos* and put your taco ingredients in it, so you can walk around while eating it. It's really good. Do you wanna try it?"

Sprinkles glances at Cody and Alex, and my gaze follows. They're both nodding enthusiastically, striking a similar appearance to a pair of bobbleheads. When Nico turns back to me, he gives me a single nod of affirmation.

"We'll get started on that then," I say, flashing a reassuring smile to Nico before leaving his side and squeezing between Cody and Alex.

"We?"

I sling my arms around both their necks. "We as in if you want to eat, you will help." A chorus of moans and groans draws a satisfied smirk out of me, and yes, this is exactly what I need right now.

Alex reaches for another handful of potato chips, but I snatch the bag away. She juts out her bottom lip, and her light brown eyes water like a child who's had candy stolen from them. "Help and you can have them back."

She continues to pout but gives in, "Fine. What do you want me to do, Chef?"

That one word - that title tacked on at the end - sends a jolt through me, momentarily pausing my thoughts. Damn does that feel fantastic. It feels right - like that title was made specifically for me.

"The three of you can grate some cheese and chop up vegetables, and I swear to god, if any food is thrown at each other, no one eats tonight."

"Aw, you're no fun!" Cody whines.

"Yep, I'm a stick in the mud," I say as I start retrieving ingredients. I pop a package of frozen ground beef in the microwave to defrost before tossing a head of lettuce at Cody. He catches it easily, along with the block of cheese which follows. The tomatoes, on the other hand, brings about a scrambling dash not to let them hit the floor.

"Thought throwing food was against the rules," he huffs.

I shrug and use his own words against him, "Rules are made to be broken."

Cody pushes the heap of coats to the floor to clear room on the dining table to set down the ingredients. I dig in the cupboards and drawers for a cheese grater and a pair of knives, and then join Cody at the table. Cody and Alex both grab for a knife, but I hold them out of reach. "Don't make me regret giving these to you," I say before handing them over.

The two of them dig right into the lettuce and tomatoes - carving them so crassly I want to cringe - so I avert my eyes to Sprinkles, who's looking even more like a lost puppy out in the rain. I lock gazes with him and motion for him to join us. His socks slide against the floor as he shuffles to my side. When I pull a chair out for him, he plops down on it, wiggling a bit to get his blanket cape situated comfortably (which may or may not be one of the cutest things I've ever seen a grown man do).

A snort of laughter has my head snapping up to glare at Cody and Alex. I am not above kicking their asses out if they giggle every time I interact with my Sprinkles, because it's going to happen a lot and I can't help it that my eyes are always on him. Although my hand on the back of his chair as I lean for the block of cheese probably isn't helping my case.

"I'll grab you a bowl to shred the cheese into," I tell Nico, leaving him with a reassuring pat on his back.

When I return with the bowl, his fingers are fumbling to tear the plastic off the block of cheese, and I can see the panic starting to flood his pupils. Placing my hand over his, I gently pry the cheese from his grasp and rip at the corner with a fingernail. When the wrapping finally tears, I hand it back to him, not releasing my grip until he meets my smile with a small one of his own.

"Earth to Liam. Your meat's beeping," Alex interrupts; and I'm about to scold her for an inappropriate joke before I hear the microwave going off.

I begrudgingly leave Nico's side, not missing how his smile falters as I step away. I pause next to Alex and lean in to whisper, "Break rule #3 right now."

Ignoring the squeal of victory that startles both Cody and Nico, I retreat to the kitchen and brace myself for the storm of embarrassing stories that's brewing in favor of browning meat that's incapable of laughing at my expense. As Alex's exclamation of *Story time!* rings in my ears, a chant of *it's for Nico* runs on repeat in my head.

"Oh, I know! Back in 6th grade..."

Here we go. Just fuck me up.

Alex continues, "...we had this crazy art teacher who always came up with the weirdest projects, and one day she had us painting faces on vegetables, but here's the catch - the paint only came off with paint thinner. Bet she didn't think that one through. Clean up time came round, and the entire class raced out to recess 'cause no one wanted to suffocate to death in a room where the windows didn't open. It was like a prison. Poor baby Liam couldn't escape though, 'cause he was a chubby little cutie pie with two left feet. He tripped over a chair leg and–"

Liar. "You fucking tripped me! If you're gonna tell the story, tell it right."

The cackling laughter that follows has my blood boiling. I'm ready to abandon the browning meat, march out there, and whack her upside the head; but then I hear it - the musical lilt that has my heart beating faster. If it can make Nico laugh, can make him comfortable being around new people, then Alex can skew the details any way she pleases.

"So maybe I did trip him. Doesn't matter. He fell and got roped into washing all the desks with paint thinner. Needless to say, he got higher than a kite. He spent the entire day getting kicked outta classes 'cause he kept laughing at everything, and it got to the point where his mom had to come in and take him home. He became a legend after that."

Cody pipes in, "And he needed all the help he could get 'cause he wasn't exactly Mr. Cool back then."

"Wait, wait! I've got a picture of baby Liam on my phone," Alex says.

No! Absolutely not. That's going too far.

I abandon my spatula and race out of the kitchen, my feet stomping against the floor. When I reach the threshold between the kitchen and the dining area, Alex cries to Cody for help. He jumps in my path, and I spin on my heel to stumble around him; but he hooks his arm around my waist to hold me back. "Let me go!" I yell, my arms flailing in a poor attempt to reach Alex as she scrolls through her image gallery.

"No can do," Cody laughs.

"I swear to god, neither of you will live to see the light of day!"

The two of them freeze - staring at me, then each other - before bursting into hysterics. "Worth it!" they cackle in unison.

"Found it!" Alex chirps as she sidles up to Nico's side.

I watch in horror as Alex shoves her phone in Nico's face. Thankfully enough, he doesn't seem too startled by the action. But fucking hell! Does she have to show him? I know exactly which picture it is too, because she sweet-talked my mother into sending it to her. In it, I'm a chubby little brat - probably ten years old or so - and I'm waiting at the table for a piece of birthday cake with a death grip on my fork and a smile that takes up half my face (showcasing a missing bottom tooth). I was an awkward little shit before I hit puberty, and the less people that know that, the better.

"He's cute."

Air catches in my lungs, and my flailing arms abandon trying to get free in favor of pounding on my chest to dislodge the traitorous air. Sprinkles - my Sprinkles didn't just say that, did he? Oh fuck, look at that gorgeous flush to his freckled cheeks! He called me cute! Or, well, he called prepubescent, awkward as fuck, chubby ten-year old me cute. But still!

"If you think he's cute there, you should see him in diapers. I bet his mom has some on her *Facebook* page," Alex says as she takes her phone back.

Fuck, shit, goddamn it all to hell. Yes, my mother does in fact have a FB album of embarrassing childhood photos dedicated to my 16th birthday. That was hell to live down at school, and I'm not letting Alex drag those relics to the surface.

I wiggle free from Cody's lax hold and lunge for the phone. Plucking it from her swiping fingers, I tuck it into my pant pocket and stroll back to the kitchen with calls of protest following me. "Rule #3 is reinstated!" I huff.

All three of them follow me into the kitchen, Nico hesitating by the entrance. As Cody and Alex keep grabbing for Alex's phone, I hear a quiet question, "What's rule #3?"

Cody, Alex, and I freeze - the two of them looking to me for some sort of direction. "Uh," I mumble. Distraction - I need a distraction. "Food's done."

"Finally."

"It's about time."

Cody and Alex latch on to the change of topic and immediately scavenge the cupboards for bowls, but Sprinkles doesn't look convinced in the slightest. I feel like I'll crumble and break under that honey gaze so I turn from him and busy myself with distributing *Doritos* evenly into four bowls. We each load up our tacos; and while the numbskulls are totally absorbed in the food, Nico keeps sending questioning glances my way.

I need another distraction - something to catch Sprinkles' attention and hold it long enough for me to think of an excuse or for him to forget about rule #3. Maybe my original plan of collapsing atop my bed and ignoring the world will work; but I can't leave Nico alone with Cody, Alex, and access to my mother's FB account. It'd be best - no, safest - to distract all of them. A movie should do the trick, and this way Nico and I can continue our *Disney* binge-a-thon.

I head to the living room without uttering a word, kneeling in front of the TV and reaching for the next DVD in the rather tall stack on the floor. Alex's squeal of *Movie time!* has her and Cody launching themselves at my couch before I even get the DVD in the player. I finish setting it up and turn to see the two of them sprawled over the couch's entire length with the blanket bundle that is Sprinkles perched on the armrest.

Yeah, no. That's not gonna happen. I only give up my couch for one person, and his probably freckled butt isn't even planted on a cushion.

I plop down atop of Cody's feet and press as much of my weight into him as possible. He begrudgingly pulls his feet out from under me, which is exactly what I hoped he'd do. Leaning on his bent knees, I scoot into him until he's squished between Alex and me.

"Alright, alright!" he concedes. After an elbow to Alex's ribs and a knee digging into my hip, Cody wiggles into an upright position with a pout of his lips.

I pat the newly available space on my left until Nico slides down from the armrest. With all of us finally situated in a reasonable manner, I press play on the remote and hope this suffices as a distraction.

The peanut gallery is quiet for the first few minutes of the movie (which is a great feat), but that glorious silence disappears as fast as their food.

"It's biologically impossible for them to be full sisters," Alex says.

"Why's that?" Cody asks between his last bites of chips.

"Cause there's seven of them, and they all have different hair colors."

"So Triton's been around the block a few times," Cody hums in response.

That's only the beginning of their sometimes comical commentary. I have to admit, when Cody mimics Ariel by brushing his non-existent locks of hair with his fork while shouting *dinglehopper*, I laugh my ass off. He mocks the animated mermaid's naivety to all things human every time she finds a new sunken object, sending the rest of us into fits of giggles.

But no matter how funny the mermaid's naivety is, her wonder and awe are still endearing. I find myself glancing at the entranced Sprinkles, and the fond smile I seem to be wearing a lot these days is back. They're a lot alike - Nico and Ariel that is. Nico's enamored by the world around him, no matter how commonplace it may be. Snow, for example. That morning - when he first spotted the falling flakes from the kitchen window - he gazed upon the sky as if he'd never seen snow before. Which I guess is quite possible since I know very little about his past, but it seemed more like he didn't even know snow existed. If Sprinkles was a mermaid, I image he'd be just like Ariel - all the way down to thinking humans brush their hair with forks.

And Skyler is definitely Sebastian. He's got to watch over and keep Sprinkles (and me) out of trouble. Emil can be Flounder - the sometimes nervous but always dependable best friend/sidekick.

So what does that make me? I'd love to say Triton, 'cause who wouldn't want to be the ruler of all seven seas, but I don't want to be Nico's father. That'd be extremely weird. If I'm choosing based off who Sprinkles is, the obvious choice would be Eric. And yeah, he's no king, but I'll settle for a prince if I can also make Nico one (which Eric does, so yay for cliché happy endings).

"This movie is hilarious when you remember Ariel's only sixteen," Alex laughs, and the fun fact has a snort of laughter coming from Cody. You know you're an adult when your response to a sixteen-year-old declaring their undying love for their crush is a roll of your eyes.

The only person not snickering with laughter as Ariel sings *Part of Your World* is Sprinkles. His gaze is locked on the screen, the honey of his orbs shining with... an almost nostalgic longing. He pulls the quilt even tighter around himself, and I feel him scoot closer into my side. I want to ask him what's wrong but instead bite my tongue against the desperate desire. If we were alone, I wouldn't hesitate to ask him; but with Cody and Alex here, I'm sure he'd tell me he's perfectly fine. So in this moment, all I can do is welcome the closeness and be his shoulder of support.

When the scene changes to a ship at sea and Prince Eric makes his big appearance, Alex chimes in again, "Cue the cradle robber."

The snorts of laughter continue, especially when Eric says love will hit him like lightning and ironically enough, guess what strikes his ship. Way to jinx it, man. He wrecked his ship and lost a gifted statue of himself to the sea. Oh well, at least he saved the dog. That's the only thing that matters.

"How high do you think he was? Like seriously - a singing savior. You don't see that without being at least slightly stoned," Cody says, to which Alex vehemently agrees the prince is a druggie.

I'm not gonna lie, when the musical number of *Under the Sea* plays; Cody, Alex, and I partake in a rather bad rendition of mumbling lyrics we don't know and screeching *under the sea* as loud as we can. I lean into Sprinkles, wiggling my eyebrows in an attempt to convince him to join in. It works, and holy fucking shit can my Sprinkles sing! He matches the melody almost perfectly, leaving my mouth agape and my ears wishing Cody and Alex would shut up. When the song ends and I'm still staring slack-jawed at Sprinkles, he shrugs and quirks his lips into a bashful smile.

His attention turns back to the movie, watching intently as Triton finds out about Ariel loving a human. He physically cringes, burrowing further into my side, when Triton destroys the statue of Eric. Tears prick at the corners of his eyes, his hands darting out from under his blanket to wipe them away.

I don't mean to take advantage of the situation, but I'd like to think I'd do the same if Cody or Alex was in tears. Wrapping my arm behind Nico's neck, I pull him snug against me and give his shoulder a reassuring squeeze. He's stiff and rigid for a short moment, but quickly melts into my side, his head falling to my shoulder. I take a chance - trailing my hand to the nape of his neck and settling my fingers within his hair. His gaze flicks to mine, holding my eyes for a long moment, before returning to the movie.

A nudge to my other side has me directing a glare at a grinning Cody. He pokes Alex's cheek to draw her attention as well, pointing a finger at me. Alex leans to see behind Cody's head, her eyes going wide when she spots Nico's head upon my shoulder and my fingers massaging his scalp. She wiggles her brows and puckers her lips in a mock make out session with air.

Assholes. I roll my eyes and ignore the numbskulls. At least they have the decency to keep their mouths shut and only mime air kisses. Glad to see they can follow rule #1. Not sure I can follow the damn rule though.

When the movie scene changes to Eric and Ariel rowing a tiny little boat on a lagoon, Cody and Alex start whispering to each other. The music of the song starts up, and oh no, they better not be planning what I think they are. I swear to god, I will kill them if they so much as...

"You wanna kiss the boy!" they belt at the top of their lungs.

For fuck's sake, seriously! What part of *don't mention Liam's undying love for his speckled roommate* did they not understand? This is not behaving. This is fucking misbehaving, and I outta kick their asses into the hallway and lock the door behind them. But if I do that, Sprinkles is going to question why; and I don't have a decent excuse to answer him. A furrowed glare does little more than make them increase the frequency of kissing sounds between the chorus.

And Sprinkles doesn't miss the swap of *kiss the girl* to *kiss the boy*. He sits up straight, his warmth disappearing from my side and my fingers slipping from his hair. He stares straight at the TV, seemingly ignoring the damn antic of the monkeys; but the flush to his cheeks and even the tips of his ears betrays him.

They're never allowed under this roof ever again. Never ever!

"You've gotta kiss the boy! Go on and kiss the boy!"

That deserves a punch to the shoulder, and since Cody's the only one I can reach, I punch him twice. He just cackles, nearly keeling over from the laughter. Alex joins in, slapping the arm of the couch and gasping for air.

I should've hit him harder.

Especially since Nico's ignoring me, and it's all their fault. To make it worse, I can't even distract myself with the movie because I can't hear it with the obnoxious laughter echoing in my ears. So I turn up the volume as loud as it can go. Grumpily crossing my arms over my chest, I settle in to finish the movie.

It's one of those cliché happy endings where the couple gets married and lives happily ever after. And okay, it improves my mood slightly, but only because Sprinkles is freaking delighted by the ending. He's blinking back tears of joy as if he's actually attending the wedding of his closest friend.

Cody and Alex hop up from the couch the second the ending credits start rolling down the screen. A part of me hopes they're heading for the door before they break any more of my rules, but I know them better than that. It doesn't surprise me when I hear bottles rattling from the kitchen. It's even less surprising when they come back in with some of the hard lemonade drinks Skyler likes.

"Want one?" Cody asks Nico and me, offering a bottle out for either of us to take.

Sprinkles shakes his head, "No, thanks."

"Nah, I gotta work tomorrow," I say, although I'd love to down one. I normally would - even with work in the morning - but I'm on damage control duty tonight.

Cody plops back down between Alex and me. "What's on next?"

I briefly contemplate putting in another movie, but with all the lovey-dovey plots of *Disney* films, I'd rather not risk an encore of *Kiss the Boy*. I have more faith in my go-to channel. "Whatever's on *Food Network*."

Which turns out to be reruns of *Chopped*. The entree round just began and the contestants are opening the mystery basket of ingredients. Duck meat, brussel sprouts, and even the veal demi glaze are pretty normal, but then they throw cotton candy into the mix. It's far from the weirdest basket I've ever seen, but it's still not ideal. At least I know what all the ingredients are this time. Hell, I'd be great at this show if the ingredients were food that any normal college kid would have in their fridge. One time, I whipped up peanut butter and jelly pasta because that's all that was in the apartment. But ask me to cook with some weird ass caviar shit and I quit. That's just nasty.

As contestants scramble to plate their final dishes, Cody says, "I feel like this is something that shouldn't be rushed. Like, would you take heart surgeons and tell 'em they have thirty minutes to perform heart surgery and then judge them on their sutures?"

I burst into laughter, because where the hell did that come from? Comparing cooking to heart surgery - that's too funny. A boast to my pride (and probably every cook's pride) but still funny. And the thought of a TV show where heart surgeons compete against each other is ridiculously hilarious. Imagine a judge being like, "Sorry, but we had to chop you because you accidentally killed your patient." It's so stupid that it's funny.

By the time the dessert round is coming to a close (the weirdest ingredient being blueberry goat cheese), Cody and Alex are pathetically plastered. I always forget that they're lightweights in the alcohol department, especially when consuming them rapidly (even if the alcohol content is a mere 5%). It's a good thing they're the kind of drunks that find everything funny, 'cause that's the best kind of drunk to be.

Alex reaches for another bottle, missing it horribly. As the responsible friend that I am, I get up and snatch the bottle from the floor. "No more," I say, to which Alex laughs out a high-pitched *okay* before sprawling out on the couch, draping her body across Cody's lap.

I gather up all the bottles - both empty and full - and head toward the kitchen. I pause, asking Nico to help gather the dirty dishes, and then continue on my way. By the time I shove the couple full bottles back in the fridge and dispose of the others, Nico is dumping the few dishes in the sink and running water to wash them.

"I'll wash them," I tell him.

He nods and moves to the side, bundling his blanket tighter around him. I feel his eyes on me as I squirt liquid soap into the water and begin scrubbing down bowls. I have a few good ideas of what could be running through his mind, so I guess I'll swallow some of my pride and mention the one I hope it is.

"Talk shit, get hit."

"Wha–" Sprinkles squeaks, obviously startled.

"Rule #3 - it's talk shit, get hit," I say. When he still looks confused, I clarify, "I didn't want them telling you a bunch of embarrassing stories from my childhood so I made it a rule that they couldn't."

"But they did."

"Yeah, well, I kinda told them to. You looked a little uncomfortable, and I wanted you to be relaxed - to be able to laugh and smile," I tell him, focusing on scrubbing away nonexistent food from a fork.

He asks quietly, "Are there other rules?"

Tread carefully - very carefully. "To behave basically. To be nice and not rude. To treat you kindly."

Sprinkles is quiet for a moment, but then I hear him say, "Thank you."

I nearly drop the fork back into the mountain of bubbles, scrambling to get it into the drying rack. I stare at Nico, because I didn't expect a thank you. There's nothing to thank me for. It's what friends do for each other, especially when one friend views the other as their world.

Okay, Liam, breathe. Yes, his honey orbs gaze fondly back at me; and yes, they are quite breathtaking. But focus, Liam. Complete sentences. "I think your couch has been stolen tonight."

He hums in agreement when I fail to go on. Come on, Liam. You've shared a bed with him before. It's no big deal. "My bed's big enough for two. And of course you know that. Anyway, I'm asking if you're ready for bed." Smooth, Liam. Nailed it.

Sprinkles nods and heads back to the living room, leaving me to flip off the kitchen lights. I follow after him and find him wiggling out of his blanket burrito. He drapes the quilt over the two sprawled out bodies, but he freezes next to Alex. I can hear her mumbling voice but can't make out any of her drunken ramblings. Whatever she says has Sprinkles' skin flushing a brilliant pink.

"Are you okay?" I ask.

Sprinkles straightens up with a jolt, nodding like a bobblehead. I raise my eyebrow at him but choose not to push it, instead heading to my bedroom. I hear Nico's feet dragging on the carpet and glance over my shoulder to spot him staring at the floor, rubbing at the nape of his neck.

What the hell did Alex tell him?

"Liam," he says, his voice both soft and secure.

I stop in the hallway, turning to face him. He takes one hesitant step toward me, staring at the ground; but then pauses to glance at my face. The honey of his eyes flickers back to the carpet as he closes the distance between us in three short strides. His gaze slowly rises, and it has a shiver running down my spine. It's as if he's looking at a priceless piece of art, appreciating every minuscule detail and stroke of a paintbrush. To have such an adoring gaze meet my eyes makes my heart skip a beat, momentarily forgetting how to breathe.

He leans in slow - impossibly slow - as if he's giving me the opportunity to step back, but I won't - I can't. My brain is lagging behind, and even if I want to - which I don't - I can't move a single muscle for fear of waking up from a dream. Because this has to be a dream - a cruel concoction my mind brewed up to torment my pining heart.

But the moment he presses his lips to mine - so soft and tender - I know this can't possibly be a dream. No dream has ever been so warm, so earnest, so real. I melt into him, but all too soon he pulls back.

"Liam," he breathes my name, his lips parting to showcase... fangs?

He gasps, his eyes going wide and his hand rushing to cover his mouth. The adoration of his orbs is replaced with a rampant fear - one which matches that of a terrified animal. Like a wild animal, he flees, darting for the bathroom.

No, this isn't ending here. The fangs - or whatever they are, because they are something - must have an explanation behind them. And you know what, I don't even care what that explanation is. Nico kissed me. My Sprinkles kissed me! Fangs be damned. If he has them, then great. They're gorgeous, because he's gorgeous. And I can't let something so insignificant take away Nico. Because fangs won't change who he is to me - how important he is to me.

"Nico, wait." My hand catches his arm, and he doesn't fight against my grasp. "Please talk to me. Tell me what this means - what it means to you. Because I won't know unless you tell me. And I want to know. I want to know you... because... because I like you. I like you a lot, so much that I love you."

IF ONLY YOU COULD SEE

"Kiss the boy. He loves you."

I jolt in surprise. The quilt slips from my fingers as I suck in a startled gasp. My muscles freeze, and I'm momentarily left with my mouth agape, staring wide-eyed at a very much awake and lucid Alex.

Soft brown eyes peer back at me, and her lips upturn in a gentle smile. Her eyes very purposefully flick to look past me to where I know Liam to be. When her gaze returns to me, there's a sheen to her orbs - one that has me placing my irrevocable trust in her.

Or maybe I'm that desperate to believe her words. I want to believe that I'm as important to Liam as he is to me, so it's easy for me to latch on to even the slightest flicker of hope. And Alex doesn't seem like a person who toys with others' emotions. She can be loud and blunt, but there's not a hint of negativity to her words. A ball of energy is probably the best comparison, and she's been nothing but kind and considerate to me. Maybe I'm too trusting in people I don't know that well; but I'm willing to bet on her words, because I want them to be true. I want them to be indisputable facts.

But it doesn't matter what I want. Sometimes wishes go ungranted just like many dreams stay in our heads - fated to never become a reality. No matter how much I desire for reciprocated feelings from Liam, I can't help but feel it'll stay an ungranted wish - like someone else used up my three wishes from the genie in the lamp or my shooting star crossed the sky while I was sleeping.

Because it's one thing for him to consider me his friend, but I can't fathom why he'd love me. I'm nothing special. I don't have remarkable talents or an outgoing personality. At best my looks are average, and at worst I have a tail. A tail! Humans don't have tails or wings. The only fangs they have are plastic costume accessories they can take off and get rid of. Mine aren't disposable. How could he love that? How could any human love a demon?

"Are you okay?"

I bolt upright, catching Alex squeezing her eyes shut to feign unconsciousness. Spinning toward Liam, I find myself unable to voice an answer without having to gasp for breath every other word, so I nod a little too enthusiastically. He raises a skeptical eyebrow but thankfully doesn't push it any further. Instead, he leads the way to his room.

Dragging my feet against the carpet, I follow him. I'm not particularly tired or sluggish; but if I trudge after him, it'll give me a few extra seconds of thought before being confined in a small space with him for the night.

What are the chances that Liam does love me or even remotely likes me more than a friend? I don't want to ruin the relationship we have now, but what if there could be so much more? Am I willing to risk it for such a slight chance?

"Liam." My voice sounds far calmer than I actually feel. It's a miracle his name doesn't come out as a trembling squeak.

He stops in the hallway and turns to me. The artificial light hits the metallic copper of his irises, and my own image reflects in their dark depths. I avert my gaze to the ground, breathe in a steadying breath, and take a single step toward Liam.

Can I do this? Can I put my trust in Alex? She's one of his best friends and has been for many years. If anyone knows Liam's feelings, I feel like she would. But even more importantly, can I put my trust in Liam - trust that even if he doesn't see me as anything more than a friend, he won't hate me after this?

I can and I will believe in him. In my mind, there's no question about if I can trust him, because I already do. So I take three steps to close the gap of space between us. Sucking in a calming breath, my mind slows down until the flurry of thoughts fades away. I don't want a muddled mind to eat away at what little courage I have, so I clear it of everything but Liam.

The way an irritated glare softened to a cocky quirk of his lips and the nickname Sprinkles rolled off his tongue as naturally as the name of an old friend even though we hadn't officially met yet - maybe it all started at that first meeting without either of us noticing it. I can't forget how flour dusted his dark undercut, especially when it happens so often and he never seems to notice it. Maybe that's why he always smells like baked goods - a scent that's undeniably comforting and reminds me of home. Not that I've ever had a place to call home, but maybe home isn't a place. Maybe it's watching movies curled up on the couch together or sharing the last chocolate chip cookie. It's waking up to find him sprawled on his bedroom carpet and him tugging me to the floor beside him. It's freezing our fingers as we ball up snow to make a snowman in the early hours of the morning. It's gaining a sense of safety and security by simply curling my fingers into his hoodie.

Meeting his gaze, I lean toward him slowly, giving him ample time to pull away. Dear god, I don't want him to back away; but if he doesn't want this - doesn't want me - I'd rather he flee now than later. But please don't flee. Please want this - want me as much as I want you.

Brushing my lips against his, I kiss him - lightly at first to test the waters. When he doesn't pull away or take a step back, I deepen the kiss. He's still for a moment - not moving a single muscle. Pounding against my ribcage almost painfully, my heart races at the thought of Liam being frozen - of him holding still to appease me - but as my thoughts begin to panic, he leans into the kiss, lips moving against mine.

Feeling his warm breath against my lips reminds me of my biological need for air, and I've never before wished for superhuman lungs until this very moment. I pull back and suck in a breath of air. "Liam," I breathe his name on the exhale.

Copper orbs widen slightly, and I figure out why when sharp points dig into my bottom lip. A gasp escapes me before I can hide my fangs behind my hand.

This can't be happening - not here, not now! He kissed me back. Liam kissed me! And now it's ruined. He'll hate me - despise me. He must be disgusted, because who'd want to be kissed by a monster? I can't talk my way out of this, can't explain why a pair of fangs would magically appear in my mouth. So I dart for the open bathroom door.

"Nico, wait," Liam calls as he catches my forearm.

Please, Liam, let me go. I can't fight against your hold when your touch is the one thing I want, so you have to be the one to push me away. Just let me go. You don't know what you're getting into.

But he holds on. "Please talk to me. Tell me what this means - what it means to you. Because I won't know unless you tell me. And I want to know. I want to know you... because... because I like you. I like you a lot, so much that I love you."

He... loves me? Liam loves me? No, he– That can't– What? Am I hearing things? Have I gone crazy, because that seems far more likely than Liam confessing to me?

I want to ask him to say it again to prove I'm not imagining it, but my voice can't be found. Words fails me. When I need it most, my mind goes completely and utterly blank. I'm not sure how I'm still breathing, let alone still standing, because my knees grow weak.

"Nico? Are you okay?" he asks.

No, I'm not. I feel like I'll pass out any second.

"Okay, that's a no. Come with me," Liam says gently. His hand slides down my forearm to link his fingers with mine. While rubbing his thumb in soothing circles against my skin, he slowly backtracks to his room, his eyes never leaving mine. He leads me to his bed and places his hands upon my shoulders to coax me into sitting upon the mattress. "Take a few breaths. I'll be right back. I promise."

His words resound loud and clear, but I barely register them. He turns on his heels to leave. I want to reach out to him - tell him to stay - but neither my voice nor my arm would listen to me. I stare after him, unable to do anything but watch him go.

When he's out of sight, everything tumbles down upon me. I want to hide - to disappear - but I have no place to go except here. There's no other place where my racing heart and heaving lungs will calm down, where my hands will stop trembling, where the strength will return to my limbs. But even here, I'm scared of what Liam will say, of what he'll do when he hears the truth.

With shaky arms and legs, I scoot further back on the bed until I'm pressed against the wall. My knees draw up to my chest with my arms wrapped around them. Dropping my head to rest atop my arms, I squeeze my eyes shut.

I'm not sure how long I sit curled up before Liam returns. It feels like hours but is probably only a few minutes. It's not the sound of his footsteps but an angry meow that has me peeking through my lashes.

Clutched under each of his arms, Simba and Furby squirm to get free. Simba wiggles back and forth, slowly slipping from his grasp. Furby, on the other hand, claws at his side and sinks its teeth into Liam's arm.

"Ah, fuck!" Liam hisses. He hurries to the bed to set the cats down at my feet. As soon as his hands are free, he rubs at the fresh bite and claw marks on his left arm, but his attention quickly shifts to me.

Liam crawls into bed beside me, leaning back against the wall with his legs crossed beneath him. He's close - not close enough to brush shoulders, but still close.

Neither of us speak for quite a while. The only sounds are the purrs of the kitties as Furby crawls under my arm to settle in my lap and Simba curls up at my side between Liam and me. Feeling the soothing vibrations has my heart rate slowing to a much more reasonable pace. My fingers uncurl from clutching my arm to bury themselves in the fluff of Furby's fur.

But I know the silence between us can't last forever, and it's Liam who breaks it. "Are you okay?"

Sucking in a steadying breath, I quietly answer, "Yeah."

Liam puffs out a breath of air, turning his head to flash a small smile at me. "Good. I'm glad." He leans forward and scoots away from the wall, twisting and shimmying until he's seated in the center of the bed. "Can you smile for me?"

No. Absolutely not.

When I shake my head, he says, "Please, Nico. I know they're there. I can see the tips of them."

My hand darts to cover my mouth; and my eyes squeeze shut as I shake my head more fervently. If only my fangs would disappear! But even if I could make them go away, that wouldn't change the fact that Liam's already seen them. And no matter how long I rack my brain for a way out of this - for a realistic excuse to explain everything - my mind blanks to nothing but static. If only Skyler and Emil were here. They'd know what to do. They'd–

"Nico," he calls my name quietly, almost in a whisper. Slowly reaching out to me, his fingertips brush the back of my hand as if asking for permission. When I peek through my lashes and meet the copper of his eyes, he cups my hand in his to gently pull it away from my mouth. He holds my hand in both of his and squeezes lightly. "Nothing you show me will every change how I feel about you. Please trust me."

The warmth I feel from his hands matches the warmth within his words. His unwavering gaze - so soft and tender - has a calmness spreading throughout my body, one that has the tension fading from my shoulders.

I do trust Liam. I always have.

After breathing in a single breath of air to steel my courage, my lips part - not necessarily quirking into a smile, but it's enough to showcase my fangs. With bated breath, I wait for even the smallest reaction.

Liam stares at first, his head tilted slightly; but then a brilliant smile chases away every doubt within my mind. His eyes light up with unabashed elation. "That's awesome. So are you, like, a vampire?"

A puff of laughter bubbles up from my throat. "Not quite, but you're close."

"Okay, not a vampire. That's good. Vampires are kinda lame. I'd say werewolf, but your fangs aren't really canine. Hmm," he hums. "Can I have another clue?"

He's so calm, not fazed one bit. How does he not see a monster sitting before him when I see a monster every time I look in a mirror? How is he so accepting? What would he do if... if I told him the truth, or maybe... showed him?

I pull my hand free of his, and he willingly lets me reclaim it. So as not to disturb Furby in my lap, I carefully scoot away from the wall and twist to face Liam. "If I show you something, do you promise not to freak out?" I ask quietly.

"I pinky swear," he says, offering his little finger. We hook pinkies and shake on it.

Inhaling deeply, I hold the air in my lungs for a short moment before releasing it, letting my control over my demon features slip away with it. The weight of my wings settle over my shoulder blades, ripping slits through my t-shirt where they connect to my skin. At the small of my back, the base of my tail materializes and its length curls around my leg until the tuft of coarse hair at its end flicks at my feet. And lastly - a feature I rarely show to anyone, not even my demon partner - a pair of horns protrude from the sides of my head, curving outward like mirrored images of the letter *s*.

Copper orbs widen almost comically as Liam gapes at me, but he quickly collects himself. He scratches at the nape of his neck and says, "Well, that was unexpected."

Combing my fingers through Furby's fur, I wait, because there must be more. Even Emil and Skyler showed more surprise and asked countless questions, some of which I had no answers for.

But Liam's silent as he reaches for me, stopping short of my tail to meet my gaze. "Can I touch it?"

I nod, watching as he hesitantly pokes at my tail - as if he's not sure it's actually there. When it doesn't disappear under his touch, he brushes his fingers along the length, trailing all the way to the tuft of hair at the end. He combs his fingers through the coarse, dark hair and draws a gasped laugh from me. "Sorry," he says, withdrawing his hand.

"Oh, it's fine. That just tickles."

His eyes glint mischievously. "I'll have to remember that." He leans forward on his knees, peering at my horns so closely that the warmth of his breath brushes my cheek. "Are these ticklish too?" he asks as his finger pokes at one.

"No. Only the end of my tail is."

"Interesting," he hums quietly. He pokes a finger at each of my horns and then wraps his hands around them. After gently pulling at them, he sits back and laughs. "So they really are attached to your head."

How is he so calm, so lighthearted? There's no way he can still believe I'm human. Right before his eyes, I materialized traits which no human could naturally possess. So why isn't he running away or kicking me out? Why isn't he calling me a monster, an atrocity, or an abomination?

Why is his smile still tender - no, even more affectionate and adoring than before?

"Can I touch your wings?"

When I nod, he crawls to my side. The pads of his fingers feather over the membrane of my wing, and it's surprisingly soothing. He pets my leathery wing as if it is the soft fur of a cat; and like a feline, the strokes make me want to purr. There's a rumble in my chest as his fingers rub over one of the bones, and my wing unfolds further under his touch.

His voice is filled with nothing but wonder and awe as he asks, "Are you the real life *Batman*, or maybe half-bat, half-human? Oh man, I'd love to meet your parents then."

There he goes again - turning what I thought would be an awkward and tense situation into a carefree conversation.

"No, I'm a... a demon."

His hand falls from my wing, and he leans back to hold himself up on his palms. Lips pursing and eyebrows drawing together, copper orbs peer at me curiously.

Okay, here we go. This is where the declarations of monster and abomination are shouted. It's when disgust contorts his glorious smile. He'll finally act like any human would and push me away.

"Cool."

What? "You're... okay with this - okay with me... being a demon?"

"Well, sure," he says as nonchalantly as if we're discussing the weather. "You're my Sprinkles; and you've shown me proof, so I know you're not crazy. And you're not a serial killer, so that's a plus. I couldn't live with a serial killer; but a cute, freckled demon is pretty great in my book."

Liam doesn't hate me. He doesn't think I'm a monster. He... he accepts me - the demon me that even I haven't accepted yet. I can't believe it. I can't–

"Nico," he quietly calls my name, reaching a hand out to me. He caresses my cheek, his thumb wiping away moisture. "Why are you crying?"

I dab at my eye, and sure enough, a tear trails down my cheek. But I'm not sad.

"Nico."

Lifting my gaze, I meet Liam's eyes, and my lips part in a beaming smile. "I love you, too."

Liam breathes out a stuttering gasp, his cheeks flushing a light pink. He wipes at his own eyes and blinks against the moisture forming in their corners. "Dammit, Sprinkles, you're gonna make me cry too."

"Sor–"

Liam shakes his head. "You don't have to apologize. They're happy tears."

My heart leaps in my chest. Never in a million years would I have imagined I'd fall for a human, but even more profound is to have that human reciprocate my feelings. And for that, he deserves to know the truth and not just part of the truth.

"Um, there are a few other things you should know," I say.

"Are you gonna tell me you have super powers? 'Cause that could be amazing."

"Well," I nervously laugh, "I guess that's one way to put it."

With a tilted head, Liam curiously peers at me, leaning forward as if he's on the edge of his seat.

"I should probably begin by saying there a different types of demons in my world, and each type has a different specialty or super power," I tell him. "For example, imps specialize in mischief, jinn are great shapeshifters, and alps deal with nightmares."

"So what kind of demon are you?"

Just thinking about it makes me want to cringe. "I'm an... incubus," I say quietly.

Liam's eyes bulge, and his mouth falls open in surprise. He almost falls forward before he catches himself on the heels of his palms. "Wait, so does that mean you– You're, uh–" He combs a hand through his hair and laughs. He laughs. "Holy shit, dude. I was so wrong about you."

"What type of demon did you think I was?"

"I don't know," he shrugs. "I guess something more innocent or shy."

A demon being innocent? I'm not sure such a phenomenon exists.

"So how does that, um, you know, work? Like, do you have a partner or something?"

Heat rises to my cheeks - not particularly because of the question, but because it makes me remember the last time I masturbated... on this bed. Right where Liam is sitting now.

"Wait, I'm sorry. That's really personal. You don't have to tell me," he backpedals and glances at the bedside clock. Before I have the chance to tell him I don't mind the questions, he says, "I have work tomorrow so we should probably go to sleep."

Liam slides off the bed and pads to the light switch. "Get comfy, Sprinkles, 'cause you get the wall side this time. And keep Furby on your side."

"Why don't you like Furby?" I ask as I scoot toward the head of the bed with said cat still clutched in my lap. I pick up Furby and set him beside me so I can wiggle beneath the blanket.

"Because he's a de– Oh my god! That's why he likes you. It all makes sense now."

Liam looks so pleased at this revelation that I can't help but smile. "It took you long enough to notice," I say, scratching Furby's head.

"How was I supposed to know you're a demon?" he asks before directing a glare at Furby. "And I'm serious about him. He better stay on your side."

"Yes, yes," I tell him, but he continues to glare at Furby until I move the cat to my other side. The furry puffball curls up next to Simba, and both of them fall asleep almost instantly.

Liam flips the light off and easily finds his way back to the bed. He crawls beneath the covers to lie flat on his back but quickly decides he'd rather be on his side. Now his bed is not big in any definition of the word. It'd probably be too narrow for the both of us if it wasn't pushed up against the wall. We'd both end up on the floor otherwise. With him so close, his warmth radiates against me, and his eyes seem like stars in the sky.

Under his gaze, I feel safe. I feel I can tell him anything, and he'll listen as if I'm recounting some epic, nail-biting adventure of the universe. I can trust him with my deepest, darkest secrets one moment and lightheartedly joke with him the next. When I'm weak or scared, he'll be there to hold onto. And I'll never hesitate to do the same for him.

For the first time in my life, I want to tell someone everything about me, no matter how minuscule the detail. I want to confide in him and for him to confide in me. I want to tell him about the demon world as much as I want him to share his world with me. I want to hear stories about his childhood and see the baby pictures Alex was going to show me. I want to know him and for him to know me.

"Liam?"

"Hmm?" he hums.

"I had a partner."

Even in the dark, I can see his eyes scrunch up. "Huh? What are you– Oh." He's quiet for a moment as he breathes in through his nose. "Like only one partner? Wouldn't that be odd for an incubus? Not that I think all incubuses - incubi? - are, um, promiscuous, just that, well, that's how all the stories go, and I'm just gonna shut up now."

A quiet puff of laughter escapes me. "Those stories are mainly right," I tell him. "Most demons - especially incubi - go from partner to partner quite easily. And there's nothing really wrong with that. It's just not... what I want."

"Then what do you want?" Liam asks.

My eyes flick to stare at the ceiling. "Something human. Like what Skyler and Emil have."

"That's a tall order to fill," Liam says, and I can hear the smile in his voice. "Although I guess I got the human thing going for me."

"Yeah, human is good," I murmur.

"Can I... can I ask you something?"

"You just did."

"Haha. Funny, Sprinkles." He pokes my cheek until I turn to look at him. "Can I?"

I nod.

"Why are you here in this world and not yours?"

I turn my head back to the ceiling. So quiet it's almost a whisper, I say, "I don't like it there. I hate being a demon."

"Is that what you meant that one day when you told me you knew what it was like, that you didn't want me to feel that way too?"

My words from then echo in my head. *I know what it's like to hate myself, so I don't want you to go through the same pain.*

"Yeah."

"Do you still hate yourself?"

My eyes squeeze shut against tears that threaten to form, and I nod.

The next thing I know, Liam wraps his arm around me - resting the limb under my wing - and pulls me flush against his chest. Slipping his other arm beneath my head, comforting fingers comb through my hair; and I relish in the touch. The feel of his heartbeat thumping beside my cheek has me melting against him. His lips brush my forehead, placing a light kiss upon my skin.

"You are the most amazing person I have ever met," he says in a whisper meant for my ears alone. "You're selfless and considerate. You're modest to the point of putting yourself down, and I wish you could see yourself like I see you. If only you could see the brightness in your smiles or the gentleness in your eyes, hear the melody of every word you speak, and feel my heart pound in my chest every time you look my way. Maybe then you'd see how amazing you are."

I hide my face in his chest, because the tears flow whether I want them to or not.

"And if it's the demon thing you don't like, I just want you to know that even that part of you is awesome. I mean, you have wings! That's pretty damn cool. And your fangs are kinda cute when the ends peek between your lips."

With stuttering breaths, my fingers curl into the fabric of his shirt - if only to have something to hold onto. I feel so bare - so vulnerable - and yet, there's no other place I'd rather be. His touch, his breath ghosting over my hair, his heartbeat echoing in my ear - they all prove to me that this is real, that I'm not imagining his words or fantasizing about the warmth of his body. He's here, and he loves me.

"Do you know why I call you Sprinkles?" he asks.

I shake my head against his chest.

"Because your freckles remind me of sprinkles on a cupcake, and I love fucking cupcakes."

My quiet laugh is muffled by his shirt, but I'm sure he hears it.

He presses his lips to my forehead. "Goodnight, Sprinkles."

"Goodnight, Liam," I whisper.

As my eyelids fall close and I breathe in the sweetness that is distinctly Liam, a calmness I've never known settles within me. It's as if every worry disappears, and the weight of the world is lifted from my shoulders. The focus it takes for my demon features to conceal themselves is minimal; there's no long struggle or frustrated failure.

It's never been so easy to drift off into a peaceful sleep as it is tonight within Liam's embrace.

Hot. Far too hot - like a blazing inferno in a scorching desert. The blanket is suffocating as my shirt and pajama bottoms stick to my skin.

But it's not the heat that has my eyes cracking open. The blaring beeps of an alarm clock ring in my ears, but even that annoyance isn't enough for me to welcome the morning. It's not until the arm I'm using as a pillow flexes and shifts beneath my head that my eyes flutter open.

And the sight before me takes my breath away. A ruffled head of hair - sticking up on one side and flattened on the other - turns enough for Liam to direct a weak glare at the alarm clock as his hand drops atop the snooze button. He sighs at the beloved silence, his eyes falling shut again before his head plops back on the pillow. Squeezing me close, he nuzzles his nose into my hair.

"Liam," I breathe his name.

"Hmm?"

"You have to get up for work."

He groans like a whining child. "Don't wanna."

My lips upturn into a smile as I say, "But you have to."

"But I'm tired and oh so comfy."

I wiggle within his embrace. "I'm not. I'm too hot."

Liam giggles, "Hot damn."

"Liam, I'm serious. It's too hot."

"Nah, it's fine."

"Liam!"

"Five more minutes," he whines.

Palms flat against his chest, I push myself back from him, but he holds me tighter. As I squirm within his toasty embrace, my foot brushes against a lump at the bottom of the bed. I peer over Liam's arm and catch a glimpse of bushy gray fur.

Perfect. "I'll sic Furby after you."

"No, you won't."

"Do you want to test it?"

Liam huffs out a breath against my hair. "No," he says in defeat, loosening his hold on me.

I lean back enough to meet his drowsy gaze. When his copper orbs meet mine, his lips stretch into a dopey grin. "Good morning." He laughs. "I've always wanted to be able to say that."

Liam's cute when he's sleep deprived. I'd love nothing more than to explore this side of him all morning, but he has to get to work. Plus, there'll be plenty of other mornings.

"Good morning to you, too," I say. "You should probably start getting ready for work."

"Fine," he relents with a yawn as he pulls his arm out from beneath my head. He sways a bit as he sits up, rubbing at his sleep-crusted eyes. "I'ma go take a shower."

"'Kay. I'll put some pop-tarts in the toaster for you," I say as he stands up.

He shuffles across the carpet and mumbles his thanks before fumbling with the doorknob. He nearly walks into the wall but somehow manages to round the hall unscathed.

When I hear the spray of the shower through the wall, I roll out of bed and pad to the door. I tiptoe down the hall and through the living room, careful not to disturb the entangled pair sleeping on the couch. After entering the kitchen, I dig in the cabinet for the box of poptarts and grab two packages of strawberry pastries. As I pop them in the toaster, I hear a meow come from behind me.

"What is it, Furby?" I ask as I bend down and beckon him to me with my hand. "Are you hungry too?" The kitty meows in response and rubs against my hand. "Okay, okay, I'll get you some breakfast."

It takes a bit of rummaging through cupboards before I find a small bag of cat food in one of the lower cabinets. I unroll its crinkled top as I walk out to the dining room. There's a little measuring cup among the kibble bits that I use to scoop a bit of food into a ceramic fish dish on the floor.

Furby munches on the meal, and it takes all of three seconds before Simba comes scrambling out of Liam's room to join him. I watch the two of them with a fond smile until I hear mine and Liam's breakfast pop up in the toaster.

After piling the hot pop-tarts on the plate, I go back to Liam's room and crawl atop the bed. Crossing my legs beneath me, I set the plate in my lap and pick up a pop-tart to munch on.

With the shower still sounding as background noise, I can't figure out why I feel so... high. Even while being alone in this near silence, my heart won't stop fluttering in my chest. My lips ache from being in a constant smile, but I can't stop. I try to wipe the smile from my face, but it keeps returning. This all feels so surreal, like it's some sort of vivid hallucination I'll wake up from.

But it's not a hallucination or a dream. It's real, and I couldn't be happier.

The shower turns off when I finish my first pop-tart. While I reach for a second, I look up to spot Liam entering the room - one hand holding up the towel around his hips and the other stifling a yawn. The pop-tart falls from my grasp as my mouth is left agape.

It may not be the first time I've seen him practically naked, but it may as well have been. This time, there's no angry scowl or exasperated shouts. His temper doesn't flare, and he doesn't lock himself in his room.

Liam must not notice my stare, or maybe he's pretending he doesn't see me gawking at his glistening abdominals. And oh my gosh! That is a tattoo on the right side of his ribcage! I can't get a good look at it, but it seems like some sort of orange bird and scripted writing.

"Liam."

"Hmm?"

"Can I see your tattoo?"

He glances down at his side. "Oh, sure." He comes to stand beside the bed and raises his arm over his head to show off the art upon his skin.

The bird's feathers blaze like a fire as it's poised to attack, its wings flared above its head. With an arched neck, its opened beak and grasping claws prepare to strike anything in its path. Long tail feathers drape down Liam's side to end just below his sharp hipbone. I tilt my head to read the two lines of script parallel to the tail feathers. It reads, *From The Ashes I Will Rise, Twice As Strong And Much More Wise.*

"It's a Phoenix," I say.

Liam drops his arm and moves to his dresser, digging around in the drawer to find a pair of boxer briefs. There's a slight smile on his face as he says, "Yeah. I always thought they were cool. No matter how many times they die, they always rise up again."

I avert my gaze as he lets the towel drop from his waist (okay, I may sneak a quick peek at his ass, but anyone would if such perfection presented itself before them). He shimmies into his underwear before turning back to me and grabbing a pop-tart for himself.

"Actually," he begins as he picks up a shirt off the floor and gives it a quick sniff, "I got the tattoo to piss off my parents, but I've never shown it to them. When I saw it for the first time after it was fully completed, I felt like they didn't deserve to see it. It's kinda, like, a daily reminder that I can persevere and make it through anything life throws my way. I didn't want them to ruin that for me."

He takes a bite of his pop-tart before slipping into a black t-shirt and searching for a clean(ish) pair of jeans.

"Thanks."

"For what?" He finally finds pants to wear and steps into them.

"For sharing that with me."

"Well, of course, we're..." He stops dead in his tracks. Averting his gaze to the side, he scratches at the nape of his neck while his cheeks flush. "...boyfriends. Or something. Or whatever you want us to be."

My temperature rises as his gaze flicks back to me almost shyly. It's hot, but a good kind of heat. "Boyfriends... sounds pretty nice."

"It sounds great," he smiles.

He finishes getting ready - finding a belt and socks to wear - and shoves the rest of his pop-tart into his mouth. He glances at the clock and nearly chokes. After swallowing properly, he leans on the bed to snatch the last pop-tart off the plate. "I gotta go, or I'm gonna be late," he says. He rises to leave but pauses at the last minute. Copper meets my eyes before flicking to my lips. Bending down, he places a quick peck on the corner of my lips. When he straightens, his cheeks and even the tips of his ears are flushed. "I'll see you later."

He turns to leave, and all I can do is stare after him. My pulse echoes so loudly in my ears that I barely hear him say, "Oh, and you can kick Alex and Cody out whenever you feel like it." Somehow I manage to nod at his words even though they're in one ear and out the other.

I stare after him long after he's gone and out of the apartment. The pitter patter of my heart doesn't slow, and I swear I may internally combust. If I don't find something to distract my mind, I'm going to end up fantasizing about Liam's lips, his warmth, and his beautiful ass all day. And that can't happen. Definitely not an option today.

I focus enough to scarf down the last of my pop-tart and walk the plate to the kitchen. I return to Liam's room and dig through the pile of books in the corner. Among his scattered textbooks are the many books Liam bought for me. No matter how many times I stack them in neat piles, they always end up as a jumbled heap after one of Liam's 15-minute study sessions. Even though it doesn't pay for me to organize them, I find myself doing just that.

I sit cross-legged while going through the books, and it doesn't take long for me to be distracted from my original goal of organizing them. Liam has a lot of textbooks - most of them about business or mathematics - and I can't help but wonder how he juggles it all in only three days a week. To have that many classes, especially with how complicated some of them look, must be exhausting.

I flip open a Calculus book, and I'm already lost on the first lesson. And it's not because I'm a demon. Even demons are taught basic math. We have to be able to blend into the human world after all. But just looking at the confusing mixture of letters, numbers, and symbols makes my head hurt. And most of his business books explain concepts, protocols, and procedures that are far too confusing for my level of education.

There's only one textbook that I'm utterly fascinated with. Colorful sticky notes mark nearly every wrinkled and worn page. They all have words scrawled across them to identify what they mark - baking formulas, recipes, and conversions. Anyone who laid eyes upon this book would immediately know how much passion Liam has for the art of baking, and it makes me sad that his family doesn't see it too.

If they supported him like a family is supposed to, would the numerous business books be specialty pastry textbooks instead? Would he have studied the desserts of foreign countries or maybe gone to a culinary school instead of Sodalis University?

As I carefully flip through the pages - learning the proper names of utensils I never knew existed - I feel a happiness that I can't quite place. There's something special about gazing upon the pictures of decadent desserts and reading about the formulas and science that make baking possible. To me, it's about as complicated as the business concepts; but I want to understand it, even if only a tiny bit. This is what Liam loves - what he wants to spend his life doing - and by gaining a bit of understanding, I feel closer to him.

I can imagine him staying up late and stifling yawns to read just one more page; and then the next thing he knows, it's 3 a.m. and he's two chapters ahead of his class. Or him making an unexpected trip to the store because he runs out of sticky notes and needs more right this moment. Or him testing recipes and begging Skyler and Emil to taste them with a nervous and yet expectant smile upon his lips.

This is supposed to be a distraction from thinking of Liam all day. I'm supposed to be organizing and stacking books against the wall, but I'm engrossed in reading the pastry textbook and imagining how Liam read the exact same words. What went through his mind as he gazed upon the photos of five-star tarts and cakes? Was he envious of the baker's skills, or did he imagine the feel of the dough against his fingers as he kneaded it? Could he smell the sweetness of baked chocolate or taste it melt on his tongue just by staring at a picture? When he skimmed the list of ingredients, did he mentally check if they were in the cupboards or fridge? Did he rack his mind for possible alternatives when he knew he didn't have an ingredient?

"Oh my god, Nico, how'd it go?"

My head snaps up, and my entire body jolts. Nearly pounding out of my chest, my heart races a mile a minute.

"Come on, come one, I wanna know everything," Alex gushes as she bounds to my side. She wraps a hand around my wrist and tugs until I stumble to my feet. She pulls me behind her to the living room, skipping and swinging her arms back and forth the entire time. As she plops down on the couch, I'm forced to do the same - finding myself between an exuberant Alex and a quietly smug Cody. "How did he react? What did he say? What did you say?"

Cody laughs, "Lex, he can't answer if you don't give him a chance to speak."

"Sorry, sorry. I'm just so excited for our little Liam." Alex flails her arms and bounces up and down in her seat. "So how'd it go?"

"Um..." I scratch at my temple. "Perfectly?"

"Oh my god, yay!" She leans across me to swat Cody's shoulder. "I told you I make a great wingwoman!"

"You better hope Liam doesn't find out, though," Cody smiles.

"What do you mean? He owes me one now."

"He's gonna kick your ass first."

"Then I'll just hide behind our new buddy," Alex says with a jubilant smile as she slings an arm around my shoulders. "You'll protect me, won't you?"

"I can try."

"Dude, don't worry," Cody says. "Liam's already wrapped around your finger. He'd do anything you'd ask."

I can't help but smile at that and hope the heat rising in my cheeks isn't as obvious as it feels. "He's not–"

"Oh, yes he is," Cody says while vehemently nodding his head. "You're pretty much all he talks about - you and baking. Nothing else is ever on his mind. Right, Lex?"

"Right," she chirps. "It's all *Nico was so cute playing with Simba this morning* and *you should have seen the smile on his face as he gazed at falling snow.* He fell so hard he can barely remember his name most days."

Oh gosh, that can't be true. I hide my flushed face in my hands. They've got to be humoring me, but... what if they're not? What if that's true, and Liam pined after me as much as I longed for him? I mean, categorizing me with baking is the best compliment anyone can receive from Liam. To say he likes me as much as his culinary passion makes my heart flutter like a million butterflies are swarming in my chest.

"So," Alex squeezes my shoulder and sidles into my side. "Details, my friend. Details."

I peek between my fingers and direct pleading eyes at Cody. Please, save me.

Cody folds his hands behind his head and leans back against the cushion. "I can't help you, Nico. The faster you tell her, the faster we get to watch TV."

"But shouldn't you ask Liam?"

Alex waves off my suggestion. "Nah, I don't wanna wait that long."

I wish she would. I don't know how much or even what I should tell. Or really what I can tell. The majority of it dealt with me being a demon. I can't exactly come out and say *Hey, I have a tail.* Liam reacted well - far better than I could've imagined - but it's still a secret I want to keep. The less people who know, the better.

"Um, there isn't really much to tell."

"Aww, that's no fun. What happened after you kissed him?"

"We went to bed."

"That's it?" Alex asks incredulously.

"Yeah... pretty much." Technically, I'm not lying.

"Fine," she pouted. "I'll pester Liam about it later."

I huff out a sigh at successfully dodging that bullet, but Liam persistently fires question after question at every chance she gets. Even after Cody turns on the TV to a cartoon channel, Alex considers every commercial to be prime interrogation time. And it does feel like an interrogation from one of Skyler's cop shows where the detective wears down the suspect's composure until they crack under the pressure and confess to their crime. It becomes increasingly harder to keep my answers to simple *yes*'s, *no*'s or noncommittal grunts, but they seem to appease Alex's curiosity a tiny bit.

I'm exhausted by mid-afternoon; and thankfully enough, Alex and Cody are content with lounging on the couch all day laughing at an animated cat trying and always failing to catch a cute little mouse. The only time either of them moves is when they run out of chips and try to find another bag in the cupboards. I'm positive they've eaten every last chip in the apartment by the time Skyler returns in the early evening.

Before Skyler fully opens the door, Cody hops to his feet and bounds across the room with a shout of his friend's name. Skyler's eyes go wide as Cody sprints at him with no intention of stopping.

"Wait, Cody, wait!"

"Nah, bro, you gotta catch me," Cody laughs.

"Cody!" Skyler warms; but Cody doesn't slow his charge and forces Skyler to drop the plastic grocery bags in favor of catching the body that jumps at him. Skyler gapes at the dropped groceries. "I had eggs in there."

"Oops, my bad."

"Yeah, your bad. You jumped at me."

"But you caught me."

"I always do, bro."

"Bro," Cody says with a fondness to his eyes that Skyler mirrors.

After a long moment, Skyler says, "But really. I had eggs."

"I'm sure they're fine." Cody wiggles free of Skyler's bridal-style hold and digs in the plastic bags until he finds the carton of eggs. He picks it up and opens it. "See, they're fine."

"They're cracked - every last one," Skyler deadpans.

"Put 'em in the fridge. Liam'll never notice."

"You put 'em in the fridge. I don't want Liam pissed at me. He cooks my meals, and I'd rather not be poisoned."

"Fine, but I'm taking full credit," Cody turns toward the kitchen.

He takes a single step before Skyler grabs him by the back of his shirt and tugs him to a standstill. Without releasing Cody, Skyler stoops down to grab the rest of the groceries and hangs the bags on Cody's arm. "Put the rest away while you're at it."

"Aye, aye, bro," Cody salutes as he continues on his merry way.

With an amused smirk, Skyler shakes his head before turning to Alex and me. "How's it going?" he asks as he plops down on the couch next to me.

I don't get the chance to even open my mouth before Alex beams with excitement. "Nico kissed Liam last night, and they're in love now."

Oh, dear god. That bullet I dodged ricocheted and is coming back for me.

Heat rises to my cheeks... again. It seems blushing like a fool is all I've been doing recently; and by the proud parent grin on Skyler's face, I'd say it's not going to stop any time soon.

"Holy shit, Nico. Congrats. Wish I could've been here to see it."

No, you really don't. Nobody else needed to see that potential wreck, because it really was a runaway train just waiting to jump off its tracks. If Liam was a less accepting person, that train would've went up in flames, but thankfully Liam's a better conductor than I am.

"Uh, thanks?" I say, because I'm not sure what a proper response to that is.

"We should celebrate," Skyler declares.

"How?"

"Video games!" Cody answers my question.

"'Kay, but Nico gets to pick the game," Skyler says.

As three pairs of expectant eyes turn to me, only one game title pops into my head. "*Mario Kart*."

Skyler has to dig around in his closet for two extra controllers. After he finds them and sets up the game, he gives me the honor of being player 1. Much to Alex's chagrin, I choose the little mushroom dude, so she chooses the baby princess instead. Skyler claims the monkey character, and Cody takes Yoshi (I only know its name because Liam loves the little green guy).

If I thought I was bad playing against Liam, I downright suck competing against Cody, Alex, and Skyler. *Mario Kart* is brutal against them. Bananas are dropped, and shells are thrown, and Alex knocks everyone off the course. But it's still fun no matter how many times I come in last, because I'm surrounded by laughter and childish bickering.

We lose track of time as we play round after round. I don't even notice Liam coming home until Alex squeals his name and abandons her controller.

"You're welcome!" she exclaims as she wraps him in a bear hug.

He blinks blankly - a weariness to his eyes. "For what?"

"For setting your pining heart free."

"Huh?"

"Who was a good wingwoman last night?" Alex coos as she pokes Liam's cheek.

He swats her hand away. "Skyler?"

"No, you dummy! Me!"

Liam squirms free of her embrace to shed his jacket, draping it over a chair. "You didn't do–" his words fall short as copper orbs brighten with enlightenment. "I should smack you upside the head for breaking my rules, but you're lucky I don't feel like it."

Something's wrong. I can hear it in the monotony of his voice and see it in the tension of his shoulders.

149

"I'll take that as a thank you. Now come and play with us," Alex says as she skips back to the couch.

Instead of following her steps, Liam heads for the kitchen. "Maybe later. I'm gonna make something to eat first."

I hand Skyler my controller and wordlessly follow after Liam. When I round the wall and stand under the entrance to the kitchen, I'm met with Liam's back as he leans against his hands on the sink, staring out the darkness of the window. His reflection reveals closed eyes of his bowed head as his shoulders rise and fall with every slow, deliberate breath he takes.

"Liam," I call quietly as I come up behind him.

Copper orbs snap open as he spins to face me. His hand raises to scratch at his neck. A nervous flash of teeth greets me, but the smile fails to reach his eyes. He steps past me and yanks open the fridge. While rummaging in the fridge, he says with a voice that is slightly higher in pitch than normal, "I was thinking of making a breakfast pizza. Do you want to help?"

"Are you okay?"

His arm freezes as he reaches for the jug of milk. A huff of air breezes through his lips. He abandons the milk and straightens. Dragging his fingers through his hair, he nods. "Yeah," he sighs. "It's just some bullshit revolving around my dad."

"Do you want to talk about it?"

He shakes his head. "Not now. Do you want to help?" He nods at the fridge and goes back to gathering ingredients.

"Sure. I'd love to."

"Then can you grab a mixing bowl and get a pan on the burner?"

"Yep," I say and do as instructed.

I wait while Liam gathers all the ingredients, noticing the carton of broken eggs sitting on the counter. Liam grabs a worn cookbook from the cupboard beside the stove and flips to a marked page. "This is the dough recipe I use," he points it out. "Can you start on this while I brown some meat and whisk some eggs?"

I nod, my lips quirking into a small smirk. Liam eyes my smile but doesn't comment.

He cuts open a package of ground beef while I start measuring flour. My movements are slow, what with watching Liam out of the corners of my eyes. When he reaches for the egg carton, I almost laugh and have to hide my smile behind my hand.

"What the fuck?" He stares incredulously at the mess of eggshells and yolks, and a bubble of laughter escapes me. Disbelieving eyes turn to me. "Did you do this?"

Trying but failing to hide my grin, I shake my head.

"Cody?" he asks, and I nod.

"Dammit, Cody! Get your ass in here and pick out every last eggshell!" he shouts.

Echoing laughter erupts in the apartment, and I can't help but join in. Even Liam fights against a smile as he stomps out of the kitchen. "I'm serious! Every last eggshell!" Liam comes back with a hunched over Cody in tow. Joyful tears form in the corners of Cody's eyes; and as he gingerly picks through the slimy egg to grab the first piece of shell, Liam turns his back – a tender smile upon his lips.

IT'S NOT YOUR FAULT

My mind wanders, thinking back to the phone call I received in the middle of my shift. I didn't answer the vibrating annoyance because I was in the middle of serving a customer. By the time I excused myself, my voicemail had kicked in. I figured it was Skyler calling to ask me to stop by the corner store on my way home, but then my phone buzzed a good five minutes later to notify me of a new voicemail.

Who the fuck takes five minutes to leave a message? Not Skyler, and not anyone I can think of off the top of my head. So during my next break, I went back to the employee lounge and dug my phone out of my front pocket. My heart nearly stopped when I saw the caller.

Mom.

Even now, as I drag my feet through the slush on the sidewalk, I don't know what to make of her message. She asked me to call her back, but no matter how long I stare at my phone - her number ready to dial with a single push of my finger - I can't bring myself to touch the call icon. My phone always ends up back in my pocket, because maybe if I ignore the issue, it'll go away.

But it's not going away. If anything, the thoughts of what my father did stew within my mind, running in circles until nothing makes sense anymore. How did none of us know what he was doing all these years? For fuck's sake, Bryce works as his right-hand man. He's my father's damn dog. How did he not know? Unless he found out and dirtied his hands to help cover it up.

No, Liam, stop. If Bryce is guilty, then my entire family is too. We all benefited from the despicable wrongdoings, living in luxury that we shouldn't have been able to afford. How did none of us notice it? How did I not notice? Where did I think all that money for expensive cars and designer clothes came from? Accounting firms are lucrative businesses, but not that lucrative.

Maybe I did notice, at least at some subconscious level. Maybe that's why I stopped wearing the designer jeans and fancy dress shirts. It was a waste of money when I preferred graphic tees and ripped jeans. Or when I refused the sports car my parents gifted me on my 16th birthday, forcing them to take it back to the dealership. As an irresponsible teenager, even I knew that was frivolous. My stubborn pride (and, yeah, my growing hatred of my father) wouldn't allow me to accept such superficial expressions of love. Did I want that car? Fuck yeah I did, but I couldn't accept it when all my friends bought their own or took the bus. The very idea didn't sit well with me.

And I guess now I know why my stomach wrenched whenever my parents paid tens of thousands and even hundreds of thousands of dollars on goddamn jewelry or watches or silverware. Because that money was never theirs to waste.

I can't duck into my apartment building fast enough, because every person I pass under the glow of the streetlights has guilt welling up in my chest, like they know my family's deep, dark secret. I want to hide away in my room and pretend I'm not my father's son. Change my name, maybe move across the country. I wonder if I would, you know, if I had the financial means to support such a venture. Yesterday, I could've; but today, I'm on my own - no longer supported by my father.

But even if I had cut all ties and ran off, it wouldn't have changed whose money I was spending. It wasn't mine, and apparently not my father's either.

I come to a standstill in front of my apartment. My hand freezes in its search for my keys when a squeal of victory echoes on the other side of the door.

Deep breaths, Liam. Don't take my anger out on anyone who doesn't deserve it. I did that before, and it got me nowhere. Well, actually it resulted in Nico moving into my room, but that's irrelevant - considering I hurt him in the process. I promised myself to never make him feel like a stranger to me ever again, and that extends to all my friends. They have done nothing wrong, so I'll put on a smile and stuff down my anger until I can think it over with a clear head.

Unlocking the door, I breathe out a sigh before stepping across the threshold. I quietly close the door behind me and slip out of my damp sneakers. Glancing into the living room, I find four pairs of eyes glued to the TV. Maybe, just maybe, I can retreat to the kitchen without being spotted.

But as I take the first step, the ring of my name has my limbs locking in place.

"Liam!" Alex beams, dropping her controller to the floor and leaping to her feet.

Shit. Busted.

She races across the room with her arms open wide, sweeping me into a tight embrace. "You're welcome!"

Uh, I don't recall her doing me any favors. "For what?"

"For setting your pining heart free," she says with a suggestive wink and an elbow jab to my side.

"Huh?"

She leans in close, poking my cheek with her fingers as she coos at me like I'm a small child, "Who was a good wingwoman last night?"

Is this a joke? Am I missing the punch line? "Skyler?"

"No, you dummy! Me!"

Well, that isn't very funny. What the fuck is she talking– Oh. But wait. What the hell did she have to do with Nico and me?

I wiggle free of her arms, finding myself to be uncomfortably hot. I shed my jacket to drape it over the chair, if only to cool my head in order to understand what Alex's hinting at. But my mind is blank. "You didn't do–"

And then it hits me like a freight train. She's a scheming, conniving little devil. I knew she wasn't such a lightweight in the drinking department, but I never would've guessed she'd fake being drunk. I let my guard down, and fuck I want to be mad. I want to be pissed, because I specifically told her not to meddle; but at the same time, I'm grateful to her. I truly am, but right now, I don't feel anything. I'm blank - a walking shell of a human being, because it's easiest to function while feeling nothing at all.

"I should smack you upside the head for breaking my rules, but you're lucky I don't feel like it." I don't feel like existing at the moment.

"I'll take that as a thank you. Now come and play with us." Alex turns from me to skip back to her position on the couch.

"Maybe later," I quickly dismiss her offer. "I'm gonna make something to eat first."

I dart for the privacy of the kitchen, because I can't keep the facade of a smile upon my lips any longer. My shoulders slump forward as I reach for the edge of the sink. My fingers curl into the cold metal as my head bows forward and my eyes squeeze shut.

Not yet. I can't collapse under the weight of this knowledge. I can't burden my friends with my own problems - can't even tell them if I wanted to. Because this can't get out. Not before lawyers get involved and figure this shit out. I can't say anything, because I don't want to be involved. I don't want to be called in for statements. And I know I'm being selfish, but I don't want my family name dragged through the mud.

God, I feel like a useless piece of shit.

"Liam."

My eyes snap open as I twist to face Nico. The poorest attempt of a smile crosses my lips as I scratch at the nape of my neck. Think, what can I– Fridge. Perfect. I step past him and yank the fridge door open. Don't panic, don't panic. I've got this. "I was thinking of making a breakfast pizza. Do you want to help?" I internally cringe at the squeakiness of my voice. That wasn't convincing at all.

"Are you okay?"

Stretched out to grab the milk jug, my hand freezes. Of course he noticed. My Sprinkles always notices, and I don't want to lie to him. I'd love nothing more than to sit down and vent to my heart's content, but I... I don't know how to begin or how to express what I'm feeling. I haven't figured it out yet.

With a sigh, I give up on hiding it, straightening to face Nico. As I rake fingers through my hair, I nod. "Yeah. It's just some bullshit revolving around my dad."

His russet brown orbs soften in a kind of silent understanding. "Do you want to talk about it?" he quietly asks.

"Not now," I shake my head. When I turn back to the fridge, my mind isn't so frantic and jumbled. "Do you want to help?"

"Sure. I'd love to."

The way his words wrap around me like a safety blanket - like he's all the protection I need from the cruelties of the world - ease my tattered thoughts, mending the pieces back together with every smile he sends my way.

"Then can you grab a mixing bowl and get a pan on the burner?"

"Yep," he chirps, and it's so easy for me to forget about the voicemail (even if only for the time being) with Nico simply being in my vicinity - being able to hear every breath he takes and feel the warmth of his skin whenever we brush arms.

I dig in the fridge and freezer for all the ingredients - collecting ground beef, an assortment of cheese, and a carton of eggs on the counter. Maneuvering around Nico, I gather everything needed to make the dough before grabbing my favorite cookbook from the cupboard. I set it down in front of Nico and flip to the desired page. "This is the dough recipe I use. Can you start on this while I brown some meat and whisk some eggs?"

Sprinkles nods. His eyes trail to the egg carton as a mischievous smirk dances upon his lips.

Weird. I didn't know someone could get that much amusement from eggs. Oh well, I'm not about to complain. His smile - even when a little devious - is a masterpiece I'll never get tired of.

I turn to the stove and focus on my own duties. Slicing open the package of meat, the frozen beef falls into the hot pan in a giant clump. After breaking it apart the best I could, I leave it to cook and focus on the eggs.

Opening the carton, I reach for an egg, but my arm freezes halfway. "What the fuck?" I breathe incredulously, staring at a dozen broken eggs in a brand new carton.

A single bubble of laughter has accusing eyes darting to Sprinkles. "Did you do this?" I ask.

He shakes his head. His lips quiver as he attempts to wipe the broad grin from his face, but it comes back tenfold.

"Cody?"

He nods.

"Dammit, Cody! Get your ass in here and pick out every last eggshell!"

A chorus of laughter erupts, echoing from the living room and even from Nico at my side. My lips quirk up into a smile, but nope. Not funny. Okay, maybe a little. But that little shit is gonna pay.

"I'm serious! Every last eggshell!" I stomp into the living room, finding the culprit doubled over with laughter between the equally cackling Alex and Skyler. Grabbing Cody's wrist, I heave until he's on his feet and haul his ass back to the kitchen. I shove him toward the egg carton, mustering up what I hope is an intimidating glare until he gingerly picks up an eggshell shard from the slimy mess.

Satisfied that he's actually doing as told, I turn back to the pan of ground beef. The smile I've been fighting against finally wins, because, yeah, that was pretty funny.

"Liam!" Cody whines. "I'm sorry. This is gross. Can I please be done?"

"Don't do the crime if you can't do the time," I say.

"Liam!"

I glance at Cody over my shoulder. In his defense, he's done a pretty good job of piling eggshells on the countertop. With a sigh, I take pity on my friend. "Dump 'em in a bowl and I'll take care of the rest." His face lights up, opening his mouth to offer his gratitude. Before he can, I add, "But you're not done."

"Anything but the eggs. I beg of you."

"Take over the meat then."

Cody wiggles his eyebrows as his lips upturn in a devilish smirk. "Shouldn't taking care of your meat be Nico's job."

I choke on my own air, sputtering for a retort, and warily eye Nico. I'm amazed by his ability to breathe calmly. His hands don't even falter in their kneading of dough, muscles flexing with every downward press. And I know he heard Cody, because the tips of his ears are dusted a glorious shade of pink.

"Shut up," I sputter, elbowing him out of the way. "That's none of your business."

But my sputtering reply only draws a string of chuckles from my bald friend. "Well, if you insist," he laughs, picking up the spatula to dramatically stir up the meat.

"Hey, don't spill any," I warn.

"Oops," he shrugs. "My bad."

A quiet puff of laughter from Nico sparks a thought within my mind - a very welcomed thought of positivity. I can say for certain now that I enjoy cooking with others, even outside of work. Hell, especially outside of work. I never thought I'd be able to say that, be able to share my special alone time with anyone else.

But thinking back on it, it was stupid of me to believe sharing my passion would somehow tarnish it. Because listening to the constant banter of Cody - while sometimes crossing the line of appropriateness - makes my chest constrict, but not out of the painfulness I'm used to. It's like a bittersweet longing for something I didn't realize I needed. Even when he falls silent and the three of us focus on our respective duties, simply knowing Nico and Cody are at my side has a comforting warmth washing over me.

It makes me want to cry, because I think of all those years I missed out on this. There's no doubt in my mind, that had I asked, Cody and Alex would've rushed over to make a mess of my parents' kitchen while trying to make cupcakes. Would they have tasted better if we had baked them together, even if Alex accidentally used salt instead of sugar? Probably, because the resulting laughter and fond memories would have been worth the bitterness of the cakes.

Now that I have this - that I know the joy of sharing my biggest passion with others - I never want to let it go.

We assemble the pizza together. Nico rolls out the crust and forms it to the glass baking dish. I pour the whipped eggs (hopefully 100% free of shells) in next before Cody unceremoniously dumps the ground beef on top. He stirs the eggs and meat together until it's evenly mixed. Then the three of us throw copious amounts of shredded cheese to cover the egg mixture.

"How long till we get to eat it?" Cody asks as I put it in the oven.

"20 to 25 minutes," I answer, setting a timer for the shorter cooking time.

"We can go play a few rounds then." Cody walks off to do just that, pausing to add, "You're going down, Liam."

"The hell I am," I retort and race after him to the living room.

Cody plops down on the couch, half atop Skyler before being pushed off Skyler's lap to the cushions. "Dammit, Cody. Now Alex's gonna win."

"I was already winning."

"Barely."

"Aw, is Skyler being a poor loser?" Alex coos as her baby Princess Peach crosses the finish line.

"I'ma kick your ass next round."

"Wait, who's all playing?" Alex asks, glancing between Nico and me.

Before I can even suggest switching every round, Sprinkles says, "Liam can."

"You sure?" I ask.

With a small smile, he nods, "I prefer watching anyway."

With the lineup decided, Skyler tosses me the last controller. I sink to the floor in front of the only available space on the couch, receiving crooked stares from everyone else; but I ignore the questioning gazes in favor of patting the cushion behind me.

Sprinkles accepts my invitation and crawls into place behind me, a leg on either side of my shoulders. Leaning back, I rest against the couch and get ready to kick some ass.

So I say I'm gonna kick some ass, but the only person in the room I can actually beat is Nico; and sadly, he's not playing. It's not eternal 12th place bad, but it's 4th or 5th place with Skyler, Cody, and Alex taking the top 3 spots. A tiny flicker of hope shines upon my sore loser ass when I convince Skyler to select the Yoshi Falls track. If I'm gonna kick some ass, this is the best chance I have.

Lined up at the starting line, I'm already in 4th place; but as the green light signals the start, Cody jumps the gun and spins out. He falls into 10th place with a string of curses tumbling from his lips. I graciously take the opportunity to claim 3rd place, but I've got my eyes on Alex's coveted 1st place. If I can just get a turtle shell from the mystery boxes, then I can knock her and Skyler from the top spots. Come on, turtle shells, don't fail me now.

Or banana peels. I guess those will work too, that is if I can get in front of them. Which I can't. So I randomly drop them on the course and hope Alex or Skyler runs into them on the next lap. And then an octopus-like character dances at the top of my racing screen, covering my vision in a blob of dark ink.

"Hey! Who inked me?" Alex demands to know the culprit as she dramatically steers from side to side.

If it wasn't obvious because of the only player screen not covered in ink, the maniacal cackling coming from her other side answers her. "Suck it, Lex!" Cody exclaims as he zooms past all three of us to take the lead.

Dammit. I'm back to 4th place as I begin lap two, and the automated characters behind me keep throwing turtle shells at me. When one hits me and my toadstool character spins off course, every little figure on their car or motorcycle leave me in their dust.

Ah, Dammit! Alex, Skyler, and Cody (in that order) begin their third and final lap; and here I am - only halfway through my second. Stupid fucking game! Stupid fucking Toadstool (damn Cody for taking my Yoshi!)

and stupid fucking course! That goddamn turtle shell, and are you fucking serious? I slip on a banana peel I dropped in lap one! Stupid fucking–

The massaging of fingers against my scalp chases away my internal monologues of frustration, along with every fine motor skill my young adult brain is capable of performing. My thumbs stop mashing buttons on the controller, and all thoughts of a come-from-behind win fade with each comforting scratch of fingertips. My head lolls back to further lean into his touch. A hum of appreciation rumbles in my chest when a second set of fingers joins in to comb through my undercut, and I suddenly know why dogs love to be scratched behind their ears.

I vaguely register Cody saying, "What the fuck, Liam?" as he laps my abandoned character now sitting in the middle of the track.

"I quit," I mumble. The controller slips from my grasp, landing on the carpet between my legs with a muffled thud.

The resulting complaints from my quiet declaration go in one ear and out the other so fast that my brain doesn't register a single word. Slumping down until my head can comfortably rest in Nico's lap, I gaze up at him - meeting the dark honey of his eyes and the soft smile that has creases forming through his labyrinth of freckles. If I could, I'd pause time so I could relish in the gentleness of his touch; because right now, nothing weighs down upon my shoulders - no father, no money, no nothing. Only Nico's fingers in my hair, his warmth beneath my head, and a smattering of gorgeous stars upon his cheeks.

"Are you sure you're okay? Do you want to talk about it now?"

My limbs momentarily freeze - my arms in the middle of pulling my shirt over my head. It takes half a second for me to shake off the renewed tension and shed my t-shirt, tossing it in the growing pile in the corner. I spin to face Nico, catching a glimpse of his boxer-clad ass as he crawls into bed - our bed (damn, it feels so good to be able to say, or well, think that).

I step to turn off the light, if only for an extra moment to gather my thoughts. "No, I need some time to think, 'cause I don't really know what I'm feeling right now. But I promise, I'll tell you when I figure this shit out."

"'Kay," Sprinkles says with a quiet yawn. He shifts onto his side as I slide beneath the blanket. "But you are okay?" he asks, wiggling close enough that I can feel each of his breaths against my cheek.

"Yeah," I nod in the darkness.

"Good," he hums and lazily drapes an arm over my torso. "'Night," he yawns again, his eyes closed. Before I can even return the sentiment, he's fast asleep.

But I say it anyway. "Goodnight, my beautiful Sprinkles," I murmur against the speckled skin of his cheek, pulling back only after leaving a kiss upon my favorite bundle of freckles just below his cheek bone - the only spot where three freckles overlap to kinda form the shape of a heart (if you squint with one eye closed while tilting your head to the right - or maybe it's just me who can see it).

Carefully - so as not to disturb him - I scoot further down the bed until my head can rest against his chest. My forehead presses to his sternum as my eyes fall shut. The negative thoughts I pushed to the depths of my mind start to resurface; but at the first mental image of my father, I shake away the very thought - forcing it back to the darkness it dragged itself out of.

My eyes snap open. Holy crap. This is the first time I haven't sunk into self-despair in the dead of night after hearing about my father and his bullshit. Because when the lights go out and I'm encased in nothing but a lonely darkness, it's so easy to fall apart - to forget I don't have to fight this alone, that I've never been in this alone. And it's not just Nico at my side. Skyler and Emil always have my back, even when I'm acting like a major d-bag and don't deserve their support. Back in high school, Alex and Cody never failed to offer me a couch to crash on after a fight with my family. Hell, I hid at Cody's house for an entire week one summer because my dad's parents were in town to visit. And if it wasn't for Eli's suggestion, I'd be following my father's path for my future instead of forging my own.

I know this is far from over. I'm going to crumble to pieces eventually; everyone does - it's a simple fact of life. But until that day comes, I'll look forward to peaceful nights like this where I fall asleep to the comforting thump of Nico's heart.

One leg hanging off the bed, I awake on my stomach with my face buried in the mattress. Turning my head just enough to catch a glimpse of the bedside clock, my eyes bulge at how late it is. 11:38 a.m. Holy shit. Why didn't Nico wake me up?

I squirm to roll off the bed, but the ensnaring blanket holds me in place. What the fuck? Why can't I–

As I attempt to pull the blanket free, I find it wedged beneath Nico's weight as he lies atop it, fast asleep. Which is odd. I can't recall a single day when I woke up earlier than Sprinkles. While I'm more of a night owl, I've noticed him to be an early bird. So many mornings, I'd trudge from my room with crust-filled eyes to find Nico cheerfully playing with the cats or sitting by the patio gazing up at the cloud-ridden sky. For him to still be in bed when time nears noon worries me.

Is it because he's simply tired from being up late playing video games? Or does it have to do with him being an incubus? If he feeds off of sex, does that mean he starves without it? Oh fuck, what if that's the case? What if that's why he's been feeling ill recently? I really need to ask him about it when he wakes up, because I absolutely will not have him starving himself. If he's not comfortable... feeding... with me, then I don't give a shit if he goes to someone else. All that matters to me is his health - both physical and mental - so if I can't give him what he needs, then I want him to go to someone who can.

But until he wakes up, I'm going to do the one thing I know I can and hope it helps, even if only a tiny bit. So I quietly struggle free of the blanket to awkwardly roll to the floor, landing on my hands and knees with a muffled thud. After a quick check to make sure Sprinkles is still soundly asleep, I tiptoe out of our room (that's never gonna get old), leaving the door cracked open for the awaiting Furby to dart past my feet.

Once in my domain of the kitchen, all foggy drowsiness vanishes to be replaced by a natural focus. I gather ingredients to make chocolate chip waffles and whip up a batter real quick. I make enough for both of us, piling two per plate and dousing them in chocolate syrup. After pouring two glasses of milk, I pin them between my torso and arm while grabbing a plate in each hand. I hurry back to our room, because I can already feel the cups slipping through my hold. Barely making it in time, I set the glasses and plates on the nightstand.

Nico's still sound asleep, lying on his back with his limbs splayed out in every direction. Furby curls up on his stomach, rising and falling with each of Nico's quiet breaths.

The mattress dips under my weight as I sit upon it and fold my legs beneath me. I stare at the peacefulness that is my slumbering Sprinkles, and I hesitate to disturb him. But I feel I must, or his sleep schedule is going to be royally screwed. So my hand settles upon his shoulder and gently shakes him. "Nico," I whisper his name, but the only response is a meow from Furby.

"Is your name Nico?" I question the feline. "I didn't think so, so shut up." But does the evil ball of fur listen? No, of course not. It bares its teeth in another high-pitched meow. "Are you back-talking me?" Another meow. "That's not very nice. I'll tell Nico on you."

A soft groan draws my attention away from Furby to the fluttering eyelids unveiling the russet orbs I love so much. "Tell me what?" Nico mumbles.

"Furby's being an ass."

His eyes blink a few times before peering at the cat perched on his stomach. He raises his hand to scratch Furby's head, and I've never heard purrs so loud from that demon cat. "Furby's a sweetheart."

A quiet puff of laughter escapes me. "Whatever you say."

While Nico is distracted with petting Furby, I twist to retrieve his breakfast from the nightstand. I hide it behind my back until I have his attention. "Nico," I say, and his eyes fall upon me. I reveal the waffles and glass of milk, holding them out for him to take.

Dark orbs widen with surprise as he pushes himself upright. Furby falls into his lap with a meow of complaint as Nico's lips upturn into a soft smile and the corners of his eyes crinkle. "Thank you," he murmurs, a light flush dusting his cheeks. He takes the plate and glass from me. "How long have you been up?"

"Like 20 minutes," I say, reaching for my own breakfast.

We enjoy our waffles and all of their chocolatey, syrupy goodness in relative silence. Furby begs for milk by pawing at my arm, but fuck if it thinks it's getting any from me. Sprinkles is a whole different story though. It takes a single meow and those big gray eyes for Nico to offer the cat his milk. He's such a softie.

When we finish eating, I take his plate and glass to pile them on the nightstand. As I turn back to Nico, he slumps against the wall. I take this chance to breach the topic of his exhaustion. "It's odd that I woke up before you."

He nods but doesn't comment.

I guess I'm going to have to pry a little. "I know you've been really tired recently and you haven't been feeling the greatest. Does that, um, have anything to do with you being an incubus?"

Nico averts his gaze to Furby, and one hand raises to scratch at his cheek. "Yeah."

"Are you starving yourself?"

His shoulders tense, and his finger freezes against his cheek. A shaky breath breezes through his lips as his hand drops to his lap. "...not exactly," he mumbles.

"Nico."

"No, I'm fine. It's just..." he trails off.

When he fails to elaborate, I prompt him, "It's just..." His eyes flick momentarily before darting back to the ball of fur in his lap. "I don't know how any of your incubus stuff works, so you have to tell me if something's wrong or if you need something. If... if you need to go to your demon partner, then I want you to."

"I can't."

"Yeah, you can. I'm okay with it."

"No," Nico shakes his head, "that's not what I mean. I can't go back to my world. I just... can't." His head drops to his hands, and I'm reminded of him saying he hated himself. I think back to when we first met and how he felt useless not helping me cook so I let him do dishes. And I still wonder why that is. How did he - the man who stole my heart without me even knowing - come to think so lowly of himself? What kind of world did he come from? What kind of life did he lead before abandoning that life to come here?

I need some air; and by the looks of it, Nico does too. "Hey," I say quietly, reaching to brush my hand against his. At my touch, his eyes flick to peer at me. "Do you want to go for a walk? I know this little park that isn't far from here. And it should be pretty deserted, since it's a Monday and all."

He nods once, short and stiff. I stand and wait for him to do so as well before walking out our room and to the entryway. Digging in the closet, I retrieve Nico's jacket, hat, and gloves; and hold them out for him to take. I slip into my own coat (I bought a new one 'cause Nico seemed to really like my other one) and grab my apartment key before ushering Nico out the door.

He waits for me to lock up, and then we quietly descend the stairs. When we step out into the light of day, the winter air momentarily stuns my system, but thankfully there's no wind today. The sun brilliantly shines overhead, not a single cloud obstructing it; and I find myself hoping the wonderful weather is a good omen.

With Sprinkles on the inside of the sidewalk, he follows a step behind me. When the occasional person passes by us, he falls in line behind me; and I can't help but check every few steps to make sure he's still there. My fingers clench and flex at my side - wanting nothing more than to interweave with Nico's - but instead, they ball into a fist.

I turn down a side street that leads into a quiet residential area, not another soul in sight. Slowing my pace, I let Nico catch up until he falls in step.

Staring straight ahead, I begin, "Um, Nico, I know this can be an, uh, awkward subject, but I think we really need to talk about it." My eyes flick to him to find russet orbs peering back. "I don't want you thinking I'm only in this for the sex; but if you need to, uh, feed or whatever you call it, then I'll do whatever you need me to. So if you have to go back to your world, then I'll support that too."

He's quiet for a moment, his eyes averting to his feet. "I can't go back. I kinda ran away, and if they catch me, I probably won't ever be able to come back here."

Wait. He's on the run? So is he... "Are you, like, a demon outlaw?"

My question has his lips quirking into a shadow of a smile. "I guess you could say that," he hums before quickly clarifying, "but I'm not a criminal or anything like that. Just a runaway."

"Whatever the reason, I'm happy you did run away."

Hesitantly, his eyes find me, and I flash him a smile so bright it rivals the glare of the sun on the snow. "And I'm serious," I continue. "If you need to feed, all you gotta do is ask me. Okay?"

163

Sprinkles nods. "Okay."

I look back to the street, catching a glimpse of the swing set behind the needles of a coniferous tree. "That's the place," I point. His gaze follows my finger, and a heartbeat later I grab his wrist. "Race you," I laugh a little breathlessly, tugging him to motion before letting him go.

All out sprint, my arms pump at my sides as my shoes crunch atop snow. White wisps of air huff from my lips, matching pants coming from Sprinkles. He's two steps behind me, but with every long stride he closes the gap. My head swivels to check the length of my lead, but I'm distracted by the avid grin that overtook the dejected line of his lips and the sparkling glint of the sun reflecting in his eyes. Nearly tripping, my pace falters as I catch myself; but Nico's already taken the lead. But you know what, I'm okay with losing, because his happiness is the best prize last place has ever given me.

I catch up to him as he hops from the sidewalk into the shin-deep snow of the playground. Coming to a stop, snowflakes flurry around his legs as he leans back and laughs. Laughs! The breathless pants of air echo in my ears like the melody of singing angels. I can't help but to stand and stare in awe of his sheer beauty as he steals every ounce of breath from my lungs.

When his gaze leaves the sky to settle upon me, there's a watery sheen to his orbs. "That was… that was so fun," he pants.

I nod, because I can't seem to find my voice.

With an equally awe-filled gaze, Sprinkles takes in his surroundings. Tall fir trees border the playground on three sides with a chain-link fence hidden by their branches. A large sandbox is buried beneath the snow in the far right corner, only the wooden planks of its sides visible. Three seesaws stand in a line on our right while a jungle gym complete with monkey bars and four slides of various sizes sits in the middle of the plot. On our left, there's a large swing set of six swings - two of which are made for babies.

"Everything's so... small," Nico says with a quiet puff of laughter.

"Well it is meant for little kids." I reach out to him and wrap my fingers around his wrist. Leading him through the blanket of snow, I forge a path to the swings. "But there's no rule against us playing here."

After brushing the snow from the seats, Sprinkles and I sit upon the swings, so low to the ground we're nearly sitting upon the layer of snow. He laughs again as he spreads his legs out in front of him, and they sink into the snow. His hands drop from the metal chains to dig his fingers in the cold flakes.

He sucks in a deep breath and releases it in a long sigh. The liquid sheen of dark honey eyes turn to me. "I hate to ruin the moment, but I, um, was wondering about yesterday, about your dad. I know you said you're okay, but I... I'm still worried about you."

Yeah, I kinda expected that eventually. After all, Nico is the only one who's witnessed my breakdowns firsthand, and the one he saw is actually mild compared to a few others I've had. And you know what, he's the reason I can face the world right now without wanting to hide away in my own isolation. So even though I still haven't figured out exactly what I'm feeling, I want to tell him; because I know he won't let me shoulder this burden alone.

"I got a phone call from my mom yesterday. I didn't answer it, and I really don't plan on calling her back so all I know is from the message she left." With a huff of air, I continue, "My dad's in deep shit. It's a long list of allegations - tax fraud, money laundering, stealing money from clients' accounts, and pretty much anything else you can think of involving the misappropriation of money. Apparently, there's evidence going all the way back to before I was born."

"I'm sorry," Nico whispers.

I shake my head, "Don't be. He's guilty. I just know it."

My head lolls back as I look to the sky. "I know none of this is my fault, but I still feel like shit. Like I've been spending money I thought was his just to spite him, but... but it wasn't his money I was spending. All I can think of now is who he stole it from. They could be struggling families or single parents. Maybe even friends I grew up with or students at Sodalis U. It's their money that's putting me through college, that's paying my rent, that's buying me groceries. And I took advantage of that. I splurge on things I don't need because I thought it'd hurt my dad, but it's..."

A tear rolls down my cheek as my voice cracks. I blink against the burn of a blurry vision and focus on the clear blue of the sky. My chest constricts painfully to think that the victims of my father's wrongdoings are under this same sky, could very well be gazing upon it and cursing my family name. But I don't blame them, and I think that's what hurts the most - that I want to scream *Fuck Holt!* at the top of my lungs and renounce my name. But what good would that do? It won't rewrite history or give back what was stolen.

My name tumbles from Nico's lips, soft and soothing. When my eyes fall upon him, unwavering russet orbs stare back. "It's not your fault."

It almost hurts to hear those words, because my mind fights against them. I want to believe part of the blame weighs down upon my shoulders; because if it did, then maybe I could've done something to prevent this. Maybe I could've stopped it before it got this bad. Maybe, somehow, I could've gone back a good decade before I was born to stop my father from ever committing a felony.

"I... I know that. I do. It's just..." Heaving a sigh, my gaze averts to my lap as my head hangs in defeat. "I feel guilty 'cause I'm being selfish. I don't wanna be involved, so I'm ignoring it. And–" my voice shakes "–and honestly, I'm more worried about what this means for me. All of my father's accounts are frozen, so I have to talk to the landlady and financial aid at the university and the cable company and the internet provider and I still have to study for finals in three weeks and–"

"Liam." Gloved fingers wrap around my trembling ones clutching to the chains of the swing. "Take a breath."

My body shivers as I force air into my lungs one shaky breath at time. When my fingers receive a comforting squeeze, my eyes rise to meet Nico's. I focus on his voice - so steady and soothing - and it possesses a magical calming effect on my racing thoughts and thumping heart.

"We can make a list of everything you have to do later. We'll write it down together so you don't forget anything, but for now, you don't have to worry about it. Just take it one step at a time, even if it's only a small step. Okay? We'll figure this out."

My eyes fall shut as I nod at his words. It's all I can do to focus on my breathing, each inhale and exhale coming easier than the last. But I don't miss how my grip grows slack on the chain links or how Nico's fingers weave between mine until our hands are a connection between us that rests upon the snow.

Staring at our connection, I hesitantly ask, "Can you, uh, keep this whole thing between us? 'Cause my parents are trying to keep this quiet. And I'll tell Skyler and Emil after I get everything figured out."

Another gentle squeeze of my fingers. "I promise not to say a word."

"Thanks."

The next deep breath I inhale is steady - a glaring contrast to that of a moment ago. All of this - the glowing sun in a clear sky, the tingling numbness of my ass from sitting for so long, the warmth wrapped around my naked fingers - makes me believe I'll be okay, that everything will somehow work out for me - for us. Because I hope Nico will come along for the ride, and I really don't want to let go of his fingers any time soon.

My gaze turns to his face, finding him staring at our intertwined fingers. A single squeeze is all it takes to gain his attention; and when those liquid brown eyes of his meet mine, I say, "I love you, Sprinkles."

As the sun reflects in his honey eyes and his lips twitch into a bashful smile - his bottom lip between the bite of his teeth - his answer, although soft enough to be carried away by the breeze, rings loud and clear in my ears. "I love you, too, Liam."

The folded paper in the front pocket of my jeans weighs heavily on my mind, but tracing its outline with my index finger gives me a static sort of peace - like the calm before the storm. It's a constant reminder of the smudge on my family name - something I'll never be able to run from no matter how hard I try - but it's also my to-do list for the next couple of days. Writing everything down truly did help to calm my erratic thoughts. So I guess it's worth having a constant reminder, if only for the new clarity of my mind.

But that clarity is muddled as I take my seat in the lecture hall of my first class of the day. The universe must be laughing its ass off at the irony of which of my classes I'm now diligently taking notes for. No longer will I question the common sense behind this Business Ethics course, because apparently there are plenty of renowned businessmen who either skipped the class or fell asleep during it.

As the professor drones on about sexual harassment in the workplace, my attention pricks when she brings up real life cases. I unconsciously slump lower in my seat, and my hand freezes in its scribbling of notes. Next semester when she teaches this course to a whole new set of students, will my father become just another example to dissuade future business leaders from following in his steps? Will my surname be forever engraved upon the pages of the latest edition of the course's textbook? Will she hand out packet after packet of quizzable material on my father's case? Will I have fellow students stopping me in between my classes to ask for extra details so they can get a better grade on their written report?

My stomach drops at the thought, but I guess I better get used to the idea of the world knowing. Because no matter how I try to distance myself from the situation, I can't deny that I'm a Holt and that yes, Christopher Holt is my piss-poor excuse of a father. And it's only a matter of time before the story breaks. If it's as bad as my mother made it sound, then there's no way they can sweep nearly three decades of baggage under the rug.

As I pick up where I left off with notes, my phone buzzes in my pocket. I finish writing the phrase before dismissing the call ('cause I'm not one of those assholes who talks on the phone in class). But as I slip it back into my pocket and reach for my pencil, it starts vibrating again.

My heart nearly stops, and my pencil rolls from my grip. When I drag my phone from my pocket, I peek at the screen, dreading to confirm the caller. The screen lights up with a blank picture ID and the name Mom above it. Nope. Not gonna deal with this. I send the call to voicemail and immediately turn off my phone.

I'm well aware it's a selfish act on my part, but I'm going to be selfish. I'm going to protect myself, and I don't give a damn what anyone else thinks of that. Let my family be pissed. Let them be frustrated and angry with me for ignoring them. Maybe they'll finally understand how I've been feeling all these years.

Stooping down, I pick up my fallen pencil and scramble to catch up with notes. Being this close to finals, I can't risk missing a single detail, because there's no way I'm retaking this class. Mentally and emotionally, I won't survive a new curriculum where my father is used as an example of what not to do. And thinking on it now, it'll be a miracle if I survive the next six months to finish my business degree. I can only imagine what people will say when I graduate. Probably shit about how my father was grooming me to follow in his footsteps - the next CEO ready to cheat customers, lie about the company's net income on tax forms, and deal with shady black market money.

At least I'll have six months to prepare for the onslaught of speculation. I may have to rethink the name of my future bakery though. No one's going to want to enter a shop with the Holt name plastered all over it. Well, I have time to think of the perfect name, so I guess it's not that big of a deal. I'll just have to get creative.

But not now. Gotta get back on track and focus.

Once I focus on my professor's words and getting the gist of them on paper, class flies by. I take my sweet time in stuffing my supplies in my bag and shrugging on my coat. Slinging my bag over my shoulder, I stand and walk for the door. I enter into a nearly empty hallway as all the other students have already left the building.

I glance at a clock on the wall, and I still have a good 25 minutes before my next class starts. If I head over to the financial aid center now, I should be able to make it to the mathematics department in time for Calculus. I just have to pick up some paper work, and I'll fill it out after Calculus while I eat lunch. I should be able to hand it in before financial aid closes at three, and I'll be able to cross one thing off my to-do list.

So I turn right down the hall and head for the double doors leading to the outside. As I come to them and reach for the handle, someone else shoves the door open and I have to jump back to avoid being hit.

"What the– Skyler? What are you doing here?" My momentary flash of anger morphs to genuine curiosity at the sight of my hulking friend, huffing and panting for breath. What the hell was he doing in the business department? His classes are all the way across campus.

"Liam," he huffs, grabbing my forearm. "You need to see this. Now." He hurries further into the building, tugging me away from the outside world.

"See what?"

"It's important."

"What is?" I ask again, but he doesn't answer. I pull against his grasp, but I don't gain a single inch of leeway. "Skyler, I really need to go pick something up. Can't this wait?"

He remains silent and continues dragging me deeper into the building, turning down halls and going up a flight of stairs to the second floor. When the strong scent of coffee beans reaches my nostrils, I dig my heels into the floor. "What the hell, Skyler? I seriously have important shit to deal with." If he needed money for coffee or a muffin, he could've just asked.

"Liam." The way he says my name so sternly raises the hair on the back of my neck. I gulp. "You need to see this."

The seriousness of his stiff line of lips and his golden eyes leaves me no choice but to follow him. He leads me right past the university cafe, not even glancing in its direction. As we get closer to a small student lounge area, I feel far too many gazes turning to stare at us. Skyler doesn't bat an eyelash and continues to drag me toward one of the TVs mounted on the wall, but I shrink under all the attention. What the fuck are they staring at? Have they never seen a person being forcibly dragged somewhere before?

I walk right into Skyler when he stops and mutter a half-hearted apology. His grip loosens until his fingers fall from my arm altogether.

"Liam," he says quietly, pointing to the TV screen.

My eyes follow his to stare at the screen. The moment they land upon the TV, my eyes widen and my breath stills in my lungs. No. Goddammit no! A little box with the word *Live* in it sits in the upper right-hand corner as *Holt Scandal* displays itself upon the news ribbon. With my childhood home in the background, a news anchor narrates as police arrest my father. Press cameras flash from every direction as my mother and brother watch on - the very image of controlled calmness.

My eyes squeeze shut as I cringe away from the screen. How the fuck was this keeping it quiet? A single goddamn day! That's all the preparation I got. No fucking warning. No, *Hey, I'm sorry but your life is gonna be a living hell because of me.* And goddammit, keep my fucking name out of it! Why must you mention me as the youngest son and display a fucking family portrait from my last year of high school?

What does this have to do with me? Why should I suffer for the sins of my father? I just want to live a happy, quiet life. Is that too much to ask?

I want to run, to sprint back to my apartment and lock the door on the world. But my limbs are locked in place. They're weighed down by lead, and I'm not strong enough to move them. It's a wonder I'm still standing with how badly my legs shake. If it wasn't for Skyler wrapping an arm around my shoulders and guiding me from the spotlight, I don't know how long I would've stood there and stared at the television screen.

I don't struggle against Skyler's support and willingly follow after him. I don't ask where we're going, because I honestly don't care. Anywhere but there. I don't want their accusing glares or whispered comments. What did I ever do to deserve this?

"Liam."

Skyler stops in the dead end of a hallway, but I can't respond to his voice, not even with a simple nod of acknowledgement. He releases me to pull his phone out of his pocket. The moment he no longer holds me up, I crumble. "Whoa, easy there!" he says as he catches me with his free hand. He maneuvers my body like a limp doll and leans me up against the wall, helping me to slide to the floor. He dials someone and speaks into his phone, but the words fail to register with me.

My knees draw up to my chest, and my head bows to rest atop them. My arms cross to hide my face as tears prick in the corners of my eyes. I blink against them and focus on keeping my breaths steady, but they're shaky and uneven.

When the static of Skyler's voice no longer rings in my ears, I feel him at my side - sliding down the wall to sit next to me. The weight of his arm settles around my shoulders, and he pulls me close until my head rests on his collarbone. "It's okay to cry," he whispers, and his words trigger the onslaught of my tears.

PERFECT IMPERFECTIONS

"Simba! I can't see!" I whine but scratch the tabby's head nonetheless. Purrs vibrate from the cat as it paws at my chest, claws getting caught in the fabric of my t-shirt. For the umpteenth time this morning, I set my book down upon the back of the couch to free Simba's claws. Laying my head upon the armrest, I grab the book on exotic animals and settle into flipping through the pages again.

Simba walks in circles upon my chest for a few more minutes before finally curling into a ball. It makes reading quite difficult, forcing me to hold the book up in the air. I'm not going to lie - my arms tremble from the strain after a mere ten minutes. I'd sit up and rest the book against my legs, but Simba seems to be comfortable and it's against kitty law to disturb a slumbering feline. So my hands are tied, and I'm stuck lying on my back beneath the weight of a tubby cat.

Not that I'm going to complain, because there's a calming comfort seeping into me from the vibrations of the purrs. I don't understand how anyone could hate cats with how soothing their presence is. Even Liam - who's more than adamant about his dislike of Furby - sits down on the living room floor to play with both fluff balls. If Mr. Prickly Pear himself melts under the glassy gaze of kitties, then the grumpiest and bitterest of people should as well.

I clumsily turn the page of my book and nearly drop it atop Simba. It falls from my grasp once - twice - before I manage to catch it; but not without jostling the tabby on my chest. "Sorry," I say with an apologetic scratch behind its ears.

A single meow answers me before Simba falls back asleep. I'm not sure how long I lounge on the couch, but it's long enough to finish reading the heavily pictured book. Maybe I should've grabbed a few more from Liam's - no our - bedroom before lying down. But I'd feel bad having to disturb

Simba.

The cat's contentedness or my freedom from boredom? Decisions, decisions. I can always join Simba in a nap. That actually sounds heavenly after waking up when Liam got up at 6:30 a.m. I absolutely adore mornings, but I just haven't had the energy to awake before sunrise; and today is no exception. But I couldn't fall back asleep after Liam left the bed to shower, and then Skyler woke up. Let's just say he's far from quiet with his morning routine. He sings in the shower... badly... loudly.

So a nap sounds lovely. My eyes fall shut with every intention of drifting off to the realm of dreams, but a loud pounding on the door has me jolting upright. Simba tumbles to the couch cushions before darting down the hall to hide. And, nope, that reaction doesn't make me want to answer the door.

I don't think I should answer it, because I'm technically not one of its residents (on paper, that is). And if it's one of Liam's family members trying to get ahold of him, then I'm definitely ignoring whomever it is. Even if he was home, I'm 99% sure Liam wouldn't answer it either.

But what if it's someone else - maybe one of his or Skyler's friends? Or what if it's an emergency? I don't... Should I..?

"Nico! You there?"

When the voice registers as Cody's, I scramble to my feet and race to the door even as his incessant pounding grows more frantic. I pull the door open, and Cody's hand freezes mid-knock. His cheeks are flushed red from the cold, and his pupils are blown wide. Chest heaving with each pant of breath, he huffs, "Let's go. Grab your coat."

Wait, what? "Why?" I squeak out, but still move to retrieve my jacket from the closet. I slip my arms through the sleeves quickly, because something's wrong. "What's going on?"

"Have you watched the news?"

"No."

"Okay, just come on then. It's about Liam. I'll explain on the way." Cody grabs my wrist and pulls me into the hallway, giving me half a second to pull the door shut.

News... about Liam. My stomach drops, because it can only be one thing. Rushing down the steps two at a time, it's Cody who struggles to keep up with me. When I race out onto the sidewalk, I pause long enough for Cody to take the lead and show the way to the university. Arms swing at our sides and feet pound against cement as we sprint around other people, nearly colliding far too many times to count.

"Is this... about his... dad?" I ask between panting intakes of burning breath.

Cody nods, and that's all it takes for me to ignore the sharpness of the winter air as it enters my lungs, begging me to slow down, to get more air with every long stride. But I can't. I won't. Screw my lungs! They can wait. They can suffer until I get to Liam, because he's in far more pain than I am. Why else would Cody come for me if he isn't?

The betrayal, the hurt, the guilt - they shone so brightly within the copper of his irises yesterday. What would've happened if I hadn't been there, if Alex and Cody hadn't stayed longer the night before? Would it have been another picture smashing incident? But he destroyed all the photographs. Would he have turned that destruction upon himself? I sincerely hope not, but there's no telling the lengths a desperate being will go to alleviate their pain for even a single moment.

And that's what scares me - the not knowing if he's okay, if he's safe from his own thoughts. So I'll run any length - as far and as long as I have to - to be by his side. If I knew the way to his university myself, I'd sprint ahead of Cody's fatigued pace to get there faster.

I ignore the strain of my calves and the tingling numbness of my cheeks. I don't know how long we run for, but it's long enough to have a sheen of cold sweat form on my brow. When Cody slows to a trudging jog, I do as well, finally noticing the change in surroundings - more open space with bare trees between brick-faced buildings and far less traffic occupying the quiet streets. We jog up a shoveled walkway - chunks of salt sprinkled atop the treacherous ice - and earn a few glances from less-hurried students as we pass them.

Cody whips open a door, and the heat from the building envelops us. By the time the door slams shut, we reach the bottom of a slick staircase, its non-slip treads the only traction giving me decent footing. He leads the way past a little coffee house and lounge area.

I glance at the screens of numerous televisions mounted on the walls. Most show a sporting event, reality show, or even a cartoon; but there's one in the middle of the room displaying this week's predicted weather. A news ribbon runs along the bottom of the screen, the day's headlines passing by one after another. Even from my distance, I catch sight of a familiar surname in bright white letters. As if I needed even more confirmation of what happened, quiet murmurs of his name are tossed between peers as if the name which makes my heart sing is some sort of vulgarity, something dirty and taboo.

Cody's hands clench into fists at his sides, and he pointedly glares at as many people as he can. I don't blame him. I'd love to do the same, but the energy required to showcase my anger will be better used to console Liam. So I stare straight ahead and quietly follow Cody down a few more halls until coming to the dead end of a corridor.

Multiple pairs of eyes - ranging from quiet relief to wretched despondency - turn at the sound of our thumping footsteps and echoing pants for air, but the metallic copper I wish to see is hidden behind his crossed arms, head hanging down to rest atop knees drawn to his chest. Even with Skyler sitting close on his left and Alex to his right with her arm slung around his shoulders, Liam refuses to lean against either one of them. Directly across from them, Emil and a shorter blond boy quietly lean against the wall.

Emil pushes himself off the wall and silently steps to meet Cody and me.

"How is he?" Cody says in a hushed murmur.

Emil shakes his head, eyes flicking to Liam before falling upon me. "He won't speak to anyone. We tried to get him to go home, but he won't budge. Please, Nico, help him."

I meet each of their gazes, finding desperation in each watering orb - silent pleas to do what they can't. It's not their shoulders Liam wants to lean on, and the fact that they're being shut behind his walls hurts them, not because Liam isn't letting them in, but because they don't have a means to get in on their own without harming his already fragile shell. So they put their last hope in me to rescue him from the burning and crumbling world he's been thrown into.

I just hope I can before he's buried under the weight of the rubble.

With a meek nod, I step over to Liam, my footfalls as soft and quiet as I can make them. Skyler and Alex both reluctantly stand to join the other three against the wall; and Liam suddenly looks so small against the pale beige and artificial lights of the corridor. But he's not small. He takes up space and should never have to curl in on himself to make the world accept his existence. No one deserves that. I want him to take up so much space the universe has no other option but to adapt to him, because people shouldn't have to change for the world; the world should change for them.

Leaning my back against the cold tile of the wall, I slowly slide to the floor with barely a centimeter of space between our shoulders. "Liam," I quietly breath his name.

His arms wrap around my midsection so fast I'm momentarily taken aback. Sobs muffle themselves against the fluff of my jacket as his fingers clutch at my back. His cries are just sharp intakes of breath - no cursing or blubbering rants accompany them.

One hand splayed across his back to hold him to me, the other finds its way into the soft prickliness of his undercut. "It's okay. It'll all be okay. You're safe," I whisper against his hair, murmuring the words over and over again to hopefully give him something to grasp onto - something to focus his mind on. Because maybe if I say it enough, he'll believe it, believe that his world isn't crashing down upon him, that he has friends to hold the weight of the sky above his head.

My fingers stroke through his undercut, brushing from the nape of his neck to the roots of his dyed hair and back again. I slowly rock us back and forth, breathing the same words of comfort in a constant string of murmurs against his hair.

I vaguely register Cody snapping at a group of passing students, protecting Liam like his personal bodyguard. In this otherwise heart-wrenching situation, it gives me ease of mind to know Liam's friends - no matter how useless they may feel right now - will do anything within their power to protect him. They're all still here, waiting for Liam to feel safe enough to lift up his head and show his face no matter how red-rimmed his eyes are or tear-stained his cheeks may be. And if that isn't a beautiful friendship, then I don't know what is.

My eyes squeeze shut as I hold him a little tighter. What I wouldn't give to take his pain away, even if it meant shouldering it myself. He doesn't deserve any of this. Liam's a good - a brilliant - person. Why would this world choose him of all people to break?

I thought the human world was different, but the same hatred and swindling and manipulation I ran from is glaringly present in this world too. It seems no matter the species, it's every being for themselves. Maybe humans and demons aren't so far apart. They both disguise themselves as something innocent - harmless - but their claws and fangs strike all the same. Their cuts reach the same depths into flesh, tearing and ripping to shreds that which others hold dear. So why is only one called a monster?

But I can't imagine labeling any of the people I've met - the friends I've made, the man I've come to love - as monsters. They are far too precious to be lumped together with the less morally upstanding members of humanity. I know it's not fair to assume every other human is a monster in disguise; but when I have the one most dear to my heart clinging so tightly to me and his broken cries echoing in my ears, it's hard to overlook the world which extinguished the fire in his once brightly shining eyes.

It's my turn to protect and nurture his dying ember while he isn't strong enough to. Because it's okay to be weak. It's okay to trip and fall under the burdens of the world. And it's okay if he needs help standing up again, because we're all here to offer a helping hand - to risk being burned to see his flame spark to life again.

. Liam inhales a deep, steadying breath as he wipes his tears dry against my jacket. One final shaky sob - much softer and weaker than all those before it - escapes his lips before he falls silent. But the vice-like grip he holds onto me with doesn't waver.

"Liam." I stroke my hand down the back of his head to his neck, trailing it to cup his cheek and gently coax him into meeting my gaze.

There's a bloodshot sheen to his puffy eyes, and his cheeks glisten with the remnants of tears. The broken despair I expect to be faced with is veiled masterfully behind a well-practiced mask. He pushes his pain to the deepest recesses of his mind, willing it to go away by focusing on something else - something that has his eyes sharpening in an all new panic.

"What time is it?" he asks, his quick words sounding slightly hoarse.

I turn my gaze to Skyler, because I have no idea. "Quarter to one," he supplies after a quick glance at his cellphone.

"I... I have to get to class." Liam's grip on me grows slack until his hands fall to his sides. He straightens, scrubs at his eyes, and scoots away from me.

I catch his wrist before he can stand, and Skyler steps into his path to prevent him from shaking me off to flee. But he doesn't fight against my touch. Liam silently stands, and I rise to my feet with him. Not meeting anyone's gaze, he stares at his feet.

"Go home with Nico," Skyler says with motherly gentleness that not even Liam can ignore. "We'll cover your classes, get any work, whatever you need. So go home and ignore the world. It'll still be here when you're ready to face it."

Liam sniffs back more tears, wiping at his eyes as he nods. When he reaches into his front pant pocket, I release his wrist to give him the freedom of motion. He withdraws a square of folded paper, clenching his fingers around it until it crumples under the pressure. Hesitantly, he holds out his fist to Skyler who opens his palm to catch the falling scrap of paper when Liam pries his fingers open to let go - to hand over control and trust to Skyler.

Skyler closes his hand around the folded square and steps aside to let Liam pass him. Liam takes a single step before pausing, his eyes flicking briefly to Skyler; but his gaze finds the floor once more. Two more steps before he plants his feet to the floor and stops again. In a breath so quiet that the slightest noise can overpower and drown out his voice, he says, "Thanks."

And then he rushes down the hall before anyone can answer.

I jolt to follow after him, but stop in my tracks when Emil calls my name. "Here. His bag," he says, grabbing it from where it sits against the wall.

Relieving him of it, I sling one strap over my shoulder before racing to catch up with Liam. He hasn't gotten far, standing at the end of the corridor like there's an insurmountable wall preventing him from going any farther. And maybe there is, but it's not a wall per se. It's those whispered comments and judging glances awaiting him once he steps out from his safe haven of friends.

I don't say a word as I walk to stand at his side, turning my body to him. Catching his disheartened gaze, my hand moves slowly to clasp his shoulder and squeeze gently. "Trust me?"

Copper eyes flutter shut as he nods.

I grab the hood of his jacket to pull it up over his head. "Stay behind me, okay?" I say, intertwining my fingers with his.

I don't let go of his hand as I step in front of him. With a gentle tug, Liam follows at my heels, his foot nicking the back of mine every few steps. But that's okay. The closer he is, the more my bigger frame can conceal him.

Backtracking through the halls, I huff a quiet sigh of relief when I breathe in the scent of coffee, thankful I took all the right turns. As we walk through the slightly less crowded lounge, Liam grips tighter to my fingers.

I squeeze back and quicken our pace, because I hear the quiet murmurs of students and the drone of the hourly recap of news too. If I could cover his ears and drown out the cruelties of baseless and unintelligent gossip, I would. But I can't.

I need to get him home - lead him past the cafe, down the stairs, and out into the bitter cold. Once outside, my brain racks my memory for the way back to the apartment. It's a pretty straight shot from what I remember. If I just stay on the sidewalk and follow its curves and crossings, we'll make it back safely.

Foot traffic is just as dense as it was on my dash to the university. I guess it could be worse considering it's the tail-end of the lunch rush. But now that my pace is slow - that I'm the leader - a prickle of doubt climbs its way up my spine to settle itself within my head. This is the right way, isn't it? Yes, it has to be. But nothing looks familiar. Did Cody and I really pass so many towering office buildings, cross in so many crosswalks, zigzag around so many people? How did we not cause an accident or get hit by a car?

After crossing a fourth street, I highly doubt I'm going in the right direction. Surely, Cody and I would be seriously injured if we did. My head whips back and forth for anything I may recognize, but there's nothing - no significant landmark that stands out. But if I'm leading Liam the wrong way, would he say something?

I glance over my shoulder to see him frantically avoiding eye contact with every person we pass. Nope, not going to ask him. I can do this. I can protect him like he's protected me.

Maybe this is a little familiar - the sleek modern storefronts of one of the shopping districts. Stopping at the next intersection, I peer down the side street and catch a glimpse of bright red and white. Thank heavens! I know where we are!

Shortly after crossing the street, the storefronts give way to old apartment buildings - their sunbaked bricks crusted with snow. This I recognize. This I can do.

When our apartment building comes into sight, I want to race for it. But I push aside the urge, knowing it would draw too much unwanted attention. Finally coming to stand before it, I hold the door open for Liam, releasing his hand as he enters. We bypass an empty lobby and climb the squeaky stairs. Liam reaches the apartment first and digs in his jacket pocket for the key.

His hand shakes as he unlocks the door.

Liam slips inside, standing in the entryway as if he's not sure what to do. So I close the door behind us and shed his bag and my jacket as quickly as I can. I step around him to stand facing him. He meets my gaze for a short second before it flicks in the direction of our bedroom.

To be honest, I'm surprised he hasn't already darted to that safe zone. Either he's still taking me into consideration or he's buried his emotions so deep that he doesn't feel anything but an empty numbness. For his sake, I hope it's not the latter.

Carefully, I pry the key from his trembling fingers and slip it back into the jacket pocket. Pinched between my thumb and forefinger, the jacket's zipper eases along its track. I nudge the hood from Liam's hair, smoothing over the sandy locks before pushing the coat from his shoulders. It drops from his figure and falls to the floor where it remains abandoned.

Cupping his hands in mine, my thumbs smooth over his knuckles as I coax him to follow me. My feet shuffle backwards across the living room carpet, into the dark shadows of the hallway, and over the threshold of our room. My hand leaves his to flick on the lights but returns to the growing warmth of his skin. When the back of my knees collide with the bed, I spin us until our positions are switched. Fingertips trail up Liam's arm to his shoulders and push him gently to the mattress. Dropping to one knee, I unlace his sneakers and slip them from his feet one at a time, haphazardly tossing them over my shoulder.

One thumps into the wall while the other has an angry hiss echoing in the silence. Liam and I both jolt in surprise. I whip around to spot a bushy gray tail exiting the room.

Straightening to my full height, I cross the room to shut the door, muttering a string of apologies to the retreating Furby. I'll have to cuddle the kitty later, because it's Liam who needs some cuddles right now - needs to be shown how loved and important he is.

I turn to find Liam lying on his back, arms draped over his eyes. I pad to the bedside, leaning one hand and knee on the mattress to swing the others over his trembling form. Peering down at him, I spot his bottom lip between the bite of his teeth, shuddering breaths escaping with every quiver of his lip.

Holding my weight above him with one hand, my other caresses his cheek, thumb running over his lip until his teeth release it. He sucks in a shaky breath, and his fingers dig into his own forearms.

"Fall apart. It's okay. I'll help you put the pieces back together again," I whisper, my words ringing far too loudly in the silence.

And he does, a whine fighting its way from his lungs. With every breathless sob, I press my lips to his arms, to his cheeks, to his neck - peppering every inch of his skin with kisses. "It's gonna be okay. Everything's gonna be okay," I murmur against his arm, massaging circles into his skin with my thumb. My hand feathers down his forearm, over his bony wrist, to fingers curled painfully into his flesh. The pads of my fingers slip beneath his, closing around them to squeeze gently.

His muscles relax enough for me to draw his hand to my lips, pressing kisses to each knuckle. "If you need to hang on to something, hang on to me. Dig your nails into my flesh, but please don't hurt yourself."

Fingers twitch within my grasp, and his other arm slowly falls from his face, reaching for my cheek but freezing halfway. Suspended between us, it's like time stops with his hand. My own heartbeats echo in my ears when his teary gaze finally meets mine. He peers through long lashes, blinking against more tears, but one forms in his left eye. The plump tear rolls down his cheek, sliding over his cheekbone and catching at the corner of his lips.

His suspended hand retreats to wipe away the salty trail, lingering on his cheek. When he reaches out again, his fingers settle upon my shoulder, curling into the cotton fabric of my shirt before splaying his fingers and rubbing over my shoulder blades. Fingertips send a shiver down my spine when they brush against the base of wings I didn't realize materialized.

A shadow of a smile ghosts over his lips, their corners upturning slightly. It barely reaches his red-rimmed eyes, but what's important is that it does.

Placing his other hand upon my shoulder, I free my own to steady myself on the mattress. Leaning down, I press my lips to his cheek - starting at the corner of his eye and following the trail of his tears, tasting the remnants of salt on his skin. Mirroring my actions on his other cheek, I end it with a kiss upon his lips - noting how they no longer tremble. I pull back to allow barely a hairsbreadth of space between us, feeling his fingers toying with the frayed edges of my wings.

When he speaks, I feel the tickle of his lips moving beneath mine. "Make me forget." His fingers flex against the smooth leather of my wings. "Please, Nico, make me forget this pain."

"How?"

His chest rises as he inhales a steadying breath through his nose. He stares straight into my eyes, and I don't see the broken boy at the university reflecting in them. I see bravery and strength, determination of a man who knows what he wants - of what he needs in this moment.

"Take me. Make me yours," he breaths.

A jolt of electricity races through my veins. Is he asking what I think he is? But I... I can't. Not now. I can't take advantage of him. He deserves so much better than what I can give him. "Liam, I–"

"Nico," he says quietly, his hand resting gently upon my cheek. "I'm giving myself to you. I want you to fuck me. I want to be enveloped by you, to think only of you. You are my everything. I trust you."

His words penetrate deep into my heart, spreading a tingling warmth through my chest. My lungs suck in a quiet gasp of air, because I never knew how much I needed to hear those words - to hear that I'm wanted. It didn't matter how many times my demon partner told me similar sentiments; they were meaningless coming from that demon. But Liam - from him, they mean so much. To know I'm as important to him as he is to me - I can't even describe how that makes me want to dance in the snow and throw handfuls of flakes above my head and watch the glinting crystals rain down upon me.

My eyes squeeze shut, and I nod, feeling a single tear roll down my cheek.

Liam's hands slide over my shoulders to rest on my chest. His palms push me back until I'm straddling his lap, Liam rising up to come with me. Wiping away my tear with his thumb, he says with a hint of amusement in his voice, "I thought I'm supposed to be the one crying."

Lighthearted humor fits him so well. Crinkled eyes and a quirky grin with a flash of teeth. A light flush upon his cheekbones. The snort of laughter at his own jokes. They're all so beautiful. He's beautiful.

Heat pools beneath my skin. "I... I might not be any good at it, but, I'll... try my best."

"We're in this together," he says, his hands falling to the hem of my t-shirt. Far too slowly, he lifts it up over my head, but it snags on my wings. He tugs lightly, but the fabric doesn't give.

"Do you need help?" I ask, chuckling at his ministrations. With my arms trapped above my head in the fabric, I wiggle my limbs to try to get at least one arm free. But my struggles work against me to entangle me in my shirt even more. "Liam!" I whine, because I'm not a fan of being visually impaired by my shirt. I want to see him.

"Uh, how much do you like this shirt?"

I stop struggling, confused by his question. "I'm not attached to it if that's what your mean."

"So you wouldn't be opposed to me ripping it?"

My shoulders shrug. "Not really," I hum. "My wings already ripped it, right?"

"Okay, hold still. I got this." The focused concentration I hear in his voice has my lips twitching into an endearing smile, because this is ridiculous. I can make this so much easier by putting my wings away, but I'd feel a little silly mentioning that idea now, so I don't. Plus, it'll probably be good for Liam to destroy something, and an already tattered shirt is perfect for that.

His hand reaches around me to grasp the shirt where my wings protrude through the fabric. He yanks roughly down on it, jostling me in the process. It takes two more sharp tugs before the threads rip, and he manages to pull the shirt (or what's left of it) over my head, tossing it to the floor.

"Hi," he smiles as I blink at the bright light of the room.

"Hi," I murmur back, sneaking a peck to the tip of his nose.

Color rushes to his cheeks as he wrinkles his nose. He sticks his arms straight up in the air, eyeing me expectantly.

Taking the hint, I divest him of his shirt much quicker than he did mine. "You made that look so much harder."

"Haha, Sprinkles. I'm sorry I don't have cool ass wings."

"I like your lack of wings," I say, wrapping my arms around him to rub my hands over his shoulder blades.

His gaze averts to the side, and he nibbles on his bottom lip. "What else do you like about me?"

I blink at the sudden insecurity, trailing my hand up his back to cup the base of his neck. Grasping his shoulder, I gently push him back, laying his head upon the pillow. He needs this, needs me to be gentle with my touch and my words. He needs me to take the lead - to take care of him while he's vulnerable.

My lips press a kiss to his forehead, lingering long enough that Liam squirms beneath me. "I love how considerate you are to your friends - to me." A kiss right beneath his left eye. "I love how you get offended when the judges of your cooking competitions choose a different winner than you would've." I nibble at his ear lobe, eliciting a sharp gasp of breath from him. "When you come back after work or school and immediately race to write down a new recipe in your cookbook, gushing about how good it tasted or how Simon demonstrated how to make it so effortlessly." A kiss to his jugular. "How you argue with Furby when you think no one's listening." A quick swipe of my tongue along his collarbone. "When you pout after losing any sort of game." My lips close around a pert nipple, sucking gently.

A breathless moan tumbles from his lips, his fingers clenching the comforter beneath him. When I lean back to take in the brilliant flush that's spread across his chest, cheeks, and ears; his body shivers beneath my gaze. A bubble of hesitant laughter escapes him. "What about my hair? Do you like my hair?"

I chuckle, pushing a few strands of ash blond hair from his forehead. "I love your hair, especially right after a shower."

His nose scrunches. "It looks like a wet dog."

"Maybe I think wet dogs are cute."

"Course, you do," he says, a lazy smile upon his lips.

Head lolling back, he stares up at the ceiling as he sucks in a calming breath. "Hey," he starts, his eyes softening. "Are you sure you want to do this? We don't have to if you don't want to."

Cupping his cheek in my hand, I lead his gaze back to me. "I do want to." And that's the honest truth. I've never wanted to as much as I do right now. And instinctual needs have nothing to do with it. My hunger isn't driving me; it has no part in this. This is all Liam and me trusting each other and giving ourselves to the other - something I never thought I'd be able to do. But here we are, flushed with each other's body heat and sharing breaths mingled between us.

"We're gonna need a few things then," he says. I lean back as he sits up and twists to reach the nightstand. He digs around in the drawer's clutter for a few minutes, muttering about how he knows they're in there somewhere. "Aha!" he exclaims, tossing a small tube of lube and a foil packet at me. He settles back into the mattress, pointing a finger at the condom. "You gotta wrap it before you tap it. No exceptions."

His words have me stifling a snort of laughter with my palm. Pushing himself up to lean on his elbows, he quirks an eyebrow at me. "What's so funny?"

I vaguely gesture, "Everything. This whole situation. It's just... not what I'm used to. But I... I like this."

"Oh really," he says, his smile twitching mischievously. "It's only going to get better."

His weight dropping back to the mattress, Liam hooks his fingers in the loops of his jeans and bucks his hips. The friction jolts through me, heat pooling in my groin. "L-Liam," I stutter.

He reaches for the buckle of my belt, fumbling a little to unhook it. Popping the button free, he drags my zipper down. Fingers fisting into denim, he yanks at my jeans with as much finesse as he had with my shirt, and it takes some fancy maneuvering on both our parts to get them off. Before I settle back between his legs, he's already unzipping his own pants and raising his hips off the mattress to shimmy out of them, dragging his boxer briefs off with them.

And oh my gosh, we're actually doing this. Seeing him laid out beneath me, his eyes hooded and tattoo vibrant against flushed skin and body reacting to mine - he's absolutely gorgeous. God, I love him so much.

He grabs the lube off the blanket, pushing it into my hands. "Get to it, Sprinkles," he says, spreading his legs wider for me.

I don't know if I'm going to last with what Liam is doing to my heart, with how my body reacts to his every word and the shifting of his muscles. My fingers fumble to uncap the bottle, and I squeeze far too much on my fingers.

"Calm down," Liam breathes, wrapping his fingers around my wrist. He guides me to him, giving me permission to continue. "It's okay. You're doing great."

Prodding at his entrance, I push one finger slowly into him, feeling him tense before relaxing just as quickly. I work my finger in and out, imagining what I would like done to me and try to replicate it - searching for his sweet spot. When I find it, brushing the tip of my finger over the bundle of nerves, Liam sucks in a gasp of breath.

His fingers entwine in my hair, combing through the strands until they bump into my horns. Huh, didn't realize those were out either. Are all my demon features visible?

"Your tail's twitching," Liam laughs.

I guess that answers my question. Weird. Normally I notice - feel - them materializing, but I'm so caught up with Liam that their added weight feels completely weightless. I feel... human - like I don't have abnormal features and I belong here with Liam.

He reaches for my tail, clutching it to his chest and playing with the tuft of fur at its end. "Liam, that tickles," I laugh, working in a second finger while I have him distracted.

"Good," he says a little breathlessly, brushing through the strands of hair to the smooth silkiness of its shaft, running his hand up and down it suggestively.

The tickling sensation turns to something warmer, hotter, needier. A moan rumbles in my chest, falling from my lips so suddenly that Liam's hand pauses in its ministrations and he stares at me, lips parted in awe.

"Interesting," he hums, squeezing a little harder.

Inhaling a shaky breath through my nose, I use my free hand to clasp his and stop his stroking of my tail. "I won't last if you keep doing that."

He shrugs coyly. "Guess you better hurry it up then." And then he resumes stroking my tail with a cocky grin upon his face.

You know what, two can play this game. My fingers press against his sweet spot, lingering before drawing almost completely out only to plunge back in with a third finger.

His grip tightens on my tail, and his other hand fists into the blanket at his side. "F-fuck, Nico. Do that again."

So I comply, loving the soft moans and mewls that my actions cause. I lean over him, catching one of his nipples in my mouth and sucking. Swirling my tongue around the pert nub, I trail my tongue across his chest, showing his other nipple the same treatment. I kiss my way up his sternum, nip at his collarbone, and lick up the side of his neck to his ear, where I nibble on the lobe.

"Nico," he moans my name; and oh god. Who knew my name could sound so beautiful when rolling off his tongue? I sure didn't, but I'm glad I know now. "I... I need you. Right now."

I don't have to be told twice, so I pull my fingers back and wipe them on my boxer briefs, shedding my underwear right after. With trembling fingers, I roll on the condom and apply more lube for good measure. Sucking in a steadying breath, I line myself up.

Liam laces his arms around my neck, and his tender gaze meets mine. We're really going to do this, and it doesn't make me loathe my existence. I feel no self-hatred or self-despair. There's not a drop of pity swirling among the golden specks of Liam's irises - only trust and longing and love. This is what I mean when I say I want something human. I want the connection that humans feel for one another. No, that's not quite right, because I already have that connection with Liam. And dear god, I'll do anything to keep this connection alive.

A single nod from Liam has me pushing into his tight heat. The scratch of his nails dig into my shoulders as he clings to me. I push in slowly, reveling in his warmth until I'm seated all the way in. I wait for Liam to adjust, leaning down to pepper kisses along his neck and collarbone, wrapping my arms around him to cling to him like he does to me.

Hooking his legs over my lower back, he traps my tail between his crossed feet to toy with it. With slightly labored breaths, his voice comes out huskier than normal when he says, "Move, Nico."

My hips slowly rock back and forth, pulling out further with each careful thrust before pushing back it. It feels so good. Liam feels so good. His heat envelops me, sparking pleasure like none I've ever felt - my heart thumping wildly within my ribcage, my toes curling with every soft moan of my name that tumbles from Liam's lips. His sharp cries ring in my ears as his fingers fist into my hair, dragging me down for a heated kiss. His lips move against mine until they part to let out a low whine.

"Are you okay?"

He nods, even as moisture pricks in the corner of his eyes. Lips upturn into a small smile and copper orbs glisten, renewed tears rolling down his cheeks.

At the sight of his tears, I freeze. "Liam, what's wrong?"

"Nothing. Keep going." He rolls his hips to entice me, but no matter how good that feels, I'm not going to continue if it hurts him.

"Li-"

I can't even finish saying his name before he buries his face in the crook of my neck. Tears wet my skin; and when his breath skims over the trails of moisture, it sends a shiver down my spine. "I just... I-I love you so much," he sobs, fingers tightening in my hair. "Please, Nico, I need you. I need to feel you. Please!"

His words stab at my heart; and in this moment, I can't deny him what he wants. "I love you too," I murmur in his ear, feeling him tremble in my embrace as I set a deliciously slow pace - my thrusts long and deep.

"Liam, I love you. You're perfect the way you are." My heated whispers draw moans and whimpers from Liam's mouth as more of his tears smear my neck. "Everything about you is gorgeous." I can feel the curling of his toes against my tail. "Don't change for anyone." His fingers tighten in my hair, nails scratching my scalp. "I love you and all your perfect imperfections."

With a sharp cry of my name, Liam tightens around me and releases onto both of our chests. It's not the tight heat that has me following after him - not the fingers pulling at my hair or the nails digging into my skin, not the quivering of his thighs around my waist or the rubbing of his feet against my tail. It's how his voice hitches with each syllable of my name, his cries echoing in my ears.

Chest heaving for breath and demon features disappearing, I carefully pull out to dispose of the condom and do a quick cleanup of both our chests. "Liam," I quietly call his name as I stretch out beside him. "You okay?"

While staring at the ceiling, he squeezes his eyes shut and nods. He twists on his side to face me, nuzzling into my chest. "I'm sorry," he says so softly I almost miss it.

"What for?"

"For... crying."

Holding him to me a little tighter, I rub some of the tension from his shoulders. "You don't have to apologize."

"But I ruined—"

"No," I quickly correct him, because I don't want him thinking he can't express his emotions. I don't care the time or place or atmosphere - if he needs to express himself in tears or laughs or shouts, I want him to feel comfortable doing so. "You didn't ruin anything. You can cry every single time, and you still wouldn't ruin it."

"Every single time? You plan on doing this often?"

"Uh, I, um. Only if... you want to," I stammer.

I feel his lips press into a smile against my chest. "That'd be nice," he hums.

We fall silent, simply reveling in each other's warmth. Our breaths even out until they're in sync. So many heartbeats pass without Liam so much as moving that I think he might have fallen asleep. And a nap sounds as lovely now as it did this morning. I'm sure Liam can use one as much, if not more, than I can. My eyes flutter shut as I breathe in Liam's scent - still sweet as a bakery even with the sheen of sweat.

"Hey, Nico,"

I jolt slightly, eyelids snapping open. "Hmm?"

"I kinda need to do something to keep my mind busy, so would you, maybe, wanna make cupcakes with me?"

"Sure, as long as I get to eat some."

"You can have as many as you want."

We slip out of bed, foregoing our t-shirts and jeans in favor of plaid pajama bottoms with no tops. Liam opens the bedroom door to both cats sitting outside it, meowing at him. "Yeah, yeah, I'll get you some food."

The cats dart between his legs the entire way to the kitchen. When he gets a scoop of their kibble bits and dumps it in their dish by the dining table, Liam lingers to pet Simba. But what surprises me is him scratching Furby behind the ears.

He straightens, spotting my arched eyebrow at his actions. "Little shit took a shoe for me," he says as if Furby is an old war buddy who stepped in the line of a bullet to save Liam's life.

"So what kind of cupcakes are we making?" I ask, following him into the kitchen.

"I don't know," he shrugs. "We'll start with a basic vanilla and see what we end up with."

Baking with Liam is an adventure in itself. He handles the wet ingredients while I measure out the dry ones. When I'm not looking, he dips his hand into the flour container and flicks it at me (which may or may not result in a childish flinging of flour at each other for a good five minutes). Liam whisks the ingredients together to finish the batter, but he leaves it to sit while scouring the cupboards.

"What are you looking for?"

"I won't know until I find it," he says, pushing aside pop-tart boxes to search behind them. He rearranges bags of rice and cans of vegetables as he glances over each shelf, standing on his tiptoes to reach as far back as he can. His hand withdraws holding a small box, and he turns it over to look at it. "How would you feel about blue raspberry flavored cupcakes?"

"Depends how old that jello mix is," I say when Liam brushes some dust off the box.

"Who cares?" he shrugs. "Jello mix doesn't expire."

I'm pretty sure everything expires eventually, but I'll take Liam's word for it. He rips open the box and tears a corner off the inner packet. Not bothering to measure, he dumps some of the bright blue powder into the cupcake batter and whisks it until its a light shade of greenish blue.

Liam swipes his pointer finger through the batter and offers it to me. With a light flush dusting his cheeks, he says, "Tell me what you think."

Have I ever said I love Liam? 'Cause I do. A lot.

A quick swipe of my tongue over his finger has a sweet tartness enveloping my taste buds. The flavor sits on the brink of overpowering - even a pinch more would be too much - but it's good in a bake sale kind of way. "I like it."

"Good. Let's get 'em in the oven then," he says as he retrieves two muffin baking pans. He sprays them with a non-stick coating before spooning the batter into the trays, ending up with eighteen cupcakes and one that will be half the size of the rest.

After putting both trays in the heated oven, he asks, "Have you ever had cream cheese frosting?"

"No. Is it good?"

"It's divine. Grab a fresh bowl and I'll whip some up," he says, already gathering ingredients.

I do as told, setting a mixing bowl on the counter. "It's super simple to make too," he continues. "All you need is cream cheese, powdered sugar, some butter, and a hint of vanilla extract."

He laughs then - a single puff of air. "You know, one time I ran out of powdered sugar and looked up alternatives online. It said you could put regular sugar in a food processor and that would work. Of course, I didn't have a food processor, so I thought a blender could do the same thing." He shakes his head, a fond smile on his face while reminiscing. "It didn't. But it might have, you know, if my blender wasn't a damn dinosaur. The frosting tasted okay, but I couldn't get over how grainy it was. The texture was just too weird to overlook, but Skyler still ate it like it was the best frosting known to mankind. I swear he's a human garbage can. Like is there anything he won't eat?"

"Probably not," I chuckle.

Liam continues talking, or maybe I should say rambling. It's like the silence must be filled for fear that it may otherwise consume him. He retells tales of his cooking mishaps - everything from nearly burning down his childhood home with an oil fire to thinking it was a good idea to make a sauce out of grapes, watermelon, and an old bottle of root beer. I love hearing these stories, because I feel like I know him a little bit better now; but it's hard to watch him be so out of his element in the kitchen - the one truly safe place where he can escape the world. His movements still flow effortlessly into the next - each flick of his wrist as smooth as a professional pastry chef - but I've watched him cook enough to know that he usually loses himself in his own little world. He's normally so focused that there's no room for conversation.

Which only proves even more how deep this newest wound of his really is. He's been cut so deep that he can't ignore the laceration, because he'll bleed out if he does. And yet he doesn't want to feel it - doesn't want to face it as reality. If he does, he'll have to come to terms with the fact that there's nothing he can do to change it - nothing anyone can do to spin back time.

The beep of the kitchen timer interrupts his story of creating a cheesecake crust out of *Froot Loops*. He pulls the cupcakes from the oven and overturns the pans until the little cakes tumble onto the counter. We let them cool for about ten minutes before icing them. I'm pretty sure we eat more frosting than what ends up on the cupcakes (Liam was right. Cream cheese frosting is divine).

We're still piling frosting atop cupcakes with butter knives when the apartment door opens and closes. Liam falls silent in the middle of another story, his body visibly stiffening when Skyler and Emil pop their heads into the kitchen. If I didn't know any better, I'd say they were pleasantly surprised to find Liam acting like his normal self; but they're not fooled. None of us are. We see how he masks his pain with a forced smile, but we go along with his act of bravado. Because it takes strength to continue living when the world is crashing down around you.

"Smells good. Whatcha making?" Skyler asks, stepping further into the kitchen.

Liam's reply is quiet, and he doesn't meet Skyler's eyes. "Blue raspberry cupcakes."

"Oh, yummy!" he exclaims with more enthusiasm than normal. "You gonna share?"

Liam nods and hands over two of the frosted cupcakes. With his goodies in hand, Skyler turns to leave the kitchen. "Oh, and Liam," he stops walking. "We've got the rest of your classes covered this week. We'll get you notes and assignments, so take the rest of the week off. The paperwork you needed is on the table, and I'll hand it in whenever you finish filling it out."

"Thanks," Liam says meekly.

"No problem. What else are friends for?"

In the darkness of our room, the silence becomes too much for Liam. Or maybe it was always too much. Maybe he's been struggling against the daggers of his own thoughts, and he's too exhausted to fend off their strikes any longer. And do I blame him for falling apart in my arms for the third time today? No, absolutely not. I'll dry his tears as many times as he needs me to. I'll hold him to me and whisper how much I love him for the rest of my life if I have to.

He tries to stifle his cries, knowing it's the middle of the night and Skyler and Emil are sleeping in the adjacent room. I wouldn't even call them cries - more like the whimpers of a kicked puppy. I can't hold him tight enough to keep his body from trembling. I stroke my fingers through his hair and rub his back through every jerk and convulsion that accompanies his gasps for breath.

As his sobs even out to soft breaths and his body no longer trembles in my embrace, I thank every divine being I can think of that he doesn't have to cry himself to sleep alone. Because how cold and empty must he have felt in the past when he bottled this stuff up and kept it to himself. It hurts me just thinking about Liam curled in on himself, clutching his pillow to his chest to replicate the closeness of another person - of someone who'll simply be with him. Because he wants to be close with people - wants to open up more - but I don't think he knows how to bridge that gap. Or maybe he's scared to. Maybe's he's afraid of giving people the power to break him, because it sure seems like those who were supposed to be closest to him did enough damage already.

Which leads me to my last thought of the night before joining Liam in unconsciousness. I want to be strong enough - confident enough - to be his pillar of support when his foundation shakes beneath him. I want to be the mortar that helps to rebuild after the earthquake. But most of all, I want to be the breath of air that ignites his ember into a blazing inferno.

LET ME BE YOUR WINGS

"You don't have to do that now."

My hand ceases its scrawling of numbers and checking of the proper boxes on the financial form lying on the dining table. Eyes flicking to Nico, I'm grateful for the momentary distraction of pop-tarts fresh from the toaster that he places atop the form. I move the plate to the side, snatching one of the strawberry pastries to take a bite out of. "If I don't do it now, I'm never gonna do it."

"But you just woke up," he counters as he takes a seat in the chair beside me.

Ugh, don't remind me. Half past one in the afternoon and I've barely been up for ten minutes. If I had it my way, I'd still be lying in the comfort of my bed with the warmth of Nico's skin against mine; but my bladder had other ideas. And I'm pretty sure Nico's arm had gone numb many hours earlier. Now that I'm up, I don't think I'll be able to fall asleep any time soon, but that doesn't mean I want to be awake. Seeing as I am though, I might as well be productive. It'll at least keep my mind distracted from my father's criminal activities. Hopefully.

"And how long have you been up?" I ask, my eyes returning to the page of tiny print.

"Since about seven."

"You stayed in bed with me for six hours?"

"Uh, not exactly. I got up, watched a little TV, and then came back around noon. I was kinda worried that you weren't up yet."

I sigh, setting down my pen and leaning back in my chair. "Yesterday was just... exhausting. Really fucking exhausting. I could sleep for a century and still be tired."

"Which is why you should fill that out some other time," he says, his hand slowly creeping closer to the piece of paper.

Catching his hand in mine, I squeeze his fingers. "Next semester is my last semester. It's the only one that's not paid for, and I don't think I'm gonna qualify for financial aid, 'cause you know, rich parents who happen to be criminals."

"Liam."

"I know, I know. I shouldn't dwell on it, but it's the truth." I let go of his hand to pick up the pen and continue filling out the form. "If I pay for the classes upfront, the university will give me a discount; so that's what I'm gonna do."

"But do you have to do it now?"

My eyes stay glued to the paper; because if I look up and meet Sprinkles' concerned gaze, I'll cave. I'll lay down my pencil and abandon the form in favor of spending the afternoon wrapped up in Nico's embrace. That I'm sure of, because in his arms is the one place where the rest of the world can't touch me. But I can't give in. I'll never get this done in time if I do.

"There's no time like the present," I say.

Nico sighs, settling back into the chair. "Okay, fine, but what can I do to help you finish this faster?"

The stroke of my pen pauses a moment for me to contemplate. "My laptop would be helpful right about now."

Nico nods and scoots his chair back to stand. Taking two steps, he stops. "Um, where is it?"

"Probably buried beneath my textbooks."

And then he disappears into our room, and I focus on reading the fine print. If I wasn't majoring in business, I'm sure I'd be lost among all the technical jargon and the hidden fees of not meeting deadlines or filling it out improperly. God, this sucks. Being an adult sucks. What happened to coloring books and playing basketball in the driveway and finger-painting for a passing grade? I miss not having a care in the world; but even if I could somehow roll back the hands of time, I wouldn't. Or maybe I should say, I can't after knowing the truth. I'd rather fast forward five or ten years to when I've got my life sorted out.

"Here," Nico says as he sets my laptop down by my elbow.

"Oh, thanks." I shake off my thoughts of time travel to open the laptop. Clicking through a few folders, I open up a spreadsheet and size it to half the screen, quickly opening up a webpage and doing the same.

"What are you doing?" Nico asks as he scoots his chair closer to me and peers at the laptop screen.

"Um..." How do I explain online banking to a demon? Do demons even have banks? Or currency for that matter? "Balancing my bank accounts, trying to decide which to use for each of my newly acquired bills."

"Humans have more than one account?"

I arch my eyebrow at Nico's curiosity. Interesting. "Demons have bank accounts?"

"Well, kinda," he says. "There's no actual money or anything. I guess it's like a trading center. You register whatever you want to trade, it stays at the center in your account, and you get a slip with an identification number and photo ID of the item. You trade or pay with the slip, and the other party goes to the center to pick it up. It's a really tedious system, but it helps a little bit to keep demons from swindling each other."

"That's really... old-school," I say as I type numbers into the spreadsheet to update my account totals.

Nico shrugs, "Currency would be easier."

"It's still a pain in the ass," I sigh. Being financially responsible is exhausting, and I don't want to do it. I've always kept track of my funds, but most of it involved transferring my paychecks from my checking to one of my two savings accounts - mainly my I'm-gonna-own-a-bakery-someday account. That was fun, because I was watching my dream slowly get closer to becoming a reality, but now I'm scared. I am terrified of losing the one thing I've been working toward, because I don't have a plan B for my future. I've been dead set on owning my own bakery for years, and I never foresaw this major hiccup getting in my way.

I don't know how long I stare at the balances of my accounts without moving a single muscle, but it's long enough to have Nico fidgeting at my side. He lightly taps my shoulder. When I turn my attention to him, his hand retreats to his lap. "Is something wrong?" His eyes dart between the laptop screen and me.

I shake my head, a small smile upon my lips. "Calm down, Worrywart. I'm just lost in thought."

But that answer has dark honey eyes widening even more with a new flash of panic. "Okay, wait wait wait," I quickly say. "I'm okay. I'm not fragile right now. I'm not gonna break." As I hold his gaze, I see his apprehension to believe me.

Heaving a sigh, I tell him what's on my mind, because maybe saying it out loud will help me decide. "I'm thinking about which account to take my tuition money from. I don't want to withdraw any from my bakery fund account; but if I take it from my main savings, it'll nearly deplete the account. I promised myself not to touch my bakery money, but I might have to."

Planting his elbow on the table, Sprinkles leans his head against his hand. "Well, if it were me, I'd take it from the main savings account. That way, you can always fall back on your other account if you desperately need to."

That's the direction I was thinking of going, and it's reassuring to have Nico suggest the same thing. "Thanks," I murmur, scribbling the proper account numbers upon the form before signing on the dotted line.

Done. I wander into the kitchen and rummage through drawers for an envelope. I find one, slip the form into it, and seal it with a lick of my tongue. After abandoning it on the table, I'm left with nothing to do.

Which I'd normally love, but now it's dangerous to be left along with my inner thoughts. And I don't want to think about anything right now. I need to do something mechanical - something that'll exhaust my body to the point that I don't have the energy to think. I'd go for a run and not stop till I puke, but there's no way in hell I'm leaving the apartment. I could cook, but it's far too early to start dinner, and I don't want to wash dishes.

Actually, that might just do the trick. I'm not one to enjoy cleaning in any form, but god knows there's plenty of that to do around here. Yeah, that's what I'll do. This apartment is going to sparkle by the time I'm done with it. Except Skyler's room. I'm not touching that.

So I stroll to the entryway closet and retrieve the vacuum, broom, and mop. The floors are going to be the easiest so I can start with them, then tackle the nasty ass bathroom, maybe clean out the fridge, do the dishes last 'cause I really don't want to do them.

"Liam, what are you doing? Sit down and relax."

"I can't," I say, dragging the vacuum through the living room to the short hall.

"Then let me help."

I'm about to say no, but the word dies on my tongue. Nico will probably feel bad if he does nothing while I clean. Plus, he'll have no problem doing dishes.

We waste away the afternoon scrubbing the apartment from floor to ceiling. You'd be surprised what you can find lying around or stuffed between couch cushions while cleaning. I swear there are at least five socks beneath the couch, and only one little demon would stash them there (hint - not Nico). And the spare change! Where the hell do all these coins come from and why are they in my couch? I'm going to keep them though. After all, finders keepers, losers weepers.

As I swat at a spider on the ceiling with the broom, the apartment door swings open. "I'm not sure I want to know what you're doing," Skyler says, his voice startling me and making me miss the spider for a second time.

"Cleaning," I huff as I whack the wall again.

"Looks like you're trying to put a hole in the wall."

"Yep. Thought we should remodel a little." Finally got the damn spider! I brush away what's left of the cobweb in the corner and spin to face Skyler, tossing the broomstick to him. "Help out."

Golden eyes sweep across the apartment to take in the spotless floors and clutter-free dining table. "How 'bout you cool it instead and take a break."

"But there's still–"

He cuts me off as he puts the broom away, "It's cleaner than the day we moved in, so stop before it starts resembling a hotel room."

Okay, so maybe I'm going a bit overboard. Maybe taking a sponge to the walls was too much, but I had no idea how dirty they were until I took a closer look. And when you clean one patch of wall, you have to clean it all or the colors will be slightly different shades of white.

"I talked to all your professors and have your notes for the week, but–" he emphasizes "–you're not getting it today."

What? "Why not?"

"Because you need to take a breather and relax. And stop cleaning. It's weird."

I open my mouth to fire back a retort, but the stare he directs at me has my jaw snapping shut. Nope. Not gonna mess with Papa Bear Skyler. Dammit, I hate when he gets all stern and parental with me. I get that he and Nico are trying to help, but this isn't something they can fight. And I don't want to fight it alone, so just let me preoccupy myself with whatever I can think of doing whether it be studying or cleaning. But both of those have been taken off the table by Skyler.

"Fine," I huff in defeat and shuffle past Nico and Skyler to the kitchen.

"Oh, come on. Don't pout about it," Skyler says as he steps to follow me.

I stop beneath the threshold of the kitchen and spin to face him. "I'm not. I'm going to cook a full course meal and neither of you–" I point at both of them, wiggling my finger between them "–is going to interrupt me."

"Or what?" Skyler dares to ask.

"Or you may find an unhealthy amount of cocoa powder dumped on your plate."

He raises his hands in surrender. "Alright. We'll leave you alone. Can I request spit-free food though?"

"I'll think about it."

I watch them retreat into the living room and wait till I hear the drone of the TV before focusing solely on cooking. I'm not gonna lie, I have no idea what to make. It doesn't help that my back is killing me and my feet hurt like a bitch. But nope. I'm not simply going to toss a frozen pizza in the oven and rest my feet on the coffee table while I wait for it to cook.

I want my body to ache, want my muscles to be as exhausted as my mind. When a reasonable bedtime rolls around, I want to crawl into bed and be asleep by the time my head hits the pillow. I don't want to cry myself to sleep again. I'm sick and tired of being weak, of having to pick up the crumbled pieces of myself over and over again. So I'm going to stand tall and ignore the broken pieces of myself for awhile. Let them stay broken. At least that way, no one else can break them again.

I'm never one to willingly get out of bed, especially when my eyes are crusty with sleep and it'll only take another two seconds for me to rejoin the blissfulness of temporary death. But as I roll on my opposite side and reach out to pull the blanket further over my shoulders, the comforter is cold - the kind of cold which shocks my system until I'm wide awake. With a low groan, I blink my eyes open to find Simba curled up where Nico should be, but my beloved incubus is nowhere to be found. No wonder the blanket is so cold.

Checking the time, I glance over my shoulder to see 10:24 a.m. on the bedside clock. I could stay in bed all day, but there's something about being awake before noon that makes me feel a tad bit accomplished. And I'd love to know where my sprinkled boyfriend went and what he's up to so early in the day. I wipe the sleep from my eyes and slowly push myself to my feet, hearing my back crack as I straighten. With every stretch of my arms, I feel another joint crack, and my muscles scream at me to take it easy. So maybe I did overdo it yesterday. It's not like I have anywhere to be today, so it's fine if I ache. Great even. Gives me a type of pain that I can actually feel - a deep ache that isn't just in my head or my heart.

"Come on, Simba," I yawn. "Let's go find Sprinkles." I scoop the tubby tabby into my arms and walk out to the hall, only to stop upon finding a bed sheet hanging down from the ceiling to block my path to the living room.

"The fuck is this, Simba?" I ask the cat, but it looks as confused as I am.

I brush the sheet to the side to pass into the living room, freezing midstep to stare at the rearranged room. With its cushions missing, the couch has been turned around so the back of it faces the TV. The four dining table chairs sit spaced out between the couch and TV, two on each side to leave lots of space for the couch cushions and a mountain of blankets and pillows on the floor between them. White Christmas lights are crudely taped to the back of the chairs and weave through the wooden rungs. And the mastermind of this makeover - he's struggling to tape a blanket to the wall above the TV.

"Are you making a blanket fort?" I ask as I walk over to assist him, setting Simba on the floor to help hold up the blanket.

With a hum, Sprinkles nods as he uses an unreasonable amount of packing tape to hold the blanket up. After testing to see if it'll stay, I release the blanket and step back to let Nico drape its other end over the back of the nearest chair, adding more tape for good measure.

"Where did you find all these blankets?"

"Skyler apparently hoards them in his closet," he says, grabbing another to create a blanket ceiling with the chairs. He catches my gaze, fond smile upon his lips, as he says, "Go take a shower and come back out in clean pajamas."

"Are you saying I stink?" I tease.

He's dead serious as he says, "Yes."

With a huff of laughter, I shuffle back to the makeshift blanket door of the hall. "Okay, I'll go get all frilly for my boyfriend."

"Thank you!" I hear him call as I shut the bathroom door behind me.

As I strip down, I give myself a quick sniff. And yeah, I guess I do stink of sweat. Probably should've showered yesterday. After adjusting the water's temperature, I step beneath the hot spray; and dear god, I really should've done this yesterday.

There's something soothing about having water pelt my skin and drip down my body. It's like everything weighing me down is being washed down the drain beside the soapy suds. The enveloping warmth makes me want to stand beneath the spray until the water turns ice cold, but there's a greater warmth waiting for me in a blanket fort. And I'd much rather indulge in my Sprinkles, so I wash away the last remnants of soapy bubbles from my hair and towel dry as quickly as I possibly can.

Foregoing any type of shirt, I slip into a fresh pair of plaid pajama bottoms and pad back to the living room. Nico works quick, having completed the blanket fort in the middle of the room. With the main lights switched off, the soft glow of the Christmas lights illuminates the entrance of the fort.

Walking to the fort, I drop down on my hands and knees to crawl into it. There's far more room than I would've guessed, and it's all covered in a soft layer of couch cushions, blankets, and pillows. Bags of chips and cans of soda are piled beside the entrance, and the cats are curled up in the middle of the blanket nest. Nico's sorting through a stack of DVD's lying in front of the TV until he picks one to pop into the player. When he swivels around on his knees and spots me, his body jolts with a gasp.

"You scared me," he quietly breathes. Crawling around the cats and past me, Nico settles his shoulders against the back of the couch and the sloping pillows until he's lying in a comfortable lounging position. The glow of the Christmas lights reflects in his russet eyes as he pats the space beside him.

That's all the invitation I need to crawl over to him and curl into his side, resting my head on his chest as he wraps an arm around my back. "Why'd you do all this? And where'd you even find some of this stuff?" I ask as I glance up at his face.

Nico peers back with a shy twitch of his lips. "I wanted you to relax, so I asked Skyler what to do, and he suggested this. He gathered all this stuff before he left this morning and told me to have at it."

"Even the Christmas lights?"

"He said it'd be romantic," he quietly murmurs.

Leaning up, I press a soft kiss to his chin. "He was right."

With a breathy laugh, Nico relaxes even further into the blankets, pulling me with him until we're both staring at a pale pink blanket with cartoon strawberries all over it (where the hell did Skyler hide that?). "Thank god. I was a little scared."

"Hmm? Why?"

"Because I wasn't sure you'd like this."

"Are you kidding me? Who wouldn't love lounging around in a blanket fort all day with you?"

Someone would have to be stupid not to love this - hearing his heartbeat beneath my cheek, feeling his breath breeze over my hair, having his arm wrapped around my shoulders. Yeah, this is perfect, and I'm definitely not stupid. Sometimes dumb, but not stupid.

"I figured we could just lie around talking or napping or watching movies or whatever else you wanted to do," he says.

Talking would be nice, as long as it's not about me. That's a no-go for a while. But Nico, now him I could listen to all day. And I want to know more about him and the world my favorite little incubus comes from. "Tell me about your world."

He's quiet for a moment and his next breath is deeper than the rest. "What do you want to know?"

"Anything. Everything. Whatever you want to tell me."

I wait patiently as he contemplates what to say, glancing at his face every now and then to spot a purse of his lips or the furrow of his brow. His nose scrunches at a particular thought until he shakes it from his mind, and I can't help but find it wholeheartedly endearing.

"Everything's kinda... cruel, I guess. Like an-every-person-for-themselves mentality. I mean, it's not all bad. There are always exceptions - a rare demon who looks out for the well-being of others - but it's still really... lonely."

When he doesn't elaborate, I ask, "How so?"

"Because our sole existence is to serve humans and their desires. We're meant to grant their desires in exchange for something of equal value. Our whole society revolves around humans, and it creates this sort of race - or competition - among demons to be the best at what they do. That wouldn't really be a problem if humans asked for good things, but it's always sex or killing or haunting or destroying. Demons are the evil-doers of the universe, and we've embraced that. We used to be good. We used to help people; but then religion depicted us as the villain and we changed to fit that image. It's just... really lonely when you're only called upon when someone needs something from you or wants you to do their dirty work."

"Nico, I'm sor–"

"No, it's okay," he shakes his head. "It's what we are. And I guess there are some cool perks to being a demon."

"Oh, like what?"

"Well, you seem to be pretty fond of my wings, so I guess they're okay," he smiles down at me.

Oh my god, this should've occurred to me sooner. "So can you fly?"

"Technically yes, but..." He bites his bottom lip and tips his head to the side. "I'm not very good at it." At my quiet chuckle, he adds, "It's a lot harder than you'd expect."

"I'm sure it is," I hum. "What about school or like normal jobs? Or the weather - does it, like, rain or is it the traditional fiery pits of Hell? Are there cities with skyscrapers or little villages or—"

"One at a time, Liam," Nico quietly laughs, the soft rumble reverberating in his chest. "We have all afternoon."

Indeed, we do; and neither of us has any qualms of letting time tick by while Nico shares his world with me. He tells me of mandatory education demons must receive before being allowed to enter the human world - something about having to blend in with human society. He tells me how his world is geographically similar to Earth. There are mountains that touch the sky and oceans which hide monstrous beasts. Seasons never change; it's stuck in a perpetual summer with hot days (but not fiery inferno) and chilly nights. It storms every few months with flashes of lightning and boisterous claps of thunder, but it never snows or hails - nothing but violent storms.

"I don't know if you'd call them cities, but demons tend to congregate around trading centers. Most don't stay in one place very long, so there aren't really any houses - not like here anyway. They're more like shacks I guess, built between trees and using their branches as a ceiling. Or some live in caves. They're normally more powerful and can defend a permanent residence without getting devoured."

"Did you have a cave?"

Nico shakes his head. "No, I'm not nearly powerful enough. In demon standards, I'm considered weak."

"Really?" I ask incredulously. I poke at his bicep, trailing my finger down the inside of his arm. "You're no *Hulk* like Skyler, but I'm pretty sure you could handle yourself in a fistfight. I mean, look at these guns. They're way bigger than my noodle arms."

He cracks a smile and catches my hand in his. "I'm happy you're human."

"Why? Maybe I want a kickass pair of wings."

"Because your noodle arms would make you easy prey, and you'd be devoured," he says quietly, voice so low I almost miss it. A forlorn sheen wets his russet eyes, and his lips tremble slightly. It's the face you'd expect on a child who has lost a beloved pet to the hands of time.

I don't want Nico to be sad or to be thinking about losing me, even if only hypothetically, so I muster up my inner spoiled brat as I whine, "But my wings!"

Dark honey eyes look down upon me with their corners crinkled. The arm around my back holds me a little tighter to his side as upturned lips part to say, "Let me be your wings. Please."

My heart beats quicker at his words, my pulse pounding so loud it echoes in my ears. I can't meet his piercing gaze as heat rises to my face, because he already is. He's my wings and so much more. When I'm plummeting over my emotional cliff with nothing but jagged rocks waiting for me below, he catches me mid-fall. He holds me steady midair until I'm ready to embark on the climb back up the cliff, and I think that's the most important part. Nico doesn't whisk me away from the jagged rocks, but instead allows me to face my darkest parts until I'm ready to move on. And if I launch myself over the same cliff time after time, he'll always be there to grab me by the back of the shirt and let me dangle over the rocks below until I no longer want to crash into them.

"You already are," I whisper. The words fall easily from my lips, but my chest constricts almost painfully.

I can't recall what life was like before Nico. Probably stagnant and monotonous and a hell of a lot lonelier. But that's what has the sharp pang constricting my heart. I don't ever want to go back to pre-Nico life. I want him to be my wings every day for the rest of our lives. He's my person (okay, demon), my confidant, my support, my best friend, my Sprinkles. Before I knew it, he was my everything. I've never depended on someone else for my happiness, but, dear god, does Nico make me happy. It may be selfish for me to think, but I never want him to return to his world.

Fuck that world and everyone in it! They don't deserve the sunshine that is Nico. And honestly, I refuse to give him back. If the demon police (or whatever they're called) come for my little runaway, they're not taking him without a fight. I'll follow him to the depths of Hell and won't leave without him.

But if I had one wish, I'd ask the universe to never take him from me in the first place. Just this once, I want the universe to be on my - our - side. Can't we have that one small piece of happiness? Please, universe, if you must fuck me over for the rest of my life, at least let Nico stay at my side. Throw every punch you can my way, and I'll graciously accept them. But don't take him from me.

"Liam," he says quietly.

My eyes hesitantly jerk to his face, widening upon the sight of crinkled eyes and a brilliantly bright smile.

"I'll try not to drop you."

Sputtering laughter erupts in the privacy of our blanket fort, my gasping breaths echoing around us. The image of Nico accidentally dropping me among the clouds - his flared wings flapping frantically to catch me - elicits another snort of laughter from me. The panic widening his dark honey eyes almost comically, the gasping chuckle which escapes him as he catches my wrist, and the apologetic smile accompanied with a breathy *Oops* - they'd make the fall worth it.

"Is me dropping you that funny?" Nico asks with a hint of amusement at my reaction.

"Yeah, 'cause I know you'd always catch me."

"But I'm not that great of a flyer."

"You can't be that bad," I tell him.

"I'm not that good either."

"One day, I'm going to take you to this secluded little spot out in the country I used to go to as a kid, and then you can show me how great of a flyer you are."

"But someone might see."

"Nah, it's private property. No one will be there but us."

"Liam," he admonishes. "Isn't that trespassing?"

I shake my head, my hair rubbing against the fabric of his shirt. "My grandma owns a little piece of land about six hours south of here."

"But I thought your grandma—"

"Oh, no no no," I quickly clarify. "This is my mom's mom, not my dad's. I'm not super close to her any more, but she sends me a birthday and Christmas card every year. And she's never called me worthless, so that makes her my favorite grandma."

"Oh, okay. Well, that makes me feel a little better about it," he says.

"So if I take a weekend off next spring, would you want to take a trip down south to visit?" I twist in his embrace to spot him worrying his lip between the bite of his teeth. Rolling on top of him, I plop my weight down to draw a quiet *Oomph!* out of him. Chest to chest, I cross my arms over his breastbone to rest my chin against. "It's just my grandma, and she lives on this quaint little hobby farm. She's got cows, horses, chickens, a dog, and even a potbellied pig that's house trained. Oh, and kittens! She always has a litter or two running around. And she's pretty nice so you don't have to worry about her not liking you and—"

The apartment door swings open with a bang to cut off my ramble of words. The sudden noise in our otherwise peaceful space causes both of us to jolt into a tangled mess of limbs. As numerous voices mingle in the air, we scramble to untangle ourselves - him pulling his arm from beneath my back and me rolling to the side.

As we catch our breaths from the near heart attacks, a head of blond hair and bright blue eyes peeks into the blanket fort. "Are we interrupting something?" Eli asks with an all-knowing smile upturning his lips.

"N-no. Not at all," I sputter, earning a quiet chuckle from Eli. "Just watching a movie."

"Oh, yeah? What movie?"

"Uh..." My eyes flick to the TV screen portraying the start menu of the first *Toy Story* movie. Fuck, we never even pressed play, and I didn't notice the soft tune of the melody playing on repeat that accompanies the DVD's play options.

Nico's breath tickles my skin as he leans closer to whisper, "It's *Toy Story.*"

"I know what it is," I whisper back, but my words are drowned out by Eli's laugh.

Eli crawls into the fort beside me. "We haven't been formally introduced," he says to Nico. "I'm Eli, a childhood friend of Liam's."

"Nico, Liam's..." his eyes flick to me as a light flush dusts his speckled cheeks, "...boyfriend."

"It's a pleas–"

"Is it safe?" Skyler's booming voice cuts off Eli's pleasantries.

"Yes!" Eli calls back.

It takes only a few seconds for Skyler's feet to cross the living room and appear in the fort's entryway. He drops to his knees and accidentally crushes a bag of chips beneath his hand as he crawls in with the rest of us, Emil right behind. "Phew," Skyler whistles with a mischievous grin. "Thought maybe you'd be getting it on in here."

If he was closer, I'd smack him for that comment. "So you sent Eli to check for you?"

As he scoops a sleepy Simba and grumpy Furby into his lap, he says, "Well yeah. He doesn't have to live with you two and be reminded of your love making every time he looks at your face."

"You do realize we work together, right?" Skyler just shrugs, more interested in passing Simba to Emil. "And it's not like I've never overheard you and Emil going at it like rabbits in heat," I add.

Emil violently coughs, choking on his own air. "Sorry," he manages to say between sputtering breaths.

"You have nothing to apologize for. It's Skyler who's so loud he wakes the neighbors."

"That happened once," Skyler defends himself.

"More like once a month," I say.

"Um, can we talk about something other than our sex lives?" Emil quietly asks.

"Yes, please," Nico pipes up.

"Why don't we watch that movie you guys never got around to starting," Eli suggests.

We can't for the life of us find the remote; and due to the who's-ever-closest rule, it should be Skyler who crawls over to press the play button. But he rivals that rule with the thou-shall-not-disturb-a-kitty-cat law. The two closest to the TV - Skyler and Emil - each pet a cat curled in their laps so they insist they can't possibly move. Eli's out because he's sitting cross-legged to my left. And Nico - my little shit - draws his knees up so my sprawled out legs are closer than his.

"Fine, I'll do it," I grumble as I begrudgingly crawl between Emil and Skyler to press play. On my way back to Nico, I make sure to bring my knee down upon Skyler's toes. His yelp of pain is worth the kick to my ass in retaliation. And even though my little shit of a boyfriend is most likely the one who lost the remote and thus is responsible for me having to manually press play, I'm more than happy to stretch out beside him and nuzzle my head against his shoulder.

When Skyler whistles at my action, I don't want to slap him; because the flustered flush and shy smile it brings out of Nico are absolutely marvelous.

It's a miracle we're all quiet enough to actually hear and enjoy the movie. Of course, this is our childhoods, and it's been a while since us *Disney* babies reminisced. Because no matter where you grew up or what kind of childhood you had to live through, *Disney* movies were a staple of our generation. We grew up on this shit, and that's something no one - not even shitty ass parents - can take from us.

We finish the first movie and move to its squeal (stupid cat rule makes me have to swap discs). At only ten minutes in, a loud knock on the door disturbs our mini-marathon.

"Who the fuck's that?" I blurt out.

"Probably Cody and Alex."

At Skyler's answer, I arch my brow. "This is starting to look like a party."

"And what if it is?" Skyler counters.

"It's Wednesday. Who has a party on a Wednesday?"

"We do. Now go answer the door before Cody breaks it down."

It doesn't pay to argue any further, so I slip pass Eli and rush to answer the door before Cody pounds a hole through it. But when I pull the door open, it's not Cody's hand suspended in mid-knock (although he and Alex are indeed present).

"Kari?"

"Don't be flattered, Liam my boy. I'm here for my Freckle Buddy," she says as Cody and Alex assist in pushing her across the threshold.

As she and Alex head straight for the blanket fort, I call after her, "The spot next to Nico is mine! Don't fucking take it!"

"Yeah, yeah, Buttercup. Whatever you say."

That doesn't sound very promising. I may have to gear up to fight her for my man. Which I will. Don't think that I won't kick her ass.

Before I can chase her down, Cody distracts me by asking, "Did you make popcorn for the movies?"

Was I the only one who didn't know about the movie marathon get together? I'm starting to regret not putting a shirt on, especially when everyone else is fully clothed. "No."

"You should make some."

"You make some. You know where it is."

"Ugh! Fine," he grumbles and trudges into the kitchen.

I move to close the door only to jolt with a start to find Fae standing before me. "Sorry, Fae, I didn't even see you."

"That's okay," she laughs - a twinkling lilt of her voice. She steps inside, slipping her sneakers off to line them neatly among the disarray of everyone else's. "Sorry for intruding. Kari wouldn't take no for an answer."

"Don't worry about it. The more the merrier," I say, closing the door and following behind Fae to the blanket fort. "I'ma kick her ass, though, if she stole my spot."

"I won't stop you," she says with a smile.

She's true to her word when we crawl into the now cramped space within the fort and find Kari lounged out beside my Sprinkles. Yeah, no. That's not gonna happen. "Move your ass," I say, directing the most venomous glare I can muster at her.

"Make me," Kari spitefully latches on to Nico's arm, and my freckled demon shrugs his shoulders with a lighthearted smile. He may be too kind to shove Kari to the side, but I'm not.

"Gladly," I say with a smirk. Crawling pass Eli and around Fae, I climb right over Kari while she elbows me in the side. At a particularly hard jab to my ribs, my weight collapses atop the two of them - half on Nico and half on Kari. I take advantage of my position and wiggle to wedge myself between them. But Kari - that persistent she-devil - pushes her weight into me until I'm uncomfortably squished between her and Nico.

"Um, guys," Nico quietly speaks up to effectively make Kari and I freeze. "I can always sit in the middle."

Peeking up at Kari, she stares back at me, her eyes lighting up with the same sudden realization which floods my mind. With locked gazes, we stare frozen at each other for a long moment before nodding in sync.

"I've got a smart Freckle Buddy," Kari grins as she shoves me over Nico.

My poor Sprinkles - I'm pretty sure my elbow digs into his gut as I roll over him; but the only discomfort he shows is a muffled grunt as he scoots toward Kari.

"Are you guys finally done being obnoxiously loud?" Skyler asks from where he's lying on his belly in front of us. He eyes us over his shoulder with one of his scolding-mom glares.

"Yep. We're all set, Mama Bear," Kari says with a lopsided grin as she leans against the back of the couch. Purposely catching my gaze, her grin twitches into a smug smirk. As if her feint of stretching out her arms would fool me!

Before her hand can settle upon Nico's shoulder, I shoo it away with a quick slap and pull Nico closer to my side. When Nico lolls his head upon my shoulder and snuggles even closer, I turn to the pouting Kari and stick my tongue out like the five-year-old that I am.

When Cody finally joins the rest of us with four bags of popcorn in his hands, he plows through the legs in the back row (Eli, Fae, Kari, Nico, and me in that order) to pass out the popcorn. After handing the third bag to Skyler, he squeezes between Emil and Alex in the front to plop down on his belly. With everyone finally settled in, all eyes turn to the TV.

As a fly on the wall - or, well, blanket - a group of college kids squished into a blanket fort to avidly watch animated children's movies is probably an amusing sight to behold. But who cares about that fly? If more people had movie marathons in blanket forts, the world would be a better place.

Nico and I may have slept in the blanket fort that night. And we may have left it up all week to lounge around doing nothing. Even when I had to drag my ass into work (thank you to all that is holy - in other words Simon - for keeping me in the kitchen), Skyler was kind enough to crawl into the fort and wake me up on time. But after a Monday of furiously finishing schoolwork for my missed classes, it was time to take it down. I'm gonna miss it. I think we all will. But on the bright side, by taking it down, we'll get to rebuild it some other day when it's rainy or gloomy or we just need a break from reality.

Going back to classes on Tuesday sucks ass. No matter which class I'm in, my skin bristles with the knowledge of eyes on me and mouths whispering my name. My glowering face is either scary enough or pitiful enough to keep any asshole from confronting me directly. Which is kinda disappointing, because I could go for a good fistfight right about now. With all my pent up and smoldering anger, I could thoroughly whoop some punk ass bitch. But the one time I'm raring for a fight, no one gives me a good enough reason to throw a punch.

The entire week, everyone avoids me the best they can (minus my small circle of friends). They have no problem whispering rumors behind my back but god forbid one of them say it to my face. Did I mention I really wanna beat the shit outta someone? 'Cause I do. But sadly, the opportunity never presents itself, so I keep my head down. No point in getting expelled the week before finals, although it would make an amusing headline that wouldn't help my father's case. It'd almost make the expulsion worth it, but I'd rather graduate sooner than later (and who am I kidding, no other college would accept me after this bullshit). So no matter how much I want to start a little trouble, I keep my mouth shut and my fists at my side.

Cramming for finals helps to keep me out of trouble, but just like the rest of my academic experience, it sucks. Scheduling a full week's worth of courses into three days seems like a great idea, and any other time of the year it is. But come finals week, I want to kick myself in the ass. Four fucking exams nearly back to back for three days straight. Who thought that was a good idea? Me apparently. And I should know better, what with having the same basic schedule for the past three years.

My brain is thoroughly fried after my final test on Thursday. Don't ask me how I got home, because I have no idea. I'm pretty sure I almost got hit by a car at least once. But miraculously, I trudge up my apartment building's stairs in one piece. I fumble with the knob until the door swings open and I can step inside.

Kicking off my shoes, I toss my bag to the side. My feet drag against the floor as I head to the living room with every intent of collapsing upon the couch for a century or two, but I walk right into a duffle bag lying on the floor. And oh look, there's a suitcase standing beside it.

I guess it is that time of year.

Following the laughs and chuckles to Skyler's room, I find Emil and Nico randomly tossing clothes at Skyler who's got a decent mound of shirts and pants surrounding him where he sits in the middle of his bed.

"When are you guys leaving?" I ask.

Skyler turns his attention to me long enough to miss a pair of jeans Nico throws at his head. Proud to say my Sprinkles has fantastic aim as the denim hits Skyler dead on. After a muffled chuckle, Skyler brushes the jeans to the growing pile and says, "Tomorrow right after class. We're not coming back till after New Year's, so you and Nico will have the apartment all to yourselves." He just has to add a lecherous wink at the end.

"Oh, just get packing," I say; and if I had something to throw at him, I would. Thankfully enough, Emil and Nico bombard him with shirts and socks and jeans.

I never used to look forward to Skyler and Emil going home for the holidays. The apartment felt cold, quiet, and far too empty without them for that month of winter break. But this year, I won't be alone. I won't have to pretend spending Christmas by myself doesn't bother me. Because it does, but I'm not going to impose on my friends' time with their families.

Now I have Nico, and we can celebrate any way we want to. Maybe we'll decorate the apartment with a tree and lights and stockings. Maybe we'll cook up an elaborate Christmas dinner for two. The blanket fort might find its way back to the living room where we can cuddle under blankets and sip hot chocolate. We could build snowmen or make snow angels or have a snowball fight in the parking lot. Staying up late, we can count down to the new year and welcome it together - end one year and begin another with a kiss.

A light bump to my shoulder brings me back to the here and now as I watch a balled up shirt tumble to the floor at my feet. "What are you all smiley about?" Skyler asks as he throws another shirt at me.

It hits me in the chest as my eyes flick to find Nico. He pauses in picking up a stray shirt to throw, and the dark honey of his eyes find mine. "Nothing," I say, smile stretching even bigger on my lips.

A MAN OF MANY SURPRISES

"Do demons celebrate Christmas? Or even any holiday for that matter?" The copper of Liam's irises meet mine as he gazes over his shoulder for a short moment before returning his attention to the omelet in the skillet.

"Not really," I say as my feet knock against the lower cabinets. I shift to adjust my perch on the edge of the sink, because my butt's starting to go numb. "Human holidays tend to be busy times for demons as there's a surge in people who summon us, so it's more of an extra burden than a holiday. Oh! Except Halloween."

"Of course," Liam chuckles as he slides the folded omelet on a waiting plate. "Because you guys blend in easier?" He hands me the extra cheesy omelet as he prepares another.

"Well, that's one reason, but it's mainly because we get more freedom on Halloween." I take a bite of my breakfast and relish in the ooey gooey-ness of the cheese and the crispness of the bacon bits.

"Freedom?"

Nodding, I swallow. "Yeah, freedom to enter the human world without a summons. We can only do that on Halloween, the Eve of May, the solstices, and the equinoxes; so I guess those can be considered holidays."

"Why though?"

"I don't know," I shrug and take another bite of the omelet. "Something about the bonds between the spiritual and physical worlds growing stronger."

Liam hums at the information as he slides his omelet onto a plate. Turning off the burner, he leaves the skillet on the stove and hops up on the counter beside me. "I've decided."

"Decided what?"

"You and me," he waves his fork in the air between us, "we're gonna go all out for your first Christmas."

"But I don't know how to celebrate a human Christmas."

"Don't worry," he smiles, soft and tender. "It's not hard. We can put up some decorations: lights, a tree - or well, not a real tree. They're a pain to clean up after. I'll cook a homey Christmas dinner, and we can hang stockings and wait for Santa to fill them with goodies."

"Santa?"

"Yeah, Santa. He's a big ole jolly guy who travels the world on Christmas Eve to bring toys to good kids and coal to bad kids. So you better behave yourself." He playfully nudges my calf with his toe as his smile stretches into a mischievous smirk.

I may not be familiar with human holidays, but I'm no fool. And I'm definitely not a five-year-old child who'd believe a single man can deliver millions of presents all over the world in one night. But if Liam wants to go all out with human traditions, then I won't stop him, especially when he's doing this for me.

"If anyone's getting coal, it'll be you."

"Me?" Liam feigns innocence. "But I'm the most well-behaved child on the planet."

"Mhmm," I hum. "And I'm an angel."

"Liars get coal."

"I guess we're both getting coal then."

"You'll have to wait and see."

The quirk of his lips and the shine to his eyes pique my curiosity to the point that I don't want to wait. I want the 25th to magically be here tomorrow when I wake up, but it's unlikely to arrive for another week and a half. Maybe that's a good thing though, because nothing's better than a growing excitement which is left to flutter in one's belly. It's a jittery glee that makes the actual holiday all the more special when it finally arrives.

Stuffing the last bite of egg and cheese into my mouth, I drop the plate into the sink behind me. The clattering of Liam's plate quickly follows, and I slip from the counter to wash them.

"Nah-uh," Liam says, grabbing me by my wrist. "We're gonna make a Christmas tree."

"Make?" I'm no tree expert, but I'm pretty sure it takes numerous years to grow a full-grown tree.

"Yeah," he confirms as he drags me to the living room. "Stay put. I gotta go get some stuff." He releases my wrist and jogs down the hall to our room.

What could he possibly be getting? I don't recall a random tree lying on the carpet of our room or propped up against the wall.

I don't have to wait long before Liam joins me in the living room once more, dropping his armful of white paper, crayons, scissors, and tape. With a clap of his hands, he says, "Okay. Where should we put this baby?" He spins to eye the back wall. "Smack dab in the middle would look nice. What do you think?"

"Um," I glance between the craft supplies on the floor and the expectant gaze he tosses over his shoulder. "What exactly are we doing?"

"Making our own Christmas tree."

Oh. Like literally making a tree. Out of paper and crayons. Alright, we got this. It'll be fun.

"The center sounds good," I say.

"Perfect," Liam hums. "You grab the crayons, and I'll get the paper."

Joining him at his side, I stoop down to pick up the box of crayons as Liam starts taping sheets of paper to the wall in a vaguely triangular shape. When he finishes, he drops the remaining paper to the floor in favor of holding his hand out to me. "Brown crayon please."

I give him the requested color. He kneels on the floor to press the tip against the paper, drawing the outline of a rectangle at the bottom of the wall. Letting the crayon fall to the carpet, he asks for the green one instead. He straightens to his full height as I hand it to him. Grasping each end, he snaps the crayon in two.

"Here," he offers me one half to take before pressing the tip of the other to the uppermost sheet of paper. "You draw that side, and I got this side. We'll meet at the trunk."

I observe for a moment as he drags the crayon across the paper in a zigzag pattern, much like a series of upside down sevens. Starting at the same point Liam did, I mirror his actions to the best of my abilities. Slow, precise strokes glide upon the paper as I work my way to the floor. As I connect the tree outline to the trunk, a bubble of laughter from my side has my hand wavering.

"Liam!" I whine, my head whipping to gape at him.

"No one will notice your squiggly line. They'll be too focused on the lopsided tree," he laughs, plopping to the floor beside me. Leaning back on his hands, he tilts his head to the right to scrutinize our art project. "Yep. Lopsided from every angle."

My gaze flicks to take in the whole outline. Liam's side is narrow with equal spacing between the points of the branches. His crayon strokes are soft - enough to leave a solid outline but not so dark it'll be glaringly obvious when the tree is colored. On the other side, my branches are wide, each point settling near the edge where paper meets wall. My lines are think and dark - bold upon the white paper.

"It's..."

"Perfect," Liam supplies for me. He reaches for the brown crayon and rocks forward to sit on his knees. "It just needs some more color."

As he fills in the tree trunk, I work to color the rest of the tree. When

Liam finishes the trunk, he joins me in scribbling strokes of green on the paper. And it takes a long time, so long that my wrist aches and my fingers cramp. We're only halfway up the tree when Liam calls for a break. But his idea of a break is only switching tasks to using excess paper to make colorful ornaments to tape to the tree.

If I didn't know before, I definitely know now that my artistic skills are a little lacking. My circles resemble ovals, and those are my more successful ones that don't look like a lumpy pizza. And my sorry attempt at drawing the star for the top of the tree turns out to be a geometric mess.

"That's your best one yet," Liam praises of my seventh - no, eighth - star.

I shrug. "You can probably make a better one."

"Nope," Liam shakes his head. He snatches the piece of paper from the floor before I can crumple up the star. "This is the one we're using."

"But–"

"This is the one," he says again, setting the paper on the floor in front of him. Reaching for the crayon box, Liam picks out a few colors and puts crayon to paper - to my star actually.

"Are you fixing it?" I ask quietly, a slight twinge in my chest as his hand obstructs my view of the star. But I remind myself that Liam can make it look like a star and not... whatever it is now.

"It doesn't need fixing," he says, glancing up at me with a twinkle in his eyes. "I'm just adding us to it."

"Adding us to it?"

"Give me a couple minutes, and I'll show you."

I go back to coloring the tree, but I can't help but sneak a peek over my shoulder every few minutes. With Liam purposely blocking my view with his arm, I see little more than the outline I drew. Even when he loses himself in the strokes of color - chewing on his bottom lip - I still can't get a good look at the star. After a while, I give up trying. He'll show me when he finishes it.

Although a couple minutes was an underestimation on Liam's end. I don't know exactly how long he spends on the star, but it's long enough for me to finish coloring the tree two different shades of green (I ran out of actual green and had to use yellow-green to finish the top of the tree). I start cutting out our colorful tree ornaments when Liam sets down his crayons.

"Tada!" he exclaims as he holds the paper out for me to see.

Within my geometric train wreck of a star, Liam drew two figures with their hands laced together. The one on the left - complete with ash blond hair and an undercut - wears a glowing white robe and simple sandals. Feathery white wings sprout from his back, and a golden halo floats above his head. The second figure contrasted the first with the flared wings of a bat, horns protruding from the head, and a tail curled up like a cat's. But most prominently - even more than the fangs portrayed in a broad smile - an abundance of freckles dot every inch of exposed skin, which is a lot considering the figure is only wearing a frayed wrap around the waist that stops at mid-thigh.

"Why am I practically naked?"

"Why not?" Liam fires back with a cocky grin.

I find my own lips upturning into an amused smile, because if the tables were turned, I'd do the same thing. "Then why are you an angel?"

"Because I'm the most angelic person on the planet." He can't even say it with a straight face.

Hopping to his feet, Liam tapes the star to the top of the tree. "Hmm... it's almost perfect. It just needs... Oh! The white Christmas lights! Where'd you put those?"

"The entry closest."

Without another word, Liam races to the closet with extra pep to his steps. As he's digging through the chaos of shoes and coats, I tape the colored circles all over the tree - making sure two of the same color are nowhere near each other. When I stick the final ornament upon the tree, Liam returns with a tangled mess of lights bundled in his arms.

"Here," he says, handing me the end with the plug-in. He struggles to unravel the rest of the bundle, but with a little persistence, he manages. Tape dispenser in hand, he secures the lights to the tree, draping it back and forth among the ornaments. "Plug it in," he says as he sticks one last piece of tape to the wall.

With plenty of extra slack, I easily reach the outlet to do as told. When I straighten back up and look toward the tree, it's not the soft glow or child-like art display which grabs my attention. It's Liam who draws my gaze as he steps back, hands on his hips, to smile upon our life-size creation. Copper orbs rise from the tree trunk to trail up over the circular balls of color to the very top. His gaze settles upon the misshaped star, the corners of his eyes softening even more.

I silently pad to his side, my eyes never leaving him as he's completely oblivious to my presence. Fingers twitching, I reach for his hand. A quiet gasp of air escapes him as my fingers slip between his. Eyes dart to our shared contact, staring for a long moment, and then rising to meet mine. He holds my gaze as he leans closer ever-so slowly, pressing his lips to mine in a slow kiss. His nose brushes my cheek as he pulls back, a light flush to his skin and a bashful smile upon his lips.

"We did good," I murmur, turning my eyes to the 2D tree.

"Yeah, we did. But we're not done yet."

"There's more?" I ask, my voice a little high-pitched and squeaky.

Liam nods, his grin spreading from ear to ear. "We have to hang stockings and make snowflakes to put on the walls and bake Christmas cookies and– Oh, wait. We have to go grocery shopping later too."

The way his words tumble from his lips in a flurry, his voice laced with excitement, the light reflecting in his irises - I love all of it. I love all of him.

"So what's first?"

Liam hums in thought, checking the time on his phone. "Stockings and snowflakes first. Then shopping. Then cookies." His hand slips from mine, and he motions for me to wait while he disappears into our room once more.

I hear the familiar scrape of wood from the old dresser drawer being wrenched open and then closed. Liam walks back to me with a single sock in each hand. "Those are clean, right?"

"They smell clean," he says, as if it's normal to throw dirty socks in the same drawer as clean ones. My apprehension must be written all over my face, because he adds, "Doesn't matter if it's clean when you're getting coal."

"Am not."

"Are too."

"Oh, just give me the dirty sock." I reach for the whiter of the two socks and snatch it from his grasp.

"It's clean!" he defends himself.

Hesitantly, I bring the sock up to my nose for a quick sniff. Okay, maybe it is clean, but my worry is warranted. Anyone who's ever seen Liam do laundry (or not do laundry) would understand.

"Well?"

With a defeated pout, I huff, "It's clean."

"And you didn't believe me," he says with a toothy grin. Before I can retort with a *Do you blame me?*, he holds out his palm to offer me a small tack. "Your sock can go on the right and mine on the left."

I watch as Liam pushes the thumbtack through the sock and into the wall. I hesitate to do the same.

"What's wrong?" he asks.

"Um, isn't this damaging the wall?" I'm sure the landlord wouldn't appreciate holes scattered on the living room wall.

"I'll fill 'em with toothpaste later. No one will know."

Toothpaste? Is that a thing that works? Liam seems to think so, and he already put one hole in the wall. So what's one more?

"Alright," Liam claps his hands together once after I hang my sock. The noise echoes around us. "Snowflake time. Grab a scissors."

Lowering to sit cross-legged on the carpet, I reach for the scissors closest to me as Liam folds a piece of paper into a small square. I watch as he starts cutting random shapes and slivers from the paper. He even wedges the scissors through the middle to cut out more pieces. When he's finally satisfied, he unfolds the paper to display a snowflake - the same pattern of missing shapes mirrored along each crease in the paper.

"Think you can handle that?"

I nod while reaching for a sheet of paper. Folding it, I cut triangles and squares and arcs in no particular pattern, randomly hacking away at the paper until its littered with holes. Opening it up and smoothing down the creases, a smile finds its way upon my lips at the simplicity of the arts and crafts project. I can't say mine looks like a snowflake - more like a piece of paper with holes hacked into is (which it truly is) - but there's a warmth spreading within my chest with each new snowflake that finds its way into a growing pile between us.

Sometimes simple is beautiful. In a time of self-doubt - when my self-worth was at its lowest - Skyler quoted to me, "It's the simple things in life that matter most." I can't say that's what I wanted to hear at the time, because I was so caught up with living a life that mattered - being useful and productive, achieving something worthy of being remembered. But now I finally understand. Who would guess an arts and craft project that I'm failing miserably at could bring me more joy than I can contain? Definitely not me, but I'm happy to be wrong. Because each cut I hack from paper is another moment of blissful peace where nothing else matters.

And Liam. He's the perfect company to have, because he makes even the most mundane tasks as exciting as watching fireworks explode in the sky.

Our pile of paper snowflakes grows until we run out of sheets. We easily have 20-30 snowflakes, and we stick a few to every wall, even one to the apartment door on our way outside.

Other than going to school and work, Liam hasn't left the apartment. Despite that, he's quite eager to step out into the cold winter air. He walks close to my side, so close there's hardly a sliver of space between us. When we venture closer to the line between residential apartments and businesses, Liam's fingers tug at my coat pocket before finding their way inside beside mine.

I don't hesitate to link my fingers with his, feeling the sharp coldness of his skin. He presses even closer into me until we're leaning on each other with every step. Knocking shoulders and stumbling around strangers, white wisps of breathless laughter flow with the chilly breeze and swirling snowflakes around us. In this moment, we're not in the human world or even the demon world, but our own little universe where the only beings in existence are us. Every other person is merely a background shadow passing through - nothing to be concerned with or distracted by.

Liam doesn't let go of my hand when we enter the refreshing warmth of a small corner store. He grabs a shopping basket with his free hand and meanders down specific aisles. He knows the place like the back of his hand, steering me through the aisles and stopping in front of exactly what he's looking for. We spend a significant amount of time trying to choose which colored sprinkles to buy before Liam says *Fuck it!* and gets them all.

He leads me to the candy aisle, asking, "What's your favorite kind?"

Is candy on our grocery list? I thought we were shopping for cookie and Christmas dinner ingredients.

I shrug. "Anything chocolatey."

Liam hands me the basket to hold. His eyes sweep quickly over the vast selection before deciding on what he wants. He tosses bag after bag into the basket - anything from peanut butter cups to miniature chocolate bars to fruit chews. It's not until the basket is overflowing that he's satisfied.

"Can I ask what all this candy's for?"

"Nope," he shakes his head, relieving me of the now quite heavy basket. "It's a secret."

A secret. What is his devilish smirk hiding and what does a cavity-inducing amount of candy have to do with it? Maybe if I bug him enough he'll tell me.

"What kind of secret?"

"The kind you'll have to wait for."

"How long?"

With pursed lips, he hums. "Hard to say. It could be a couple days, a week, maybe a month." The corners of his eyes crinkle as his lips upturn with amusement.

"Liam~," I draw out his name in a childlike whine.

My petulance proves to amuse him even more as he shakes his head. "Whine all you want, but I'm still not telling you."

"You're no fun," I pout, directing the strongest glare I can his way, but it does little to help my case.

"And you're as cute as a hissing kitten trying to be all scary."

"I can be scary."

"Not to me you can't," he says, setting the basket on the checkout counter and offering the cashier a smile in greeting.

"Why not?"

"I don't know," he shrugs. "You're just not."

"But I am."

"You're as scary as a child dressed as a ghost on Halloween."

"That can be pretty scar–" His eyes light up as they spot something among the candy and knickknacks for sale at the counter. His hand lets go of mine in my pocket and rushes to cover my eyes. "Liam, what are you–"

"It's a surprise. Just shut your eyes," he says, words all jumbled together.

I try to push his hand to the side to get a peek at whatever he grabs, but he's adamant about hiding it. He spins me around to face away from the counter and finally uncovers my eyes.

A quick glance over my shoulder doesn't go unnoticed by Liam. "Nico," he warns.

My head whips back around, staring at the aisles. "But Liam! Surprises aren't fun!"

"They are for me," he says smugly.

A soft giggle startles me, and this time when I turn around, I'm not admonished. "You two are really cute together," the girl behind the counter says as she hands Liam a small paper bag compared to the numerous plastic ones with our groceries.

Liam's hand freezes in taking it, stunned for a moment before tucking the little surprise into a pocket on the inside of his jacket. "Th-thanks," he says meekly, ears tinted red and his smile bashful.

As we both gather our few bags, the girl says cheerfully, "Have a good day." And I think she genuinely means it.

Liam's unusually quiet as we leave the store and head home. An intentional shoulder bump gains his attention. When his eyes flick to me, there's still a light flush to his cheeks, but I don't know if it's from what the girl said or from the chill of the winter air.

"You know," I start, lazily colliding with Liam again. "According to the cashier, I'm both cute and scary."

"She didn't say that. She said we're... cute together. As in you and me, not just you."

"Do you agree with her?"

"Of course," he doesn't hesitate to say. "Do you?"

"Yeah," I say a little breathlessly. How can I not when her words make my heart flutter like a butterfly? "But I am scary."

A rush of air passes Liam's lips in an amused breath of laughter. "Okay, Mr. Demon, you're scary. But not to me. You'll always be my Sprinkles, and sprinkles don't scare me."

Video games have become a type of bonding time for Liam and me. When we're bored and there's nothing decent on TV, we rely on video games to entertain us. What ensues is usually an afternoon of *Mario* or *Wii Sports*, but this time, Liam digs his old laptop out from Skyler's closet. He plops down beside me and turns it on.

"You're gonna love *Sims*," he says as he presses an icon on the desktop. "You make your own people - or sims - and let them run loose in a town. They do some crazy shit at times, so it's pretty amusing. We can start a new game and create a sim you and move you in with me, Skyler, and Emil."

"A sim me?"

"Yeah. I have a whole bunch of add-ons and downloads, so I'm sure we can figure something out."

I'm still not sure what he's talking about. From the little he's explained, it seems like it's a game where you can create characters to live out their lives. Is that really exciting? He seems to think so, but wouldn't it get boring watching them do the same thing over and over? But maybe there's more to the game than just that.

It takes a bit for the game to load and even longer once Liam selects a new town to play. As it loads, he gives me a basic rundown - a spiel about saving every 15 minutes in case the game crashes (it apparently does that a lot), some basic cheats to remember (he emphasizes *motherlode*), and something about added mods he has (whatever those are).

"Okay, let's make a sim Nico," he says when everything finally loads.

A screen pops up with a character that looks... questionable. At least in fashion taste. "I hope that's not me."

"Oh no, of course not. Randomized sims are fucking weird," he says.

Liam clicks a few buttons and drags some slides to adjust the skin tone, weight, and muscle definition; but I still can't say the guy looks like me. The outrageous sunglasses and hair that looks like it was cut with a lawnmower need to go. Thankfully enough, Liam gets rid of the sunglasses before focusing on the hair.

"How 'bout this one? It's not perfect, but I think it's the closest we're gonna get."

Liam must have high standards for perfection, because I think the new hair is a million times better than the last. And it's pretty spot on if you ask me - parted in the middle, not too long. "Yeah, that works," I say.

With my go-ahead, Liam starts to alter facial structures, moving slides with practiced ease. For every change, he asks for my stamp of approval before moving on. By the time he adds the freckles, I'm pleasantly surprised to be staring at a video game version of myself.

"Pretty cool, isn't it?" Liam asks, proudly displaying the virtual me.

"Yeah, but..."

"But what?"

"You're going to do something about the clothes, right?"

"Of course," he says a little too mischievously, a dangerous twinkle to his eyes. "I've already got the perfect idea."

I'm not sure I like the sound of that. "What are you–"

"Don't worry. I got this." He turns the screen away from me. When I lean in closer, he leans further away. It becomes a game of hide and seek - him hiding the laptop while I try to get a glimpse of what he's subjecting sim me to. His bubbles of laughter spur me on, but all I catch is a quick view of pastel purple.

"Liam, come on! What are you doing?"

"N-nothing," he laughs. "It's a surprise."

He sure has lots of surprises for me lately, and I'm not sure I'm going to like this one.

"Would you consider yourself a neat person?" he asks after a while.

"Neater than you."

My jibe doesn't faze him as he asks another question. "Indoor or outdoor?"

"Um... in?" Is this part of the game?

"Favorite color?"

"Blue, I guess."

"What shade: turquoise, aqua, or blue?"

"...aqua."

His questions continue. What's my favorite food, my favorite genre of music, my star sign? Even after I answer all of them, he still won't show me the sim. Shouldn't I - the muse for this particular sim - have the right to make changes or at the very least see it? According to Liam, that's a no. He hides the screen as he merges my lonely household of one with the household of him, Skyler, and Emil. Only after the loading screen returns does Liam scoot back to my side and situate the laptop to sit upon both of our knees.

"If I don't like your fashion choices, can I change them?" I ask.

"No. Well, yes, but I'm not gonna show you how."

"That's not fair."

"Doesn't matter. You won't need to change it."

With an arched brow, I ask, "And why's that?"

"Because it's cute and dorky and compliments my sim perfectly."

That scares me ever more. Knowing Liam, his sim is probably really cool, or at least Liam's version of cool. Does that mean mine's going to be a walking atrocity? If it is, I'll find a way to change it with or without Liam's help.

Finally done loading, the game zooms in on a house and four sims standing in its front yard. As it focuses, I easily make out the too bright hair of Skyler and his obnoxiously pink long sleeve. Liam obviously had fun making that one. Emil's the next one I spot with his dark red jeans and a flannel shirt - the most normal one of the four. I'm not going to lie; Liam's undercut doesn't translate well into the *Sims* universe. It kind of looks like he's got a short bowl cut, but the many earrings and button-up with the sleeves rolled to the elbows are pretty cool. And then there's sim me. At least it's not as obnoxious as Skyler.

"What about me screams pastels?" I ask, watching as the figures explore their new home, specifically sim me and his pastel purple tee and pastel blue jeans.

"Pastel compliments punk, so why not?"

I wouldn't necessarily call Liam's sim punk, but I won't argue over it.

Pastel isn't so bad. It's soft on the eyes and the purple and blue do look nice together. I guess Liam didn't do too bad of a job choosing outfits... so far.

"So what am I supposed to do now?" I ask.

"They'll kinda do whatever they want, but you should keep a watch on their basic needs. And you can gain lifetime points by granting their wishes. Like if they want to chat with a certain sim, make them talk and it'll improve their mood," he explains as he shows me what all the tabs do.

"Um, why is there a llama man on the porch?"

"He's the university mascot. You can ignore him.""

"Okay, but what should I do first?"

Liam glances at the sims' wishes. "Make 'em get jobs."

Liam shows me how, making each sim choose a career from the newspaper. Emil and I join the medical career, Skyler becomes a cop, and Liam, of course, is a cook. They each meander off to do their own thing. Ironically enough, the activity of choice is playing video games with Skyler making angry faces in the background because there's no space for him on the 3-person couch. After some incoherent shouting, he walks away to play games on a computer.

"So we're playing a game where the characters are playing games. Do you think they're playing games where the characters play games?"

"Oh my god, Nico, stop. You're gonna make my head hurt." Liam bumps my hand with his when he takes control of game, choosing other tasks for the sims.

I side-eye him for his choice. "Really? Is making out more important than food?"

"Well yeah. Skyler and Emil are already boyfriends on here, but we're not 'cause I had to merge the households. I can't let you find some random sim to marry and have kids with," he says with more seriousness than the situation requires.

"See it worked. Now they wanna go on a date." Little hearts circle around our sims' heads. "Where do you wanna go?"

"I don't know. The beach, maybe."

After changing the view to a map of the town, Liam clicks on the nearest beach. A car materializes from thin air to drive to the ocean. When they arrive, the beach is surprisingly crowded, but not with people.

"What's with the horses?"

"They're wild and run all over the town."

That's a little... odd. I hope they don't get hit by cars.

As I'm scanning the few faces, one looks rather familiar. "Is that Darin?"

Liam glances at the three other sims at the beach, spotting the one I'm talking about chatting with sim me. "Yeah, that's— Don't let him kiss you!

You're on a date with me!" He cancels the motion before I can even react to sim Darin. As the proper adult that he is, Liam chooses to rudely introduce his sim to Darin, and the two get into a shouting argument.

"As I was saying before I was interrupted–" he directs a glare at sim Darin "–I made sims of most of my friends and co-workers."

"That's cute," I chuckle, referring to both the fact he made his friends into sims and that he's so serious about a virtual date between virtual us.

"Nah, it's weird when they randomly start making out. Or fucking Kari and Fae. Like literally fucking. My sim was walking through town and those two were fucking on a bench."

"Wait, what? Sims can have sex?"

He nods. "It's called woohooing. They wouldn't normally do shit like that on a bench, but I have a mod downloaded that has lots of woohooing add-ons."

Woohooing. That's a fun word. It sounds so much better than sex. It's more innocent, although I guess sex isn't exactly innocent. But still, woohoo elicits excitement, like I won some sort of prize.

We mess around with *Sims* all day, and I have no idea why it's so addicting. What's so fun about watching Sim me break the kitchen sink three times or Liam paint stick figures on a canvas? Why am I on the edge of my seat when sim Liam asks sim me to be his boyfriend and why do we cheer when the answer is yes? Why does my heart swell at the sight of our sims sleeping in the same bed and occasionally cuddling throughout the night? The most exciting thing to happen is Liam fighting with a burglar and embarrassing himself by losing. Yet, I don't want to stop playing. I want Skyler to get his promotion and Emil to rank higher in his nerd social circle. I want Liam to master cooking and painting while I'm on call at the hospital in the middle of the night.

"Watch this," Liam says as he directs his sim to paint a still life. With sim me sleeping in the same room, Liam angles the view just right to capture my sim's sleeping face. "And now we fast forward until... Tada!"

"Aw! You're not going to sell that one, right?"

"Of course not," he says, dragging the canvas to the wall. "The entire bedroom can be decorated with paintings of you."

"What about you?"

He shrugs his shoulders. "We can take a romantic photo together and hang it up."

Liam speaks as if we're discussing reality and not a video game. He treats the sim version of me as well as the real me, and if that's not adorable, I don't know what is.

With a nudge to his shoulder, his copper eyes turn away from the butterfly boxers and bunny slippers my sim walks around in. "Hmm?"

"We should do that too."

"Do what?" he asks with a tilt of his head.

"A picture."

"Oh yeah. That's– Yeah," he stumbles with his words, his eyes blown wide; but then his lips soften to a smile with each passing moment of thought. "That'd be great."

"We have to go to bed."

"But it's only ten."

Liam grabs my wrist to pull me up from the living room floor. With an angry meow, Furby tumbles from my lap. "Santa won't come if we stay up all night," Liam says, pushing me toward our room.

"But, Liam!"

"It's tradition," he insists. "Go to bed." With a gentle push, I stumble into the hallway only to turn around when his hands leave my back.

"What about you?" I ask as he heads toward the kitchen. Why should I go to bed if he doesn't?

"I'll join you after I leave Santa his milk and cookies."

Human traditions never fail to baffle me. If this Santa guy eats milk and cookies left by every child on Earth, wouldn't he be comatose from all the sugar? And what if he's lactose intolerant? He's got to be in quite poor health, what with the sugar intake and massive stress from his one night of work. No wonder he only comes once a year. Any more and he'd probably be dead.

I leave Liam to his odd traditions and crawl into my side of the bed. Furby's quick to follow me, curling up atop the blanket at my feet. Liam, on the other hand, is rather slow. I'd understand his tardiness if he had to bake a batch of cookies, but we already did that. How long could it possibly take him to put them on a plate and pour a glass of milk?

"Liam, hurry up!" I call.

"Give me a sec."

A second turns into a minute, and still Liam's footsteps don't get any closer. They shuffle back and forth upon the living room carpet, retreat into the kitchen; and is that plastic ripping that I hear?

When Liam finally does flip off the lights and joins me beneath the covers, he grins broadly. He attempts to train his features into something more neutral but fails miserably.

Turning onto my side to face him, I whisper in the darkness, "What took you so long?"

"Nothing," he breathes, scooting closer to press his lips to the tip of my nose. "Go to sleep or Santa won't come."

His eyes fall shut, but he's further from sleep than I am. He fidgets - a twitch of his leg, constant tossing and turning, splaying his arms out only to tuck them back into his sides. I can feel the giddy excitement electrifying his skin, if only because his twitchiness makes me twitchy too. With him wound up like a child on a sugar high, neither of us will get any sleep.

Liam turns once more with his back away from me. Draping an arm over his middle, I pull him closer. "He'll only come if we're asleep," I murmur against his ear.

Liam relaxes into me, weaving his fingers with mine. It's as if the tingle to his skin dissipates, or maybe it spreads to me as well. Either way, his restlessness disappears, so maybe we'll fall asleep before Santa comes.

"-co. Nico. Nico!"

The crust breaks on my eyes as I squint against the artificial light. Through the blurriness of my vision, Liam's a little fuzzy around the edges. He reaches out to me and pulls me to my feet. After a moment of unsteadiness, I gain enough balance to stand upright. "What time is it?" I ask, voice a little raw as I rub the sleep from my eyes.

"Five thirty." Clasping my wrist, he leads me out to the hall and into the living room. "Santa came!"

His exclamation has my eyes snapping open and suddenly I'm wide awake. He no longer has to pull me as I willingly follow him to our 2D tree. Beside the soft glow of the Christmas lights, the questionably clean socks sink toward the floor with their overabundance of candy stuffed into them. They probably would've fallen by now if it wasn't for an extra thumbtack holding them up.

I pull the tacks from the wall to retrieve my overflowing stocking, a few pieces of chocolate falling out. Stooping down to grab them, I find they're the same kind Liam bought the other day. Actually, now that I think about it, I don't know what happened to all that candy. It magically disappeared. Only I have a feeling that I've found the missing candy. No wonder it took Liam so long last night.

"I told you Santa's real. He even took a bite of the cookie," Liam says, holding up the plate for me to see.

I can't go against that giddy grin of his, so I play along. "Did he drink the milk too?"

"Actually," he drags the word out with a quiet chuckle. "Furby and Simba got to it first."

"Of course, they did," I laugh, spotting the culprits at our feet. "Did you get candy too?"

Liam glances at his stuffed sock as he rounds the couch to sit upon its cushions. "Looks like it, but Santa might've hid something at the bottom. You should check yours too," he says, biting his lip to stifle a smile.

I join him on the couch. As I start piling the candy in my lap, I feel

Liam's eyes on me. Glancing at his face, he already abandoned his candy-filled sock and perches on the edge of his seat, his leg bouncing with impatience. As I dig at the bottom of the sock, my hand bumps into something hard. My fingers wrap around what feels like a globe of glass atop a little pedestal.

Pulling it from the sock, my fingers uncurl as white glitter floats in the globe. A spherical ball of glass sits atop a red base that's decorated with snowflakes. Within the globe, a tiny snowman holds its stick arms out at its sides. Mittens serve as its hands. A matching red scarf wraps around its neck, and a black top hat sits atop a smiling face.

"Liam, this is–" my voice breaks. Clearing my throat, I try again, "Thank you."

"Don't thank me. Thank Santa." Despite his words, his grin holds an immense amount of pride, and his eyes sparkle with a wet sheen. "I'm sure he saw our sad little snowman on the balcony and wanted to give you one that won't melt."

"Oh, yeah? Did he tell you that?" I shake the snow globe and watch the blizzard of glitter swirl around the snowman.

"It's just a hunch," he shrugs, but his smirk betrays his whole nonchalant act. "Merry Christmas, Nico." The softness of his lips brush my cheek, causing a quiet gasp of surprise to slip from me.

Human traditions may be a little off and their stories defy logic, but they're fun. And isn't having fun the only thing that matters? Maybe if demons celebrated holidays and told silly tales of a man who breaks into houses to leave gifts, my species wouldn't be so cruel and self-centered. But that's their loss, not mine.

"Merry Christmas," I return the sentiment.

We forgo breakfast in favor of munching on our candy, and Liam boots up our *Sims* game. Around noon - after the game crashes for the third time - Liam decides to start this elaborate dinner he has planned and leaves the lives of our sims in my hands.

Liam's one to enjoy playing god and making the sims do whatever he wants, but I prefer to sit back and watch them do their own thing. That's when the sims' personalities truly shine. For instance, Skyler enjoys skinny dipping in the hot tub even when it's winter and he has the flu. If Emil isn't at work, he's reading or playing video games; and he's always the first to go to bed. Liam works afternoon shifts, so he's always up till 3 a.m. painting and doesn't wake up till the other three have already left for work. My sim loves playing catch. After buying a frisbee, a football, and a baseball, sim me put them in his inventory and would play with random strangers. My sim is always making new friends, whereas Liam starts arguments more often than friendships. He and Skyler argue once every few days, and I tear up when he has his first and only fight with sim me. But everything works out when they watch the stars together.

What I think is the most interesting, though, is the dynamics of the woohooing. I'll be watching Liam paint a picture of a squirrel; and when I go to check on the other sims, I'll find Skyler and Emil woohooing in the kitchen or against the wall by the fireplace. And poor sim me walks in on them in the dining room. At least he has the courtesy to ignore them and eat breakfast on the deck.

I enjoy watching the thought bubbles while the sims sleep. Sometimes they'll worry about getting a promotion or (if you're sim me) dream about washing the dirty dishes. A new bubble - one I'd never seen before - pops up above my sim's head. I audibly gasp at the sight, because a pair of intertwined golden rings can only mean one thing.

"Hey, Liam!" I call. "Would you say yes if I proposed?"

A loud clatter echoes from the kitchen, and I nearly drop the laptop at the sudden noise. "Wh-what? Isn't it, uh, way too early. N-not that I haven't thought about a future with you, but, uh, we should probably move out and I should graduate first and–"

"Liam, wait," I can't help but chuckle. "Sims. I'm talking about the sims."

"O-oh." He hesitantly peeks his head around the corner. With tomato red cheeks, he scratches at his nape. "Would it be possible to forget what I said?"

How could I? Liam's thinking of a future with me. With me! A demon! After a life of never feeling wanted or needed, there's no way I can forget his jumbled words as they rushed past his lips. It's impossible.

I save our game before setting it aside. Standing, I cross the carpet to where Liam waits, anxiously nibbling his bottom lip. I step past him into the kitchen and stoop down to pick up the fallen utensil. Holding the wooden spoon out to him, I say, "What if I can't forget because your words make me incredibly happy?"

Slowly, his fingers curl around the spoon's handle. "Well, I guess it wouldn't be fair to ask you to forget it." He laughs then - a single breezy breath. "But for future reference, you should probably be in the same room when you ask me. There'll be a better chance of me saying yes." He ducks around me, returning his attention to one of many pots on the stove. His eyes flick back to me - waiting, searching.

"I'll take note," I beam, lips twitching into a giddy grin. That same electrifying static I felt rolling off Liam last night dances upon my skin. It sends my heart into a beating frenzy, my pulse pounding in my ears, and my skin tingling. My fingers twitch at my side, and I have this uncomfortable itch to move - to do something, anything.

"Can I help?" I ask.

"It's actually almost done," he says, turning off a burner. "But you can start setting the table if you want."

Christmas must be incredibly special if we're eating at the table instead of the couch, or maybe this is Liam going all out for me. Either way, it's an experience I won't take for granted.

I lay out utensils, plates, and cups at adjacent seats, turning around in time to catch one of numerous potholders tossed my way. After setting them upon the table, I join Liam in bringing the food out. Dear god does it look good, and it smells even better! To be able to make all this on his own in one afternoon is astounding. When he said he was going to cook Christmas dinner, I thought it'd be something simple, but he outdid my wildest imagination - ham, mashed potatoes and gravy, stuffing, and buns. And I'm pretty sure he just put a pan of something into the oven.

As I take my seat, Liam brings out cans of soda from the fridge. Popping the tabs, he pours them into our glasses with a remark of, "It's classy if it's in a glass."

We pile our plates high as we exchange Christmas sentiments. Eyes like a hawk, Liam watches as I take the first bite of ham. His anxiousness rolls off him in waves, but it disappears the moment I hum with delight. He digs in then, and neither of us have the energy to speak. Our communications come in the form of silverware knocking against plates and satisfied groans as rich, smoky ham or creamy mashed potatoes pass over our taste buds.

When the timer goes off in the kitchen, Liam excuses himself to take care of it. I can't imagine what more he could possibly bring out to top this meal, and if I'm being honest, I don't think I'll be able to eat another bite I'm so full.

"It's not Christmas cake," Liam says, returning to the table with two new plates, "but who doesn't like brownies?"

I take that back. There's always room for dessert, especially when it's a moist fudge brownie. I relish each chocolatey bite and leave not even a crumb behind.

"That was amazing, Liam."

"I'm glad you think so, 'cause this is all we're gonna be eating for like a week."

I'd eat like this every day for the rest of my life if I could. It is that good, and Liam is incredibly talented to be able to produce such quality. There's not a single shred of doubt in my mind that Liam will fulfill his culinary dreams someday. He'll flourish and be able to stand on his own and hold his head high when sharing his creations with the world. I, for one, can't wait to view his prideful smirk after all his hard work pays off, and hopefully, I'll be standing beside him to see it in person.

Liam is a man of many surprises. As if the candy and snow globe aren't enough (sorry, Liam, I know it was you and not Santa), come bedtime, Liam pushes me back upon the bed to straddle my hips.

"Liam, you don't have to." I lean up on my elbows to watch Liam scoot further down, situating himself between my legs.

He reaches for the waistband of my pajama bottoms. "I know I don't have to, but I want to. It's my Christmas gift to you."

"But the snow glo– Ah!" His hand dips below the waistband of my pjs, his touch feather-light, too light.

"As I keep telling you," he smirks, "that's from Santa. I haven't given you anything yet."

"But I– I haven't given you anything either."

"Give me your dick in my mouth, and we'll call it even."

I sputter for breath at his words, my eyes blown wide and my face flushed. That doesn't seem like a fair deal, but who am I to talk when the proposition goes straight to my groin.

"So is that a yes?"

When I nod, Liam's grin grows even wider. He grabs the waistband of my pjs, waits for me to lift my hips, and shimmies both my pants and underwear down my thighs. Copper eyes never leaving my face, he strokes me - long and slow - until I'm squirming atop the sheets. He leans down, lips parted enough for his tongue to lap at my length.

"L-liam."

Eyes bright with pride, he smirks at me as he drags his tongue along the underside. When he ascends back to the tip, the warmth of his mouth engulfs me.

With a stuttering moan, my back arches off the bed, head thrown back in a heady breath. Liam's fingers dig into my hips to push them back to the mattress as he takes a little more of me in with each bob of his head. His heat, the tightness of each suck, the rush of cold air with each purposeful inhale - they all have my fingers curling into the sheets and my hips bucking against Liam's hold.

Heat coils in my gut, building with each flick of his tongue and every suck of his lips. "L-liam! I'm gonna–"

He takes me all the way in, sucking even harder to pull me over the edge of ecstasy with a breathless cry of his name. Sitting back on his haunches, his eyes lock with mine. He smirks, tongue darting out to lick his lips. "Merry Christmas, Nico."

"Is this still fun when you stay up this late every night?"

Liam snorts at my question. Pinching my thigh beneath our shared quilt, he says, "It is when my sprinkled little smartass is with me."

When I pinch him back, he jolts with a yelp. "I was asking a serious question."

"And I gave you a serious answer," he retorts, grumpily settling back into the couch. "This entire winter break is only fun because you're here."

Liam's cute when he's grumpy, his bottom lip jutted out and his arms crossed over his chest. Leaning into his side, I lay my head upon his shoulder and nuzzle into his neck. "Every day's fun with you," I murmur against his skin.

Goosebumps prick his flesh and a shiver racks his body. He sits frozen in his grumpy state for a moment longer before sighing. Sitting up straighter, he tosses his arm behind my head and hooks my shoulder to hold me close.

"Are you done being grumpy?"

"No," he grumbles, but the upturn of his lips betrays him.

"But you don't want to start the new year off on the wrong foot."

"Nothing wrong with being grumpy."

My hand leaves the warmth of the blanket to poke Liam's cheek. "You have about thirty seconds to change your mind."

His eyes dart to the countdown timer in the corner of the television screen. He shrugs, "I guess it's gonna be a grumpy year for me then." He stares at the TV with an air of indifference, but his gaze flicks to me - a gleam to the irises that dares me to change his mind.

Hand caressing his cheek, I coax him to meet my eyes. As I hold his gaze - watching his lips twitch in an effort not to smile - I press a kiss to his cheek, the tip of his nose, his other cheek. His hand finds the nape of my neck, and fingers curl into my hair. He leans closer to meet me halfway. With the final seconds counting down around us, he smiles - eyes half-lidded as our lips touch.

A high-pitched ring has both of us jumping with a start. Hearts beating out of our chests, we stare at each other with dumbfounded shock as the shrill ring goes off not once, but three more times.

"Sorry," Liam laughs, reaching into his pocket to retrieve his phone. A few swipes of his finger and then he's showing me texts from Skyler and Emil, Cody and Alex, Eli, and Kari and Fae - selfies in various states of drunkenness wishing us a happy New Year.

Wrapping one arm around me, he holds his phone out in front of us with the other. "Smile, Sprinkles," he says, leaning in to press a kiss to my cheek.

He snaps a picture and sends it to our friends. Before showing me, he sweeps his finger across the screen and taps a few icons. "Now I'll see you every time I use my phone." He tips the screen my way so I can see.

As his background image, I stare at a moment forever captured and remembered - his prideful smirk as he holds eye contact with the camera, his lips pressed to the freckles of my cheeks, me gazing upon him out of the corners of my eyes.

Who would've guessed something as simple as a picture could bring me to tears? But this isn't just some picture. It's our picture - one in which it isn't Liam the human and Nico the demon. It's just Liam and Nico - the fools in love.

DON'T TAKE THE BOY

Some people thought I was absolutely insane to have a loaded class schedule for the past two and a half years. I recall Cody writing a satirical eulogy for the funeral he and Alex began planning the day they first saw the schedule, and there have been times I wanted them to bury me six feet under. But it was all worth it to graduate a year earlier than normal, and it's a plus to only have three classes for my last term. They're two literature composition classes and an international taxation course, but they're nothing I can't handle with the help of coffee and energy drinks.

My lightened class load is what has me wandering into the Scout's kitchen after a Saturday evening shift. Simon is easy enough to find as he scrubs down a prep table with a soapy sponge. His gray gaze flicks to me as I walk over to him before returning to his task at hand.

"Do you have a minute to talk?"

Without turning to look at me, he says, "I'll listen when you grab a broom and help sweep up." After retrieving one, I return to Simon and start sweeping from the corner closest to him. "I'm listening," he says.

Ignoring the fact the few other kitchen staff can freely listen in, I focus solely on sweeping up every speck of dirt and particle of flour. "I'd like to pick up more shifts."

Simon hums at that. "Shifts in the front or in here?"

"It doesn't matter. I'll take anything I can get." It does matter, at least in which I prefer, but beggars can't be choosers.

"What days are you available?"

"Any day other than Wednesday or Thursday." I sweep around Simon and under the prep tables. He doesn't respond for quite a while, long enough that I consider telling him to forget I ever asked. But I'd rather get more hours here than try to find a second job, so I keep my lips sealed and my words in my head.

I sweep the entire kitchen, ending in the opposite corner from where I started. After disposing of the tiny dirt pile, my eyes wander around the kitchen. Sven changes the oil for the deep fryer, Konrad stacks clean plates and cups in their racks, Simon rotates stock in the walk-in cooler, and Stephanie fills a mop bucket with soap and water. The four of them are a perfect well-oiled machine as each of them completes their list of tasks with practiced ease. Compared to them, I don't belong here standing awkwardly in their space.

Shifting my weight, I glance at Simon exiting the cooler to my left and swallow the lump in my throat. "Uh, Simon, I—"

"Are you a morning person?" he asks, picking up conversation as if we had been talking this whole time.

I fidget, scratching the nape of my neck and shifting my weight once more. "It depends what I'm getting up for."

Simon sighs. "Alright, listen. I'm only offering this to you because I think you'll take it seriously. I don't want to hear a single complaint come from your mouth. Got it?"

I don't know what I'm agreeing to, but I say, "...yes, Sir."

"Mondays and Fridays. 4 a.m. to 8 a.m. You'll assist me in baking desserts for the week. Sound good to you?"

My mouth falls open to speak, but a short circuit in my brain keeps me from forming a single word. I'm lucky I remember how to breathe properly, or Cody might've had to dig out that eulogy he wrote. Simon arches a thin eyebrow at my gaping fish demeanor until I manage to answer with a single slow nod.

"Can you start this coming Monday?"

I swallow the lump in my throat. "Y-yes, Sir. Thank you so much!"

He turns from me to return to the walk-in cooler. "You're welcome. Now get out of here before I change my mind."

I flee faster than a rabbit with a fox chasing its cottontail. No way in hell am I giving Simon even a single second to reconsider his offer, so I stumble through the swinging door to leave quiet chuckles behind me. I never thought I'd be saying this, but I can't wait to wake up at 3 a.m. on a Monday morning.

"Does it really pay to go to bed now if you won't fall asleep till midnight?"

The clock barely strikes nine thirty on Sunday night, and I - along with Nico and Skyler - am not the least bit sleepy. But whether I'm ready to go to bed or not, I'm gonna lay my ass down and hope for a relatively decent amount of sleep before having to wake up at the godawful hour of 3 a.m. If it was anyone but Simon - any other job than the one of my dreams - I wouldn't give a flying fuck about how cranky and tired I'll be in the morning, but it is Simon and is my dream job. I doubt he'd let me stay if all I do is bitch and moan about being tired. And god forbid I oversleep and show up late!

I stand from the couch and look back at Nico. With a flick to his forehead, he squeaks in surprise before swatting my hand away. "If you don't want to join, you don't have to," I say, stepping to round the arm of the couch.

Half a step is as far as I get before Nico catches my wrist. My lips twitch into a smirk. After schooling my features into something hopefully neutral, I turn back to him.

"I never said that." Nico stands, placing his hand in the middle of my shoulder blades to push me toward the hall.

"Have fun, boys," Skyler calls as he stretches out across the whole couch.

"We're sleeping! Sleeping!" I retort. My head whips back to scowl at Skyler, but my eyes meet the corners of Nico's crinkled ones. The breathlessness of his awkward laugh and the flushed constellations on his cheeks derail my thoughts until my head is filled with nothing but my Sprinkles and his touch upon my back and the shrug of his shoulders disregarding Skyler's comment.

"Goodnight, Skyler," Nico says, urging me into our room and closing the door behind us.

His hand falls from my back as he crosses the room to crawl beneath the covers and shimmies to his side. I stand frozen for a moment, simply watching him roll onto his side and tuck the comforter around his shoulders. When his brow furrows with confusion, a flip switches in me that reminds me to move. After turning off the lights, I join him beneath the warmth of the blanket.

Snuggling into his chest, my eyes fall shut. I listen to his breathing - soft and even - and the rhythmic thumping of his heart. The weight of his arm settles over my torso, and his breath brushes the ends of my hair.

It'd be so easy to fall asleep, you know, if I was actually tired. But my heart beats out of sync with Nico's, and it's annoying as fuck to try to slow mine to match his. And the muffled drone of one of Skyler's game shows travels down the hall and through the bedroom door to echo in my ears. On top of that, blood rushes through my veins so fast it resounds in my head. And then paws scratch at the door with a high-pitched meow.

Nope. Not gonna get mad. A deep breath fills my lungs. I hold in the air for a moment before releasing it in a drawn-out sigh. But before my sigh even ends, the pawing at the door starts up again.

"I'm gonna kill that cat," I grumble.

"No, you won't," Nico murmurs.

"What's stopping me?" Another shrill meow attacks my precious peace, and I seriously consider strangling the furry asshole.

"You won't because you love me."

"But I don't love the fucking fur ball."

"But I do." The pawing at the door continues. Nico sighs, "Just let him in, and he'll stop."

"Ugh!" I groan. I feel more than hear the quiet chuckle that reverberates in Nico's chest. "Stupid fucking cat." Dragging myself from my warm comfort that is Sprinkles, I trudge to the door. Barely cracking it open, Furby forces his way into the room and darts past me with a meow of victory. The cat jumps onto the bed and curls against Nico's chest, purrs echoing in the little space.

"Taking my damn spot. Stealing my boyfriend," I grumble under my breath.

"Hmm? Did you say something?" Nico asks as he strokes Furby's fur.

Padding to the bed, I slip under the covers, lying on my side with my back to Nico. "No. Nothing."

The ruffle of fabric behind me is accompanied by a meow of protest before Nico shuffles closer, his body heat spreading to caress my back. His breath tickles my earlobe, sending a shiver down my spine, as he says, "Are you jealous of a cat?" The amused twitch of his lips is evident in his voice.

"No," I huff.

"Are you lying to me?"

"No."

"Are you sure?"

"God, Nico, yes!" Reaching behind me, my palm presses to his cheek to push him away.

"Whatever you say," he chuckles, pressing even closer to me. Wrapping an arm around my middle, he holds me to him. "For the record, I love you more than Furby."

"...how much more?" I ask in a whisper.

"Hmm," he hums as if in deep thought. "Like a tiny bit more. Maybe an ounce or two."

Sarcastic little shit. But he's my sarcastic little shit. "Go to bed," I grumble, but there's no heat to my words, only an overwhelming endearment for the little shit I call my boyfriend.

It's not my alarm clock which wakes me a mere three hours after I had finally managed to fall asleep. No, that'd be too simple. Fifteen minutes before I'm supposed to be woken by the beeping blare of my alarm, a certain cat decides to sit atop the nightstand and cries with the most innocent sounding meows I've heard from the ball of fur. Its paw reaches out to my forehead, thankfully with claws retracted as it brushes my skin.

"Please, shut up," I beg, voice thick with sleep.

But does Furby listen? Absolutely not. It'd be out of character if the cat did.

Another meow is the final straw, and I can't ignore the damn cat any longer, or I'll give myself an aneurysm. With the groan of a five-year-old, I push myself up. The weight of my limbs feels heavier than normal as I stand, as if they're bags of bricks instead of lumps of flesh. Furby hops to the floor as I switch off the alarm. The cat beats me to the door, darting through it before I manage to pull it open all the way.

I step into the hall, flicking on the light only after I close the bedroom door behind me. Just because I have to be up at this deplorable hour doesn't mean Nico should abandon the bliss of sleep as well.

I head straight for the bathroom. Hopefully a scalding shower will bring some life to my bones and wash away the thoughts of sleep from my mind.

A shower both does and doesn't help. Once I'm under the pelting spray, I never want to get out. It's only when the water turns ice cold that I reluctantly drag my slightly less tired ass from the shower and towel-dry my skin.

Upon exiting the bathroom, I spot light spilling from the kitchen and detect the scent of coffee brewing. The bedroom door is wide open, and I flick on the lights to find the bed empty. Nico is insane to willingly get up at this hour. If I was him, I'd stay in bed for at least another six hours. But, hey, if he's going to make coffee for me, I'm not going to complain.

Because of my dawdling in the shower, I'm left with only ten minutes to get out the door - five if I want to be sure I'm not late. So I dress with record speed, pulling a white polo shirt over my head and stepping into a pair of black slacks. After slipping my phone in my pocket, I rush down the hall and take a moment to pop my head into the kitchen.

"Hey, I'm gonna head out in a minute."

Nico pauses in reaching for the coffee pot, turning his head to me with a lopsided smile that's brighter than the sun. "Oh, good morning." How is he so chipper this early in the day? "Do you want coffee to take with you?"

"Oh god, yes please." I could drink the entire pot, and that still wouldn't be enough.

"'Kay, I'll put some in a thermos for you."

"Thanks." I force my eyes from Nico's lazy smile and his ruffled bedhead, because I'll never leave if I keep staring.

I grab my jacket from the dining table and slip into it after tugging on my sneakers. As I straighten, Nico joins me at the door and holds out a silver thermos. "Thanks," I say again. The thermos warms my fingers as I take it and bring it to my lips.

"Have a good day," Nico beams. He leans forward to kiss my cheek, and the press of his lips sends a shock through my system that wakes me up more than the coffee does.

Clutching the thermos in both hands, my eyes flick from it to Nico who's all smiley and cheery. "See you later." I tip forward to kiss the corner of his mouth before spinning around to leave, because I really need to go.

As I descend the stairs and exit the building, thoughts of how domestic this whole situation is flood my mind. He made me coffee - got out of the glorious comfort of bed when he didn't have to. And I know he didn't make it for himself because he hates coffee (his scrunched nose and tongue sticking out when I gave him some come to mind). He saw me off with a kiss and a *have a good day*. That's some sappy romance movie kinda shit, and I feel like a hypocritical jackass for enjoying every minute of it when I roll my eyes at couples in the movies for doing the same thing. But damn if it doesn't feel great to be loved!

By the time I reach the diner, my coffee's long gone, and my fingers are freezing from the cold. I leave the thermos and jacket in the breakroom before wandering through the dimly lit kitchen to the brightness of Simon's mini bakery.

"Morning," I greet Simon with as much enthusiasm as I can muster at 4 a.m.

His eyes flick to me as he washes his hands in the sink. "Good morning," he returns the sentiment. When the remaining soap bubbles disappear down the drain, he grabs a paper towel to dry his hands and steps to the side.

As I replace him at the sink and start scrubbing my hands, he explains how this little arrangement is going to work. "You're going to start out mixing doughs, measuring ingredients, washing dishes - the easy stuff. Once you familiarize yourself with the recipes and the equipment and prove to me you're responsible enough, I'll let you fly solo. Sound good to you?"

I turn off the tap and wipe my skin dry. "Sounds great."

"Good. Let's get started." When I twist to face him and our workspace, Simon tosses a white apron at me.

As I tie the strings around my back, Simon quietly disappears into the back office and comes out with a small binder. He snatches a clipboard which hangs from a tack on the wall and sets both of them on the prep table in front of me. His finger taps the top sheet on the clipboard, and my eyes follow to stare at a table-like grid with three columns - the first a recipe name, the second a number, and the third a blank square.

"When you're working back here, this is your god. It tells you exactly what we need to complete for the day, so if you don't know what to do, check the agenda. If it's being worked on, draw a slash in the empty box; and when you finish it, put an *x*." I nod at the information as he continues with a run-down of how everything works.

Once he's satisfied that I've had enough explanation, he sends me to the far wall of dry ingredients with the recipe binder and an empty mixing bowl. He calls out a cookie recipe and a batch quantity for me to measure and mix dry ingredients.

It takes a little practice to figure out where everything is located, but soon enough I fall into an easy rhythm of scooping flour and sugar into the bowl. Simon shows me how the mixer works - how to switch the attachments and lock the bowl - and supervises as I dump in the ingredients. He lets me search the fridge for butter and eggs without pointing them out. Once I find them, I cut the butter and toss the chunks into the mix to let it incorporate before adding the eggs and remaining few ingredients.

When the cookie dough is thoroughly mixed, Simon takes over, scraping the dough into a smaller bowl on the prep table. He forms the dough into identical balls and lines sheet trays as he says, "You have to wash the mixer's bowl and attachment every time you switch recipes to prevent cross-contamination."

Yep. 'Cause of health issues - allergies and such. "'Kay. Got it."

I've never had a more relaxing experience at a job than I have today, especially after Simon turns on classical music to play in the background. It's a peacefulness that tricks me into believing I'm cooking at home but with industrialized equipment. It feels surreal to even be here in this professional space, beside a professional of my dream career.

But is it still a dream? Can it be considered such when it's no longer a figment of my imagination? It's real - I can see it, touch it, experience it. No longer is it an ideal I may never reach, because I'm doing it right now. It may be the first day and my only duties include measuring ingredients and washing dishes, but everyone starts at the bottom. Simon said it himself - once I gain more experience and prove I can handle more, he'll give me more substantial tasks.

So I'm not mad or even disappointed to spend four hours washing dishes and measuring ingredients and placing color-coded stickers (red for Monday) upon the plastic-wrapped sheet trays lined with goodies or upon the side of a pie tin. They're menial tasks, but they have to be done. And in my opinion, it's better to start at the bottom and work your way up. You gain a sense of pride from doing so - like, yes, I started there and through my own hard work and determination, now I'm here. And the skills I gain from being at the bottom will only improve my performance when I reach the top.

I'm almost sad to mark the last x on today's agenda, to hear Simon tell me to sweep up while he moves the trays of desserts and breads to the walk-in cooler. Time ticked far too quickly with four hours passing in what seemed like five minutes. But even though my heart aches at the idea of calling it a day, my lips stretch into a fond smile.

This is what I'm meant to do. No amount of number crunching and filling out financial forms has ever brought me such a feeling of accomplishment and pride as today's menial tasks have. All those times when I doubted my resolve and debated giving up make this moment taste even sweeter on my tongue. I could've fallen back on accounting - that is my major after all - but no matter how good I am at completing simple mathematical formulas, it's never been fun for me. I never enjoy it. Hell, it's more frustrating than anything. And, yeah, accountants make a decent chunk of change. Being a son from a major accounting firm, I know that better than anyone. But I don't care about the riches. If my father's taught me anything, he's taught me that.

Let me bake - give me a kitchen and a salary to support a modest future with Nico - and I'll show you the happiest man alive.

When I finish sweeping, I exchange my broom for a mop as Simon wipes down the prep table. I wish I could say I'm not surprised when Quinn pokes their head into our workspace, but I jump with a start when they clap a hand on my back.

"Congrats on surviving your first day!" they beam at me, wide grin and sparkling golden brown eyes behind the rims of their glasses.

"Was there an outcome where I didn't?" I ask, raising an eyebrow.

They laugh - loud, body-shaking laughs. "You never know with Simon."

"Oi!" Simon raises a hand to point to the main kitchen. "Get out. You know you're not allowed back here."

"Aw, come on," Quinn pouts. "I won't touch anything."

"That's what you said last time," Simon grumbles.

That piques my curiosity. "What happened last time?"

Simon sighs, shaking his head as if I shouldn't have asked; but Quinn perks up like a kid in a candy shop. They grab my shoulders, staring so intently at me that I feel they're seeing straight into my soul. "Have you ever heard of molecular gastronomy?"

"...yeah."

"Well, you see—"

But that's as far as they get before Simon marches over, grabs my forearm, and tugs me away from Quinn. "Finish cleaning, would you?" he drones as he pulls me through the main kitchen and into the break room.

Stephanie and Sven both look up at our sudden appearance, staring for a moment before nodding to themselves. "You asked," they say in unison, a certain amount of wisdom to their voices to suggest they've made the same mistake.

"Should I not have?" I say a little meekly as I reach for my coat.

"By all means, feel free to go back there and ask again if you have a week to listen to their reply," Simon says, also reaching for a jacket.

"Nah, I think I'm good." After zipping my coat, I grab my empty thermos and bid my farewell to the others. It takes a minute to process Simon following me out the side door to the parking lot.

For a split moment, I think I must've forgotten something, but then he heads to a car parked beside a lamppost. In my stumped state, I miss a stride and stumble over a nonexistent crack in the sidewalk. But then reality catches up with my sleep-deprived brain; and, duh, of course Simon has days off like everyone else. As much as I'd like to believe he lives at the diner 24/7 (like how it's weird seeing high school teachers outside of the school), it's reassuring to know Simon's human too, that even he needs breaks and vacations to keep from burning out.

Speaking of breaks, I can really go for a nap right about now. Without my hands constantly moving and my brain busy adding up measurements, the exhaustion from this morning returns tenfold. The cold wind against my cheeks makes me long for the warmth of my bed and Nico's skin against mine. But then there's the brightness of the morning sun that's fucking with my internal time clock. My body says it's time to catch some z's, but my mind's like, nah bruh, it's daytime so go do some shit.

If anything good comes from my messed up internal clock, it's that it keeps me awake long enough to navigate the sidewalk without colliding into some hasty businessperson. I trudge back to the right apartment building (after stopping in front of another which turned out to not be right) and enter into the heated lobby. The rush of warmth blankets my limbs with a sluggishness that reflects my lack of sleep, and it takes immense concentration on my part to drag my feet up each stair without falling flat on my face.

I eventually make it to the right apartment and unlock the door. Slipping inside, I huff a silent sigh as the door clicks softly shut behind me. While toeing off my sneakers and jacket, I glance up to spot Nico sitting on the couch - pillow in his lap, Furby sleeping on the pillow, and a book lying open upon the armrest. His eyes follow the words of the story, so absorbed in his fictional universe that he hasn't noticed my entrance.

After the little incident with Furby last night, I'm feeling rather needy. I'll blame it on my exhaustion (yep, definitely not competing with a damn cat for my boyfriend's affections), so I quietly pad across the floor to the couch. Nico's eyes flick up as my shadow passes across the page he's reading.

"Welcome ba—" his words cut off when my hands slide beneath Furby. The cat meows in protest at being picked up and set on the floor, but thankfully it walks off to Skyler's room instead of mauling me.

Plopping down on the couch, I stretch out upon the cushions and lay my head on the pillow in Nico's lap - still warm from Furby's body heat.

An amused puff of air breezes through Nico's nose as his fingers settle into my hair - rubbing and scratching all the best spots on my scalp. The skilled fingers have low moans rumbling in my chest, and suddenly it makes sense why Furby loves my Sprinkles so much.

"Did you have a good day?"

"Mhmm," I hum, eyes falling shut with another brush of his fingers.

Winter comes and goes. The incessant cold that's stuck to the city since last fall finally releases its grip with the beginning of spring. I, for one, am truly grateful for the changing of seasons, especially for my early morning walks before the sun rises. No more below freezing temperatures which make me question whether or not I'll ever be able to feel my fingers again. Hell, I'm ready to break out the shorts and sing my praises to the heavens.

Although the decor inside the apartment would make someone think I'm unwilling to let go of the last remnants of the winter spirit. I never did get around to cleaning up Nico's and my holiday creations (minus the socks - I needed to wear those last week). An apartment with a crayon-drawn Christmas tree and paper snowflakes still decorating the walls definitely needs to check the calendar, but I can't bring myself to take them down. Even after Skyler scolded Nico and me for leaving them up so long, neither one of us could find it in ourselves to dismantle our little creations. I figure one of these days Skyler will get fed up with asking and do it himself.

Just in case that is what happens, I removed the star - our star - from the 2D tree and placed it in my nightstand for safe keeping before leaving for my Monday shift with Simon this morning. That star is the one thing I don't want anybody damaging or throwing away. Skyler can do what he wants with the rest of it as long as I get to keep the star, because it's more than enough to remind me of the memories Nico and I made that day.

I'm also proud to say I gained Simon's respect rather quickly. I've gotten to the point where he trusts me with a recipe from start to finish. It's no longer menial tasks for me (although I still do those too). Simon and I divide and conquer the clipboard agenda, helping each other when asked. Even those snail pastries I used to struggle with have become a normal routine for me. I still have to twist them against the prep table, but at least they don't fall apart on me anymore.

Some recipes, like the garlic herb rolls, go faster when we work together - a two-person assembly line if you will. I dump a large batch of dough on one end of the prep table while Simon lines the other with greased baking trays. With a dough cutter, I portion relatively equal chunks of dough - weighing one every so often to check my accuracy - and toss them in front of Simon. He cups his hand to roll the dough blobs into balls and then lines them on trays. When a tray is full, he brushes the tops with butter and a sprinkle of cheese before putting them in the oven.

As we're working, Simon says, "You're graduating soon, right?"

"Yeah." I toss another dough blob his way.

"Are you majoring in the culinary field?"

I shake my head with a quiet tsk. "I wish, but nope. It's accounting."

Simon hums, seemingly understanding the connection between my major and my family name. "I can't imagine you'd actually enter that field."

"No, not that anybody would hire me anyway. They'd be fucking idiots to trust a Holt with their money." If my tone holds a bit too much heat, Simon doesn't mention it.

"So, what do you want to do then? You probably have some back-up plans."

"Accounting was my back-up plan. I never really wanted to do it to begin with. I only agreed to because I figured having business knowledge would make starting and operating a successful bakery easier. But who knows if that'll ever happen."

I don't know why I'm so willing to tell Simon my biggest insecurities about my future. Maybe it's because I look up to him as a teacher or because he's already successful in a career I want. Maybe because I know he'll listen objectively, or it could be he's more experienced with life and its many curve balls.

"A bakery, huh?" A timer beeps, and Simon moves to pull a tray of rolls from the oven, quickly replacing it with another. "That's not a bad idea."

I cut the last two dough blobs and walk to set the cutter in the sink. "Doesn't mean I'll ever be able to do it."

Simon hears my mumbled words and sighs. "You know, kid, have some faith in yourself. Dreams don't happen overnight. Do you think I got to where I am now right out of school? Because I didn't. Fuck, I didn't even go to culinary school till I was twenty-five. I wanted to be a vet until I flunked my board exam and dropped out. I moped around for a year before going to Europe to study culinary arts. After graduation, I thought being a celebrated 5-star chef would make me happy; but it didn't, so I came back here to rent this little diner. And this is what I love. It took me over thirty years to figure out what I wanted to do, so you're already ahead of the game. Give yourself some credit."

My hands shake as I slowly turn to face Simon, but he continues sprinkling the last tray of rolls with cheese as if nothing happened. Blinking against the burning moisture forming in my eyes, I open my mouth to speak, but nothing comes out.

Everyone always wondered why Simon chose this little diner. Well now I know, and it's one of the most reassuring things anyone has ever told me.

High school doesn't prepare you for the real world. It preaches choose a career, go to college, and get a job in that career field; but it never tells you it's okay to change your mind - to feel uncertainty, to not know what you want to do. Goddamn, I wish someone would've told me that sooner! Maybe then, hearing it from Simon wouldn't feel like such a revelation, wouldn't bring tears of relief to my eyes.

"I'll finish this. Start cleaning up."

I nod, swallowing the lump in my throat as I reach for a washcloth. "Thanks."

"Do you know what you're doing?"

"Yes, now get out." I physically shove Skyler from the kitchen as Emil and Nico laugh.

Skyler whines in protest, "But why does Nico get to help?"

"Because he won't burn water."

Skyler grumbles under his breath about letting go of the past as he drags Emil with him to the living room, abandoning the idea of cooking in favor of video games. And thank god for that, because I'd rather not have to order take-out tonight.

With Skyler out of the way, Nico joins me by the counter and skims the recipe for homemade noodles lying open before us. "So what's first?" he asks.

"I think I'll have you make the noodles, and I'll start the meatballs." I dig in one of the lower drawers and grab an apron for Nico. "Here. Have at it."

I start gathering ingredients for him as he ties the apron behind his back. While I slide the flour container across the counter, Nico turns - hands on his hips and a jovial glint to the honey of his eyes. "Liam," he says with a breathless laugh, pointing at the words written across his chest.

Following the point of his finger, I snort at the apron I gave him. Out of the many stuffed into the drawer, of course that's the one I had to choose. With a small shake of my head and an amused smirk, I step closer to Nico. Leaning up, I brush my lips against his, because how can I disobey what the apron clearly states in thick, bold letters across his chest.

Nico's breath of laughter breezes against my skin. "You were wearing this the first time I met you."

"Really?" I don't remember what I wore that day. I was more focused on not making an ass of myself.

"Yeah," he nods, as we busy our hands with making dinner. "I remember, because I was so scared to meet the roommate."

"The roommate?"

"Well, I didn't know your name at the time, and I was scared you wouldn't like me."

I chuckle at the irony of that, because I had been thinking the same thing. "I'm not gonna lie. I thought you were a serial killer."

"What?" Nico squeaks, his hand pausing in cracking an egg. He glances over his shoulder at me. "But, why?"

"Okay, hear me out. I had no idea who you were, and your story sounded kinda fishy. But what tipped me off the most was Furby. The evil fucking cat adored you, so I assumed you were evil too. Turns out you're both just demons."

"A cat," he says disbelievingly. "A cat made you think I was a serial killer."

My hands stop combining the meat mixture as my lips purse. "Well, when you say it like that, it sounds ridiculous."

"I'm glad you realize that."

He kneads the dough as I roll out miniature meatballs. I toss the balls in the oven to cook and put a saucepan on the burner to start the tomato sauce.

"How thin am I supposed to roll this?"

With a glance over my shoulder, I spot Nico pulling and pushing a rolling pin across the dough. "As thin as you can get it without ripping."

"'Kay." I watch as he works the dough, putting more of his weight behind the rolling pin.

Returning my attention to the stove, I put water on to boil before focusing on the sauce. I dump canned tomato sauce and paste into the saucepan, mixing them with a dash of water to get the desired consistency. A pinch of salt and pepper, a little oregano, thyme, basil, and a couple cloves of garlic get tossed into the mix and left to stew on the stove.

"Liam, is this good?"

I step to stand beside Nico and check the dough. "Yep. That's perfect. Now you can cut the noodles." I retrieve a pizza cutter and cut a few long strips through the dough before handing the cutter to Nico. "When you're done, leave them to dry for a little bit."

Nico nods as he takes the cutter. After a minute of watching him cut thin strips, I return to the stove to stir the sauce, but a loud knock on the apartment door distracts me.

"Skyler, can you get that?" I call, adjusting the heat on the sauce.

"No can do. I'm in the middle of kicking some ass."

Heaving a sigh, I wipe my hands on a dish towel before heading to the door. Another series of loud knocks echo in the apartment. When I pull the door open and meet the silver gaze waiting on the other side, I don't recognize the man standing across the threshold. And frankly, he doesn't look like a man I'd like to know, what with how his lips curl as his eyes scrutinize me from head to toe.

"Can I help you?" I ask with a stiff bite to my tone.

The stranger runs a hand with painted black nails through his black hair, letting his arm fall back to his side as he huffs an exaggerated sigh. "Yeah, I'm looking for Nico."

My blood runs cold at the name which passes through this bowl-cut bastard's lips. There's only a handful of people who know Nico lives here, and this guy isn't one of them. Him and his flip flops and loose-fitting tank top and sweats aren't getting anywhere near my boyfriend. I move to slam the door in his face, but his hand darts out incredibly fast to hold it open.

"I'd listen to what I have to say if I were you," he says nonchalantly, as if I hadn't tried to slam the door on him. He cracks a sickeningly sweet smile with a tilt of his head. His silver eyes purposely flick up, and my gaze involuntarily follows.

If my blood ran cold before, it's fucking frozen now as I watch two dark horns materialize from his forehead to curve up along his head.

Fuck, fuck, fuck. He's a demon, and Nico's on the run from demons. He'll take Nico - my Sprinkles - back to the demon world, and I'll never see him again.

No, fuck that. Goddammit, I am not losing the one person I love who loves me back just the same. Take anything else; I don't care what. I'll give up my apartment, my job, every last dollar to my name. Take my clothes and my laptop. Take away my cooking skills and my ability to speak. Take fucking Furby if that's what you want, but god-fucking-dammit, don't take Nico.

HE'S MY HOME

Boiling bubbles pop in the tomato sauce, and a few drops spray on the stove. "Liam!" I call as I abandon cutting the noodles to stir the sauce. Some of it sticks to the bottom of the pot, so I turn the heat down to prevent it from burning. I call his name again, because I really don't want to ruin dinner.

But he doesn't reply. And actually, I can't hear the revving of engines from Skyler's and Emil's video game. When did they pause that? Is someone special here? Maybe Cody and Alex dropped by, or even Fae and Kari. No, that can't be it. It's far too quiet for them. Naomi maybe? Or Eli?

I turn both cooktops as low as they can be while still producing some kind of heat. Abandoning our hopefully not burnt dinner components, I wander from the kitchen, wiping my hands clean on the *Kiss the Cook* apron. It only takes two steps for me to spot the backs of Skyler and Emil in the entryway - the tufts of Liam's hair visible between the other two's shoulders.

"Who's here?" I ask, stepping closer to the three blocking the view into the hall.

Liam jolts at the sound of my voice - as if it's a shock of electricity coursing through him - and Emil's head whips back to stare at me, eyes blown wide and sweat glistening his brow.

"No one." There's a bite to Skyler's tone - a promised threat that sends chills down my spine - as he stands with squared shoulders between me and whoever's waiting in the hall.

"Well that's rude." My breath stills in my lungs. I know this voice. "I'm not no one. Right, my little runaway?"

No, no, no! This can't be happening. He's not actually here, right? Right!? I'm dreaming - no, having a nightmare more like it - and soon enough all of this will fade once consciousness hits me. Anytime now... Please... Body, I'm begging you to wake up. Open your eyes to see the peacefulness of a slumbering Liam - his breath warm against my neck, the scrunch of his nose as I try to free myself from his embrace, his hold growing tighter until I relent to hold my bladder for another half-hour. Please go away - fade to the hole in the bedroom wall or Liam's dirty socks abandoned on the floor.

Change to anything but this. One of those nightmares where I'm falling and falling and never stop falling - yeah, change to that. Let me hit the ground for once, so hard it'll jolt me awake.

"W-why–?" But I can't finish the question, can't formulate the right words, can't wrap my tongue around the syllables, can't force my voice to cooperate.

"Why am I here?" His head - horns quite visible - comes into my view as he takes a single step into the apartment until a whack to his chest stops him.

Liam... hit a demon. He holds him at arm's length, palm flat against the demon's sternum. A venomous *Don't!* is spit in the demon's face.

But Liam, that's what I want to tell you. Don't put yourself in danger for me. He's a demon - a demon. No sane person stands up to a demon, let alone hits one. Don't hold on to me if it means getting yourself killed.

But don't let me go. Dear god, I don't want to go. Don't take me away from the happiness I've found here. I may not deserve it, but damn do I want it!

I want game show marathons with Skyler and in-depth book discussions with Emil. I want sleepovers with Cody and Alex. I want Kari to shout Freckle Buddy while wrapping me in the tightest bear hug I've ever felt and Fae reminding her not to suffocate me.

I want to stay with Liam - with his smile that sends my heart into a beating frenzy and his touch that's so gentle it makes me want to melt. His grumpiness in the mornings, his jealousy of a cat, his tears when he's reminded of his father - I want it all: the good and the bad, the ups and the downs, the extreme highs and lows.

Is it too much to ask for forever? Because even forever doesn't seem long enough when I'm with him. Give me an eternity of lifetimes spent by his side, and I'll never tire of the everyday mundane - of sending him off in the mornings with a cup of coffee, of dates spent on a much too small seesaw at the park, of watching the same reruns of *Cutthroat Kitchen* and *Cupcake Wars*.

I just want an eternity. Is that too much to ask?

"Easy, buddy," my old demon partner says, raising his hands in front of him. "I come in peace. I'm not here to take him back. Do you really think I would've knocked on the door if I was?"

"Why should we believe you?" Skyler questions, the demon's attempt at innocence doing little to quell the heat to his words.

The demon shrugs his shoulders. "I guess you don't have to, but you probably should. That is, of course, if you want to save our precious little runaway from a lifetime of torture in the dungeons of Hell. By all means, I'll leave, but I figured–"

Liam's hand fists into the demon's tank top and slams him against the door frame. "What did you just say?"

The demon doesn't so much as flinch. His fingers curl around Liam's, dark nails digging into flesh, until Liam is forced to release him. "We can either talk civilly inside, or I'm leaving."

Liam cocks his arm and swings for the demon's face. His fist would've connected with the demon's jaw save for Skyler grabbing his arm to stop him. His head whips to scowl at Skyler - betrayal burning in his irises - until Skyler grasps his shoulder to pull him back.

"Let's hear him out."

"But–"

Skyler ignores Liam's protest, stepping in front of him to glare down upon the demon. "You so much as lay a single finger on Nico, and Liam won't be the only one throwing punches."

"Like I said," the demon emphasizes, his irritation finally coming through. "I'm not here to hurt him." Piercing silver eyes land upon me, his lips curling in a shadow of a smile. "Have I ever hurt you before?"

The other three gazes turn to me as well. Each waits with bated breath for my answer, ready to strike should I label the demon a liar.

But he's not. Never once has he raised a hand or voice to me in hatred. Through our years of knowing each other, he's been nothing but considerate, even taking into account his insufferable teasing at times.

"Well... no."

"See?" He steps further into the apartment, this time without any retaliation from Liam. "Nico and I go way back, don't we? Dare I say friends? Hmm, maybe not, but consider this a gift from a... from an acquaintance."

With another step in - far enough to nonchalantly kick the door shut behind him - my ex-partner approaches even closer. But Liam beats him to me, placing himself between me and the demon.

"Ah, you must be the reason Nico doesn't visit me anymore. I'm not gonna lie; it saddens me a little. But as long as you make him happy," the demon shrugs.

Liam's palm twitches at the words. It's not hard to put two and two together, so I commend Liam for not trying to throw another punch. Because if he's jealous of a cat, I hate to imagine what's racing through his head now.

Instead, he demands an answer to his question, "What was that about the dungeons of Hell?"

"Well, you see," the demon leans back against the dining table, "Nico's a wanted criminal in our world - him being a runaway and all - and runaways aren't taken very kindly to. He'll be lucky to get a few lashings at the very least, but I doubt Avon will let him off that easy. It's not often demons evade the apprehension unit for as long as he has."

"Are you–" I swallow the lump in my throat and try again. "Are you saying they're closing in?"

Silver orbs lock with mine - an unwavering seriousness to the metallic eyes. "It's worse than that. They know you're here."

No, they can't. It's not possible. I've been careful. I never go out without Liam or Skyler or Emil. I'm careful to keep my demon features in check. I stopped traveling between worlds, so my trace should be long gone. I've been careful!

What more could I have done? Move from place to place every week, never staying somewhere for too long? I can't do that. That'd be no different from my life in the demon world. I ran then, but I don't want to run now. I have reasons not to run now, but what other option do I have? If I stay, I'm putting my friends in danger. But if I leave... if I leave...

I don't want to leave. I don't want to run away. I don't want to be alone again.

Please, don't take my happiness away.

Fingers brush the back of my hand, and a gaze so soft and tender you wouldn't believe he tried punching someone moments ago meets mine. "Hey, breathe," Liam whispers. "I won't let you go. They'll have to take you over my dead body."

I want to scream at him, to tell him that's what I'm afraid of. Demons have killed for less. But the thought can't pass my lips. If I don't say it - refuse to believe it - then maybe Liam'll stay safe.

"How long do we have?" Skyler asks.

"Avon is still rounding up his team, so I'd say a week at most."

One week. Seven days. 168 hours. That's the most I can ask for, and that's a best case scenario. Worst case, they could show up in the next five minutes. Maybe I should make this easier on everyone and surrender now. Accept my fate - it was bound to happen eventually.

"Two days." My eyes dart to Liam, but he's staring at the demon. "Give me two days. By this time Thursday, we'll be long gone."

"But, Liam–"

"No buts," he interrupts, turning his gaze to me. His eyes are steady - unwavering in his conviction. "I– We won't let them take you, so let us protect you."

He leaves no room for refusal, turning back to the demon before he can see the single nod of my head. "Can you stall for two days?"

My ex-partner straightens, stretching his arms above his head and arching his back. He exhales a long sigh, then walks for the door. "I'll give you that, but I can't promise anything more." He stops in the entrance and gazes over his shoulder until his eyes lock with mine. "Good luck and farewell." Then he's gone, walking through the door without opening it.

No one moves. We stand frozen in time, eyes darting between one another, silently asking the same thing. Did that really happen? Was he really here?

We dare not breathe - too afraid to break the temporary calm before the storm. The ticking of the clock on the kitchen wall rings in the air around us, its rhythm the only thing proving that it's not time which stopped, but us. Water boils in the kitchen, and its bubbles pop with the occasional drop falling upon the burner and fizzling with the heat. A fly repeatedly runs into the light above us, its wings buzzing like a never-ending echo shouted into a cave.

As quickly as the curtain of silence fell over us, it's torn by a meow from Simba and the scratch of his claws at an empty food bowl. Everyone jumps into motion at the same time, words falling from mouths in a jumble and feet rushing back and forth.

"You're not staying here." Liam tugs me to our room, Skyler and Emil right behind.

"But where should I go?"

"Anywhere but here."

"But, Liam—"

He releases my arm and rushes to the closet, wrenching the doors open. "We're leaving." He digs around among the clutter until he finds two duffle bags and throws them atop the bed.

"We need a plan."

"There's no time," Liam disregards Skyler's words as he paces back and forth across the room, grabbing random articles of clothing as he goes.

"But where will you go?" Skyler catches Liam's forearm and yanks him to a standstill. "Where will you guys go and—"

"I don't know!" Liam rips his arm from Skyler's grasp. Inhaling a shaky breath, he forces the panic from his voice. "I don't know," he says quieter. "That's what the two days are for - to figure it out. But Nico can't— We can't stay in this apartment, because this is the first place they'll look."

"But you two can't sleep on the streets."

Liam goes back to packing, and I join him; because I need the distraction. "I'll book a hotel room or something," he says, tossing a pair of jeans at me.

"What about my dorm room?" Emil suggests. "You two can stay there, and I'll stay here."

Liam pauses for a moment before nodding. "Yeah, that'll work. Thanks, Emil."

Emil digs a key from his pocket and passes it to Liam as Liam rushes from the room. "Can we take the car?" he calls from the bathroom.

"Keys are on the table," Skyler calls back.

Skyler joins me beside the bed, handing me a sweater lying atop the comforter to stuff into the bag. "You okay?"

I shake my head; because if I speak, I fear my voice will break.

Skyler grabs my hand as I try and fail to zip the bag shut. With a steady touch, he guides my trembling fingers along the zipper's path. "It'll be okay. We'll think of something."

I want nothing more in this world than for his words to be true. I want to believe everything will miraculously work itself out, but that's not how the world works. Sometimes, no matter how you struggle, you still lose.

And that's what scares me. What if after all this - after successfully fleeing and spending months hiding in dark alleys before being found by Skyler and Emil - it's all taken away from me? Am I even capable of going back to an isolated life without them? I shudder at the mere thought, because I'm not. I've had a taste of the human world, and it's the sweetest thing I've ever experienced. To be forced to abandon the place where I belong, I can't do that - not after spending my entire life trying to find it.

But one wrong move and I'll have to.

Liam returns, stuffs toiletries into his bag, and slings it over his shoulder. "Are you ready to go?"

I nod as I grab my bag. Skyler - with a bittersweet sheen to his golden eyes - wraps his arms around my back to pull me into a tight embrace. "This isn't goodbye," he says with a heavy voice.

"Not a goodbye," I choke out, feeling the sting of tears in my eyes.

We're both reluctant to let go, but we do. One warm embrace is exchanged for another, and instead of clinging to Skyler's back, I cling to Emil's. "Stay safe."

I nod, letting go before the waterworks have a chance to overflow.

Liam reaches for my hand, intertwining our fingers with a reassuring squeeze. "I'll call you when I figure something out." Liam leads me to the door where we slip into our shoes and coats.

"We'll try to think of something too," Skyler says, holding the door open for us. "Text us to let us know you're okay."

"Will do. You guys stay safe too."

With that, we're out the door and racing down the stairs. We take them two at a time, rounding the landing and nearly sprinting out the door. It's only when we reach the car that our hands separate to hastily toss our bags in the back seats and buckle our seatbelts.

Once in the vehicle, Liam struggles to get the key in the ignition. His entire arm trembles, and each failed attempt leaves his fingers shaking even more. After what has to be the fifth time, his hand falls to his lap and his fingers grip even tighter to the key.

"Li–"

"I'm sorry," he blurts out. His eyes squeeze shut, and his lips quiver. Leaning to rest his forehead against the steering wheel, a trembling breath passes his lips. "I'm sorry. I just... need a minute."

In this moment, I'm reminded how weak Liam is. He's not exactly strong or courageous, and sometimes he's hotheaded and acts before he thinks; but all of those things - they're not necessarily bad. Being weak can be a strength in itself, because he understands what it's like to feel powerless - to abandon hope only to try to find it again. It's because of this - because I see the same pain etched into his face, the way his hands curl into fists in his lap, how he swallows a gulp of air as if it may be his last - that I trust him.

He feels pain - maybe not identical to mine but similar enough. He understands, and that simple fact calms me.

My heartbeat slows until it no longer echoes in my head, and the thoughts of my impending capture turn to ones of escape. It wouldn't be fair to solely rely on my friends for my safety or to assume they aren't as scared as I am. Liam has held it together up to this point - physically put himself between me and danger - so it's only fair I do the same.

I reach for his hand, feeling the trembling beneath my touch. Rubbing my thumb over his knuckles in soothing circles, I say, "It'll be okay. I won't leave you."

Whether either of us believes those words is up for debate. I can't guarantee any of this will work out. I can promise not to leave, but that won't stop Avon's unit from forcibly taking me.

But maybe if we say it enough - scream it to the heavens until our voices go hoarse - then maybe the world will get on board our ship too.

We sit in the silence of the dark car for longer than a minute, but I don't mind it. Whatever minutes or hours or days I have left, Liam can have them all.

I'm not sure how long it takes for his trembling to cease, but it eventually does. He lifts his head and uses his jacket sleeve to wipe at his eyes. With a final deep breath, his grip on the key loosens. My hand releases his as he lifts the key to the ignition, slipping it in much easier this time. With a flick of his wrist, the car rattles to life.

When Skyler's cheerfully bubbly music sounds from the speakers, neither of us turns it off. Despite its obnoxious volume, it's merely background noise on our short drive. Three and a half songs later and Liam's parking in what's probably the last space in the lot.

With a tight grip, he grabs my hand while we walk to the building. My gaze darts back and forth - zeroing in on every rustle of a tree branch or footfall upon the walkway. Briefly, my eyes meet those of everyone we pass, scanning their faces to confirm they're not demons. A few greet Liam as we pass, and he replies with variations of grunts and the occasional forced smile.

I want to rejoice when I recognize the number plate beside the door Liam stops in front of to unlock. He ushers me inside and flips on the light. As I toe off my shoes, Liam tosses his duffle bag beside a desk before stepping back into the hall.

"I'm gonna go find us some food. Don't leave this room." He doesn't close the door behind him until I promise to stay put.

A sense of nostalgia washes over me as I turn to face the small dorm room. With barely enough space, two loft beds with desks situated beneath them are pushed up against the right wall. The one nestled in the corner directly to the right of the door had been the first bed I ever slept in, and I remember my first night of sleep on it. Compared to concrete or dirt, it was so soft I wanted to cry (actually, I did cry). Two tiny closets - each with a single shelf for storage - line the left wall, stopping just shy of the door to the bathroom shared with the adjacent room.

This is the first place I called home, but to be back here under these circumstances has it feeling as foreign as it did when I first stayed here. Without the calming and protective presences of Emil and Skyler, I find myself wanting to hide in a corner or burrow under a blanket. Seeing as the latter option sounds far more comfortable, I climb up the metal frame of the nearest loft bed to settle atop the mattress. My head knocks against the ceiling a few times as I rustle the blanket from beneath me to wrap it around my shoulders. Even up here - slouched against the wall with my feet dangling awkwardly over the edge - the feelings of home don't return to me. But on the bright side, I'm warmer than I'd be crouched in the corner.

Minutes tick by as if each is a separate eternity. Every approach of footsteps in the hallway has my heart pounding and my breath hitching until they fade further into the dormitory. One set slows to a stop on the other side of the door. When the doorknob jiggles, I burrow even further into the blanket cocoon to make myself as small as possible. Maybe I can disguise myself as a pile of pillows jumbled atop the mattress, and whoever it is won't even know I'm here.

As the door slowly opens, I chance a peek over the bed's metal frame. A familiar copper gaze meets mine. He pauses in the doorway with an arched eyebrow and a cup of ramen in each hand. "What are you doing?" he asks as he nudges the door shut with his foot.

"Um..." I sit up as straight as I can without my head hitting the ceiling. "Imitating a pile of pillows."

"Hiding in the closest would probably be more successful." He kicks off his shoes before walking over to me and passing me both cup noodles to hold.

"Where'd you get these?"

Liam scales the frame and crawls to my side. Taking back one of the styrofoam cups of instant ramen, he says, "The communal kitchen."

"So you stole them?"

"If there's no name, it's fair games." He shifts his weight to pull a pair of plastic spoons from his back pant pocket, offering one to me. "Plus, communal means community, and I'm part of Sodalis U.'s community."

"So you stole them," I repeat.

With a lopsided smirk, he shrugs, "Sure, if that's how you want to define it, but communal sounds so much... nicer, like we're all looking out for each other."

Laughter bubbles up my throat and overflows from my lips. Tension fades from my shoulders with each giggled breath. Liam arches a brow at the sudden outburst, an amused glint to his eyes; because even he knows his words weren't humorous enough for gut-wrenching laughter. And maybe it's not hilarious, but it feels right. It feels... normal, like we're sitting on the couch back in the apartment and he made some sarcastic side comment about one of Skyler's reality shows.

As my laughter dies down to leave a lazy grin in its place, I relax into Liam's side. Long after we've finished our impromptu (and probably stolen) dinner, we're still slouched against the wall cuddled beneath a single blanket. Even with a dull ache in my lower back from my poor posture, I'm more than comfortable and would be happy to doze off nestled into Liam's side.

But we both know there's a more pressing matter than sleep. "What are we gonna do?" I ask, barely a whisper but it rings loud and clear in the silence of the room.

"I don't know." He breathes out a sigh. "We can leave tomorrow morning and just drive till we run out of gas."

That won't happen, or more accurately, I won't let it happen. "Liam." I direct my best interpretation of Skyler's mom-stare at him.

"So I'll miss three tests. Who cares?"

"Midterms aren't normal tests. You said so yourself."

"I'll skip them, no big deal. You're more important to me."

Yeah, that's not going to happen. I refuse to let Liam throw away his blindingly bright future for me, especially when it's not necessary. "We have two guaranteed days."

"So you trust that demon at his word?"

There was a time I'd hesitate to answer. Due to that run-in at the fast food drive-thru a couple months ago, I'd probably say no to Liam's question. I truly thought my ex-partner sold me out to his co-workers, but now I know I was wrong. The run-in was pure coincidence, because why else would he risk himself to warn me?

"Yeah, I do."

Liam groans and slumps even further down the wall. "But I don't wanna take the midterms," he whines.

"There, there," I coo while patting the top of his head. "You'll survive."

"But, Nico~" He twists to wrap his arms around my middle and bury his face against my chest.

"You can do it," I say with a light chuckle, but Liam only groans louder.

Tipping over upon the mattress, I pull Liam with me and turn to lie on my back with him lounged atop me. He crosses his arms over my abdomen to prop his chin on the backs of his hands. Eyelashes bat at me, and his bottom lip juts out in a pout. "Take it for me?"

"I'd fail them."

"Same here." He groans again and drops his head to my belly. Sigh after exaggerated sigh falls from his lips, and it's one of the cutest and most childish things he's ever done. My hand finds its way into his hair. With each scratch of my fingertips, Liam's obnoxious sighs quiet to softer and more content puffs of air.

I know there should be more important issues on my mind (the possibility of being captured, maybe?), but the sharp chill of fear which racked my body is completely gone. It's been replaced with the warmth of a midsummer day, and the dorm finally feels like home again. Feeling Liam's fingertips brush along my sides with added pressure that has me squirming with laughter, I can fathom why that may be.

Liam pushes his cellphone into my hands, adamant he'll feel better leaving if I have it. He slips into his coat and reaches for the door handle. "If anything happens, call Skyler or Emil, or hell, even Cody. They'll let me know somehow."

"Kay." I clutch his phone as he reluctantly leaves for his first of two midterms today.

Glancing around the room, there's not much I can do to entertain myself for the next few hours. It takes barely a minute to toss the styrofoam cups from last night's dinner and this morning's breakfast in the trash can. I can always read one of Emil's books lined on his desk, but after scanning the covers, I realize I've read them all multiple times. So instead, I crawl back into bed and snuggle beneath the covers with the intention of playing games on Liam's phone all afternoon.

My lips curl into a smile as the lock screen lights up to the New Year's selfie of the two of us. Even while being alone, my cheeks flush as my finger traces an N pattern to unlock the phone, and the background image changes to one of me - lips parted and eyes closed in the bliss of sleep. I wouldn't call it the most attractive picture of me; but it's cute and endearing to know Liam was getting ready for bed one night, saw me sleeping, and thought the moment was worth capturing.

I flick through the list of apps and waste away the day switching between games, most of which are themed around cooking (and the occasional doodle game). When I get bored of assembling digital pizzas, I switch to cakes or cookies or even sushi. I swear Liam has every possible version of more or less the same game, but the apps keep my attention long enough for Liam to return.

Thankfully, he brings real food with him so we don't have to live on stolen instant noodles. He drops his armful of juice boxes and bagels on the spare desk with a sigh. Running a hand through his already disheveled hair as he straightens, he heaves another sigh. "So I've got good news and bad news. Which do you want to hear first?"

My gut tightens as I swallow a nonexistent lump in my throat. "The bad."

Liam dramatically sucks in a deep breath and exhales through his nose. "I failed. I didn't know a single fucking answer on the stupid tests."

A shaky breath of laughter eases the anxiety which tightened my muscles. "Oh, well I'm sure you didn't do as bad as you think."

He chuckles humorlessly at my words. "That would take a miracle, but let's forget about my failing future because I've got glorious news." After a pause for emphasis, he continues with a much more cheerful voice, "I know where we're gonna go."

"And where's that?"

Liam tosses a pair of juice boxes on the bed before climbing up beside me. "I'll tell you once I okay it with our temporary landlord."

The smug glint to his eyes makes me want to pester him to let me in on the secret, but before I can, he plucks his phone from my fingers. I'm polite enough to stay quiet while he dials Simon and asks for the weekend off (apparently he's going out of town for a family emergency). As soon as he hangs up, all politeness is tossed aside while I try to wring his almighty plan out of him.

Liam keeps his lips sealed tight. By Thursday morning, I feel he's staying quiet just to ruffle my feathers. Even after he finishes his last midterm early and we pack our few things, he refuses to tell - a self-satisfied smirk plastered to his lips the entire time.

Sitting in the passenger seat of the car, I fiddle with the radio, surfing through stations to find something to help distract me from the dizziness of other vehicles zigging and zagging across lanes on the freeway. I don't know how Liam manages to navigate through the barely controlled chaos, let alone focus when driving straight for so long. Liam chuckles when I settle on classical music, but doesn't change the station.

I lean back in my seat and stare straight ahead. My eyes search the lanes for something to focus on, but once we're out of the city limits, there's nothing but trees or rolling plains bordering the highway. The best I can do for a distraction is read the signs of cities and towns I don't recognize, constantly wondering if one of them is our final destination.

Liam's phone vibrates in the cup holder between us, and I reach for it. After reading the incoming text, the corners of my lips curl up. "Skyler wants to know where we're going."

"Oh does he?" Liam side-eyes me with obvious skepticism. "Or is this your sneaky way of tricking me into telling you?"

Now that I think about it, that would've been a great idea to try yesterday. Liam might've fallen for it then. "No, I'm serious. He actually wants to know. See?" I hold his phone out for him to take a quick glance at the screen.

He huffs upon seeing that, yes, Skyler truly wants to know and it's not me trying to trick him into telling me. "You're lucky I'm busy driving and love you enough not to text him back myself."

Aw, he loves me enough not to be stupid. That's precious.

"So where are we going?" I ask, fingers hovering over the screen to reply to Skyler.

Eyes staring straight ahead, Liam's smile slips from his lips as he worries his bottom lip between the bite of his teeth. "Can you promise you won't freak out?"

"Um, I'll try not to."

His fingers drum on the steering wheel as he looks everywhere but at me. "I may have told my grandma I'll be visiting for spring break, and I may have mentioned bringing along my boyfriend."

"Oh... Oh!" So I'll be... meeting the family, or one member of the family, but still! I won't be introduced as a friend, but a boyfriend. Oh god, what if she doesn't like me? What if I say something dumb and make a fool of myself? Because that is a completely plausible possibility. Is there going to be an awkward silence over dinner or worse, an interrogation of if I'm good enough for her grandson? Will she make Liam and me sleep in separate rooms? Or what if–

"Nico, you're freaking out."

I bristle at his voice and offer a quiet, "Am not."

"Yeah, you are. I can tell."

"...sorry. I can't help it," I say, slouching further into my seat. My eyes fall to the phone clutched in my lap as my fingers breeze over the screen to reply to Skyler. Once the message is sent, I drop the phone back into the cup holder.

Before my hand can return to my lap, Liam catches it with his and weaves his fingers between mine. Our connected hands settle between us as he says, "If it makes you feel any better, I'm anxious too. I've never exactly brought a date home to meet the family, not even in high school, so this'll be a first for me."

Simply knowing Liam's nervous too eases the thoughts in my head. It's a continuous reminder that I'm not in this alone, that he'll be beside me with support and assistance if I need him. A repetition of *I trust him* plays in my mind. That's all I have to remember when my thoughts start to go haywire, and those three words rein my thoughts back from the negative to the positive.

From the little Liam's told me about his grandmother, I'm sure I'm overreacting. She sounds like a sweet old lady; but if worse comes to worst, I hear she has a menagerie of animals I can play with.

Oh wait. I should probably focus more on thinking of a plan to evade imprisonment instead of freaking out over whether or not Liam's grandma will like me. But, hey, there's enough room in my head for me to stress over both.

Which is exactly what I do for the long car ride, or at least until Liam pulls off the highway at an exit for a town whose name I can't pronounce. Instead of heading in the pointed direction toward the relatively small town (compared to Sodalis at least), Liam turns the opposite way. Not long after that, he turns again to a gravel road, and we're surrounded by fields and farms and clear blue skies. Liam maneuvers the back roads from memory, and it leads me to believe he's closer to his grandmother than what he told me, especially since the further into the countryside we go, the less road signs we see. I'm almost positive whatever road we're on now doesn't have a name, and I haven't seen a residence in quite a while.

When we enter a small path into a dense forest, alarm bells sound in my head. "Uh, Liam." I've watched enough horror films with Skyler to know this is how dumb humans die after a masked killer emerges from the trees. "You do know where you're going, right?"

"Huh? Of course. We're almost there."

So Liam's grandma lives in prime serial killer territory. That's... nice, as long as the car doors are safely locked.

"This is her driveway. The house is right up ahead." Liam points to the end of the path where it opens up with the brilliance of the early evening sky.

I take it back. Liam's grandma lives in paradise.

She has her own personal meadow, the surrounding forest far less ominous once you see the white two-story farmhouse and the red barn straight out of a storybook with beds of blooming flowers and even a few apple trees overhanging a fenced pasture of horses. A few cows graze within the boundaries of the trees, and I'm pretty sure that's an... alpaca... or llama... in the same turnout. Chickens peck at the grass beside the house as a golden-colored dog wakes from its nap on the porch to bark at our car.

"Fuck," Liam murmurs as he parks behind a fancy-looking silver car.

"What's wrong?" I ask, completely perplexed by his distasteful grimace.

"That–" he nods toward the car in front of us "–is my mom's."

"We can always leave if that's–"

"No, it's fine," he turns off the car and pulls the key from the ignition. "They already know we're here anyway." Liam pockets the key before stepping out.

I follow after him, being greeted by a wagging tail and the weight of a 70-pound dog jumping on me. "Well, hi there," I chuckle as I ruffle the dog's golden fur.

"Kronos, down." The dog perks up at Liam's voice, bounding from me to him and jumping at Liam too. "That's rude, you know," Liam scolds, the laughter to his voice only exciting the dog more. "Yeah, hi hi. I missed you too," he coos as he strokes the dog's head.

"Kronos?" I ask with an arched brow, opening the car's door to retrieve our duffle bugs.

"Grandma's really into mythology."

"Don't act like you didn't name the dog." My head snaps at the new voice, spotting what has to be Liam's grandmother stepping down from the porch.

Only about an inch shorter than her grandson, the woman easily tosses her arm around Liam's neck and pulls him into her side. Her fingers card through the darker hue of his undercut - the same shade her short wisps of unkempt hair would be in her younger days before the gray set in - and brings his head closer to kiss his cheek. "It's good to see you, Liam," she beams, tawny eyes crinkling with youth that doesn't match her age.

"Granny, why didn't you tell me–"

With the same genial grin on her face, she doesn't let him finish before countering, "Would you have come if I did?"

Liam huffs, his bottom lip jutting out.

"That's what I thought," she says with a smug nod before turning her sights on me. "You must be the boyfriend."

"Uh, yeah. Nico. The boyfriend." I internally cringe as I shift my weight.

"It's a pleasure, Nico." She steps to my side and wraps me in a tight embrace - one I don't expect. With me frozen from a moment of shock, she releases me before I can return the gesture. Just as I recover from the hug, she surprises me again by taking the duffle bags from my arms and tossing them at Liam. "Why don't you and I go for a walk around the yard while Liam takes your things inside."

"O-okay," I stammer.

She heads off toward the apple trees, pausing momentarily to glance over her shoulder. "You coming?"

"Ah, y-yes, Ma'am." I stumble forward, barely catching myself before tripping.

Her smile never wavers as I stumble like a newborn fawn to her side. "You can call me Granny Mae."

Not wanting to embarrass myself further by opening my mouth, I nod.

As she leads the way across the grass, she casually calls over her shoulder to Liam, "She's in the kitchen." There's a quiet authority to her tone - one that says Liam better not join us until after he has a nice long chat with his mom.

Meanwhile, I'm left alone to fend for myself with his grandmother. Am I scared? A bit, yeah.

I'm sure Mae can sense my discomfort - anyone with functioning eyes could see that - but she simply smiles with a softness that reassures me. But then again, she smiled while ordering Liam around too. She's probably a badass who would slit someone's throat while smiling like an innocent angel.

"You ever been on a horse?" she asks as she heads to the turnout on the right side of the barn.

"Um, no. I've never actually been around them."

Mae hums at that - the sound a little raspy - before clicking her tongue a few times. All five horses - coats painted and spotted by nature - perk at the call, a few nickering in reply. Leaning against the white-washed fence, she extends her arm to the nearest horse and greets the animal with a scratch on its forehead.

Three of the other horses meander over to us as well. A spotted black one - its coat resembling a Dalmatian - nudges my arm with its muzzle. "Hi, um..." I trail off as I stroke its cheek.

"That's Apollo," Mae supplies for me. "You and him will be well acquainted over the next few days."

"Huh?" I squeak, turning wide eyes to her.

She doesn't miss a beat saying, "He's the one you're going to ride."

"B-but I can't ride."

"Nonsense," she waves off the notion with a flick of her wrist. "All my grandbabies learned to ride on him, and you'd be safer on him than on Ares - Mr. Antisocial himself." She nods toward the only horse not vying for our attention - a chestnut with a single white sock on its left hind leg which grazes on the far side of the turnout. "I guess if you really want to, you could try him; but Liam would probably fight you for him."

"Is he Liam's horse?" Of course, Liam's favorite is the least social one of all.

"He might as well be. The only people he ever behaves for are Liam and my late husband. I wouldn't feel comfortable letting anyone else ride him."

"I think I'll stick to Apollo then." My hand smooths over the spots on Apollo's forehead, fingers combing through its white forelock.

"Ah, good," she chuckles, pushing off the fence to continue our little tour of the yard. "I'd hate to have the first boy Liam's ever brought home get hurt by one of my horses."

Hearing it again - Liam's first - has my cheeks flushing as I rub at the nape of my neck. As we walk around the back of the house - Mae showing me the small pond for her ducks and the substantial garden she tends to - my nerves slowly fade away. She welcomes me and treats me as a member of the family, and it warms me from the inside out. Judging by the light lilt to her voice and the twinkle to her tawny eyes as she introduces me to her family of pets and plants, I believe Liam bringing me here is a truly special occasion for Granny Mae. It leaves no doubt in my mind that Liam is her pride and joy. If nothing else, at least we have that in common.

FORMAL INVITATION

Okay, Liam, you can do this. How hard is it to say "Hi, Mom. How's it going"? No, no, no that's wrong. I can't possibly do that. I should apologize... right? Or am I the one receiving an apology?

I shake the thought from my head as I climb the porch steps. I'm not the one who needs an apology, at least not from my mother. She's not the reason for my anger or my pain. She hasn't hurt me to the point of betrayal. She's not my brother or my father, and I can't treat her like she is.

But isn't that exactly what I've been doing? My hand hovers over the doorknob, freezing with the sudden onslaught of guilt. How long have I been ignoring her phone calls and texts with the premise of protecting myself when in reality I'm simply a jackass? A damn long time - too fucking long. I know being an asshole is kinda my thing and my skills include running away from my problems, but isn't this a little too much? I should be old enough to know how all this will end if I keep ignoring it; and I'd rather not force Nico to sleep on the bedroom floor because I threw a tantrum and couldn't make it to the bed. There's no doubt in my mind that he would, but that's not a scenario I want to become reality.

Two words - I'm sorry - that's all I have to say. How hard can that be?

As they curl around the doorknob, the trembling of my fingers answers my own question. I can do this. I can do this. I have to do this.

Pushing in the door, I step inside to a calming comfort that can only be described as the warmth of grandma's house - a childhood nostalgia of a house that hasn't changed in years. Before the door fully closes behind me, I'm greeted by an oversized pork chop headbutting my legs. It was cute when he was a piglet, not so much now that he's a pot-bellied battering ram.

"Cut it out, Bacon," I say far too loudly in the quiet atmosphere and cringe at my own volume. If Mom didn't know I was here, she definitely

258

knows now.

The black and white spotted pork chop ever so rudely forces himself between my legs for the shortest path to the door. He nudges his snout against the door before pointedly staring back at me.

"Rude little bastard," I mumble, reaching to scratch the coarse hair on the pig's head. "Go find Nico. He's gonna lose his shit when he sees you." Especially after Granny tells him she let me name a piglet Bacon because I wanted to fry him up and eat him. Obviously, that never happened; but, hey, the pig's got plenty of years left for me to heat a skillet over the stove.

The pork chop doesn't wait for me to yank the door all the way open. Instead, he forces himself through a space far too small and squeals like a wild hog caught in a snare trap when it takes a moment too long for me to wedge the door open far enough. He scurries down the porch steps and across the yard like I personally scandalized his virtue.

And, yeah, my cover has definitely been blown. Unless my mother has somehow lost a significant amount of her hearing since I've last seen her, but that's unlikely.

I guess I can't dawdle in the doorway anymore, but you bet your ass I take my sweet time slipping off my shoes and meticulously lining them beside the rest. Each of my steps further into the house is unreasonably slow, and I stop altogether when the short entryway opens up to a dining room and kitchen ahead of me and the living room to my right.

Spotting the slender frame of my mother across the room, my eyes lock on her back and don't wander even as I slowly bend to place the duffle bags on the floor - my movements so calculated and precise you'd think I'm trying to avoid laser tripwires. While padding around the dining table, I manage to stub my toe on a chair and knock it over with an echoing clatter.

"God-fucking-dam—"

"Language, Liam."

My jaw snaps shut at the motherly scolding, and I completely forget the throbbing of my pinky toe. Warily glancing at my mom, I huff a breath to find her back still to me.

Which means she's mad... or maybe hurt would be more accurate. A mixture of the two? Probably.

After righting the chair, I slink closer to my mom, stopping at the little island countertop to slide atop a stool. Not gonna lie, it's weird seeing my mother in such a domestic setting - a perfectly pressed blouse and dress pants exchanged for a wrinkled flannel shirt, frayed jeans, and an apron discolored from decades of use. She tends to a couple pots on the stove with practiced ease all the while measuring ingredients for another course into a mixing bowl. When I lived at home during high school, I never saw her so much as step foot in our kitchen of stainless steel and white marble; but she looks completely in her element surrounded by scratched wooden countertops and appliances that haven't been changed since before I was born.

I can sit here and watch her for hours - the flicks of her wrist, the scraping of excess flour from the measuring cup, the small twitch of her lips when she fully focuses on the meal in front of her. My presence is completely irrelevant, but that doesn't bother me. Because I get it. I understand how easy it is to forget the world when in the sanctuary of a kitchen.

Which is why it physically pains me to disturb the peace (yeah, it has nothing to do with me wanting to run away from my problems... again).

"I– I didn't know you liked cooking." Well, that's not an apology.

Without missing a beat, my mom says, "We used to cook together all the time when you were younger."

Sure, when I was like eight, but I guess she's technically right. Way to hit where it hurts, but whatever. I deserve a little resentment for acting like I'm not her son. Can't really blame her for not wanting to look at me after these last few months. I wouldn't want to look at a spitting image of the man who betrayed her either, even more so when knowing I abandoned her to deal with all the bullshit herself.

"She didn't tell me you were coming."

"Me either," I murmur.

"That old woman's as cunning and conniving as ever."

"...yeah."

More silence. You'd think after so long, we'd have more to say to each other. No wait. I do have more to say. An apology actually. The sooner I apologize, the sooner I can see the brilliant smile of my boyfriend as Granny introduces him to the resident pets.

Oh fuck. Nico. Mom doesn't know I have a boyfriend, that I'm in a serious relationship, not like the guys and girls I was with in high school.

Okay, I can do this. Apologize - two simple words - and then I can tell her I'm okay - I'm really fucking happy with Nico - and ask her how she's been and everything will be okay.

"Mom... I..." I swallow the lump in my throat as she stills at my words. "I'm sorry for... everything."

For everything? Really, Liam. Way to take the coward's way out. Can't even tell my own mother what I'm sorry for, how pathetic is that? It's not for everything. It's for ignoring her calls, never coming home to visit, forgetting she's not the same as my father, and abandoning her under the pretext of protecting myself.

Let's try this one more time.

"Mom, I–"

The words catch in my throat as I glance up to meet her eyes - shiny from the threat of tears yet to fall. Forgetting the meal, she rounds the island. All I can do it watch as her hands reach for my cheeks, settling upon my skin with the same warmth they've always had. Her thumbs against my cheekbones, she tips my head forward to kiss my forehead. When she pulls back - the corners of her eyes crinkling with endearment - she doesn't release my face.

"Honey, children don't need to apologize for their parents' mistakes."

Her words don't match the tears forming in her eyes or the gratitude in her voice. She needed an apology (even if it was a piss-poor one), and I think she knows that. Maybe she didn't want an apology from me, but from someone - anyone - because we both know my douchebag of a father hasn't uttered a single word of remorse in his entire life.

"So... we good?"

With a breathy laugh, she nods. "Yes, we're good." She pecks my forehead once more, beaming with the broadest smile I've ever seen on her delicate features as I swat her away in protest. Just like old times.

"So~" she draws out the word as she returns to the other side of the kitchen island. "Granny didn't tell me you were coming, but she said we're having two visitors. Is there something you'd like to tell me? Something like - I don't know - a future in-law maybe?"

I choke on my own breath, nearly falling from the stool in a fit of coughing. "I– You– Uh..."

"What's their name?"

Oh dear god, Mom's enjoying this way too much. The knowing smile is evident in her smug tone, and I don't think I prepared well enough for this. I didn't prepare enough for an apology, let alone Nico. Damn Granny! She could've given me a little warning.

"It's uh... um..."

"Did you forget it?"

"Nico!" I blurt out and immediately hide my face in my hands. "It's Nico."

"Hmm. That's a nice name. Is he cute?"

Peeking through the slits of my fingers, I'm met with tawny eyes and a quirk of amused lips. And you know what. Fuck it. My hands drop to the countertop, and I lean forward on my elbows. With the biggest shit-eating grin, I lock gazes with my mom.

"He's fucking adorable."

Her brow furrows at my vulgarity. "Do you kiss him with that dirty mouth of yours?"

"I sure do."

With a click of her tongue, she shakes her head. "You really should clean up that language of yours. It's unsettling."

I shrug. "Maybe you should try saying fuck every now and then. It's great stress relief."

"Oh, is it?"

"Why don't you find out for yourself?"

"I think I'll pass." She turns down the heat on what smells like a stew before spinning back to me. Coming to stand on the side of the island, she leans against the counter. "So," she cracks a smile, "how did you and Nico meet?"

"Well," I chuckle, "he slept on my couch one night and never left."

"You do realize how odd that sounds without any context, correct?"

"He's a buddy of Skyler's and you know him. He can't say no to a friend in need, so long story short, Nico ended up moving in."

"So you live together?"

"Yep."

"I see. You two are being... safe, right?"

"Oh my god, Mom, stop." I feel my cheeks heating up involuntarily. "I know how condoms work. We don't need to go over this."

"Sorry, sorry," she placates. "Mothers worry, you know. It's our job."

"You know what else is your job?"

She purses her lips and peers at me - somehow managing to seem both curious and threatening at the same time, as if a stupid remark will be rewarded with a slap upside the head. "No, why don't you tell me?" Her voice is so calm and smooth, daring me to say something idiotic.

"To make sure our food isn't burning."

It takes a moment for my words to sink in before her senses catch up. Her eyes widen when she catches a whiff of the bitter burnt smell coming from the oven. "Oh, shoot!"

She's got the oven door open and a mitt on a second later. "Liam, open a window," she pulls a tray of what were dinner rolls from the oven. They look more like hockey pucks now.

"This is a great time for stress relief swearing." I hop to my feet to yank the dining room windows open.

"It's not going to happen," my mom grumbles as she dumps the tray over the wastebasket. Huffing a deflated sigh, she drops the pan in the sink with an echoing clatter. "So burnt even Bacon wouldn't eat them."

Rounding the island, I brush past Mom to push open the window above the sink. After retrieving the abandoned sheet tray, I set it on the island countertop. "Second times the charm."

"Don't you mean third?"

"Not when you've got a genius baker for a son."

"Oh?" she hums and hands me a measuring spoon. "You think you can do better than your mother?"

"You didn't exactly set the bar very high."

Her mouth opens to retort but quickly closes again to purse her lips. "I can't argue with you there."

As my hands move from memory, the only thing that keeps them from trembling is knowing I can't do much worse than a burnt hockey puck. All I have to do is take them out of the oven when they're golden brown and wa-lah, I prove myself to be a genius baker. Easy, right?

Except it's like I'm a teenager all over again who'd go out of my way to avoid being in the kitchen with others. Nights of waiting for everyone else to go to bed so I could make a batch of cookies, counting down the minutes until my parents got off work and crossing my fingers for the casserole to be done in time, blasting my MP3 so loud I don't hear the snarky comments from my brother - it all comes back to me like I'm a little kid again.

"So, uh..." I glance over my shoulder, spotting my mother doing the same at the sound of my voice. "How have you been?"

After a deep inhale of breath, she releases it in a drawn-out sigh. "You don't need to worry about me, Sweetie. I'm okay."

My eyes turn back to the ingredients in front of me. "Mom, you can tell me what's going on."

"I just don't want you to–"

"I'm gonna worry more if you don't tell me."

A short moment of nothing but the clanks of utensils and our quiet breathing passes before she deflates with a sigh. "Liam, there's nothing I can tell you that you don't already know. Our accounts are still frozen, assets are seized, Bryce is trying to salvage what's left of the company, and your father is undoubtedly going to jail where he belongs. I'm sorry, but there's no home for us to go back to anymore."

"It's okay, Mom. I already have a home."

"Oh, Honey." I can hear the smile in her voice. "Are you going to say something sappy about Nico being your home?"

My fingers freeze momentarily - for a single breath of air - before diving right back into the forming dough.

"Bingo, huh?" she quietly laughs. "Good. That's the kind of relationship you should be in. Cherish it and never let it go."

That's what I'm trying to do. It's why I'm here - to hold onto our future and protect it.

"I can't wait to meet him. He must be something special to have my prickly little boy head over heels."

"Prickly? Who, me? I'm a fucking teddy bear."

"I'll believe it when I see it."

"No, it's true." My head whips up at the familiar voice, lips twitching into a grin when I spot a mirrored smile upon starry cheeks. "He takes me on bookstore and playground dates. I'm Nico, by the way," he adds a little sheepishly.

Eyes landing upon Nico and Granny in the entryway, Mom tilts her head as she peers at my Sprinkles. Nico's smile wavers under my mom's scrutinizing gaze, but he manages to hold eye contact with minimum fidgeting.

Nudging me with her elbow, my mother finally releases Nico from her appraisal. "You're right, Liam. He's downright adorable."

"Eh?" Nico squeaks, his face flushing.

"I believe I said fucking adorable."

"Liam," Nico whines.

Seeing his bright cheeks and his lips fighting to stay neutral and not upturn into a bashful smile, I smirk.

"Ah, leave the poor boy alone," Granny scolds Mom and me. She pats Nico's back and effectively pushes him further into the house. "Or at least introduce yourself before embarrassing him."

"Oh, I'm sorry," Mom says, wiping her hands on her apron. "It's a pleasure to meet you, Nico. I'm Annette, Liam's mom; but you can call me Anne."

Shyly, Nico smiles and nods in acknowledgement. "It's my pleasure as well," he says quietly.

"Good." Granny claps her hands together, and the noise startles my poor boyfriend. "Now that we all know each other, why don't you two get settled in before dinner. Anne and I will finish up here."

"Just don't leave Mom in charge of the rolls," I say as I wash off the dough that sticks to my fingers.

"Did she burn them again?"

I arch a brow and side-eye my mom. "Again?"

"Oh, just go!" she huffs and ushers me out of the kitchen.

I put up little resistance, especially when honey eyes peer at me from behind long lashes. "Okay, Sprinkles, I'm gonna give you the grand tour. Follow me." With one hand, I grab the straps of our duffle bags, and the other finds Nico's fingers to give him a reassuring squeeze.

I show him the rest of the first floor - a bathroom and craft room off the left wall of the living room with the door to the staircase in between them, Granny's bedroom off the far wall, and a sliding door to the front porch in the far right corner.

Once we head up the staircase with the door shut behind us, Nico breaths a quiet sigh. "Meeting family is rough."

"Yeah, sorry 'bout that." I definitely don't envy Nico, especially since he had even less of a warning than I did. My poor Sprinkles, I'll be sure to give him extra cuddles later.

"What did you tell your mom about me?"

"Just that you're fucking adorable and I love you."

As I round the top of the landing, Nico tugs me to a standstill. Before I can fully turn to face him, he ducks closer to press soft lips upon my cheek.

"Me too," he whispers, breath hot against my skin. "I love you, too."

"How you doing back there?" I twist in the saddle to peer over my shoulder. My lips twitch into a smile at the sight of Nico sitting atop a horse that has as many spots as he does.

His wandering gaze leaves the expanse of the quiet forest surrounding us to lock with mine. The few rays of light that shine down through tiny gaps in the leaves draws pictures upon the freckles of his cheeks. "I think I'm getting used to this whole riding thing," he says, eyes flicking to Apollo's ears as he scratches the horse's neck. "Where are we going anyway?"

"On a picnic."

"I know that. But where?"

"Somewhere we can brainstorm without having to worry about being overheard. I figured we could call Skyler and see if he or Emil thought of anything too." After all, that's kinda the whole reason we're here (although a relaxing week of horseback riding and stargazing is a huge plus).

A gentle breeze rustles the leaves, and the sound is comforting to everyone but the little shit of a horse beneath me. Ares jolts forward when a branch brushes his rump, and he hops a few steps before settling down. A quick peek over my shoulder and I breathe a sigh of relief that Apollo behaves and takes care of my inexperienced boyfriend.

Bending over Ares' neck, I whisper, "Go ahead. Act like you've never seen a leaf before. I'll take every opportunity to impress Nico, so do your worst."

As if on cue, the chestnut gelding tosses his head and tries to run through his bit. It takes a firm grip on the reins and a tight circle turn to keep him from bolting down the forest trail.

"Are you okay?" Nico worries from behind me.

"Yep. Doing great." Impress Nico with my mad horse skills - check. I'd scratch Ares's neck if it didn't reinforce the bad behavior. Maybe I'll give him an extra treat as a reward when we get back. Then he won't know it's for helping me impress my Sprinkles.

Another fifteen minutes of fancy footwork on Ares' part pass before I can hear the babble of the creek. Reining Ares to a standstill, I swing from the saddle.

"Are we there?" Nico follows suit. As both feet hit the forest floor, he does a little wiggle of his hips and a sashay of his legs.

Dear god, if that isn't the cutest fucking thing I've seen!

"Is it normal to not be able to feel my legs?"

"Yeah. You'll get used to it after a while." I rub some of the ache out of my thighs as I swap Ares' bridle for a halter and lead rope. After loosely tying it around a tree trunk, I loosen the saddle's cinch and retrieve the bag with our lunch in it from the saddle horn.

Nico watches my movements and mirrors them, leaving Apollo comfortably tied at the trail's edge to follow me through the unmarked brush. We stop when a small creek crosses our path. Even though the clear water is barely shin-deep, we stay on our side of the forest (mainly because of the fallen log that makes for a perfect perch).

"So what do you think?" I ask as I sit upon the log.

Despite the beauty of nature all around me, my eyes are drawn to Nico. He stares out into the trees, soaking in each branch and twig with awe-inspired eyes. His gaze turns to the sky - the soft blue of a clear spring day peeking through the cover of browns and greens. At the sound of a chirping bird, honey eyes dart to find its source; but he's quickly distracted by clovers and ferns and tiny white wildflowers at the base of a tree trunk.

Still not taking his eyes off the tiny flower petals, he asks a little breathlessly, "Can we stay here forever?"

I quietly chuckle. "I'd rather not live with my mom and grandma, but we can come back and visit."

"I'd love that," he sighs and finally comes to sit beside me. "That's if I'm still here."

"You will be." But he's not looking at me. He's staring at his hands in his lap. "Hey." I touch his cheek and wait until his eyes meet mine. "I won't let you go."

"But what are we going to do? Keep running for the rest of our lives?"

His voice is so small and quiet it physically breaks my heart to hear it. If it's the last thing I do, I will protect this man with everything I've got.

"No," I shake my head and dig for my phone in my pant pocket. "Me, Skyler, Emil... we'll think of something. Hell, they've probably got this all figured out already." My exaggerated cheerfulness fools no one, because the words are heavy in my throat. It takes every ounce of concentration to choke them out and to forget the far greater possibility that Nico may be taken from me and he'll slip through my fingers and I won't be able to hold his hand any longer.

But I can't say that. I can't feed into his anxieties and send him into a full-blown panic. Holding back the tears at the mere thought of losing my Sprinkles is all I can do right now. I need to squash his doubts with overwhelming positivity, but I'm not exactly a glass half full kinda guy.

So I scroll through my contacts list to call in the reinforcements via *FaceTime*.

Skyler answers a single breath later with Emil leaning against him to fit on the screen. Skyler's smile is soft and warm, but his hair is unnaturally mussed - in the same disarray of raking his fingers through the strands in an attempt to think rationally and calmly that is often associated with group projects and procrastinated essays. "Are you guys oka– Whoa! Where the hell are you?"

"I told you. We're at my grandma's."

"You get service in the middle of the goddamn woods! I can't even get it in the fucking bathroom!"

Some of the tension fades from my shoulders with my next exhale of breath, and my lips upturn into my usual smug smirk. "Why don't you call the service provider and complain?"

"You know what," Skyler looks at me in all seriousness, "I'm gonna do just that! Give 'em a piece of my mind!" He shakes his fist in the air, and the image of him and Emil wobbles a bit until Emil takes the phone from him. But he continues to whine, "It's not fair. You get to show off your romantic forest adventures, but I can't even text while taking a poop."

"Please don't ever use the words romantic and poop in the same sentence ever again," I say.

"Would you prefer shit?"

"Actually, yes, I wou– No, wait." I shake my head. "This isn't what we wanted to talk about."

Emil peeps up, "Are you two okay?"

Nico nods. "What about you guys?"

Skyler grabs the phone back from Emil and holds it unreasonably close to his face. "We had a pizza delivered here for a Mr. Nico Moore, and Emil here thought the delivery girl was a demon; but nothing too out of the ordinary happened."

It says a hell of a lot about Skyler that he considers a demon delivering pizza to be completely within the realms of ordinary. If Nico's future wasn't on the line, I'd laugh my ass off.

"A girl?" Nico asks, leaning closer into my side to see the screen better. "What'd she look like? Medium height. Light brown hair, kinda wavy, to about here." He holds his hand up horizontal to his chin to measure.

"Yep. That was her. She brought pretty good pizza."

"You ate it!" Who in their right mind would eat pizza from a demon?

"It was free," Skyler defends himself with a shrug.

Okay, maybe he has a point, but still!

With a roll of my eyes, I dismiss the turn this conversation has taken. "Forget the pizza. Have you thought of any possible solutions to our current predicament?"

"Well," Skyler crookedly smiles, "while you two lovebirds have been having the time of your youthful lives, I put a great deal of thought into a solution–"

"Liam, we think you should formally summon Nico, like with a ceremony or ritual," Emil thankfully interjects Skyler's long ass monologue.

I look to Nico, and he stares back at me with mirrored amazement at how simple of a solution that is. It was right in front of us the entire time, but we completely overlooked it.

"Have you ever been summoned before?" I ask.

Nico shakes his head. "I don't even know how we would go about it," he says quietly, eyes downcast and hand reaching to scratch at the nape of his neck.

Something's wrong. I get the feeling he's not telling me something.

I turn back to Skyler and Emil, both of them glancing toward Nico as well. "Looks like we have some research to do. We'll get back to you, so why don't you take the time to call up your service provider and complain, yeah?"

Skyler takes the hint. "They're gonna get a fucking earful."

"Yeah, yeah, bye." I end the call without waiting for a reply and quickly pocket my phone.

"Nico," I say, twisting on the log to perch pretzel-legged atop it. "Is summoning... not an option?"

Wringing his fingers in his lap, he shakes his head. "No, it's not that. It's just..." he trails off.

I remain silent and patiently wait for him to go on. When he doesn't, I simply reach for the abandoned saddlebag propped against the log and dig out two juice pouches and a bag of slightly squished *Doritos*. Nico accepts his juice pouch and meticulously stabs the straw into it. After that, he simply holds it in his lap without taking a single sip.

But I don't push him. I take a long drag from my juice pouch and rip open the chips. Munching on cheesy goodness in silence isn't exactly what I had in mind for our picnic, but I think figuring out the Nico's-a-demon-fugitive thing is more important than my idea of the perfect picnic date.

Half the bag of *Doritos* is gone before Nico finally moves again. He tips his head forward and brings his juice pouch up to his lips to take a short sip before letting his hand fall back to his lap.

"I'm scared, Liam," his voice breaks on my name.

"Ni–"

"I'm scared," he repeats. "Summoning... it takes away a demon's freedom. We have to obey the contractor no matter what they ask of us, and that scares me."

Freedom. I've never given it much thought, but Nico, he fled from his world to gain the freedom to live life on his own terms. To give that up after fighting so hard to get it, even I'd be scared.

Hell, I am scared. I don't want to lose him, but I also don't want to steal his free will. I didn't fall in love with a robotic puppet who obeys every command given to it. I fell in love with Nico and his sassy side comments and his overactive imagination (yeah, he told me about serial killer territory), and his unconditional support and his puppy dog eyes and his gentle kindness and I could go on forever. I want my Sprinkles - the man who had the courage to kiss me and show me how cute he is with a blush to his speckled cheeks and fangs peeking between soft lips. I want the man who took care of me when I was a broken mess of shattered pieces and the man who let me put myself back together at my own pace. I want the one person who loves me as much as I love him.

I reach for his hand and drape my fingers over his. "I won't take your freedom. I'll always, always, ask for your permission no matter what it is. I'll give you a chance to say no. Always, no matter how insignificant it may seem. Instead of *Come help me do dishes*, I'll ask *Do you want to help with dishes.*" I swallow the lump in my throat and bat my eyes against forming tears. "And... and if someday... you decide I'm not who you want to be with, I won't force you to stay. You can go wherever and do whatever you want. I'll be happy just knowing you're safe."

His hand turns beneath mine - palm to palm - and our fingers interlock. He twists to angle closer to me and reaches with his opposite hand to wipe a stray tear off my cheek. Even while smiling, his lips quiver as his own honey eyes water. "Okay," he sniffles. "But I want to make something clear. I love you, and that's not going to change any time in the future."

I love him. I love him so fucking much! What did I ever do to deserve this glorious man's love? I have no idea, but my god, I am so fucking grateful to call him my boyfriend!

"Goddammit, Sprinkles, you're making me cry," I say through a smile and a voice thick with emotion.

"Me too," he breathes, leaning closer to brush his lips against mine. He pulls back to leave barely a hairsbreadth of space between our lips - the tip of his nose touching mine. His eyes fall shut as he drops his head to my shoulder and nuzzles into my neck. "Can we stay like this for a while?"

"Yeah," I wrap my arms around his back, one of my hands resting at his nape to scratch through his hair. "We're not expected back till dinner."

Warm breath tickles my neck as he hums. His fingers curl into the back of my shirt, and we stay like that, simply holding onto each other and the fleeting moments before we put this possible solution to the test. And maybe this is the perfect way to spend a picnic - surrounded by the beauty of nature and in the arms of the one I love. So I'm in no hurry to head back to the house.

"Uh, this site doesn't seem very reliable," Nico says, absentmindedly petting the tiny black kitten curled up on his belly.

Lying on our backs in a bed plenty big to comfortably fit the two of us, we google how to summon a demon on my phone. As I hold my phone above my head and scroll through the obnoxious red text, I soon come to the same conclusion. "Yeah, I'd rather not have to petition Satan."

So I backtrack to the google search results and click on the next link to skim over the text. "I'm guessing you don't want me using human blood to paint a 6-pointed star," I say, tipping the screen to let Nico read as well.

Even with the only light being the dull illumination of the phone screen, I see Nico scrunch his nose. "Please don't do that." He glances further down the paragraph and gasps in horror. "We're not using animal organs or live human sacrifice."

I purse my lips when I read the same passage he did and immediately switch to a different site. "*In order to summon a demon, all you really need to do is put out an open invitation,*" I read aloud. "Well that sounds easy."

"But it also says summoning a demon is a bad, bad idea," Nico quotes.

"Every site said that."

Nico sighs and turns onto his side, facing me and cradling the orphaned kitten to his chest. "Maybe every site is right. Maybe it is a bad idea."

Turning to face him as well, I set my phone on the pillow. My eyes turn to the tiny ball of fur between us, watching its back rise and fall with each breath. Poor thing. A neighbor dropped it off while we were on our picnic and said its mother abandoned it. He brought it here knowing my grandma takes in and rehabilitates sick and unwanted pets in hopes of finding them a better home. Some, like the potbellied Bacon, grow on Granny to the point of becoming permanent residents, but what about this tiny black kitten? It doesn't even have a name yet.

"It probably would be a bad idea, you know, if I was summoning some random demon," I say, gently stroking the soft fur of the kitten's head. "But I'm not. I'm summoning you - my boyfriend."

"Doesn't human sacrifice sound like a bad idea?" he counters.

"Of course," I quietly chuckle, "but this site says nothing about sacrifices. Why don't we give this one a shot? The worst that'll happen is it won't work."

Nico contemplates it for a minute before huffing, "Fine. But no blood or organs or anything like that."

"Aye, aye, Captain Sprinkles," I salute, and he finally cracks a smile.

Retrieving my phone, I continue reading. *Demons have rules...* yada yada. Already know that. *The stronger the intent, the easier it is to summon.* Well, that's good. I don't think my intent and connection to Nico could be any greater. A formal welcome - that's where the summoning "spells" come in. They can be custom-written, thank the heavens, because there's not a book of ancient scripture lying around to reference from. Uh oh...

"Do you speak Latin?"

"Um... no."

Primary language my ass.

You must invite the demon in, but then you must send the demon home (with your words and intentions) before closing the connection to the other side. This is very important. The ceremony must be done properly. Remember how I said that demons have rules? Well, one of those rules is that if you close the gateway between worlds and you haven't asked the demon to leave - guess what - you got yourself a demon.

Yes! Good! That's exactly what I want.

I finish reading the article, completely skipping over the section of sending the demon home. "Okay, this actually sounds quite simple. All I need to do is formally invite you here with a spell that I can write myself. No special symbols or candles or sacrifices needed. Just a strong connection to you, and I already have that. So I just have to write a formal invitation spell and wa-lah! We're done and you're no longer an outlaw."

"Are you sure you want to do this? It might not even work."

"It will work; and if it doesn't, I will try again." I wiggle closer to him - careful of the slumbering kitten cradled between us like a baby - and press my lips to his forehead, a few strands of his hair tickling my cheek. "I'm a million percent sure I want to do this, and I'm gonna stay up all night if I have to to write the perfect invitation that can't possibly fail. And then tomorrow morning, we're going back to the creek, and I'm gonna summon you, and we're gonna live happily ever after. If that's okay with you, of course."

His answer comes as a quick nod and his lips pressed tenderly to the side of my neck.

"It's a date then," I smile, settling back into the pillow.

Nico falls asleep not long after I turn the brightness of my phone as low as it will go. The kitten even wakes and crawls further up the bed to snuggle right in the crook of Nico's neck. What I wouldn't give to be that kitten right now, but I've got some writing to do and it has to be perfect.

My eyes crack open at the incessant light streaming in from the window. With a groan, I peek at the clock on the nightstand. 8:04 a.m. Too fucking early for someone who was up till 4 a.m. I blindly pat the mattress beside me in search of the fleshy warmth of my Sprinkles to cuddle up to, but he's not there.

Pushing myself up, I rub the crust from my eyes and blink at my surroundings. Soft pink wallpaper with a gazillion flowers in its design greets me good morning. Glancing around the room, there's no Nico or nameless kitten. On any normal occasional, I'd drop my head back to the pillow and burrow beneath the blanket till well past noon, but today's special. Today, I safeguard my future with Nico.

So despite my mild sleep deprivation, I roll out of bed and change into a pair of jeans and a light sweater. I push up my sleeves and head down to the main floor. Before I even enter the kitchen, I hear three different voices going *Awww!*

With a yawn, I step into the kitchen and take a seat at the only free stool at the island - Nico to my right, my mom next to him, and Granny standing next to the stove tending to blueberry pancakes. Sitting on the counter, the tiny black kitten dips its face into a saucer of warm milk, still unsure of how to drink properly.

"Right on time," Granny says, pointing a spatula at me. "I was about to send Nico up to get you."

"Mhmm." I don't have enough energy to reply with actual words.

But Granny doesn't mind. She's actually a huge help when she sets a mug of steaming hot coffee in front of me. "Nico tells us you two plan on going on a morning trail ride."

The coffee scalds my throat on the way down, but it does its job of waking me up. "Yep. That's the plan."

"When do you plan on being back?" she asks, setting the first stack of pancakes and three plates on the counter to be divvied up.

"Probably around noon. Why?"

"Anne and I are going to head into town to do some shopping this afternoon, and I don't want to leave little Cupcake here all alone. She seems to have taken a liking to Nico, so I was hoping you two could keep an eye on her."

I pause in cutting a piece of pancake to glance at the kitten still trying to swim in the milk. "Cupcake?" That's not mythology related.

Nico jumps at a playful elbow nudge from my mother. "Nico named her."

"Oh, did he now?" My lips quirk into an amused smile as I stuff a syrupy bite of pancake into my mouth.

With cheeks tinted pink, Nico says, "I think it's cute."

"It is, Sweetie," my mom pats Nico's arm.

What I find cute (other than Nico naming the kitten Cupcake) is how familiar my mom and grandma are with Nico. I mean, *Sweetie*. My mom's never called a significant other (not even any of Bryce's girlfriends) so fondly. Yet, it's only taken two days for Nico to fit right in. That acceptance only makes me ache for Nico even more as the words from my formal invitation spell echo in my mind.

As soon as we finish breakfast and help clean up, Nico and I are out the door and tacking up Ares and Apollo. It takes every ounce of control I possess not to race down the forest trail at a full gallop, having enough common sense to know Apollo can't match Ares' pace and Ares would most likely get too frisky and buck me off. Even at a brisk trot, the pace feels far too slow, but a glance over my shoulder tells me it's about as fast as Nico's inexperience can handle.

My impatience with the passing of time is eased only by repeating the same words over and over again in my head. The spell to release Nico from a life as a fugitive - in my own words - echoes in my mind as if I shouted it from a mountaintop. Each sentence, each word, every single syllable - I remember it all like one remembers their name, as if the words have always been a part of me.

While focusing only on the words that will forever connect Nico and me, time passes without me even realizing. We slow our horses and leave them tied in the same spot we did yesterday before trekking to the babbling creek.

"How are we going to do this?" Nico asks, glancing around as if a magical portal to Hell will open any second.

But the ceremony doesn't require any physical magic. There's no drawing of circles or stars, lighting of incense, or sacrifice of any kind of living being. The entire ritual depends on my state of mine, my ability to focus, and the proper wording of the invitation.

But no pressure, right?

I wave Nico to me so we're facing each other and slip my hands into his. With a squeeze of my fingers, I lose myself in the liquid honey of his irises. "All you have to do is focus your mind on me - only me - and listen to my invitation. I'll take care of everything else, okay?"

Holding my gaze, he slowly nods. Lips slightly parted, his chest expands with an inhale of the crisp forest air that he exhales through his nose. Despite the tiny tremors of his fingers, his grip doesn't falter as his thumbs rub over my knuckles. He stares back at me - seeing straight into my soul to leave me mesmerized in the galaxy of his eyes.

I suck in a breath, feeling the air circulate through my system before slowly releasing it. "You ready?" I softly ask.

"Yeah," he responds just as softly.

Okay, nothing but Nico. Only Nico. My Sprinkles. His true demon form - pearly white fangs, curved horns protruding from his temple, flared wings like a bat, and a silky black tail with its ticklish tuft of fur. The smooth lilt of his voice. The deftness of his fingers. Contoured abdominals that are still soft enough to make the perfect pillow. Arms with the strength to embrace gently and bring a feeling of safety to even the most dangerous of situations. Thighs, oh god his thighs - thick and fleshy and perfect. Every date we've been on - the storytelling of *The Hungry, Hungry Caterpillar*, the swing set in the park, the snow angels in the car lot, *Disney* marathons in a blanket burrito, homemade meals eaten at a cluttered dining table.

The words written in the dark of night return to me so easily, even without opening the notepad app on my phone.

"I, Liam Holt, call upon the demon Nico Moore. I ask of you to lend an open ear to my request. I invite you to share in my world and to be a part of my future. You are welcome in my home, and I wish for my home to be your home as well. I invite you to be a part of my family. In exchange for your willingness to leave your world and enter mine, I give to you my love, my heart, myself. I am yours for as long as you'll want me. Nico Moore, I wish for you to be able to call my world your home. That is my only request."

Holding my breath, I wait. I'm not sure for what. For anything, I guess. Like some sort of pillar of light or, hell, even a fucking 6-pointed star appearing in the dirt and grass. Fucking fairy dust, I don't care. Anything to tell me whether it worked or not. Anyth–

"Ni...co."

The warmth of his hands in mine has turned icy cold as my fingers hold onto nothing but air. His galaxy of stars upon his cheeks and rays of the sun in his eyes left me to stare at tree bark and branches. The imprints of his sneakers in the grass prove he stood before me, but now they're like after images of a ghost. He's gone. Disappeared right before me in the blink of an eye, not slow enough for me to grab his wrist and anchor him to this world.

Nico, what did I do wrong? Did I send you right into the arms of your captors? Oh god, I'm so sorry. Please come back. We can try again, try something else. Maybe we really did need a sacrifice or candles or ancient scripture. I'll learn Latin for you, Nico. I'll light candles and burn this forest down. I'll go rob a grave for sacrificial bones, so just come back to me.

"Nico."

Dammit! Please, please don't leave me. How am I supposed to sleep without you beside me? Who will place a thermos of coffee in my hands and kiss my cheek when I leave for work? Where will I find another smile that makes me forget about every shitty thing that's ever happened to me? Who am I supposed to give my heart to if not for you, Nico. You're the only one who's seen inside my soul and loved me despite the *Band-Aids* and tape and glue holding me together. You became my glue, Nico. I need you. I don't want to live without you, not when we've finally come so far, so please don't make me live in a world without you in it. I don't want anyone else. I only want you, Nico.

"Nico!"

I'm sorry, Sprinkles. I failed you.

HE'S A KEEPER

"All you have to do is focus your mind on me - only me - and listen to my invitation. I'll take care of everything else, okay?"

A mind filled with nothing but Liam, that's something I can do. Staring into the shining copper of his eyes, I nod. His hands in mine, I hold onto him as tight as I can; because maybe I can absorb some of his infallible confidence to still the trembling of my fingers, you know, like osmosis... or something.

How does he stand so tall in the face of the possibility of failure? Despite knowing he's a tad bit shorter than me, it feels like the other way around. Looking straight ahead with squared shoulders, I swear he could touch the sky. I admire it - the immense concentration in the furrow of his brow, even the stiffness to his stance that might be viewed as tension but resonates with me as strength.

It's his strength to calmly breathe and meet my gaze with an unwavering and blind trust in information from a random website that has me murmuring a quiet *yeah* when he asks if I'm ready.

But to be honest, I'm not ready. I want to stay here in this limbo period - just Liam and me in this beautiful slice of the world. I'd have no problem living in a secluded cabin by this creek and in the shade of the entwining tree branches with the chirping of birds singing in the background. That happens, right? Singing and dancing while little animals help clean the house happens, right? If Snow White can do it, why can't Liam and me?

"I, Liam Holt, call upon the demon Nico Moore. I ask of you to lend an open ear to my request."

Always, Liam. No matter what you have to say, I'll always listen. When you need to complain about a rude customer or an unreasonable amount of schoolwork the professor assigned, I'll put down the book I'm reading and give you my full attention. When you gush about a new recipe you stumbled upon on *Pinterest*, your excitement washes over me until my dopey grin matches yours. Even your muttering of profanities at Furby is music to my ears. Your voice - a little raspy, but always clear and precise - will always be my favorite.

"I invite you to share in my world and to be a part of my future. You are welcome in my home, and I wish for my home to be your home as well. I invite you to be a part of my family."

Yes, Liam, yes! Yes to everything! I don't want to have to distinguish between your world and my world. I want it to be our world. Our home. Our family.

"In exchange for your willingness to leave your world and enter mine, I give to you my love, my heart, myself. I am yours for as long as you'll want me. Nico Moore, I wish for you to be able to call my world your home. That is my only request."

I accept, I accept, I accept! That's how this works, right? Liam requests me and I accept the invitation, right? Well, I do. There's no other place I'd rather be, no other world I'd rather explore, no other man I'd rather love. I want to be able to live with my friends and to find my own place in this world - the world I call home.

So yes, Liam, I hear you loud and clear. To your request, I say - with all my body, heart, and soul - yes, I accept.

Bright copper eyes with flecks of gold - the eyes I could stare into for the rest of eternity - fade from my vision, morphing to a sea of endless plain, the grass more brown than green and in the far off distance, a concentrated clump of worn down shacks standing around a pristine fortress of precious metals and gems. My home town, I guess you could call it. Or more like, an old town I used to know, for my home - now and forever more - is not of this world. This barren expanse with the mentality of every demon for themselves, I give it up. I release my ties from this world.

This is goodbye. Goodbye to the dry air that scratches my lungs with every breath and the months of endless lightning and rain falling from a gloomy sky. No more hiding in the shadows or slinking from settlement to settlement in search of a place to rest my head. No more living in fear of crossing paths with a demon more powerful than me and praying to gods I don't believe in to let me survive the accidental meeting. Goodbye to running away, to not having a place to call home, to being all alone.

My surroundings fade once more. The dry plains and dull sky grow transparent until all I see is a white nothingness. When color gradually returns - bolder and brighter with each passing breath - it comes in the form of filtering sunlight through crisp leaves and the soft reds, browns, and grays of the pebbles scattering the creek bottom. Tiny white flowers bloom in little patches, some by the trunk of a tree, a few bordering the quietly babbling water, even more growing around the fallen log. Beyond that - through the entangling branches of leaves and twigs - the spots of Apollo's coat stand out far more than his chestnut companion.

"-co."

Liam. Before, I stood facing him with my own reflection in the glory of his eyes; but now it's the tension and panic of back muscles and stiff shoulders while he stands in a small patch of clovers - the fallen log separating us. Like an owl, his head swivels from left to right and back again - eyes wide and red-rimmed, tears staining his cheeks, lips parted with his quickened pants of breath.

"Nico!"

"Liam."

He spins so fast he nearly falls over his own feet. Frozen in a moment of shocked paralysis, widened eyes lock on mine, and the world stills around us. Or maybe it doesn't, but who cares. None of that is important. What is important - who is important - he's what matters.

That single moment of stillness breaks like water from overflowing floodgates. Liam's tears fall anew as he scrambles to hop over the log, stumbling and barely managing to catch himself. In the next blink of my eyes, Liam runs straight into me and wraps his arms around me in a tight embrace. I stumble backward - one step, two steps before tripping over my own feet. Breath is knocked from my lungs once when my back collides with a jutted tree root and again a millisecond later when Liam lands on top of me. But Liam doesn't give me a moment to breathe before his lips are on mine, salty and wet from fresh tears.

As my hands find the small of his back and the nape of his neck, his urgent and needy kiss abruptly ends in favor of him burying his face in the crook of my neck. His fingers curl into my shirt and dig into my skin almost painfully. "I– I thought... I thought you were..." his voice cracks as a sob racks his body.

"Shh. I know." My fingers comb through his undercut as I hold him tighter. "I'm here, and I'm not going anywhere. It worked, Liam. It worked."

Liam sniffles and wipes his nose on my shirt. I shouldn't find that adorable and endearing, but I do. "It did?" he hiccups, lifting his head to peer at my face.

Staring back at puffy cheeks and red-rimmed eyes, I nod as a smile easily finds its way to my lips. Physically, there's no proof the ceremony worked. An insignia wasn't burned into my flesh, and there's no mark of ownership on me to prove I'm Liam's. We didn't share in a blood pact or sacrifice a part of ourselves. But mentally and emotionally, I feel it. Lighter and freer, it's as if the binds of the demon world have been lifted, as if shackles and chains have fallen at my feet.

Liam sucks in a shaky breath and exhales it with a teary smile. His head drops to my chest, ear above my heart, and he sighs. "Can we stay like this? Until it sinks in?"

Even with the tree root digging uncomfortably into my lower back, I hum, "Yeah." I could be lying on shards of glass and it'd still be worth the pain to feel Liam's weight atop me. Simply knowing - feeling - that he's here proves all this is real and not some fantasy I dreamed up. I'm not going to wake up all alone in a dark alley to find all of this - the friends I've made and the life I finally love - to be nothing more than a dream. So despite his weight making it a little hard to breathe, Liam can lie atop me for as long as his heart desires.

Liam's breathing slows, and the erratic pounding of his heart evens out to a rhythmic beat. He wipes his face on my shirt again, smearing tears and snot into the fabric. He stares at the soiled spot before shrugging and wiggling to rest his head on the other side of my chest.

"So romantic," I chuckle.

"It's your fault," he mumbles.

"Yes, yes," I placate, my fingers stroking through his hair. "I'm sorry."

How was either of us supposed to know I'd disappear and then reappear? We weren't prepared for that. It's not like the internet was overly helpful in preparing us for this. Most of the not-so-helpful information revolved around sacrifices and rather disturbing grotesque acts. Maybe that works with some demons, I don't know; but that will never work for me. I will never answer such a call upon my name, but Liam's invitation, I'll answer that every single time.

"Hey, Liam."

"Hmm?"

"It's our world now."

As he shifts to plant his elbows against my ribs, I wince. But when he beams at me with bright, crinkled eyes; the pain fades away. Or, well, it doesn't, but it's bearable.

"You know what this reminds me of?"

"What?"

With a cocky little smirk, Liam says, "*The Little Mermaid. Disney*'s version though, not Andersen's."

"There's more than one version?"

"In Andersen's story, the sea witch cuts out Ariel's tongue so she can't speak. And when she gets legs, each step she takes feels like she's being stabbed with a knife. And the prince doesn't choose her, so to become a mermaid again, she's told to stab a dagger into his heart; but she can't do it. So she died."

Sucking in a breath of air, my mouth hangs open. "That's... really sad."

"I know. That's why I said *Disney*'s version."

I feel... betrayed... tricked. Where's the happily ever after? "Has *Disney* been lying to me this whole time?"

Liam snickers, trying to hide his amusement but utterly failing. His entire body vibrates with laughter, and his squirming atop me isn't helping the ache in my back.

In one quick motion, I roll until Liam is squished between me and the dirt. Splaying out my limbs, I trap him under my weight and relish in the oomph that breezes through his lips. "Can't... breathe... Nico!" he wheezes.

Propping myself up with my elbows on either side of Liam, I give him enough leeway to breathe but not enough to wiggle free. "It's not funny. *Disney* betrayed me."

Liam snorts with laughter, and I seriously consider flattening him like a pancake beneath my weight. "Nah, they just made the stories more child-friendly."

"This is a serious matter, Liam. What else have they lied about?"

Liam purses his lips as he thinks for a short moment. "Um, Cinderella's stepsisters cut their feet to fit into the glass slippers and later have their eyes pecked out by doves. In *Snow White*, when the prince finds her, she's actually dead, so the prince is a disgusting douchebag who has a thing for dead chicks. Uh, Rapunzel gets knocked up, and her prince falls on thorn bushes which poke his eyes out. The frog prince is an inconsiderate prick who doesn't know the meaning of the word no; and in some versions, the princess cuts off his—"

"Okay, okay, that's enough."

I roll off of Liam and plop onto the ground next to him, the same tree root digging into my back again. Draping an arm over my eyes, I groan. "But what about the happily ever after?" I whine.

Maybe a happy ending wasn't important to this Andersen fellow and whoever else wrote these fairy tales, but I need to believe there's a tale of happiness waiting for me. I need to believe that all of life's struggles will lead to the happiness I desire. Why else would life be worth living if that isn't the case? Who would want to live a miserable life and fight to gain the warm euphoria of happiness only to have fate say fuck you? Not me. I want my happy ending.

"Well, if it makes you feel any better, Rapunzel and her prince do live happily ever after with their kids."

Tipping my head to the side, I peek under my arm to spot Liam's tender gaze and soft smile. "Really?"

"Yep."

I breathe a quiet sigh of relief. Rapunzel is my new favorite *Disney* princess; if only because I want a happily ever after with Liam, although I hope for a happy middle leading up to the happily ever after.

Suddenly, Liam gasps and bolts to his feet. "I just thought of the perfect idea!"

I slowly sit up, a little wary of the mischievous glint to his copper irises. "And what may that be?"

Liam's grin broadens, flashing me his pearly whites as he yanks me to my feet. "Flying, my dear Sprinkles. What better way to celebrate than to soar through the heavens?"

Soaring? More like falling. Dangerous. Very dangerous with so many obstacles to fly into. It's a horrible idea. One of us - maybe both of us if we're unlucky - is gonna end up with a black eye or bloody nose or broken bone. Or even all three!

"Please, Nico, will you be my wings?"

It's too late. The moment he directs sad puppy eyes at me and juts his bottom lip in a childish pout, I know I'll give in. How can I say no to large, glassy eyes begging like a child ready to throw a tantrum? And, oh my god, his lips are quivering.

"Fine," I sigh. My boyfriend is so spoiled. "But if we die, it's your fault."

"Worst that'll happen is we run into a tree," Liam brushes off all the potential mishaps as if he's the one with wings. But if that were the case, he'd know how hard it is to fly and not run into something.

Liam holds out his arms to me and wiggles his fingers to entice me closer. I comply, but instead of letting him latch onto me like a monkey, I scoop him up princess-style. "Wha– Nico!" he whines, color flushing his cheeks.

"We are hovering. That's it. And don't move too much, or I might drop you."

Liam laces his arms around my neck. "You call it hovering. I call it flying."

There is a major difference between hovering and flying, as in I'll hover an inch above the ground and not fly above the treetops. But I'm not about to tell Liam that, because he's not getting the chance to turn his puppy dog eyes on me and convince me to do something stupid.

Releasing the control on my wings comes far easier than it ever has. They rip slits through my t-shirt as they sprout from my shoulder blades. Their weight settles easily on my shoulders, and for the first time in a long time, they feel like they belong.

Adjusting my grip on Liam, I jostle him a bit to hook my arm under his knees and get a better hold on him. "I'm serious," I tell him. "Don't move or I'll drop you."

"Yes, yes," Liam says, but he's already squirming in anticipation.

Oh, boy. This isn't going to end well. I can feel it deep in my gut. We're going to fall, or I'm going to drop him. That's how all of this is going to end. But I sufficiently warned him, so he can't blame me for whatever happens.

I stretch out my wings, giving them a few test flaps to warm them up. It's been a long, long time since I've actually used them, and I swear I can hear them creak with every flap. They're going to ache after this, that I'm absolutely sure of.

Focusing my mind on the movement of my wings, I gradually increase the tempo and power of each flap. The grass around us blows with the whoosh of air my wings create, and I feel my sneakers leaving the ground. Swaying a bit back and forth, I shift my hold on Liam again to balance both our weights better.

But Liam's excitement has him twisting in my arms to gawk at the ground and then my wings and back to the ground. "Holy shit, this is cool," he says, eyes wide with awe.

I chuckle at that. Liam could jump higher than this on his own, but I guess this is special to someone without wings. Maybe... maybe I could... No, that's a bad idea.

"You're fucking amazing, Nico," Liam beams, his face lighting up like a child receiving the toy they wanted most.

Oh, that smile! Those eyes as bright as the stars in the night sky. The arms wrapped around my neck - his grip loosening as he grows more comfortable. I want to make him happy, even if it means doing something stupid and slightly dangerous. After all, the worst that can happen is running into a tree, right?

The flaps of my wings quicken as I stretch my wingspan even further. We slowly rise higher, but I keep it within reason, no higher than five feet. A fall from this height shouldn't hurt too bad, so we should be okay.

But the one problem with maintaining a higher height is it requires more focus. I don't know how flying works for birds - maybe it's all animal instinct - but I have to consciously think about flying. The speed and power of my flaps, maintaining a constant balance, visualizing potential obstacles around us - it all requires immense concentration and focus, which isn't easy with a squirming and chattering boyfriend in my arms.

"Oh my god, this is awesome. Can you fly backwards? Or upside down? Dude, aerial tricks like spins and somersaults would be fucking sweet!"

Tricks aren't going to happen. Neither is flying upside down. Would that even work? I feel like that would propel us head first into the ground. Or maybe it'd be more like doing the backstroke in water. Either way, I'm not risking a concussion. But backwards. I think that's something I can handle.

But before that, I need to refresh myself a little on the basics. So I entertain Liam by flying forward in short bursts and adding the occasional jerk to the left and right. Liam laughs at my *bad driving* - his chest rumbling with each chuckle - and he jokes about having whiplash. To save a tiny bit of my pride, I play along as if it's a joke; but my flying skills are truly this terrible. Liam says it reminds him of his first driving lesson with his mom when he was 15, and that's probably the best analogy for my terrible attempt at flying.

By the time I'm ready to give flying backwards a try, I'm out of breath. Panting for air, I hover while trying to catch my breath. Birds make this look effortless, but constantly flapping my wings is exhausting. I feel like I've completed my exercise quota for the year.

Okay, flying backwards. There has to be some sort of science to it. Do I have to flap my wings in a special way? Maybe shift the balance of my weight? Or is it more about momen–

Warm, pliable lips pressed to mine short-circuit my thought process. My brain shuts down as Liam and I share the same breath. We're suspended in air for a single moment before my wings vanish, air whooshing past us and the ground closing in. Liam clings to me while my legs flail, but to no prevail.

Water splashes into the air as we fall to the creek. Pain shoots through my backside and all the way up my spine on impact with the stony creek bottom. Liam lands atop me, his momentum toppling me back. I gasp when cold water touches my neck and soaks into my hair, bolting straight up after only a second. Wide-eyed and panting, I gape at Liam's wet form, not nearly as soaked as I am.

He stares back with equally shocked eyes before his surprise softens and the corners of his eyes crinkle. Throwing his head back, he laughs. "At least you didn't drop me!" he guffaws.

His obnoxiously loud laughter is contagious. Flicking water into his face, I fight to hold back my smile. "This is your fault."

"My fault?" he snorts. Cupping water in his palms, he throws it at me. "You're the one with the wings."

"But you distracted me."

"I kissed you."

"Which was a lovely distraction, but it's still your fault."

"Fine. I guess I'll have to take responsibility then," he smirks and suggestively waggles his eyebrows. Palms flat on my chest, he pushes me back.

I stutter a gasp at the bite of the water against the bare skin of my neck, ears, and cheeks; but Liam simply chuckles. His palms leave my chest to plant on the pebbles beside my head as he leans closer to me. When he presses smirking lips to mine, a shiver runs down my spine at the warmth. The heat spreads as his tongue darts out to taste my lips, and his nose presses into my cheek. I melt beneath him, relaxing into the chilly creek.

Water drips from my arm as I lift it from the creek. My fingers brush against his cheek - his skin burning hot compared to mine. With a hiss,

Liam jolts at my touch.

"Holy shit, you're freezing!"

Am I? "Maybe you're just hot."

"I'm smoking hot, thank you," Liam laughs, leaning back and pushing himself to his feet. He offers me his hand, which I graciously take as he helps me up. "But you are indeed freezing, and we need to get back before you catch a cold."

The air hits my wet clothes, and I have to suppress a shiver. "I wasn't cold with you in my lap," I mutter.

"Wha–" Liam croaks, color dusting his cheeks. "Don't tem–" he stops mid-sentence. His brow furrows in thought before correcting himself, "Please, may I ask you not to tempt me?"

Right. He summoned me, so I have to obey his every order. But he caught himself, reworded what he planned to say. Our little loophole - he's consciously aware of it, using it, exploiting it. And I couldn't be happier. Actually, it makes me want to tempt him more.

"But Liam~" I moan his name, cocking my hip and raking my hair back.

Liam laughs. He laughs! "You can't be sexy and look like a wet dog at the same time."

"I don't look like a wet dog!"

"You kinda do." Chuckling, he slips his hand in mine and tugs. "We really should go back and get out of these clothes."

I follow after him, each step heavy with water weight. My socks squish with every footfall, like I have soaked sponges strapped to my feet. "All this was probably your plan to get me naked."

"Oh, you got me. You foiled my elaborate scheme to see your freckled ass."

"You could have simply asked."

He flashes me a brilliant smile. "Where's the fun in that."

When we reach the horses still tied by the forest trail, Apollo greets us with a whinny. Ares, on the other hand, pointedly ignores us, but that in itself is a relief. An hour ago, I didn't know if I'd ever see them again. Anything could've gone wrong with the summoning, but thankfully, all went well. So if I take an extra minute to trace the spots on Apollo's neck, can anyone really blame me?

Apollo and I follow behind the other pair. I'm eternally grateful for Apollo's smooth gate, because Ares' trot looks extremely bouncy, and poor Liam keeps shifting in his seat. That can't be comfortable while wearing wet jeans. If my thighs are chafing against denim, Liam's must be rubbed raw by now. And even if it is his fault we fell into the creek, he doesn't deserve chafed thighs.

By the time we reach the stableyard, my teeth chatter and my toes are numb. I waddle through the barn to hang up both horses' tack while Liam puts them back in the pasture. We meet up in the yard and waddle like a pair of penguins up the steps.

The door creaks as Liam pushes it open. I follow after him, and we leave our shoes to dry by a vent. Both of our socks squish upon the hardwood to leave a trail of wet footprints in the entry hall. Liam peeks his head into the kitchen, finding it empty, before slinking into the living room.

"Oh my gosh, what happened?"

We both freeze, turning in unison to find Anne sitting in a plush rocking chair in the corner, book lying open on the armrest.

"We, uh, fell in the creek," Liam supplies.

"Oh? Is that so?" She tilts her head, gazing between us with a knowing smile. But whatever she thinks we were doing, she's probably only half right. After all, who would guess her son and his demon boyfriend fell out of the sky?

Liam points to the enclosed staircase and slowly creeps toward it. "We're just gonna go get changed."

"Alright, Sweetie. Granny and I won't interrupt."

Liam groans while ushering me up the stairs. He slams the door a little too hard. "We are not having sex in my grandma's house," he clarifies as he stomps up the steps behind me.

"Aw, but your mom gave us her blessing."

Liam rolls his eyes. "Oh, just shut— Goddammit, I can't say that. How do I phrase *shut up* so you have the option to not shut up?"

"Ask me nicely, maybe?"

"Ugh, I'll think of something."

I round the top of the landing and continue until the hall comes to a *T*. Turning to the right, I stride a few steps to the door at the end of the hall. With a quiet squeak, I push the door open.

"I got it!" Liam exclaims as he follows me into the soft pink room. He clears his throat a few times until I turn my eyes to him. "If it so pleases you, would you kindly shut your pie hole?"

With his puffed-out chest and chin tipped up with pride, I can't help but laugh.

Liam frowns, brows creasing. "I thought that was perfect," he grumbles.

"It was. Thank you." Ducking down, I press a quick peck to his cheek. "Really, thank you so much."

I will never be able to express my gratitude to him for giving me my freedom. It would be so easy for him to take it away - a single command could do it - but nothing has changed. He still treats me as a human, the same as he always has. If anyone else had summoned me, I may not have been so lucky.

After fiddling with my zipper, I manage to peel the damp denim from my legs. With the heels of my palms, I rub some warmth back into my thighs. That helps a tiny bit, but I really want to curl up in a blanket burrito right about now.

"Well, of course. It's the least I can do." Scratching his nape, Liam's eyes avert to the side.

The least he can do? No, he's done more than enough. He has opened up an entire new world for me, and what's bigger than the whole world?

I pause in pulling my shirt over my head. There is something I can do - or, well, say - to express my gratitude. After all, I may have answered Liam's invitation, but not out loud. He didn't hear my answer, and it's only fair that he does, right?

Dropping my shirt to the floor, I abandon the idea of getting a clean one in favor of reaching for Liam. I catch his wrist as he unbuttons his pants. Slipping my fingers between his, Liam's momentary surprise fades as his fingers curl around mine.

Swallowing the lump in my throat, I steel my courage. "I'm happy - so very happy - and I owe it to you. It scares me, because I've never been this happy before and I've never relied on someone so much; but you - Liam, you make me feel like everything's going to be okay. You make me feel safe and loved and wanted, and I can't thank you enough for that." A tear rolls down my cheek, and I have to clear my throat to continue. "You said you wanted your home to be my home too, but, Liam, you are my home. I think you have been since the first day I met you."

Liam sniffles a breathy laugh. His fingers squeeze mine. "I said the same thing to my mom the other day - that you're my home." He chuckles again as his eyes trail down my chest. "Although, I was fully dressed at the time."

I glance down between us, Liam shirtless with his pants unbuttoned and me clad only in dark red boxer briefs with *KISS THIS* written on the cheeks (that's what happens when you go shopping with Skyler). But all of this moment's imperfections is what screams us, and I can't imagine it any other way.

Tearing his eyes away, Liam groans. "You're making it really hard to keep it in my pants."

"Well, your mom gave–"

"No, not gonna happen. It's just... weird. Like this was my aunt's room, and that's not my bed, and it's just, no. Absolutely not."

"It is a nice bed," I laugh.

"Yeah, for sleeping. But will you please put me out of my misery and put on some damn pants? I will do anything if you just put on some clothes. Please."

"Anything?"

"Within reason."

"Hmm." Rolling my shoulders, I feel the strain and ache in the muscles. "A massage would be nice."

"Deal."

Turning my back to Liam, I hook my fingers in the waistband of my underwear. Swaying my hips with each step, I slowly peel the damp fabric from my skin. Pride swells in my chest at Liam's grumbled *Goddammit, Nico,* and I chuckle as the boxer briefs fall to the floor. When Liam starts murmuring a string of quiet profanities, I take pity on him and slip into a fresh pair of underwear, but not without a little shimmy of my hips.

After I finally don plaid pajama bottoms and a t-shirt, Liam huffs a sigh. "You're gonna be the death of me."

"I have no idea what you're talking about," I say innocently.

"Your hips know exactly what I'm talking about."

Liam slips into pajama bottoms that match mine before snatching the top blanket off the bed. Coming up behind me, he wraps the blanket around my shoulders and hugs me. "As much as I'd love to curl up under the covers with you, we have a kitten to babysit."

"We can't keep her waiting, now can we?" I tip my head to the side and kiss the corner of Liam's lips.

With his arms still wrapped around me, I shuffle out of the room and down the hall. When we reach the stairs, Liam refuses to let go. His adorable stubbornness has us almost tumbling down the steps, but we somehow manage not to die.

When we step into the living room, we find it oddly empty. No Anne in the plush rocking chair, no Granny Mae, no Cupcake, no Bacon, and no Kronos. It's far too quiet for this house, that is until I hear the squeak of the front door and the stampede of hooves and paws running down the hall. Bacon reaches the dining area first, looking from side to side until he spots me. Then he's running again.

Uh oh. Sidestepping, I barely manage to avoid the pot-bellied battering ram, but poor Liam howls when Bacon headbutts the back of his knees. Liam spins me around to face Bacon, using me as a shield.

"Seriously, you little bastard! I'm gonna fry you up for breakfast!"

"You will not," Granny Mae scolds from the dining area, Kronos sitting beside her while she pets his head.

"But he headbutted me!" Liam whines.

"And who was it that taught him that?"

I hear more than see Liam's lips smack as his jaw snaps shut.

"Exactly," she says with the same smugness I often associate with Liam. She grabs her purse from the edge of the table, which seems to be why she came back in the house. "Cupcake is in my room. You know what to do, so just try not to burn the house down." She waves as she heads back down the entry hall.

286

"No promises!" Liam calls, his words ringing in my ears.

After the door squeaks open and closed and we hear the car drive away, Liam finally releases me. "If it pleases you, would you lie down on the couch so I can pamper you with that massage you wanted?"

"But we're supposed to be kitty-sitting."

"We can do both." Liam disappears into his grandma's room and reappears with a sleepy kitten cradled in his palms. "She can nap while I give you the best fucking massage of your life. 'Kay?"

That sounds lovely, like heaven, so I quickly comply. I ball up my blanket to use as a pillow before lying down on my belly. Crossing my arms over my blanket-pillow, I rest my cheek atop the backs of my hands. After a little wiggling to get comfortable, Liam gently sets Cupcake by the crook of my neck. Her fuzzy black fur and tiny whiskers tickle my skin when she nuzzles against me.

"She really has taken a liking to you," Liam says as he perches himself on my lower back, his bent knees framing my hips.

"It's gonna be hard saying goodbye." I stroke Cupcake's head with my pointer finger. At my touch, the kitten's whole body vibrates with its purring. It's a wonder such a tiny kitten can purr so loudly.

Liam hums as his hands press against my shoulder blades. His touches start out as gentle pushes and pulls, thumbs rubbing circles over the exact spots my wings sprout from. His kneading fingers elicit quiet moans and deep sighs of content from my lungs as they roam from the small of my back up to my shoulders and neck. Hands feathering up my neck, Liam massages his fingers along my jawline and to the base of my ears.

With a deep inhale of breath, my eyes fall shut. Liam's magical hands ease the day's stress from my muscles and leave me sinking further into the couch cushions. The kneading of his fingers is more than enough to lull me to sleep; but add to that him absentmindedly humming a soft melody, and it's guaranteed to send me to the realm of dreams.

We spend a full week at Granny Mae's, and we fall into an easy routine. After breakfast, Liam and I go out for a morning ride. The day after the successful summoning, we return to the creek. Liam digs a pocket knife from the saddlebag and carves our names into the fallen log. The days following that, Liam shows me around the rest of the property. On more than one occasion, I swear we're lost in the woods, but Liam knows the trails like the back of his hand. He knows every short cut and every clover patch and the favorite grazing spot of does and their fawns.

With wobbly legs and aching thighs, we return from our ride every day around noon. Liam's greeted by Bacon headbutting him the moment he walks through the door. Even trying to hide behind me doesn't protect

Liam, because Bacon scurries around me to slam his weight into Liam. And he only ever targets Liam. With Granny Mae, Anne, and I, Bacon is the most well-behaved pig on the planet.

After lunch, Granny Mae always has something fun planned for us, although Liam sometimes calls it torture. Like when Granny Mae brings a mountain of scrapbooks from her craft room, Liam begs her to put them back. Despite the light blush to his cheeks, Liam grumbles in his spot on the couch next to me as I flip through photos of his childhood. Anne and Granny Mae gladly share stories that go along with the pictures, like one where toddler Liam stands crying in his diaper - his left eye black and blue. Apparently, little Liam loved jumping from the couch to the chair and didn't make it once, knocking his little noggin on the armrest. Or twelve-year-old Liam covered from head to toe in mud after chasing a calf that escaped the pasture and slipping in the forest. But on the bright side, he did catch the calf.

If it isn't photo albums and story sharing, it's spending the afternoon with Granny Mae in the craft room. I never would've guessed Liam knows how to sew, and I don't believe him until he picks up needle and thread, plops himself in front of a work table for three hours, and then proudly shoves a plush robot into my hands. Complete with mismatched button eyes, the felt robot is one of the cutest things I've ever seen. It earns Liam a peck on his cheek from me and a ruffle of his hair from his grandmother.

I can't compete with Liam's sewing skills. No matter how many times I try, I always end up pricking my finger. My stitches are crooked and inconsistent, but Liam insists they're pretty great for a beginner. He walks me through the process of making a plush robot, from cutting out a gazillion felt squares to attaching the button eyes and assembling the body. Mine turns out nothing like Liam's. But even with its head looking ready to fall off and its arms being uneven, Liam's adamant about how much he loves it.

Over the days, I learn how skilled Granny Mae is in the craft department. She's like a jack-of-all-trades. She sews quilts and makes tiny fairy houses out of flower pots and clay. Sheets of watercolor landscapes hang on the wall, and I recognize them as the forest surrounding her home. Pendants and beads made of colored clay are meticulously organized, waiting to be assembled into necklaces, bracelets, and even earrings. And she's so patient in explaining her process and helping my hands mimic hers.

Our evenings are quiet and peaceful. We congregate in the living room, watching whatever TV show draws our attention the most. Bacon and Kronos settle down on their respective dog beds (pig bead?) on the floor. Cupcake chases after a piece of yarn and jumps at my toes until she's too tired to even stand, which is when I scoop her into my lap. By 10 p.m., we all retire to our rooms, Cupcake coming to sleep with Liam and me.

So when Thursday rolls around and we're packing our things to leave, I really don't want to go. With duffle bags hanging from our shoulders, we trudge down the stairs and to the dining table where Anne and Granny Mae wait to see us off.

Anne wraps an arm around both of us and pulls us into a tight embrace. She kisses each of our cheeks. "Come back soon," she tells Liam. When she releases us, her tawny eyes fall onto me. "It's been a pleasure getting to know you, Nico. Please take care of our little Liam."

Liam lets out a low whine of *Mom!*, but I nod with a smile. "I will."

Granny Mae steps forward, Cupcake squirming in her arms. Glancing at our duffle bags, she asks, "Aren't you boys forgetting something?"

I look to Liam. "Are we?" But he doesn't answer. He beams at me - eyes shining bright - as he takes Cupcake from his grandma.

Liam hands the kitten to me. "Surprise, Sprinkles. We've adopted our first baby."

Cradling the kitten to my chest, my heart beats faster at Liam's words. Our baby. Hearing it has warmth blooming in my chest. "Really? It's okay?" I look to Granny Mae.

A fond smile upon her lips, Granny Mae nods. "Liam asked a few days ago."

"And you don't have to worry," Liam says. "Everything she'll need is already in the car."

"Thank you," I say to both Liam and Granny Mae.

"You're welcome. Now get over here and give me a hug "

I don't have to be told twice. Careful of Cupcake in my hand, I hug Granny Mae with my free arm. Her embrace - so warm and secure - feels right. It feels like...

"Welcome to the family," she whispers.

Family. That's what it feels like. And it feels so good.

When she releases me, she turns her sights on Liam. She pulls him into a tight embrace, her eyes falling shut as she breathes a deep inhale. Her lips move in murmurs too quiet for my ears, but whatever she says has Liam nodding one moment and flushing a deep red the next.

His eyes glance at me, and his lips upturn into a tender smile. Loud enough for all of us to hear, Liam declares proudly, "Yeah, he's a keeper."

It's my turn to have heat flush my cheeks. Butterflies flutter in my chest, and I have to blink against the moisture forming in my eyes.

Liam pulls back from the embrace to join me. His hand grasps mine as he leads me down the entry hall. With his other hand, he waves over his shoulder.

"Drive safely!"

"Will do," Liam calls back.

The front door squeaks behind us, and it's bittersweet to hear it. We settle in the car - Cupcake sitting in my lap - and Liam slowly backs out of the yard. We leave behind the house nestled in the meadow, the morning horseback rides, the pot-bellied battering ram, and the soft pink wallpaper with a dizzy flower pattern. But what I'll remember most lies in the forest beside the babbling creek, our names carved at the very place I gained my freedom. And more important than that freedom - a family.

COTTON CANDY

It's a miracle the three of us make it back in one piece, what with our baby - our cute little Cupcake - deciding a six-hour car ride is perfect for kitten playtime. For an animal that sleeps most of its life, this rambunctious little shit doesn't so much as yawn or rest her eyes the entire way home. That wouldn't be such a big deal if we weren't, I don't know, going 75mph down the highway; but with that being the case, her climbing up my arms and pawing at my face isn't the best idea. But I don't dare scold her or ask Nico to reign in our child; because for once, Nico isn't squirming in his seat and fiddling with the radio and desperately trying not to watch the world race by out the window. He's smiling and laughing and completely distracted from being in a moving vehicle.

He's never explicitly admitted to suffering from carsickness and I never flat out asked him about it, but by now I'd be a complete jackass if I didn't recognize the signs. I normally do my best to stay below the speed limit and not complain about the classical music he likes, because it seems to soothe him a tad bit. But with the newfound distraction of Cupcake, Nico doesn't even notice the movement of my arm to switch the radio station or that I'm speeding enough to catch a cop's attention.

So if I almost crash the car into the fucking guard rail because Cupcake slips on my shoulder and digs her claws into the side of my neck, then at least I can die with my Sprinkles' tender smile that crinkles the corners of dark honey eyes fresh in my mind.

But as luck would have it, we miraculously make it back to our apartment building safely and fully intact.

"Hands are full," Nico cheekily grins as he cradles Cupcake to his chest.

"You're lucky you two are fucking adorable," I say, hefting the second duffle bag over my shoulder to rest against my back right next to the first one. Leaning into the vehicle's back seat, I load my forearms with plastic bags, most of which are toys for our soon to be very spoiled little girl and even one full of Granny's homemade cookies for Skyler and Emil. The plastic handles slide into the crook of my elbow and dig uncomfortably into my skin, but I am not coming back for a second trip. Second trips are for people who lack resolve and creativity, and I refuse to be one of those people.

Shoving the car door shut with my hip, the plastic bags knock together and tangle around my arms. Each step has a different cat toy squeaking or lighting up, and Cupcake perks at the sounds. She squirms in Nico's hold, her tiny legs scratching for traction on his shirt and her claws getting stuck in the fabric. It's almost poetic justice to see Nico struggling to keep her from leaping out of his hands. He kinda deserves it for sticking me with all our bags.

As we trek up the stairs, Nico glances over his shoulder at me. "Did you tell them about Cupcake?"

"Nope."

"Liam~" he manages to sound whiny and scolding at the same time. "What if they don't want another cat?"

"Have you met Skyler? He's an old cat lady trapped in a young hunk's body."

"True but... But it's kinda a jerk move to not tell them."

"Too bad," I shrug. "I'm doing the same thing he did when he brought home Simba and Furby, so it shouldn't be a problem." Hell, I didn't throw a shit fit even after Furby mauled my leg for the first time, so Skyler can't bitch about our little girl who is the sweetest thing since cotton candy.

When we get to the apartment door, I reach for the keys in my front right pant pocket; but the plastic bags slide down my forearm to block my hand. A few failed attempts have me ready to break the door down with a body slam. That is until gentle fingers coax their way into my pocket, the tips digging into my thighs in search of the metal keyring. The fingers linger and prod longer than necessary while I try - and utterly fail - to suppress the shudder that runs down my spine.

Keys in hand, Nico withdraws his fingers. He turns to the door as if he hasn't just worked me up on purpose, but the quirk of his lips tells me he knows exactly what game he's playing. A turn of his wrist has the door unlocking with a soft click, but he doesn't push the door open. Instead, he casually slips the keys back into my pocket. His fingers curl into my waistband with a firm squeeze before retreating just as fast.

A low groan rumbles in my chest at the lack of his touch, and dammit I sincerely hope Skyler and Emil aren't home. Chances are, they're probably watching TV dramas on the couch with overly-greasy delivery pizza from the place a few blocks down. But a guy can dream, right?

Following behind Nico into the apartment, my dreams are crushed the moment Skyler's booming voice shouts *Welcome home!*. Another step and I'm walking into the solid back of my boyfriend where he's rooted to the floor.

"What's—"

Wrong.

Leaning around Nico's shoulder, my eyes spot one too many people littering the living room. Skyler bounds forward - eyes blown comically wide at the sight of Cupcake - and transforms into his inner old cat lady. Emil stands from his spot on the couch, warily glancing between me and the person - no, demon - casually sitting beside him like the demon owns the damn place.

My blood boils as silvery eyes lazily turn from the TV screen to peer at Nico and lips upturn into a far too friendly smile. "What the fuck is this asshole—"

A firm hand splays across my chest to stop me from stomping around Nico. My eyes dart to the freckles of his cheeks, but Nico doesn't meet my gaze. The tension in his shoulders slowly fades as he exhales a steady breath and meets the metallic gaze.

But despite Nico's calmness, my pulse echoes in my ears like waves crashing against the face of a rocky cliff. My palms twitch, but I can do little with the burden of a million bags hanging from my arms. Even so, if it wasn't for Nico's firm touch holding me at bay, I'd drag the demon to his feet by his stupid bowl cut hair and throw him off the balcony.

His words from our last meeting echo in my head. *Dungeons of Hell. He'll be lucky to get a few lashings at the very least, but I doubt Avon will let him off that easy.* This demon, he's part of the unit after Nico, part of the unit ready to send my Sprinkles to a lifetime of torture and punishment. Fuck him. Fuck every last one of them.

I don't give a damn that he helped us get away. Am I grateful? Yeah, but this asshole shouldn't be here. He has no reason to show up like this and lounge on my fucking couch like it belongs to him. *Goodbye and farewell.* That's what he said, so why is he here? This isn't exactly farewell, now is it?

If he thinks I'll let my guard down because he helped us once, then he better guess again. I will never allow him or anyone else of the demon police to get close enough to snatch Nico away and whisk him off to a promise of eternal pain and suffering. I won't let anyone take away Nico's smile, and if that means being damned to Hell, then so be it.

"Easy buddy. I can feel your bloodlust all the way over here." The demon lolls his head back and settles further into the cushions of my couch. Crossing his hands behind his head, his eyes sweep over me. "I don't recall doing anything to deserve such animosity. In fact, don't you owe me a thank you?"

"Why, you—"

"Liam."

Nico's steady voice silences me, as if I'm the one bound by contract to obey his every command. His thumb rubs over my sternum in an attempt to calm me, and the simple action does wonders to cool my fiery blood. "It's okay."

Fucking hell, what part of this is okay? He shouldn't be here, simple as that. And, yeah, maybe some of my hatred stems from jealousy, and maybe I should be more grateful to this demon; but I can't get over the whole he's-a-demon-officer-whose-job-is-to-take-Nico-away thing.

My glare darts from the demon to Skyler cooing at Cupcake. I don't give a flying fuck what the reason is, Skyler shouldn't have let the demon into the apartment. What was he thinking?

"Listen, you have our gratitude, or mine at least. But you still shouldn't be here. Liam–" his fingers curl into my t-shirt "–is my contractor. Thank you for everything you've done up till now, but I don't need you anymore."

"Ouch," the demon feigns hurt, his smirk still plastered to his face. He rolls his back and leisurely stretches his arms into the air. "I'm well aware of your new contractor," he says, standing from his perch and slowly sauntering toward us. "Avon is well aware of it too, and let's just say he's not too happy. If I were you, I'd hope Mr. Contractor never retracts his invitation. You should take this opportunity to grow old and die in this world." My skin prickles when the demon's hand clasps Nico's shoulder. "Because if you ever come back, Avon will make you wish you were dead."

If my blood was a fiery inferno before, it's ice cold now. My breath stills in my lungs.

A silver gaze locks with mine. "That's all I wanted to say." He brushes past me, our shoulders knocking together and setting off a series of squeaky cat toys.

I spin to watch him leave, but he's already gone. Heaving a sigh, my lungs remember how to function. Dropping my arms to my side, I let the bags fall to the floor and shrug off the duffle straps.

My narrowed gaze turns to Skyler. "The fuck, dude?"

He reluctantly tears his attention away from the baby fluff ball. "What?"

"You let him in!"

Skyler rolls his golden eyes at me and returns to fawning over Cupcake. "I didn't want to be rude."

Are you kidding me? "You threatened to punch him last time!"

"That was before I knew he was on our side."

"And what would you have done if he wasn't on our side, huh? What if he had been lying? Would you take responsibility for putting Nico in danger?"

"Oh my god, chill," Skyler says. "You told us the summoning worked, so there's nothing to worry about. And even if he was lying, I'm more than capable of kicking some demon ass. Isn't that right, little cutie pie?" Skyler coos to Cupcake and scratches the white patch of fur beneath her chin. "Big ole Uncle Skyler can protect your demon daddy."

Nico stifles a laugh at Skyler's baby voice, but his words - or word - have me cringing. "Please never use the word daddy ever again."

"Little darling, you should tell your other daddy to take the stick out of his ass." Skyler's lips upturn into a devilish smirk.

"Cupcake, sweetie," I steal the kitten from Nico and Skyler, holding her up to talk directly to her. "You should tell Skyler he no longer gets any of Granny's cookies."

"Wha–? No, I'm sorry. Don't take the cookies hostage!" Skyler scrambles to apologize, his eyes glancing at the heap of plastic bags and probably trying to find the one with the cookies. They linger over a bag beside my foot, but before he can dart for it, I step on the plastic handles to trap it.

Skyler huffs, crossing his arms while giving me the stink eye. But this is one time when Skyler won't win a stare down, and he knows it. He deflates with a pout. Dragging his feet like a toddler, he swings his arms at his sides while slowly turning toward the living room.

He spins back so quick I don't have time to register Cupcake being snatched before she's already gone. Skyler cradles the kitten like a newborn baby and casually strolls off.

"That's playing dirty!" I protest.

"Is it, though?" Skyler stops, one foot on the living room's carpet and the other still on the hardwood. "I have something you want, and you have something I want. Let's make a deal."

"It is against democratic policy to negotiate with terrorists," I drone. I'm not worried about Cupcake in the least; the old cat lady in Skyler won't allow him to hurt a single hair on her head.

"Did you hear that?" Skyler cranes his head at Cupcake. "Your daddy #2 doesn't want you back."

"Oi, that's not–"

"Liam, don't abandon our daughter," Nico nudges my shoulder, pushing me toward Skyler. "Give the kidnapper his cookies."

"Fine," I huff. Bending down, I dig the colorful tupperware full of cookies from the plastic bag. "Cupcake first. Then you get the cookies."

Skyler shakes his head. "Nah-uh. Cookies first."

"Absolutely not. You'll take the cookies and keep Cupcake."

"Well, you'll take Cupcake and keep the cookies."

"Oh, well. I guess you don't want the cookies." I shake the container, cookies clattering in its confines.

Skyler's gaze softens as it turns back to Cupcake. He scratches her belly, and her tiny paws swat playfully at his fingers. "Daddy #2 cares more about his pride than getting you back from your dashingly handsome kidnapper. Dad of the year, right?"

"I do not! And why am I dad #2?"

Nico takes the cookies from my hand and crosses the room to Skyler. "Because you were gonna leave our baby with her kidnapper."

"Pleasure doing business." Skyler takes the offered cookies and lets Nico scoop Cupcake into his embrace. Smug, golden eyes and a victorious smirk rub salt in my wound. "That's why Nico's daddy #1."

"I have no problem taking those cookies back," I warn.

Skyler saunters to the couch and plops down not-so-gracefully. "Oh, really? You think you can take me?"

Staring down the solid wall of muscle that is Skyler Rosenberg, I am 110% sure he could kick my ass. There's no doubt in my mind a wrestling match with him will end with him pinning me to the floor and dangling a wad of spit over my face that he plans to suck back in his mouth, but because he's horrible at it, I end up with a glob of spit running down my cheek while he laughs his ass off. I am no longer as young or as dumb as I was then, so I'm smart enough to not let history repeat itself.

I puff out my chest and stand a bit taller. "Yeah, I do, but because I'm a great role model and deserve the title of dad #1, I will not fight in front of the baby."

"Oh, we can go in the other room," Nico suggests, dark eyes bright and lively. "It's probably about time for Cupcake's bedtime." As if on cue, Cupcake yawns, her eyes squeezing shut and her tongue curling up at its end.

A chorus of *Aww* follows Nico as he takes Cupcake to our room. But despite how cute and adorable my two favorites are, I still mutter a quiet *traitor* under my breath.

"Well?" Skyler's lips curve into an evil smirk - the kind super villains wear when they're staring into the hero's eyes with a gun pointed at the hero's head. "I'm ready when you are."

"Uh, I..." I am not getting a wad of disgusting spit dropped on my face again. Never again! "I'm going to be a good dad and an amazing boyfriend by helping put the baby to sleep."

"Uh-huh. Whatever you say, Daddy #2."

Ugh. When Skyler says daddy like that, it really is cringe-worthy. If we ever have actual human children that are capable of speech, they won't be allowed to call me daddy. Literally anything but that.

I gather the heaps of bags and drag them with me to my room. The squeak of fake mice and the jingle of balls with bells in them makes it hard to hold my head high as I retreat with my tail between my legs, especially when I hear Skyler snickering at me. He's lucky I'm afraid of his spit, or I really would wrestle those cookies from him.

Furby and Simba sit outside my closed bedroom door, both with their heads craned to peer under it. I nudge them out of the way with my foot and slip into my room. Simba darts to follow after me, but he runs into the door as I shut it.

I'm not stupid when it comes to introducing new animals into a household, especially when the new one is so much more vulnerable than the cats already here. I've seen Granny do it plenty of times, so little Cupcake will not be introduced to the resident asshats until I'm positive they won't eat her.

I toss the duffle bags in the corner to be unpacked later (or never, who knows?) and dump out all the kitty supplies to sort through.

"Dad #2, you're disturbing the baby," Nico shushes me from where he's curled beneath the covers with Cupcake sprawled on my pillow. Her ears perk at the chorus of squeaks, and soft blue eyes zero in on the rainbow mouse that flashes a different color with each squeak.

"I'm not dad #2," I grumble. "I'm the fun dad; so if baby wants to play, I'm gonna play with her." I wave the toy mouse by its tail and relish in the weak glare Nico sends my way.

"Doesn't Mr. Fun Dad have to be to work by 4 a.m.?"

"Oh, crap." I didn't forget. It just... momentarily slipped my mind? Yeah, that sounds about right.

Ever so carefully, I place the cat toy on the carpet so it doesn't go off again. I strip to my boxers and flick off the lights. Shuffling my feet, I manage not to step on a forgotten plastic bag or a laser pointer toy on my way to the bed. After turning on my alarm, I wiggle beneath the blanket.

Squinting into the darkness, I locate the little bundle of fur on my pillow. "Goodnight, my little Cupcake." My lips press a soft kiss to the kitten's head.

Then my gaze turns to the man watching me, his eyes reflecting the moonlight streaming through the cracks in the blinds. Leaning over Cupcake, my elbow plants itself on the mattress to hold my weight as my head tips forward. Foreheads touching, I quietly ask, "Can I kiss you?"

"Are you going to ask every time?"

"Yep," I smile.

His quiet puff of laughter caresses my lips. A shining gaze meets mine. "Yes, you dork. You can kiss me."

When our lips press together, I'm not sure it can be called a kiss. It's more smiles and breathless giggles and the occasional playful swipe of a tongue. And yet, I wouldn't change it for the world.

There's something ethereal about blinking awake to the slumbering face of the one you love, his cheek squished against the fluff of his pillow and his mouth hanging open to let soft snores pass through. Add to that the black ball of fur sprawled precariously on his neck and cheek, and it's enough to make my heart burst. I don't have it in me to disturb either of them, so I slip out of bed as quietly as possible and turn off my alarm before it gets the chance to blare.

I tiptoe through my morning routine, having to shush Simba multiple times when he meows in protest of being locked out of my room. He retaliates by winding between my legs with every step I take, and it's a miracle I don't trip over the little bastard. Before heading out, I duck back into the bedroom and kiss both Nico and Cupcake on their heads. Nico doesn't stir, but Cupcake blinks her big blue eyes at me. She stares for a moment until she recognizes it's only me; and then her eyes fall shut again, and she hides her face in her tiny paws.

My heart melts to goo at the sight. I leave before the urge to call in sick and spend all day cuddled up with these two overpowers my logical thinking. After taking an entire weekend off, I doubt I'd still have a job if I play sick today. So snapping a quick pic with my phone will have to suffice.

The early mornings are warm enough that a light sweater keeps the chill at bay. By the time the sun rises above the cityscape, it'll probably be hot enough for a t-shirt and shorts. But for now, the piping thermos of coffee is greatly appreciated as I navigate the slumbering city.

Seeing the bold red letters of Scout's sign, my pace picks up as I cross the cracked pavement of the parking lot. I won't admit it out loud - because I really did have an amazing spring break - but I did miss this place. Not necessarily the customers or the hours of waiting on them, definitely not that. But the familiarity - the off-white aprons hanging on the wall, the clipboard of the morning's bake list, the thrum of the mixer running, the baking timer beeping, the smell of freshly baked bread mixed with the sweetness of confectioneries - that's what I miss. I miss the early hours of Friday and Monday, not the shifts of Saturday and Sunday.

Simon's disrobing his jacket when I slip into the breakroom. "Mornin'," I say a little livelier than usual.

As I set my thermos on the table and shed my outer sweater, Simon returns the greeting. Simon waits for me before we both head to the back workroom. He tosses an apron at me and watches, head tilted slightly with observing gray eyes, as I tie it around my back.

A moment passes before Simon ties his own on and grabs the clipboard hanging from a hook on the wall. He scans over the morning's workload, but his gaze wanders to me again. Before I have the chance to ask if there's something on my face, Simon says, "You're awfully... cheerful... for someone who had to deal with a family emergency. Can I assume everything is okay?"

"Oh, uh, yeah." That's right. Family emergency. But he doesn't seem mad or suspicious, like he doubts there was an actual emergency (which there was). It's more like... concern? "Everything's okay now. I, uh, actually made up with my mom, and Nico came with so he was introduced to the family." I take a breath to stop my quick rambling before it turns to word vomit. "So, yeah, everything's pretty good now."

Simon nods at that, turning back to the clipboard with the faintest of smiles upon his lips. And his stance softens when he exhales his next breath.

Was he truly that worried? It's not like I–

Oh god, of course he'd be concerned. I can't say family emergency without people assuming it has something to do with my father, especially when I don't offer further elaboration. And it's not like I openly talk about the whole my-dad's-a-criminal-scumbag thing, so it's fair to assume an unelaborated family emergency would involve him.

But to think Simon was worried about me - even if his assumption was wrong - that adds a bit of extra pep to my steps as I measure dry ingredients to toss in the mixer. And yeah, if I'm being honest, I missed Simon too. He's not always the most forthcoming when it comes to small chitchat, but he never complains when I bitch and moan about classes or some stupid prank Cody pulled on me. Every now and then - if I'm lucky - I can drag a story or two out of him from the good ole days as he puts it. Turns out Simon was a stupid teenager just like the rest of us, or that's the conclusion I draw from hearing about the shenanigans he and his friends used to get into.

And let's not forget the occasional advice based off life experience he dishes out. Like damn, he could be a philosopher if this diner ever goes belly up or maybe a motivational life coach for people who don't mind the excessive use of profanity.

But for me, he's not any of those. I guess he's the male role model I wish my father had been. Yeah, that sounds about right. Hell, if I had a choice in the matter, I'd choose Simon over my old man any day. Of course, I'd choose a fuckin rock over my father, but still. Simon, I owe him a lot and I'm truly grateful for everything he's done for me.

So if I'm a little disappointed to place the last tray of dinner rolls on the cooling rack, can anyone really blame me? I could keep going till the sun sets below the cityscape, and I'd be grateful for the sore feet and aching back.

That is until Quinn bursts into our space like a whirlwind. They catch me mid-sweep, trapping me in a too tight embrace as the broom clatters to the floor. "I missed you so much!"

"Uh, me too?" I squeak as the breath is squeezed from my lungs.

"Thank god you're back!" Quinn's voice echoes off the walls. They release me only to grab my shoulders and spin me to face them. "Simon was such a grouchy old man while you were gone!"

From somewhere behind me - probably by the sink if he didn't move - Simon clicks his tongue. "I was not."

"Was too! You made Otto cry."

I glance back at Simon in time to see him roll his eyes. "Your point?" he questions.

Quinn spins me again and throws their arm around my shoulders to squish me into their side (I feel like a damn puppet). "My point being you were a major dickface without your little prodigy to brighten your godawful baking hours."

"I was not a major dickface," Simon huffs as he chucks a soggy sponge at Quinn's face.

Thankfully, Simon has great aim so as not to hit me; but much to his annoyance, Quinn ducks out of the way. The sponge hits the wall with a wet splat, momentarily sticking before falling to the floor.

"With all due respect, Sir," Stephanie pops up in the doorway, poking her head in the room to flash me a smile, "you were grumpier than usual without Liam."

Simon unties his apron and strolls over to us. Stopping in front of Quinn, he tosses the apron at their face before brushing past. "Is it a crime to enjoy an employee's company?" he grumbles as he heads for the breakroom.

Quinn elbows my ribs and flashes me a gleaming grin. "That's his way of saying he missed you."

The smile that breaks out on my face rivals Quinn's. Scratching at the heat rising to my neck, I chuckle. "I am quite loveable, aren't I?"

I may brush it off with a stupid joke on the outside, but on the inside, I fucking explode. Pride swells in my chest, because Simon fucking Hoover enjoys baking with me! If I'm dreaming, don't pinch me. Let me bathe in this glory for the rest of my life. Or maybe another few hours. That works too.

"If you don't want your fries, I'll eat 'em."

"Touch them and I kill you," I hiss at Alex. Not bothering to look up from the blank word doc mocking me on the laptop screen, I swat Alex's hand away from hovering over my tray of nothing but fries.

"Rude!" she huffs, settling further into the cushioned booth seat directly across from me. "Wake up on the wrong side of the bed today?"

"Excuse me for not being a ball of fucking sunshine." I slap away her hand again, this time with more force. "And don't you have someone else to steal food from? Like Cody? Where is that cue ball anyway?"

"I'm gonna tell him you called him that," she says between bites of fries.

Wait, what? When the fuck did she take my fries?

"Go ahead. Why don't you go find him and tell him right now?" I drone, pinching the bridge of my nose.

"No need. He's gonna join us in a bit."

Great, just great. There goes my lunch break, not that I'm being very productive anyway. That stupid blinking line on the word doc attests to my lack of productivity, but I can at least look like I'm getting something done. Fake it till you make it, right? If I act like I'm writing a 5-10 page essay, maybe I'll eventually get around to starting it (what with it being due in three days). But nope, today's not gonna be that day. I'll cross my fingers that I'll get around to it tomorrow. Probably not, but I can hope future me is slightly more responsible than current me.

With a sigh, I close my laptop and slip it into my book bag sitting between me and the wall. I reach for my tray of fries, finding only a few stray fries left. "Really, really?"

Alex swallows a mouthful of my fries. "What? You weren't eating them."

With a snap of my fingers, I point in the direction of the cafeteria. "You are going to buy me more fries, or I'm telling Cody it was you who pulled the fire alarm and blamed it on him."

"Come on, that was in middle school!" she protests and glares at me. Weighing her options, she shrugs it off. "He probably doesn't even remember that."

"He swore vengeance upon the perpetrator even if it took him his whole life to find them. And I quote, *I'ma find 'em or die trying.*"

"Yo, Lex!"

"Speak of the devil," I smirk as I watch Alex bristle at Cody's shouted greeting.

"Fine, I'll buy you more fries," she mumbles as she scoots out of the booth seat. "But this is the last time I ever do anything nice for you!"

Nice for me? More like repaying her debt. Unless she plans on getting an extra order of fries. Now that'd be–

My eyes follow Alex's departure, narrow at the tongue she sticks out at me, and then warily gaze in the direction she points. Ah, there's the cue ball - it's hard to miss the shine of his head - but far more lovely than the stupidly grinning Cody, in a maroon hoodie a size too large for him (probably Skyler's) with one hand in the pouch pocket, Nico raises a hand to wiggle his fingers in this cute little wave, and dear god do I swoon!

With a smirk, Cody slings an arm around Nico's shoulders and saunters the two of them over to me. He squeezes Nico closer to his side and beams his most shit-eating grin at me. "Surprise motherfucker. I accept thank you's in the form of cash, video games, and homemade cupcakes."

My hand reaches for Nico's sleeve on its own accord to pull him into the booth beside me. With my other, I push the remaining handful of fries across the tabletop to where Cody slides in across from me. "If this isn't sufficient, you'll have to send me a bill for the rest."

Cody's eyes rove over Nico. "Hmm," he rubs his chin, "I feel like Nico is worth more than a few stray fries."

"Then what else do you want?"

"You got a pencil and paper?"

I dig in my book bag and hand over a crumpled scrap of paper and a pen. As he busies himself with scribbling his demands, I lean into Nico and place a quick kiss to his cheek. "Did he kidnap you?" I whisper.

Nico chuckles, "No, I came voluntarily."

I feign a surprised gasp. "So you willingly left our child all alone and unsupervised?"

"Um... no?" he smiles innocently. Dark honey eyes glance down at his belly, and he pulls our clasped hands close enough for him to nudge the fabric of his hoodie pouch.

Craning my neck, I peer into the pocket and spot the curled up fur ball that is our baby. The pastel purple of her harness perfectly contrasts her dark fur, and the matching leash is bunched up in Nico's other hand as his fingers comb through her soft fur.

My fingers release their hold on Nico's to burrow inside the pouch. With the warmth of Nico's body heat and the fuzziness of the inner fabric, it's no wonder Cupcake fell asleep without a fuss. I stroke through her fur, my fingers brushing and entangling with Nico's fingers as he does the same.

"Oi, Lovebirds. I hate to break up such a precious family moment, but my demand list is complete."

Cody glances around the corridor, making sure no other students are looking our way, before not-so-sneakily sliding the piece of paper over to me. I pick it up, skimming over the short list and scoffing at his demands.

"Don't laugh!" he blurts. "This is a serious matter! Don't make me take Nico back!"

"No, no, it's just..." I wave the scrap of paper in the air as if it'll speak for me. "This is all you want? A baker's dozen of cookies 'n cream cupcakes? Do you even know what a baker's dozen is?"

"Yeah, it's—"

"And a week with my gaming laptop to binge *Sims*? Or probably my favorite, a full course meal on the day of your choice followed by a back massage and a night of free alcohol."

"What's so funny about that?" Cody squawks.

I drop the paper to the table and settle back against Nico. Within the hoodie pouch, my fingers playfully feather over Nico's as Alex joins our booth with a heaping tray of fries. "Well, considering it's Nico you're bartering with, your demands are a little... cheap. Like cupcakes and a meal?

I cook you food all the time. And when's the last time you supplied your own alcohol? That's always me too. So why would you ask for shit you already get?"

Alex smacks Cody's shoulder. "We talked about this! Why didn't you ask for eternal servitude?"

"Lex, listen," he quietly placates, hands gesturing to Nico and me. "You should've seen them being all gross and disgusting, gazing lovingly at each other and fawning over their furry baby - oh yeah, Cupcake's in the hoodie pocket! How fucking cute is that? And you expect me to ruin their disgustingly sweet family by enslaving daddy #2?"

"Oi! It's Fun Dad to you!" Fucking, Skyler. I am not daddy #2.

"Yeah, yeah, daddy #2. You should be grateful we - the famous kidnapping duo - are taking pity on you and not demanding your enslavement," Cody boasts.

"Nah-uh, it's too late for that," I counter. "Your demands have been submitted and accepted. No takesies-backsies."

"Dammit, Cody! How could you ruin our chance?"

"Look at them, Lex! Look at them for five minutes and tell me you'd be willing to tear them apart."

"You're just weak," Alex mumbles as her gaze turns to Nico and me.

Joke's on them, because I'd have agreed to eternal enslavement had they asked. Okay, maybe that's a lie. But if Nico's life was actually on the line, you best believe I'd agree to damn near anything to get him back and protect him.

But the kidnapping duo already submitted their demands, so no eternal servitude for me. And if Alex thinks I'm gonna make this easy for her, then she's got another thing coming.

Disgustingly sweet, huh?

"Sprinkles, dear, darling, honey, love bug, sweetie pie." Nico chokes back his laughter, and I struggle to keep a straight face. "Can I kiss the stars on your cheeks and your nose and your chin?"

"Of course... stud muffin." A quiet chuckle escapes Nico as he says it.

Cody gags - loud and definitely exaggerated. I hear Alex choke down a groan, but she hasn't admitted defeat yet.

So I nuzzle into the crook of Nico's neck, inhaling the faint scent of apple blossom body wash still lingering. Tipping my head up, my nose trails along the side of his neck until the tip touches his jaw while I blow a soft stream of air on my way up. Nico's skin trembles, and he squirms as he bites his lower lip to hold back his giggles. I pepper kisses to his jaw - soft, lingering presses of my lips - and work my way across his cheek, over his eyelid, stretching to reach his forehead and feeling his eyelashes brush against my cheek. He turns his head to give me better access to kiss down the bridge of his nose, and we lock gazes when I press my lips to the tip.

Liquid honey eyes crinkle at their corners, and soft lips - ones I'm more familiar with than my own - stretch into a breathless smile. Letting my eyes fall shut, I trail lower until our noses touch and our foreheads rest against one another.

"Okay, okay, that's enough. I'm getting cavities just watching you."

My eyes snap open at Alex's admittal of defeat. A few breathless puffs of laughter pass my lips, because wow, that was easy. For good measure, I rub our noses together before pulling back from Nico and settling in the cushioned seat with a smug smirk upon my face.

"But we were just getting warmed up," I say.

"Ooh?" Cody hums. "I didn't know you were an exhibitionist."

My nose wrinkles at the thought. Fuck that, I'm the only one who gets to see Nico when he comes undone. "Does that make your kink voyeurism?" I counter.

"Are you kidding me? Watching you two would probably give me diabetes."

I roll my eyes. "You inhale sugar on a daily basis."

"Exactly, so I can't handle the sweetness of..." He flails his hands toward Nico and me, trying to find the proper words. "Your cotton candy asses."

Nico snorts a laugh beside me. "What's so bad about cotton candy?" he asks.

"Ugh, it's because you guys don't even realize it."

Nico turns to me, lips pursed in confusion, and I shrug. "What's that mean?"

Alex and Cody share a disbelieving look before Alex plants her elbows on the tabletop and points a fry at me and then Nico. "Liam, you've been a damn grouch all month - glaring at your laptop like you're gonna murder it, snapping at some poor freshman who bumped into you, and scaring the living shit out of everyone who even glances your way."

"Hey now, that's because–"

"Yeah, yeah, because you're graduating in a couple weeks and have lots of essays and presentations to finish. My point," she emphasizes, "isn't to call you an asshole, because you're not. We get it, right Co?" She looks to Cody for support, and he nods his agreement.

"So what's your point then?"

"The moment we bring in Nico, you get all soft and you melt into this puddle of goo. It's cute, really, seeing you all head over heels."

I open my mouth to say something, but nothing comes out.

"Am I wrong?" she raises an eyebrow in question.

"Ah, um... no."

"Dude, you whipped."

Nico tries and utterly fails to suppress his laughter. His body shakes and his chest rumbles, and I can't help but join in.

Yeah, I'm whipped as fuck. Nico has me wrapped around his finger, and he doesn't even know it. Some might say he has me on a leash or he's got me by my balls, but that's bullshit. I willingly handed myself to him. He doesn't need a leash to tie me down, because there's no one else I'd rather be with.

"Oi, Liam."

My head pops through the proper hole as I slip into my sweater. Smoothing down the fabric, I turn to see what Simon wants. Did I forget to put the broom away or empty the mop bucket? No, I don't think so.

Simon has on his coat, a double-breasted black jacket, and he beckons me to follow him with a wiggle of his finger.

I quirk an eyebrow but don't question him. Silently, I follow him out the side door and into the parking lot. He continues down the sidewalk and turns onto the main street. With the morning foot traffic, I'm forced to fall into line behind Simon.

Where is he taking me? We're walking the same path to my apartment, but I doubt he's walking me to my doorstep. But what else is there that he'd want to show me? An office building? Unlikely. A little antique shop? Probably not. A mom and pop store? Maybe. But nothing in particular comes to mind.

Simon stops so suddenly I nearly walk right into him. "What do you think this building is?"

My eyes turn to the worn - sun-bleached and chipped - bricks of the building we stopped in front of. The large window is pretty useless, what with it being boarded up on the inside. The door - a dull and faded red - has a *For Rent* sign taped to it.

"Uh, abandoned?"

Simon snorts. "It might as well be."

When he doesn't elaborate, my gaze turns back to the burnt orange bricks. Trailing upward, it seems the second story is a residence, that too abandoned. "So what is it?"

Simon inhales a deep breath through his nose. His gray gaze leaves the building and lands upon me. "It's a proposition."

A TASTE OF SPRINKLES

Liam doesn't attend his graduation ceremony. Even with the earful Skyler gives him about regretting skipping such a major event in his life, Liam shrugs it off with a simple, "I have work." And that's the end of the conversation.

His grandma doesn't fare any better in convincing him to go. Her stubbornness clashes with Liam's, and they face off to a stalemate. And his mom, despite wanting to watch her baby boy walk across the stage with his accounting degree, leaves the decision up to Liam. Once more, he shrugs it off by saying, "Who the fuck schedules graduation in the middle of the day on a Saturday? Some of us have fucking jobs."

That's his fallback excuse. Every time Skyler or his grandma brings it up, he says his hands are tied. His job trumps a boring ass ceremony. But then Cody pipes up and says Simon would give Liam the day off no questions asked, and Liam changes the topic so fast you'd think Cody suggested murdering puppies.

It left me stumped as to why. That is until I lie awake at night, unable to fall back asleep. I curl closer to Liam's back, draping an arm over his middle and feeling Cupcake's fur at my fingertips. A single brush of my fingers has Cupcake's purrs filling the silence of night, and that's when it hits me.

The answer is right there on the opposite wall. A hole yet to be fixed - and probably won't be fixed until the landlord finds out about it. It was right there the entire time. Maybe Skyler wouldn't understand its meaning, but I do. After all, I helped clean up the broken shards and distinctly remember the photographs - the faces, the backdrops, the lack of Liam.

I can't possibly understand what he's feeling, because no one truly knows the pains of another, but I can understand why he's feeling and acting the way he is. This once in a lifetime event was never once in a lifetime for him. It was a near annual reminder of the growing gap between him and his brother. In his mind, Bryce kept climbing higher and higher while he remained at the bottom of the ladder. And you can only stare at someone's back for so long before you grow tired of chasing after them.

So maybe he grew tired long ago and resigned to the ridiculous idea that his achievements can't possibly hold up to his brother's. Which is ludicrous, but if that's how he feels, no one has the right to tell him he can't feel that way. No one has the right to tell him his emotions are wrong, because that won't change his lingering feelings of inadequacy. Add to that his father's nationwide scandal, and it's understandable why he'd want to avoid the public eyes of a graduation ceremony.

I tuck my head against his shoulders, pressing my lips to the base of this neck. My body curls to fit his like two puzzle pieces made for each other. "I'm proud of you," I murmur against his skin. No matter his decision, no matter what anyone else has to say about it; I'm proud of everything Liam has accomplished, and I'll support him through it all.

"I'll probably be late tonight, so you don't have to wait up for me," Liam says, ducking down to kiss my cheek.

My eyes flick away from the *Super Mario* level on the TV long enough for my Toadstool character to run off an edge. "Again?"

He scratches his nape. "Yeah, sorry. I can't turn down Simon's offer to stay late and cook."

"No, no, that's okay. Go have fun and level up your skills."

"Thanks, Sprinkles," he smiles, ruffling my hair with a chuckle as I run into an enemy turtle. He turns to leave, bidding farewell to Emil and me before heading out the door.

Thankfully, Emil is leagues above me when it comes to *Super Mario Bros*, and he's still alive in our multiplayer level. Jumping over turtles and eating mushrooms, Emil's Mario makes it to the flagpole first. After I jump for it and the little tune starts playing, I settle back into the couch cushions with a sigh.

Emil folds his legs beneath himself and drops his hands to his lap. Fingers fiddling mindlessly with the controller's buttons, he stares off to the side. "...it's the 22nd today."

"Yeah."

"Do you... do you really think he's working late? Or is he avoiding–"

"No, I believe him. Liam wouldn't lie to me, but..." With a soft sigh, my head tips back to the couch cushions and my gaze turns to the bumpy texture of the ceiling. A tan splotch stains the otherwise creamy color, and I can't help but wonder how it got up there.

"But he's not telling the whole truth?" Emil hesitantly finishes my thought.

"Kinda," I murmur, eyes falling shut. "I don't doubt he's actually working late. It's more the why that I'm worrying about."

A flick to my nose has my eyes snapping open in time to see Cupcake's belly as she's placed on my face. My little sweetheart is kind enough not to claw my face to shreds and wait patiently for me to put her in my lap and scratch her chin.

"Avoidance. Denial. Getting his mind off things," Skyler lists as he shuffles to round the couch and plops ungracefully on the other side of Emil.

How I manage not to hear a giant muscle man clad only in pink boxers with obnoxiously red kissy lips on them sneak up on me is a wonder I'll never understand.

Skyler sidles up to Emil's side and cups his cheek with one hand. The other inches toward Emil's lap while he wetly smooches Emil's lips. When Skyler wraps his fingers around his acquisition, he pulls away with a loud smack of his lips and a prideful grin upon his face.

Emil's so used to Skyler's not-so-sneaky tactics that he doesn't so much as bat an eye. He plays along and feigns shock to humor Skyler when Skyler presses a few buttons to continue to the next level of *Super Mario Bros*.

Leaning forward, Skyler rests his elbows on his knees and transfers into his competitive gamer mode. Which is a bit unnecessary considering he can't breeze through this level without me matching his pace. And that doesn't happen. Far from it actually. Skyler's Mario races forward but is stuck running in place on the right side of the screen.

"Come on, Nico. Get the lead out of your ass," he impatiently huffs. His meaty fingers jab buttons as if that'll somehow convince the game to leave me behind and let him continue on. But his impatience leads to Mario's demise when he runs into two enemy turtles, one right after the other.

He mutters a string of colorful profanities as he waits for Mario's recovery bubble to drop from the sky. The moment the bubble floats into view, he demands, "Let me out, let me out, let me out."

"Don't rush me," I counter back, focusing instead on the two turtles which took out Skyler. Jumping atop one, it retreats into its shell. My blue Toadstool kicks it, killing the second turtle in the process. But foolish me fails to see the green pipe sticking up from the ground. The spinning shell ricochets off the pipe and races back at Toad. In a panic, my thumbs smash every button they can reach; and I vaguely register Skyler yelling, "Jump, Nico, jump!"

...I don't jump.

"Ugh!" Skyler throws his hands up in the air, and it's a miracle the controller doesn't go flying across the room. Slumping back into the couch, his arm drops to Emil's lap to abandon the controller there. "This is too stressful for my fragile heart."

Emil and I both snort a laugh. "And playing with Cody and Alex is a cake walk, huh?" I ask.

"Exactly."

I beg to differ, but then again, I'm not the greatest gamer.

Emil picks up the controller, and we start the level from the beginning. Which is perfectly fine by me. I prefer playing with Emil anyway. He's more laid-back and patient, not all gung-ho about beating records and racing each other.

As Emil and I slowly work our way through the levels, Skyler outstretches his hand toward Cupcake. Snapping his fingers and clicking his tongue, he entices the kitty off her perch on my thigh. She walks across Emil and settles on Skyler's lap. Her little purr motor works overtime at the brush of Skyler's fingers through her silky black fur.

Cupcake's delightful purrs attract Simba and Furby to Skyler as well. About a week after we brought Cupcake home, Liam and I introduced her to the boys. I'd be lying if I said I wasn't a little worried (or a lot), but thankfully, it went off without a hitch. Furby was a little apprehensive at first, going so far as to hiss at her; but he ran off, calmed his bushy tail, and got over himself quite quickly. Simba, on the other hand, welcomed her with open paws and a lick to her head.

Simba leaps into Skyler's lap, landing with enough force to draw a quiet oomph from Skyler. The tubby cat circles around Cupcake a few times before plopping down with as much grace as his owner, nearly lying atop my little girl. It's comical to see, what with Simba being three times her size, and the cuteness distracts me enough to be hit by a flying fish.

To which Skyler cackles like a hyena, because yes, he can do better. So much better. But he sits back and watches, never once stealing Emil's controller. Eventually Furby joins the cat pile in his lap, albeit with definite space between him and the other two.

With both hands alternating between which cat to pet, Skyler quietly hums, "Liam'll be fine."

I somehow manage not to kill my poor Toadstool... again. You'd think I'd get used to Skyler dropping bombshells out of thin air, but nope. It never ceases to surprise me.

I school my features and focus on the game at hand. If I'm playing worse than normal, no one would think Toad being in the recovery bubble as odd. I guess that's one perk to sucking at video games. "I know."

"I know you know."

My lips purse at Skyler's words. "So~" I droll.

"Just reinforcing what you know."

I peek at Skyler to find golden eyes peeking back. Unlike me, his gaze doesn't dart away; I feel it on my face. It's like he has laser vision with how it burns my skin. "Th-thanks?"

"No problem, Mr. Worrywart."

"I am not—"

"You kinda are," Emil says, and I can feel Skyler's smile radiating smugness at the back up.

I huff a breath that ends with a childish pout. My gaze fixes on the characters on the TV. Fueled by pure spite and frustration, I breeze over pipes jutting from the ground and jump atop every turtle and angry mushroom in my path. With a running start, Toad leaps for the flagpole and grabs onto the very top. Mario stumbles to catch up and barely manages to reach the bottom of the pole before the celebratory sequence starts.

Huh. Spite's a great motivator. I could probably beat Alex right now, and she's the queen of everything Mario related.

"Dude, have you been hustling us this whole time?" Skyler gapes at the TV screen. "Innocent little Nico acting like he sucks at video games. You were waiting for us to let our guards down."

Completely ignoring his mini outburst, I huff a sigh and sag into the couch. "I am not a worrywart."

"Uh-huh. And I'm not overly dramatic." Emil grunts at an elbow jab to his ribs. "And Emil's not a sweaty giant."

"Rude," Emil elbows him back.

Okay, so maybe I do worry... a lot. But I feel it's warranted. Liam's track record for dealing with problems - especially emotionally fueled problems - isn't great. And today is the day of graduation, so you'll have to excuse me if I worry about my boyfriend's mental state. I don't want him overworking himself because he's running away again.

A flick to my cheek has me glaring at Skyler's arm where it snaked its way around Emil. "Nico, chill. Trust me, he's fine."

I can't chill. It's impossible, and Skyler won't let me leave to check on Liam. Which, okay, is a little excessive, but I'm restless. My legs itch to move, and I can only pace the room so long before Skyler snaps at me to sit my ass down. But then the details of one of his crime-solving dramas don't add up, and my nitpicking gets me banished to my room for the rest of the evening.

Like the adolescent child I am, I brood and pout and impatiently wait for my figurative parents to go to bed. When I hear the TV turn off and see the hallway light beneath the door become darkness, I slink to the door and press my ear to the wood. Skyler says something about how I'm probably asleep, to which I stifle a dry chuckle and wait for their bedroom door to click shut. I tell myself I'm gonna wait fifteen minutes just to be safe, but by seven minutes, my patience runs dry.

I crack the door open as slowly as humanly (demonly?) possible and peek my head out into the hall. Finding nothing but darkness, I tiptoe out of my room.

A loud meow startles me, and I flail to bring a finger to my lips. "Shhh," I shush Simba as he meows again.

I slink around the furry tattletale. When the hall opens up to the living room, I shuffle - one hand splayed on the wall to guide me - to find the lamp tucked in the far corner. My toes bump into the lamppost. It sways a bit but thankfully doesn't crash to the ground. I feel around under the lampshade for the knob, twisting it on once I locate it.

The lamp illuminates the corner of the room in a soft orange hue. While not being strong, the light's enough for me to navigate around the couch without stubbing a toe and to find the TV remote with relative ease.

I press the power button on the remote. Before the TV has the chance to roar to life, my finger rapidly smashes the volume button until the only sound is my heart beating like a jackhammer.

With a quiet sigh, I drop to the couch, hand over my heart to calm its thumping. When my adrenaline no longer spikes through the roof, I lie down and try not to kick Furby sleeping on the other end of the couch.

Absentmindedly, I flip through the channels and settle on some whale documentary. I can barely hear what the narrator says, but the whales in their ocean habitat are breathtakingly beautiful to watch. If they're this magnificent in HD, I can't even imagine what it'd be like to see them in person, to be in the same ocean as them, to swim beside them. It'd probably be scary as hell with how enormous they are (not to mention dangerous), but how many people can say they've swum with whales? Like how cool would that be!

It's too bad whales don't come in a pocket size. I would adopt a whole pod of them and build a gigantic tank for them to call home, and the tank will be so big that I can swim in it. And each of my whales will have a handpicked name that suits their personality. And it'll be perfect.

Yeah, that'd be the life.

Somewhere between dreaming about my pocket-sized whale pod and a really, really long commercial, I drift off - not fully, but to this semi-conscious state of lucidness. I'm pretty sure the whale documentary is long over, but who knows? The blue-ish blur of the TV kinda looks like an ocean backdrop, but the colorful pops of color make me doubt it's about whales. Maybe coral reefs? Or some species of tropical fish?

"-kles." The blurry light of the TV is blocked by... a head? "Sprinkles." A touch presses against my shoulder, growing more incessant until my eyes blink to clear my vision. "You with me, Nico?"

Even I'm not sure with how magical Liam's little laugh sounds in my ears. It seems pretty dreamlike to me.

My arm's heavy and groggy as it reaches to touch Liam's face. Fingers poking his squishy cheeks, I feel his smile stretch even bigger under my touch. "Mmm, what time is it?"

"Way past your bedtime. What are you still doing up, or well, half-asleep on the couch?"

Ah, his voice is so nice. So soft and quiet and soothing. "Been waiting for you."

Liam's hand covers mine on his cheek, his thumb mirroring my stroking. How long have I been stroking his cheek? "Come on, Sprinkles." He stands up straight, his face disappearing from my line of vision.

"Mmm, where are we going?"

"To bed," Liam chuckles as he grasps my shoulder to sit me upright.

I sway a bit as I try to get my bearing. Couch beneath me. TV still on some ocean documentary. The lamp's off. The overhead lights are on though. Huh, where'd Furby go?

"Come on, Sprinkles. You gotta help me out here, cause we both know I'm not strong enough to carry you." Liam grabs my wrists to pull me to my feet, but my dead weight doesn't leave the couch.

"You could try," I mumble.

"Okay, how 'bout this?" Liam releases my wrists and turns his back to me. He squats low and holds his arms behind himself, wiggling his fingers to entice me.

As if I need to be enticed.

My arms drape around his neck, and my legs wrap around his waist. His fingers dig into my thighs to get a firm hold before he straightens with a soft grunt. I nuzzle into his neck, inhaling a faint muskiness of the day's sweat; and my body sags against his.

"Hey, Sprinkles? Help me out and get the lights?"

I hum at that, vaguely wondering if we're gonna leave the TV on all night. I guess that's a yes as Liam walks toward our bedroom. He pauses long enough for me to fumble with the light switch before continuing to our room. Liam takes me to the bed, backing up till he safely deposits (drops) me on the mattress.

"Don't squash Cupcake and Furby," he says as he moves to close the door.

Found Furby! He's sleeping at the foot of the bed, butt to butt with Cupcake.

It takes too much energy to remain upright, so I let myself fall to the mattress. My eyes close before my head hits the pillow.

"You're not leaving me much room, Sprinkles," Liam says, voice light with amusement.

Eyes still closed, I hold open my arms.

A quiet puff of laughter escapes him before Liam slips into the little space available to him. He scoots and wiggles closer, and I encircle him in my arms. "Well, aren't you downright adorable tonight?" he says, forehead pressed against my breast.

"Missed you. Worried about you," I murmur.

"Hmm? Worried?"

"Yeah."

"Why?"

"Graduation."

"Oh." He reaches up to flick my nose, and then his hand settles over my heart. "I don't care about that anymore."

"You sure?"

"Positive."

Liam works... a lot. More than usual. Even on days he's not scheduled. I guess it's to be expected with him being out of school, but I didn't think I'd be this lonely. There are only so many books to read and so many games to play and so many shows to watch. They're not as fun by myself.

And it's not like I can get a job. I'd actually love to be able to pull my own weight around the apartment and help with bills; but as Skyler helpfully pointed out, I'm a demon. I don't have any form of identification. There are no records of me in this world - no birth certificate, no paper trail of my life, and no way to legally acquire them. So for our own safety, we deemed me getting a job as a bad idea.

But on the bright side, the apartment is spotless. The floors are swept and vacuumed. The dishes are washed. Laundry's done - folded, hung, and put away. The trash has been taken out. The toilet's scrubbed clean. The odd stain on the living room ceiling - gone.

I'm ready to break out the *Sims* game and redesign Liam's sim to be dorkier when there's a quick, unending series of knocks at the door. I've heard it enough now to recognize the knocks as Cody.

I hop up from my perch on the couch so fast Simba goes tumbling from my lap. I'm at the door a breath later, and one more breath unlocks it to yank it open. "Hi, Co–"

Cody waves his hand in tight circles before tucking his arm against his abdomen. A deep bow smoothly follows. "Commoner of the land, I present to you the great Alexis of Barnes." His arm sweeps out to the side as he steps back to reveal Alex.

"Thank you, my dear court jester," she addresses Cody. As she turns her blindingly bright smile to me, she reaches to her back pant pocket to pull out... nothing? She holds an invisible something up in front of her and acts out unraveling it.

She clears her throat as she reads off invisible words from an invisible... scroll. "The Liam is feeling like a complete assnugget and sends his apologies for neglecting his precious Sprinkles. But no worries, my friend, we have been sent to chase the loneliness from your heart."

I stifle a snort at *assnugget* and watch as Alex rolls up her nonexistent scroll to stash it in her back pocket. She steps closer and wiggles her finger for me to lend her my ear.

"And between you and me," she dramatically whispers, eyes scanning the hallway for eavesdroppers. "The peasant Liam is being quite secretive with his recent activities, but no worries, my friend. He's not cheating."

"We'd skin him alive and hang him by his balls if he was," Cody pipes up a little too enthusiastically.

I cringe at the mere thought of Liam hanging by his balls. It's a good thing he'd never cheat - or even think about cheating - on me, because Cody sounds more than ready to fulfill that promise.

"Uh, thanks?" Should I be thanking them for the promise of skinning my boyfriend alive? Probably not, but it's the thought that counts, right? Even if it's a morbidly gruesome thought.

"No problem, buddy. What else are friends for?" Cody strolls over and slings an arm around my neck. He leads me from beneath the threshold and pulls the apartment door closed behind us.

"So where are we going?"

Alex skips down the stairs two or three at a time. "Courtesy of Liam's wallet, we're going to the movies and then out to eat and then to the mall to spend whatever's left."

I perk up at the mention of the movies, running ahead of Cody to catch up with Alex. "Can we see the animated one about the bunny and the fox?"

"Funny you say that. Liam suggested the same movie."

Of course, he did. I melt to goo every time a commercial for it comes on, because the animals are so freaking cute! And maybe Liam has me conditioned to love all things *Disney* and *Pixar* (even if *Disney* lies to me). It sucks that Liam can't join us, because he's really excited to see it too. But I guess that means I'll have to go again to see it with him. Or he'll probably buy it the moment it comes out on DVD, and we'll watch it a billion times in a row.

Cody catches up to us on the sidewalk outside. He and Alex sandwich me between them, Cody slinging an arm around my neck and Alex linking our arms together. With a mischievous grin, Cody leans in close. "My buddy, my pal, my man, you gotta have an idea of what Liam's been up to. Why don't you share it with your bestest friends in the whole wide world?"

My gaze flicks between Cody's waggling eyebrows and Alex's puppy dog eyes. But I'm not exactly sure what they're after. "Working, I think."

"We know that, but doing what?"

Shouldn't they know more than me? I mean, they're his co-workers after all. "Cooking, probably."

"Nah-uh. That's a bunch of bullshit," Cody says.

"Huh?" He works at a diner. What else would he be doing?

"Oh, Nico, my poor naive child." Alex shakes her head back and forth with feigned pity. "Looks like you've been left out of the loop too."

"Or maybe there's no loop to begin with?"

"Nah man, there's definitely a loop. Like those late nights, what the hell are he and Simon doing?"

"Cooking. Cause they're chefs. At a diner. Where they cook."

"You don't cook in someone's office," Alex counters. She releases her hold on my arm to skip ahead of Cody and me. Her arms swing at her sides while she spins to face us. Continuing down the sidewalk backwards, it's a miracle she doesn't walk into traffic. "And I know something's up, cause even Quinn has no idea what they're doing; and they know all the juicy dirt in the diner."

"Maybe they're developing recipes or, you know, talking, like people tend to do," I suggest.

"Or~" Cody emphasizes as he joins Alex in skipping backwards. "They're having an illicit love affair."

A snort of amusement escapes me before I can stifle it with my hand. "Uh-huh, sure. That's exactly what he's doing," I say between bursts of laughter.

"Actually, it's a threesome, cause I saw the owner heading back to Simon's office before we left," Alex says.

"Ugh damn! Liam gets to fuck Mr. Handsome! That's not fair! I wanna fuck Mr. Handsome!" Cody's exclamation has a few bystanders glancing warily in our direction, and I think an elderly businessman may have had a heart attack.

"Me too!" Alex chirps.

"I'd say me three, but I don't know who Mr. Handsome is."

"Ah, if you saw him, you'd be A-okay with Liam fucking him. He's that handsome," Alex nearly swoons.

Absorbed in their fantasy soap opera, I grab their wrists and yank them away from the car that could've flattened them into pancakes. But almost walking into traffic can't snap them out of their ongoing narratives. It does have me wondering about this Mr. Handsome though.

But between my snorts and gasps of laughter, I can't form a coherent sentence. The more detailed their theory gets, the more ridiculous it sounds. From late night rendezvous to getting saucy in the kitchen, their imagination knows no bounds. They could probably entertain Skyler for hours on end, because it's really starting to sound like the soap operas he marathons.

Thankfully, they put their script writing on hold when we get to the theater. Which is a godsend considering how many children are here with their parents.

It turns out, Alex really does have Liam's wallet, or well, Cody does, but only because it's too big to fit in Alex's pant pocket. We buy our tickets and a mountain load of snacks before heading to the correct theater. I breathe a sigh of relief to find we're the only three there - a perk to waiting a few weeks after opening weekend to see it - because I really don't want to cry in a theater full of children. Liam told me of when he went to see *Big Hero 6* opening weekend; and he, Skyler, and Emil bawled their eyes out while all the little kids stared at them because they didn't understand (spoiler alert) Tadashi died. And my record with *Disney* movies is far from tear-free.

Although by the looks of the opening scene, I'll have to control my *Aww!* reflex more than my tear ducts, because oh my gosh the tiger cub and bunny kit are so freaking cute! I just wanna pet them and hold them and oh gosh, how am I gonna handle the rest of the movie if the first two minutes have me gushing?

And the animation! Oh gosh, the animation! It's breathtaking! So smooth and beautiful and the attention to detail! Ugh, I love *Disney* so much!

"It's called a hustle, sweetheart," Cody mimics the fox with a laugh.

With how much we're laughing and the amount of side comments being tossed around, it's great we're by ourselves. Otherwise, there's no doubt in my mind we would've been kicked out by now.

An hour and a half later, we're watching the ending song sequence and dear god those tigers have moves. As Cody so eloquently put it, "I'm not a furry, but damn those tigers got some stripper hips." And I mean, he's kind of right.

As it turns out, Liam was quite generous in his funding of this outing. A nice restaurant and a trip to the mall later, I have to convince Alex to give me his wallet back before she breaks out the credit cards. I'm sure she's only joking about draining his bank account dry, but I still feel better having the wallet in my possession.

By the time we're on our way home, the sun has set and the streetlamps have switched on. Cody and Alex walk an extra few blocks out of their way to drop me off at my apartment building, waving goodbye as they backtrack to their own apartment.

When I turn the knob of the apartment door, I'm both relieved and appalled to find it unlocked. On one hand, thank god because I didn't bring the spare key with me. On the other, it's dangerous with how late it is. Hasn't Liam or Skyler ever heard of the serial killer who would only kill people who left their doors unlocked? No? Well, I have, because you come across a lot of useless facts and information when surfing the internet.

I push the door open slowly and peek inside before committing to facing a potential intruder. My gaze sweeps across the apartment, noting the lights turned on and the low volume of the TV murmuring from the living room. No sign of a serial killer present, unless the sound of sloshing water and utensils clanking against the sink basin in the kitchen is the intruder doing our dishes. Which would be extremely polite and considerate of them. And I'd have to thank them before yelling for help.

Slipping inside, I flip the lock of the door before quietly wandering to the kitchen. Maybe even more surprising than seeing an intruder being kind enough to do the dishes, I stare upon Liam's naked back - the wings and tail of his Phoenix wrapping his side - and navy boxers snug against his skin. Soapy suds clinging to his hands, he stifles a yawn against his forearm, eyes squeezing shut and moisture collecting in their corners. He blinks a few times as if to chase sleep away before glancing at the glare in the window, lips upturning into a soft smile at my reflection.

"Hey," he sleepily greets as he angles his body toward me. "How was the movie?"

I close the last few steps of space between us and press a quick peck to his cheek. "It was so good," I say as I grab the towel lying on the counter to help finish the dishes faster. "And super cute! There's a fennec fox in it that dresses up in an elephant costume and oh my god it was so adorable! I want seven of them!"

"Seven?" Liam quietly laughs. "Where are you going to keep them?"

"Hmm, I don't know. I'll figure it out after I get them."

Liam hums softly at that. His hands dip back into the sudsy water, his movements a little sluggish and slow as he scrubs a plate clean. Eyes half-lidded, he sways a bit on his feet. He blinks his eyes wide and shakes his head.

"If you're tired, you should go to bed," I say.

"'M not tired," he finishes with a yawn.

"Sure you're not." I flick the towel at him, and he yelps when it snaps against his butt. "Go to bed."

Liam's eyes narrow - a sheen to his copper irises - as he sends a weak glare my way. "Why don't you try to make me?"

My lips purse as I consider doing just that. The few remaining dishes can wait, and honestly I won't be surprised if Liam passes out before we finish them. So yeah, I can make him.

Deliberately slow, I set the towel on the counter as my lips upturn into a cheeky grin. Before Liam can even register my actions, I sweep him off his feet princess-style. He startles with a shrill yelp as his hands scramble for purchase in my t-shirt.

"What are you doing? Put me– Ugh! If you want to, I'd greatly appreciate being put down!" Liam kicks his legs and squirms in my hold.

"Nope. Don't wanna," I singsong, striding from the kitchen. "Be a dear and cooperate."

"Nico!"

"Hush, dear. You'll wake up Skyler."

"Good! It can be payback for having to hear his sexy times," Liam huffs, crossing his arms over his chest.

"Yes, yes. Whatever you say."

Liam ceases all struggles when we reach the bedroom, even if he's a little grumpy about it. But his grumpiness fades away the moment his head hits the pillow. He groans his contentment and melts into the mattress like his bones are liquid goo. "Are you gonna tell me a bedtime story too?" he sleepily mumbles.

"Hmm," I consider as I let Furby and Cupcake into the room before shutting the door (Simba must've gone to bed with Skyler). "Alex and Cody told me a story today you'd absolutely love to hear."

"Would I, though?" Liam rolls onto his stomach and buries his face in his pillow.

"I'm sure you'll appreciate it," I say.

He groans at that as I join him in bed. Turning his head enough for me to hear, he says, "Try me."

"Once upon a time, in a land not so far away–"

"They told you a fairy tale?"

"Hush. Interrupting is rude." I flick his cheek and purposefully clear my throat. "As I was saying, there once lived a peasant by the name of Liam."

"Once? What happened to him?" The corner of his lips turn up as he peeks at me from the corner of his eye.

"He kept interrupting his boyfriend until the boyfriend smothered him in his sleep."

"Well, that's rude."

"Anyway," I flick him again, "the peasant slaved away day after day, or so his poor lonely boyfriend thought. Until one day when the peasant's friends saw him enter his boss's office. The boyfriend thought nothing of it - cause he, of course, trusted his lover - but the peasant's friends let their imagination go wild with images of the peasant bent over his boss's desk."

"Ugh eww!" Liam's face twists in disgust as he pushes himself up on his elbows. "I'm gonna fucking kill–"

"Wait, there's more." I press a finger to his lips to shush him. "Apparently, while your boss had you bent over his desk–"

"Oh my god, stop!"

"–a Greek god of a man joined your illicit love affair to make it a dirty threesome."

"Greek god? Who the fuck's that?"

"Uh, Alex called him Mr. Handsome."

"Oh, Dietrich." Liam's eyes soften to something dream-like. "He's the reason I now differentiate between pretty, handsome, and beautiful. Like there's a difference. He's not pretty or beautiful. He's fucking handsome - probably the most handsome man on the planet."

"What am I then?"

Liam hums and turns to lie on his side, facing me. Without missing a beat, he says, "Beautiful. Absolutely stunning. Takes my breath away every time."

I wonder if this skipping of my heart and the fluttering of butterflies in my chest will ever stop. A year from now - five years, ten - will my cheeks still flush with heat at such words? God, I sure hope so.

"You're so sappy," I breathe out with a quiet laugh.

"You love my sap."

"Yeah, I do."

"And I'm not having an illicit love affair with Simon and Dietrich," he huffs.

"I know, but Alex and Cody think you are."

He's quiet for a long moment - long enough I'd think he fell asleep if his eyes weren't still open. But then he sighs as if he's come to some sort of conclusion to his own thoughts. "I wanted to keep it a secret a while longer - until it was completely done and finalized - but I should probably tell you before the monkeys convince you of my fictional love affair."

"Tell me what?"

"Um, I haven't exactly been working overtime, per se. Simon's been helping me with a... um, project."

"A project?"

"Yeah. It's nothing bad, I swear. And it's not a love affair." Liam pulls the blanket up to his chin and burrows beneath it like a turtle. "It's, uh, probably easier to just show you, so if you don't have any plans tomorrow..." he trails off.

"Seems like I have a date with you," I say, smiling through the darkness.

Liam stifles a yawn and nuzzles his head into the pillow. "It's a date then."

"Wah!" I jolt upward with a startled shout, eyes flying open as my heart races in my chest. Blanket pooling at my waist, I jerk back at the face mere millimeters from mine, nearly falling back to the mattress. My eyes blink for clarity as my mind registers the body straddling my lap.

"Morning sunshine."

Rubbing the sleep from my eyes, I wearily peer at the out of the ordinary smile, albeit a tad nervous, welcoming me to consciousness. "Morning. What are you doing?"

"Waking sleeping beauty, obviously," Liam says as he swings his leg over me to stand.

My gaze follows him, taking in his appearance of dark jeans, a fitted tee, and sneakers. I glance at the bedside clock, but it only adds to my confusion as to why Liam - wide awake so early on a day when he can sleep in - jumped on the bed to wake me up. "Are we going somewhere?" I ask as I swing my legs to the floor.

"Yeah. My surprise, remember?"

Ah, yes, our date. But at 7:15 a.m.? When he said tomorrow, I had thought something more along the lines of mid-afternoon or early evening. But, hey, if Liam wants to go out an hour and a half after the sun rises, then that's what we're gonna do.

"Yes, yes, I remember. But why so early?"

Liam helpfully tosses a shirt and jeans at me. "Because I'd rather not have to bring Skyler along. I want you to be the first to see it, so we gotta go before he wakes up."

I slip the shirt over my head and wiggle into the jeans - the pair Liam says make my butt look good. "We both know he doesn't get out of bed till noon during summer break."

"Don't wanna risk it." Liam extends his hand to me, fingers wiggling in invitation. "Shall we?"

"Hold that thought." I brush my fingers against his as I walk past him to make a quick trip to the bathroom. I rush through my morning routine - minus the shower - as quick as I can, because there's no way I'm leaving the apartment without brushing my teeth and combing my hair, especially when I don't know where we're going or what we're doing.

As we leave, Liam swipes two keys off the dining table - the apartment key and one I'm not familiar with. But I think nothing of it. For all I know, it could be a key to a padlock or even a spare for the diner (he's there early enough and late enough to warrant one). Whatever it opens, I'm sure I'll find out soon enough.

Liam's fingers twitch and fidget in my grasp, his palms growing clammy the further we walk. "You know," I say, squeezing his hand firmly and swinging our arms between us, "you don't have to show me if you don't want to."

"Ah, it's not that." He wiggles his fingers, brushing them against my knuckles. "It's a good kind of nervous. The excited kind - like the night before a school field trip and you're so excited and jittery you can't sleep."

My eyes roam the buildings around us as the apartment complexes are replaced with the older, brick-faced businesses I've become quite familiar with. "So this is gonna be as fun as a field trip?"

"Better." Liam's eyes sparkle - *sparkle* - as they light up with the elation of a child. "So much better."

Liam picks up his pace, pulling me along as we dodge people out on their morning jogs. We nearly run into a man with his nose buried in his phone, but we pivot last minute to avoid a collision, although the man looks up to glower at us before continuing on his way. The minor interaction doesn't damper Liam's spirit in the slightest. If he's any more chipper, he'll be skipping down the sidewalk while singing inspirational *Disney* songs.

He skitters to a stop so suddenly; I walk right into his back. "Sorry," I laugh a little breathlessly as I take a step back.

But Liam barely notices my blunder, his eyes locked on the building he stopped in front of. My gaze follows his. Pristine brick - probably from a fresh coat of paint - contrasts its worn and weathered counterparts of the buildings on each side. Windows so clean there's not a single speck or fingerprint on the glass flank a shiny red door. As my gaze travels up, I spot a circular sign hanging above us to be easily read by passersby on the sidewalk. Craning my neck, I read the words wrapped around a colorful cupcake.

My breath hitches on the last word, and moisture quickly pools at the corners of my eyes. "O-oh my god, Liam. You– It–" my voice fails me as I turn my watery gaze to Liam.

He stares off to the side, his eyes momentarily flicking to my face. A light flush of pink dusts his cheeks as a hand reaches up to scratch at the nape of his neck. "What do you think of the name?" he asks, bottom lip between the bite of his teeth.

A puff of laughter escapes me as my eyes look once more to the sign hanging above us. "It's a little naughty, don't you think?"

"A tad bit, maybe," Liam says, his voice soft and tender.

When my eyes return to him, I find him staring back, as if he never stopped gazing at my face to begin with. There's a fondness to his metallic eyes that shines when the sun catches it at the right angle; and if I wasn't already on the verge of tears, the gaze he looks upon me with would've done the job. Because here we are standing in front of Liam's dream - tangible and real and finally reached - and the man is looking at me as if I'm the last star in the night sky, as if this is the moment where his dream has finally been achieved.

"*A Taste of Sprinkles,*" I test the words on my lips, feel how they roll off my tongue.

"Has a better ring to it than Holt's Cupcakery."

Ah, I can see it now. The customers are probably gonna have a good laugh when they overhear Liam call me Sprinkles, and they put two and two together. And Cody's going to have even more whip jokes, and Alex will want to try one of everything. Skyler's gonna be the boasting dad who'll brag about Liam to everyone he knows. Emil will quietly offer a helping hand in his free time; and Kari'll offer to taste test everything to check for poison, to which Fae will remind her that Liam might actually poison her if she keeps stealing frosting. Stephanie and the other cooks from the diner will drop by with their congratulations, and the guys will inquire about a former colleague discount.

"There's more," Liam says. He fishes for the mystery key in his pocket and unlocks the shiny red door. Squeezing my hand, he pulls me into his dreams.

Soft blue walls engulf us as we step on checkered black and white tiles. Square tabletops and chairs of blue and red and yellow and green give off a childlike and whimsical aura. It's welcoming without the colors overpowering the senses.

"This... this is amazing, Liam," I say in awe. I stumble to keep up with him - far too busy admiring the cartoonish cupcake cutouts on the walls - as he leads me behind the counter and display case. "Liam, hang on–"

"Later," he says, pushing through bright blue saloon-like doors. The room opens up to what must be heaven for Liam. After spending the last couple years baking in a cramped apartment kitchen with outdated appliances, this is like a gold mine with pristine ovens and mixers and worktables.

My voice comes out breathless when I ask, "How did you–"

"Questions later. There's more."

More? What more could there possibly be? I am staring at Liam's dream - his future. How can there be something more important he wants to show me?

He doesn't so much as glance at the shiny metal of the appliances as he leads me to the back. But then again, how long has he been keeping this a secret? I would've loved to see the look on his face the first time he saw this place. Did tears of joy - built up from the years of believing it was only a dream that'd never come to fruition - trail down his cheeks? Or was he at a loss for words, standing and staring for who knows how long until it finally sunk in?

There's a staircase hidden in the back, one you'd likely miss if you didn't know it was there. The steps squeak a little under our weight as we climb them. At the top, Liam pushes open a door, walking through it and glancing back at me expectantly.

I stop dead in my tracks, one foot still on a step, as my eyes take in the image before me. One large living space - completely open concept - stares back at me. Kitchen cabinets and a prep island are in the far left corner, but otherwise it's completely bare of furniture. The white walls - only interrupted by a door directly to our left (a second entrance from the alleyway?) - lead into a high ceiling. In the middle of the room, a black iron spiral staircase winds its way to an open loft where matching black railings serve as a safety precaution to keep anyone from falling into the potential dining room.

"Oh, Liam." I turn my gaze to him. He's a little blurry from the tears clouding my vision, but I'll always recognize that tender smile of his - the one that's accompanied with a fond sheen to his eyes.

"Surprise, Sprinkles." He squeezes my hand and coaxes me all the way into the space. "It's a little bare at the moment, but I figured we could fill it together. Although I'm not 100% sure how we're gonna get a bed up to the loft."

I snort a laugh at the mental image of Liam and me utterly failing to get a mattress up those stairs. Much less a dresser or two.

"How did you..?" I trail off, not really sure which question I want to ask first.

"So Mr. Handsome, right," Liam goes into full blown story mode. "He's the owner of the diner and a whole bunch of other property in the city. He finally got the last guy who rented this place to leave, which apparently was a huge battle cause the dude thought he was high and mighty, and even Gordon Ramsay couldn't have redeemed this guy's cooking skills.

"Anyway, Dietrich told Simon about this place, and Simon, he–" Liam clears his throat as his emotions start to catch up to him. "He offered me a deal. Or well, a partnership. He put up most of the money and said I can pay him back after we get this cupcakery up and running. After a few profitable years, we both hope I'll be able to buy him out, and then it'll be ours."

Ours. All of this - he wants me to be a part of it. I'm a part of his dream.

"So all the late nights…"

"Weren't me having an illicit love affair with my boss," he laughs, the sound echoing in the empty space around us. "We were working out recipes and finances and interior design. All that fun stuff. We wanna be ready to open next month, so it'll probably be even more hours spent fine tweaking everything."

"And how long until we move in here?"

"Whenever you want. We just gotta steal my couch from the apartment, because I am not leaving that there."

"Even if I said today?"

Liam leans in close to my side and presses his lips to my cheek. "Yeah."

"Today then."

"Alrighty. It's time to wake up a bunch of friends and force them to help us move our shit." The radiance of Liam's smile rivals that of the sun, and I'm not sure if it's because of how happy he is we're moving into a place of our own or if he's excited to wake up a bunch of college kids on summer break who probably just went to bed a couple hours ago.

"It's barely 8 o'clock. Don't you think we should wait a few hours?"

"No time like the present." He lets go of my hand and heads for the staircase. Holding the door open with one hand, his other gestures to the stairs. "Shall we?"

One more glance at the space - imagining it with pictures on the walls, cat toys on the floor, our coats hanging by the door - before I walk down the stairs. And I wonder if Liam sees the same thing as he gives our home - *our home* - a final glance before pulling the door shut behind us.

HEARTS

"This... is weirder than I thought it'd be."

My breathless laugh caresses the skin of Nico's neck, and I feel his body shiver beneath mine. "Is it the no-door thing?"

"Yeah. What if Cupcake comes up here?"

"She won't," I murmur against his earlobe. "She's sleeping on the couch."

"But what if she does?"

The genuine concern in his voice has me choking back a chuckle. I straighten from leaning over Nico and sit back on my haunches. My fingers still inside him momentarily cease their prep work. "I can lock her in the bathroom real quick if you're that worried."

Nico feigns an overdramatic gasp. "You'd lock our baby in the bathroom to satisfy our physical desires? No wonder you're daddy #2."

"I swear to god, Nico." I flick his forehead with my free hand.

He accepts the flick without swatting my hand away, probably too busy laughing at my expense to care. The laughter runs through him - his chest rumbling, his wings fluttering lightly against the mattress, his tail swishing like a cat's. Moisture pools in the corners of his eyes as fast as he can wipe it away.

With a single flick of my wrist, he's gasping for a completely different reason. "Not fair," he pouts, and dear god his cheeks puffed out and his fangs poking between his lips is the cutest thing I've ever seen.

"You know," I drawl, continuing from before I was so rudely called the inferior caretaker of our fur baby. "We can ask Skyler and Emil to lend us our old room for an hour."

Nico's nose scrunches at the idea. "How 'bout we don't?"

"So I can continue?"

"Please do." Nico hooks a leg around my waist, heel at the small of my back.

I don't need to be told twice.

My fingers resume their strokes to work him open as my lips find his neck once more. Mere brushes against his freckled skin, my lips roam his neck before traveling lower to his collarbone, latching on to suck my mark upon his flesh. Nico's hum of approval spurs me to suck similar marks all across his chest, his abdominals, his hips.

Nico's fingers find purchase in my hair, nails scratching my scalp. "L-liam." Oh god, I'll never get used to the breathless lilt of my name - *my name* - upon his lips. It has my body heating up even more, the warmth spreading from my core. "E-enough teasing. I'm ready."

My lips leave the junction of his vee with a slight pop. "Oh hell no. I wanna savor this."

"But Liam~" he moans with a playful smile and a glint to his honey eyes. "I want you."

"Oh fuck," I groan, because his words go straight to my groin. Sprinkles isn't playing fair. "But we're christening the new bed."

"Can't we just break a bottle of champagne over it later and call it good?"

"Haha, no. That's a waste of perfectly good alcohol. But I guess—" my fingers curl to rub against Nico's sweet spot, eliciting a drawn-out whine from him "—since you seduced me so nicely, I have no choice but to comply."

"Aw, aren't you so sweet?"

I snort a laugh at the hint of sarcasm lacing his words. "The sweetest," I whisper, before catching his lips in a slow kiss.

My fingers withdraw from him as I lean back on my knees. Reaching for the foil packet abandoned on the bed, I tear it open and roll it down my length.

When my gaze returns to Nico spread out before me - the heat coloring his skin, onyx wings stretched out beneath his back, the tuft of his tail tickling my calf, his heel digging into my lower back to draw me back in - my breath catches in my throat at the beauty of it all, of him. No matter how many times I've seen his naked body or have been allowed to look upon his demonic features, it never ceases to amaze me how each time feels like the first.

"Liam," Nico says so quietly I almost miss it over the blood pounding through my veins. He averts his gaze - head tilted to the side - and chews on his bottom lip. The flush to his skin - his cheeks, the tips of his ears, all across his chest - deepens.

Ah, my Sprinkles. He so easily casts adoring eyes upon me; but when the tables are turned, he gets adorably flustered. Of course, I'm not one to talk. All he has to do is exist in my general presence and he leaves me breathless by simply being.

"You ready?"

He quirks a mischievous grin. "I've been waiting 84 years."

I physically facepalm. "I thought we agreed no memes in bed."

Nico shrugs his shoulders and sticks out his tongue at me like a fucking five-year-old. He's such a little shit sometimes; but you know what, I wouldn't have it any other way, because sex would be so damn boring if we couldn't laugh and joke and push each other's buttons.

With a firm grip on his waist, I ease myself into his heat, a low rumble in my throat at the tightness. Breathless sighs and quiet gasps slip through his parted lips as eyelids fall shut. His fingers find purchase in the pillow, their nails scratching the fabric when I'd much prefer them to be marking up my back or twisting in my hair.

Fully seated in him, I seek out his touch - the feel of his skin against mine, chest to chest, leaning my weight upon my forearms. My forehead drops to his shoulder, eyes squeezing shut 'cause, fuck, it feels so damn good. "Ahh, fuck, Nico,"

Nico's breathy laugh caresses my cheek. "That's the plan."

Despite having the urge to roll my eyes, the corners of my lips upturn into a fond smile. "Haha, very funny, Sprin– Ahh!"

The leg hooked around my waist yanks me forward, drawing me as close as physically possible, as a gasp falls from my lips. Ugh, goddammit, it's not fair. One little action from him, and I'm falling apart at my seams. Okay, so it's not one action - it's the heat of his body seeping into my skin, his tail wrapping around my ankle and snaking its way up my leg, each stuttered breath stoking the fire within me - but still. Nico never fails to unwind me one thread at a time, but nothing sends me over the edge like Nico crying out his love for me as he finally loses it.

So let's turn the tables and work some magic to hear Nico choking back moans and writhing beneath me and tugging at strands of my hair.

Lips latching onto his collarbone, I suck another mark among his freckles as I draw my hips back only to roll them forward again. Slow, shallow at first but gradually deepening with each thrust, that's how Nico likes it - a steady buildup of heat and friction and emotions until it all bubbles over - and that's what I give him with each slow, almost lazy thrust.

When his arms finally wrap around my shoulders, I hum my appreciation against his neck. "Mmm, Nico," my voice comes out rough with a pointed roll of my hips, "I love you."

My words have a shiver running through Nico. A low whine catches in his throat as his nails dig into my shoulder blades. I murmur my adoration and love for him between every broken moan; and with every spoken sentiment, Nico clings to me tighter - his legs wrapped around my waist, his fingers clawing for purchase in my skin, his wings fluttering to encircle us in our own little world. The wings' frayed tips brush against my sides with soft, teasing touches that leave my skin tingling and begging for more.

"Li~am."

Moisture pools in the corners of his eyes as he bites back another whine. His head tilts back into the pillow, and honey eyes fall shut to the pleasure. With the enticing sheen of sweat to his skin and his neck bared, my lips seek out contact - kissing, sucking, nipping every inch of it. My arm snakes under his neck to cradle him closer; because no matter how close we are, I want more. I want to feel all of him, touch all of him.

My lips trail a path of wet kisses up the side of his neck before blowing a soft stream of air upon it. The shiver that runs through him is accompanied by a breathless moan. And when I feel his thighs stiffen around my waist, my lips quirk into a prideful smirk. He's close.

I nip at his earlobe, relishing in the sharp gasp it draws from him. "Ah god, I love you so much," my voice a little raspy, I pant each word millimeters from his ear. "Love every, ahh, part of you. All of you. Only y–" my voice cracks on a groan when Nico suddenly tightens around me. His nails claw into my back as my name falls from his lips in a sharp cry.

He draws my own climax effortlessly. It's not explosive or forceful. It's familiar like the lyrics of a favorite song, refreshing like a breath of cold air, warm like the embrace of his arms.

We're both left panting to catch our breaths, stupidly silly grins on our faces as we stare at each other. Nico leans up to catch my lips in a slow, lazy kiss before relaxing back into the fluff of the pillow. And the one simple kiss has the butterflies in my stomach aflutter, because goddamn I love this man so much. The shiny glint to his irises as they gaze up at me has my forehead dropping to Nico's shoulder and a whimper coming up my throat.

"I seriously love you."

"I know," he says softly as his fingers massage the back of my scalp.

"But like a lot. A lot a lot. Like one heart isn't enough to contain it."

If you would've told me a year and half ago that I was gonna fall madly in love with a demon, I would've called you crazy and probably a handful of obscenities. Hell, take away the whole demon thing. If you would've told me I was gonna be in love, I would've laughed in your face. But here I am - here we are. And I still can't fathom how all of the pieces miraculously fell together - how he just happened to pick this city, how he happened to run into Skyler and Emil, how Skyler and Emil happened to be my friends. So many variables came together, and changing any one of them could've prevented me from meeting Nico.

Maybe that's why I'm still so weak to him - to his every little action I find endearing - because I'm grateful to even know him, let alone love and be loved by him. I hear it all the time - how relationships fail because the initial spark isn't there anymore - but this spark between Nico and me, I don't think it'll ever die. Because we aren't just boyfriends or lovers; we're best friends. First and foremost.

I want his smile to always leave me weak in the knees, his laugh to always brighten my mood. When I wake up in the middle of the night, I want to cuddle up to his back and share his warmth. I want to spend every Christmas making a paper tree with him and never get tired of coloring outside the lines. I want our playground and bookstore dates to never lose their charm, to always be as fun and exciting as the first time. On nights spent watching movies on the couch, I want to always have the mischievous urge to press my cold toes to Nico's skin and cackle when he yelps in surprise. I never want to grow complacent or bored in our relationship. So call me a hopeless romantic, but I'll never stop searching for new things about Nico to love.

"Good thing you have my heart as well."

Ugh! Why is he so smooth? It's not fair!

But when I tilt my head to peek at his face, he's sporting a flustered blush upon his cheeks.

"We're gonna need more hearts 'cause mine just melted."

Nico's chuckle rumbles in his chest and runs through his entire body. But the sound is cut short when he winces. He shifts uncomfortably beneath me, his smile turning a bit lopsided. "Could you, uh..?" His eyes purposely glance down before returning to my face.

"Oh shit, sorry." I pull out as carefully as possible and shimmy backwards off the bed. After the quick clean up, I turn back to Nico and can't help but laugh.

Lying on his side with one wing tucked comfortably behind him, his other wing flares out to curve over himself. The wing flutters as he pats the empty space of the mattress next to him.

Ducking beneath his outstretched wing, I sidle to him. Before I'm comfortably situated, his wing drapes over me, its frayed ends flapping against my back before settling against me.

I heave a light sigh, my gaze meeting Nico's. "So the no-door thing. Still weird?"

He hums in thought, the sound echoing in our little bat-wing cocoon. "A little."

"You know," I poke at the leathery membrane of his wing, "these wings of yours make great cover."

"True, but I feel someone walking in on sex would be more appalled by the wings than the lack of a door."

"Well, they can go fuck themself. Your wings aren't appalling. They're breathtaking."

A puff of amusement escapes Nico. "So you'd be more offended by someone calling my wings appalling than them walking in on us having sex?"

"Fuck yeah, I would."

Nico's tender smile widens, becomes even more endearing when he chews on his bottom lip. He tips his head forward until our foreheads touch, and his eyes fall shut. "I love you too. Like a lot a lot."

Did I say one heart wouldn't be enough to contain my love for this man? I meant all the hearts - every last one in the universe. Add the amount of love each of them can contain, multiply it by a gazillion, and even that wouldn't be enough to express my love for him.

I watch the last customer leave for the night, waving them off with a polite smile. After waiting a moment for the mother and son duo to cross the street and continue down the sidewalk, I step from behind the counter to lock the door. As I fiddle with the blinds, I heave a sigh - not exasperated or exhausted, more calming, like a release of the day's energy. When I turn back to my cupcakery (ah, that's never gonna get old), I spot Alex on the other side of the powder blue saloon doors.

She waves a half-eaten red velvet cupcake in the air to get my attention, white frosting staining her lips. Thankfully, she finishes chewing before saying, "Nico wants to know when you'll be up for, uh, dinner."

"Why do you sound like you're hiding something?" I question with a quirk of my brow.

"Wah! I'm not! I swear!"

Uh-huh. Very convincing.

I round behind the display cases - only a few of the day's cupcakes remaining unsold - and watch Alex from the corner of my eye. "If you're trying to hide the fact that's not your first cupcake, it's fine. I already said you can eat the older leftovers."

"Oh, uh, yeah. That's it." She takes another chomp out of the cupcake as if to calm her nerves. "Mmm, but really," she swallows. "Nico wants to know when you'll be up."

"In a few minutes. I just have to put the money in the safe, and then I'll be right up."

"What about sweeping the floors? Cleaning the display cases? Wiping the windows? Tidying the chairs?"

"I can do it all tomorrow." I have all day tomorrow and Monday to tidy the chairs, what with being closed those days.

"Yeah, that's not gonna work," she mutters.

I forget about emptying the till to stare at her quizzically. I arch a brow, watching as she shoves the last bite of cupcake into her mouth. Her chews are slow, methodical. She swallows like it's the last thing she'll ever eat, never once breaking eye contact. But then, like a startled animal, she darts back through the kitchen.

I sprint after her, eternally grateful for my dorky ass nonslip shoes as I run through the swinging doors. Zigging around a worktable, I'm quick enough to see Alex disappear up the stairwell as she slams the door shut. I skid to a stop and yank at the doorknob. But no matter which way I jiggle it, the knob won't turn.

"Goddammit, Alex!"

I stomp back to the front and angrily grab the phone from its cradle beside the register. My fingers jab the buttons to dial my cellphone's number. Bringing the phone to my ear, my foot taps impatiently as I wait for an answer.

Three rings later and I hear Nico laughing out a hello.

"Alex locked me down here."

"I'm sor–"

"Tell him to use the alleyway if he wants up here so bad!" Alex shouts in the background.

"Shh. Don't give him any ideas."

Okay, I'm gonna count the people who should be upstairs. 1) Nico. 2) Alex. 3) Cody. That's it. Hmm, did I see Skyler on that list? No? Then why the hell would I hear his voice in the background?

Nico clears his throat and speaks louder to say, "Sorry, but could you hang out down there a little longer? Pretty please?"

"Ugh, you're pulling out a pretty please?"

"Please~" he drawls.

"Fine," I pout. "I guess I'll stay down here all by my lonesome. Being alone. Lonely. Crying my heart–"

"Thanks." He hangs up, leaving me to listen to an annoying dial tone.

"Rude," I mutter as I place the phone back in its cradle.

I glance around at the pastel blue walls and the cartoon-style cupcakes decorating them. Huffing out a breath of air, a smile finds its way to my lips. Whatever they're scheming, it better be good or I might decide to sleep on the checkered tiles tonight.

Instead of driving myself crazy imagining what mess will await me upstairs, I get a head start on all that tidying up chairs business. I count the day's profits before storing it in the security of the safe that's hidden away in the tiny office beneath the stairwell. It's a pretty nifty space to disappear to when I need to balance the accounts or fill out order forms, even though it's barely big enough for a small desk and chair. But I'm not complaining. I'm bragging, 'cause I have an office!

Okay, so maybe I don't tidy up the chairs or wipe the fingerprints off the glass of the display cases. I sweep the floor, get bored after five minutes, and bring my spinny wheely chair into the kitchen to glide around the center worktables.

I wonder if Alex and Cody (and apparently Skyler) have taken my Sprinkles hostage. Nah, they wouldn't risk me taking away their cupcake rights. Maybe we're having an impromptu sleepover? I'd welcome that with open arms, because I could really go for a relaxing night with friends.

A Taste of Sprinkles has been open for about a month now; and don't get me wrong, I love it, but it can be overwhelming at times. If I didn't have the support of friends and family - Simon and Dietrich helping with financial management; Alex, Cody, Skyler, and Emil taking turns to help serve customers; Fae assisting in the kitchen while Kari is *emotional support*; my mom and grandma saying they're proud of me; and Nico treating my dream as his dream as well - I don't think I would've survived the first week, let alone the first month.

Every second of it - no matter how overwhelming it may be - is worth it. Seeing people bite into my cupcakes and savoring their flavors, my chest puffs out with pride every time. My eyes still prick with tears when I hear a kid tell their parent they want another while having frosting and sprinkles all over their face. I wonder if that pride and gratitude and raw emotion will ever fade.

Fuck, I hope not.

In the quietness of the kitchen, the click of the door being unlocked resounds in my ears. I stop mid-spin, glancing over my shoulder to see the door open barely a crack. Whoever crept so quietly down the stairs now stampedes up them like a herd of wild elephants, and I hear the door at the top slam shut.

This is getting... creepy. Maybe I should reconsider the whole they-kidnapped-Nico thing. Or are they trying to scare me as a pregame to a scary movie marathon?

I scoot over to the door on my wheely chair and cautiously pull it open. At least they were kind enough to leave the light on so I don't have to wonder if there's a trap at the top of the landing. Which there isn't. But I wouldn't put it past any of them to don a scary mask and scare the crap out of me.

Climbing the stairs ever so slowly, I listen for talking or murmuring or hushed laughter - anything to give me a clue as to what's awaiting me. But it's complete silence except for the ominous squeaking of the steps bearing my weight. And yeah, that makes this whole experience about ten times creepier than it should be.

I swear to god, if they're all waiting to jump-scare me and I fall down the damn stairs, I'm revoking their cupcake rights for the rest of eternity.

With a slight tremble, my hand grasps the knob. I steel myself with a few deep breaths, utterly determined not to shriek like a little kid when they attack me with clown masks. Squeezing my eyes shut, I push the door in and take a hesitant step into my home.

I wait for... I don't know what. Something. Hands latching onto my ankles, a bad imitation of an evil laugh, maybe even Skyler or Cody shouting *Boo!*

But there's nothing, not a sound to be heard or a movement to be sensed.

I peek open an eye, making out a hazy Nico standing a few strides in front of me. Blinking both eyes open, I breathe a sigh of relief at the lack of a clown mask adorning his face.

"What's—" my question dies in my throat when my gaze is drawn to the far wall over Nico's shoulder.

This afternoon, when I came up here to have a quick lunch, that white wall was just that - a plain old white wall. But even with Nico and his dopey smile blocking some of the view, I spot the tastefully clustered photographs in their silver picture frames.

I'm drawn to them, stepping further into the loft before I notice the other walls have gained new additions as well. To my right - past the alley entrance and the coat hooks - two canvas paintings brighten the stark white. My cheeks heat up when I'm hit with the recognition of them being my works from that single art class I took in college. I glance away to the left wall, to the sparse living room where the single couch is overloaded with people. But I skim over the familiar faces, drawn instead to the thick dark frame holding a series of three photos side by side.

"Surprise! Ow!"

"That was Nico's line," Skyler backhands Cody upside the head.

The words snap me out of my trance. I blink, watching Cody sheepishly rub at his head from where he perches on the nearest armrest. Alex knees Cody in the ribs from her seat on the back of the couch, muttering something about Cody being the reason we can't have nice things. To the left of Cody, Skyler sighs like a disappointed mom while Kari throws her head back with cackling laughter. Fae shushes her while Eli and Emil - sitting on pillows on the floor - offer me timid smiles.

It's hard for me not to join in on Kari's boisterous laughter, because honestly, they should've known Cody would jump the gun. Nothing short of duct tape over his mouth would've prevented it.

Bubbling laughter - so quiet and docile compared to Kari's cackles - draws my gaze to Nico. Head bashfully ducked to the side, he sways back and forth on his feet, his hands hidden behind his back. His honey brown eyes shift to me. When they find me staring back, their corners crinkle to accompany the most heartwarming smile that has ever graced his lips. "Surprise," he says softly, yet the single word has silence falling upon the loft.

He closes the short distance between us. Worrying his bottom lip between the bite of his teeth, he rocks back onto his heels. When he rocks forward - as if needing the momentum - he thrusts his hands toward me, holding out a bouquet of...

Hearts.

Meticulously stitched - yet still a tad crooked in some places - white thread binds the plush hearts together. One of baby blue with a ribbon bow at its center, another a dark purple with mini pastel hearts decorating it. A third that's a deep red with pink buttons outlining its edges has a few stray threads hanging loose. The sunny yellow one and spring green one are overloaded with buttons and bows, one looking like stars in the daytime and the other like grass on a country hillside.

I stare at the little plushies on their multicolored dowels and the pink ribbon tying the dowels together. Hesitantly, I reach for the bouquet. My fingers brush Nico's, lingering for the touch before gingerly curling around the bundled dowels.

When Nico's hands fall back to his side, he says, "We have some spare hearts now."

The sound that leaves my mouth is a laugh and a sob mixed into one. My eyes don't want to look away from the crooked stitches and stray threads and rough edges, but I duck my head to the side to rub at my eyes with the back of my hand.

"Aw, Liam, are you crying?" Alex coos from behind her cellphone, probably snapping pictures like crazy.

"Maybe," I sniff. I blink against the moisture in my eyes and wipe away the few strays that trailed down my cheeks. "What else do you expect when you guys do all this?"

"Actually, Nico did most of it," Eli says.

A beautiful flush to his freckled skin, Nico's smile turns bashful again as he rubs at the nape of his neck. "That's not true. All of you helped hang the pictures, and Kari got the paintings–"

I send a weak glare in Kari's direction, but I'm probably as scary as a wet kitten right now because she grins back at me with pride.

"–and Emil chose the frames, and Alex helped pick out pictures, and–"

"I brought the pizza!" Cody waves his hand in the air as he shouts.

Nico finishes with a laugh, "And Cody brought the pizza."

I don't know whether to laugh or cry. "You guys," my voice is thick as I clutch the heart bouquet tighter. "You didn't have to do all this."

"Of course, we didn't, silly," Alex hops down from the back of the couch. "We wanted to. Consider it a late housewarming gift from all of us."

"Is this your way of not having to buy us a blender we'll never use?"

"Yep, you got us," Alex laughs. She strides to my side and grabs my forearm. Dragging me toward the left wall, she says, "But seriously, take a closer look at your gifts. You're gonna love them." She steers me in front of the 3-photo frame before stepping back to give me some space.

My eyes zone in on the cursive white lettering spelling *Family* centered below the pictures. There's a pang in my chest - a preconditioned response that has my throat tightening. I swallow against the feeling, but it lingers. That is, until I ignore the word that's brought me so much pain in the past to look upon the pictures above it.

The first has fresh tears welling in my eyes, not because of the picture itself but because of the memory it brings to the forefront of my mind - an evening spent at the dining table with my mother, looking through old photos for a class assignment. When she showed me this one, her smile softened to a fondness grade-schooler me couldn't understand. At the time, I saw nothing special about pudgy little baby me being rocked to sleep in my mother's arms.

But then she turned to grade-schooler me and said, "You were such a fussy baby. Always crying and screaming at the top of your lungs. You kept the entire neighborhood up half the night." She laughed at that, such a tender sound I'll never forget.

The waterworks I try to hold at bay flow freely when my eyes move on to the middle picture. A face I haven't seen since my freshman year of high school has my chest aching for a completely different reason. His thinning hair and a trimmed beard graying from age - it's been so long I almost forgot them. But the moment captured in print - him holding the lead rope attached to Apollo's halter as five-year-old me hangs on to the saddle horn for dear life and my grandma cheering me on from the fence line - I can never forget it.

The last one has my tears slowing as a moment of clarity soothes the lingering ache in my chest. The eyes I so easily lose myself in don't stare at the camera. They peek at me from their corners while I kiss his cheek on New Year's Eve. And it shouldn't surprise me that this picture is in a frame etched with *Family*. Of fucking course Nico is family.

As I turn back with watery eyes, not even trying to hide my tears at this point, each of my friends' smiling faces relieves the hurt buried deep inside my heart.

Maybe they're not family in the traditional sense of the word, but when the fuck have I been traditional? Maybe by the traditional sense, I am missing a few faces; but do I want them here? Hell fucking no. Because I've come to realize family is not determined by blood or by the name you're born into. It's bonds created and nurtured by all parties involved, friendships lasting the test of time, the people who've seen you at your worst and stayed to help you through it. So fuck blood. I have everyone I need right here - in this loft I call home, in the pictures on the walls, in the parts of my heart I never thought I'd feel again.

Oh god, I'm gonna need the hearts held in my hands, because I don't know how much longer mine can take all of this... love. Yeah, love. Because fuck, I love my friends so much.

"Save the waterworks. You're not done yet," Skyler says, but I swear through my blurry vision he's blinking back tears of his own.

I move on to the back wall, barely hearing the footsteps following me. But I see their reflections in the glass, and their beaming smiles and teary eyes would have you believing the surprise is for them.

The silver frames accent the white of the wall. Horizontal and vertical, the photos form a cluster of memories - the majority being group selfies or surprise shots by Alex - but about half the frames remain empty.

"Don't tell me you guys ran out of pictures?"

"Are you kidding me? Have you met your mother?" Skyler chuckles.

"Yeah, she sent us so many pictures we got tired of looking at your face," Cody quips.

I snort at that, because yeah, I can totally see my mom going overboard in the photo department.

"That too," Alex giggles at Cody's remark. "But we wanted to leave room for new memories."

I have such sentimental friends, and I fucking love it.

"Now Liam," Kari slinks to my side and throws her arm around my shoulders. She turns me to the right wall with an impish smirk. "Be a dear and tell everyone the significance behind your bowl of fruit painting."

I take it back. I love all my friends but Kai. She's been downgraded to a level-five friend.

"There is no significance to it. It's fruit for fuck's sake."

"Nah. Why you gotta be such a liar?"

"Why'd you even have my paintings to begin with?" I counter, wriggling out of her hold.

"For a moment such as this, obviously." She tries to catch me again, but stops dead in her tracks when I hide behind Fae. My victory warrants sticking out my tongue at her, but the action sparks a dangerous glint to her eyes.

"Ladies and gentlemen!" she calls far too loudly for someone who already has the room's full attention. With a dramatic sweep of her arm, she directs everyone's eyes to the fruit painting. "The gallery of Liam proudly presents to you this piece entitled *Liam's in Denial of Being a Thirsty Ho for Freckled Dick so He Paints Spotted Bananas Instead of Tappin Dat Ass.*"

That's it. Cupcake rights have been revoked.

"That's your–" the cacophony of laughter drowns out my voice, so I give up trying to defend myself.

Among the boisterous cackles and deep chuckles, a single laugh eases my irritation at Kari. It's soft, a tad bit reserved, as he holds the back of his hand to his smiling lips. Quiet bubbles of laughter escape him even as a light blush colors his cheeks. And goddamn if that isn't worth the embarrassment, I don't know what is.

"Come on, Liam, admit it. You're a thirsty ho for my Freckle Buddy," Kari barely manages to get out between fits of laughter.

Her Freckle Buddy.

Nico tries really hard not to join in the obnoxious cackling, but his hand isn't enough to stop the chuckles from overflowing into unabashed laughs. The sound has my lips upturning and my heart melting to goo.

I duck under the arm Kari tries to drape around my shoulder and escape to the safety of Nico's side. When my arm snakes around his waist, I feel the quiver of his body as his laughter runs through him. Leaning up on the balls of my feet, my lips press a kiss to his cheek to silence his laughter as his eyes widen with surprise.

"Fuck yeah, I'm a thirsty ho for my Sprinkles." Thirsty for his touch, his companionship, his sleepy good morning's, his quiet conversations with Cupcake, his hand to hold, his freckles to play connect the dots with, his excessive knowledge on every random animal and plant showcased in nature documentaries, his everything.

Kari quirks a daring eyebrow. "My Freckle Buddy."

"My Sprinkles."

"My Freckle–"

"I can be both," Nico says with a laugh.

"Tsk, I'm his favorite," Kari mutters.

"Oh yeah? I don't think he sewed hearts for you!" My gaze turns to Nico for confirmation. "You didn't, right?"

He huffs a quiet puff of amusement. "Only for you."

"Ha! See!" I wave my bouquet at her as if it's all the proof I need that Nico likes me better. As if being his boyfriend and knowing he's a demon and hearing him tell me I love you aren't proof enough.

Kari pouts as she retreats to Fae, wrapping her smaller girlfriend in a bear hug. "Kari my love, dear, darling, tell asshat to stop rubbing it in. Put 'em in a vase or something."

"Never. I'm gonna hold these for the rest of my earthly life, and then my ghost ass is gonna hold them until I get reincarnated, and then reincarnated me is gonna be buried with them in a golden casket 'cause that me is gonna be filthy rich."

"Fae!" Kari whines, but Fae merely pats Kari's head as Kari cries obnoxious crocodile tears.

"Now seems like a good time to break out the pizza."

Kari perks up at Cody's mention of pizza. The two of them race to the kitchen, fighting to open the freezer to get the pizzas with their favorite toppings in the oven first. I turn away when Cody rips open the plastic wrap on one pizza and frozen cheese falls all over the floor, because I can't watch them desecrate my kitchen. They're definitely going to clean up after themselves, or they're never allowed in this building ever again.

Or I guess Cupcake will eat the fallen cheese. They're lucky my baby can hear a piece of food fall from a mile away, or they'd be cleaning it up themselves. And losing cupcake eating rights. Oh wait, they already lost that. I'll reinstate it so I can take it away again.

With everyone vying to get their preferred pizza in the oven, Nico leans closer. His lips brush against my ear as he asks, "Do you like them?"

I follow his gaze as it flicks to the plush hearts in my hand. Holding them to my chest, I sigh contently as I rest my weight against him. "Of course, I do. I'm completely serious about never putting them down."

His arm wraps around my shoulders. He squeezes me to his side and rests his head atop mine. "Thank god," he quietly laughs, breathless.

My eyes fall shut as I relish the closeness, letting everything slowly sink in. "How'd you manage all this without me knowing?"

"Alex happens to be a great party planner, and your mom and grandma were all too willing to help."

Ah, it makes sense. Granny probably sent Nico heart patterns and tips for sewing. And of course, my mother was all too eager to show everyone my childhood pictures. I used to be embarrassed having my mom always waving a camera around, but now I am truly grateful for it. I wish I could go back and tell younger me to stop hiding his face or scowling in them, because one day - today - he'll be thankful to be surrounded by the memories.

"Okay true. But where'd you hide all this?" There's not a single closet in the loft, and the only closed off space is the bathroom on the second level. All these picture frames and sewing supplies couldn't possibly fit in the vanity cabinets.

"Skyler's and Emil's place. Oh, and we didn't tell Cody till this morning."

"Oi! I could've kept it a secret!" Cody shouts to defend himself.

"You almost told him three times today," Alex deadpans.

"Well, I... uh... I was excited, okay!" he sputters.

"And that's exactly why we didn't tell you," Kari pipes up. "And earth to the lovebirds, we're gonna start the movie with or without you."

My eyes snap open, and my head whips to see Kari grinning at us from the couch. Actually, it's not just her making kissy faces at us. How the hell did everyone decide on the pizzas so fast and beat us to the couch?

"I can and I will kick you out if you so much as press play," I threaten.

"Hmm, for some reason, I'm not scared," she smirks, waving the remote as if she holds all the power. Which, okay, she does.

Nico kisses the top of my head before pulling away. As much as I want to be a stubborn asshole and not move a single inch from this spot, I'm weak against the fingers which intertwine with mine. I let Nico pull me along to our little TV corner. With the couch overloaded with bodies - Fae sitting in Kari's lap, Skyler (with Cupcake perched on his shoulder) squished into Emil's side, and Alex claiming an armrest - I make a mental note to go furniture shopping with Nico. We could really use another couch or a few recliners.

Nico eases himself to the floor beside Eli, and I begrudgingly give up the idea of kicking someone off my couch and join them in sitting on pillows. I settle into Nico's side, resting my head upon his shoulder, and I quickly come to love my spot on the floor. Our thighs pressed against each other, our fingers linked together, and the heart bouquet set in my lap - I've got the best seat in the house.

When Kari starts the movie, everyone's side comments and conversations die down. Maybe it's the silence - I don't know - but everything - the pictures, the time and effort everyone put into this, the emotions and feelings and sentiments, the love - it all hits me at once.

My eyes sting with tears. I squeeze Nico's fingers, and a stray tear rolls down my cheek when he squeezes back.

I had given up on this - on a family, on a future of my own, on happiness. It was so easy to lose sight when my world was constantly falling to pieces. Or maybe it was never that bad. Maybe I needed to open my eyes and see the love that already surrounded me - the friends that stood beside me, the colleagues that saw something in me, the family that didn't abandon me.

It took Nico - my Sprinkles - to open my heart to those around me. Who would've guessed the awkward, assumed serial killer would've become my best friend; that my best friend was a demon; that my demon best friend would become the love of my life? With him, my friends, my family, I can do anything, survive anything. Because I'd be naive to think life won't have a billion more obstacles to throw at me - many of which might crush me beneath their weight - but I'm not alone.

I'm not alone.

"What's wrong?" Nico whispers, his words barely audible.

When I glance at his face - seeing the freckles I've long since memorized and the worry bright in his honey brown eyes - I smile. "Nothing. Absolutely nothing."

ABOUT THE AUTHOR

Morgan Briese always had a wild imagination and indulged in storytelling from a young age. She dabbles in a little bit of everything and has experience writing poetry, short stories, and novels. She enjoys horseback riding, playing with clay, watching anime, and experimenting in the kitchen.

For more information and bonus content, visit her website.

morganbriesewrites.com